THUNDERER

THUNDERER

Felix Gilman

Bantam Books

THUNDERER
A Bantam Spectra Book / January 2008

Published by Bantam Dell
A Division of Random House, Inc.
New York, New York

Book design by Virginia Norey

Library of Congress Cataloging-in-Publication Data

Gilman, Felix.
Thunderer / Felix Gilman.
p. cm.
ISBN 978-0-553-80676-2 (hardcover)
I. Title.

PS3607.I452T47 2008
813'.6—dc22   2007033756

Printed in the United States of America
Published simultaneously in Canada

www.bantamdell.com

BVG 10 9 8 7 6 5 4 3 2 1

To Sarah

Acknowledgments

Thanks to all at Bantam Spectra, especially my editor, Juliet Ulman, and to Howard Morhaim and Katie Menick. Thanks also to my family for their support and patience; and to Bill Thompson, whose feedback improved this book greatly, and whose advice and help were instrumental in getting it published.

THUNDERER

ONE

He came to the city at the end of summer, over the sea; leaning out over the boat's plain prow, scanning the horizon, nervously telling beads of scale and bone through his thin fingers. He'd crossed half the world to come there.

The sky over the Bay glittered with white gulls, diving and threading between blue air and sea, scavenging on the harbor's busy life. Those birds were the city's first sign, and they were a bright and lively one, lifting his spirits.

"Into the city soon, Mr. Roon." The captain clapped him on the back, giving him a gappy brown grin. "Already are, you could say. The birds' city, too, isn't it? Scared, a little?"

In fact his name was Arjun, but he was quite well used to being mispronounced, and not too proud to let the error stand. He smiled mildly back and said, "Hopeful," but the captain had turned away, and was calling out orders in a rhythmic sailor's cant to his tiny crew of dark-skinned brothers and sons. And the city sketched itself in distantly on the horizon: a smudge of rooftops, a gauzy tobacco-brown cross-hatching of bridges and spires. Shifting and shaping in slowly, distorted by heat-haze, by its own density. A great mountain rising behind it all, a daub of distant blue. The fetish of scale and bone rustled over his knuckles. In his mind he was composing a letter to his Mothers and Fathers: *Here we begin at last. The city is a puzzle box to be cracked open. Let me describe it to you....* But he wasn't sure how, yet.

In every place he'd passed through on his journey, he'd heard stories of Ararat. He thought of them as the city's echoes; that was how he'd been raised. In some places, they said the city was blessed. In others, they said *haunted*. In one such village, in the hills, in the pines, he'd stayed for a season with Ama, the doctor's daughter; she had begged him to stay, or turn back. When the snows lifted, and he had had to move on, she'd given him that charm, softly pressing his fingers over it. It would protect him, she promised. Her father had made it.

Perhaps it had some power. But he had come to search among the city's gods, not to hide from them. He let it slip from his fingers. It floated for a moment on the bright foam, then the hull forced it under.

The boat creaked and clanked as the crew worked.

A shimmer of spray rose from the water. The crew's rhythm faltered. The captain cried out. Arjun turned, to see one of the squat sea-brothers point to the sky with a yelp of delight, and another tilt his head back and moan deep in his throat. *Look up.*

Out of the Bay's high sun, curving steeply down over the water, opening out ample wings: in the first instant of perception, it could be a cloud unfolding from the cloudless sky, streaming across the firmament like a white pennant. At once, it becomes a great bird, driving forward. Its wings are wide white planes, beating slowly. Nothing so huge should be able to fly, but it seems weightless. The sunlight shivers ecstatically in its wake.

As it soars across the water, the Bay's birds gather around it, circling it with boundless fluttering adoration. It turns in a loose, free arc, and beneath it, fish leap from the water, hanging for a second amazed by the air. The Bird-God brings the gifts of flight and freedom with it. It casts no shadow.

The Bird drives over the Bay and in toward the ancient city. A single brightly painted barque bobs here, waiting, far out in the Bay. A red flare fires from its deck. A moment later, an answering flare appears over the shore, and deeper into the city, another follows. As the Bird passes overhead, the barque's sails burst with sudden air and it sets out after the god; but for all the craft's borrowed speed, it's a hopeless pursuit.

A close-packed, shifting maze of vessels sits before the docks. Under the Bird's wings, every sail applauds, snapping full for a moment. A babble rises from below: cheers, screams, canting charms and imprecations. Quickened into sudden motion, ships drift unpredictably in the crowded harbor.

The harbor's crews fight to recover control. Word of the Bird's return has gone out, and they are well-prepared. The Countess Ilona's office crafted *Rules and Regulations for the Ships of Ar-Mouth Harbor in the Event of the Return of the Great Bird, Praise Be,* and for weeks her men have been posting them in every public house, flophouse, pleasure barge, market, and church in the docks; and then, stung by this presumption—Who is Ilona to claim jurisdiction over the docks? How dare she?—the Marquis Mensonge, the Gerent of Stross End, and a dozen other lords all had their agents post their *own* regulations, tearing each other's notices down or papering them over.

It's been a difficult few weeks for the landlords of the docks; each of the city's great Estates wants to see their own rules posted up behind the bar, and no one else's; so they've had to nail up the Countess's poster, ready to swap it quickly for the Gerent's if they saw his men come shouldering in the door, or vice versa. Of course, they're used to that sort of thing. The city's Estates are so very jealous, and there are so damn *many* of them.

The docksmen mostly prepared themselves in their own way anyway. The old hands remember the last time the Bird came to the city, and what it brought with it.

But nothing can be done to make the great Bird's return altogether safe. The harbor is full of foreign ships, and too many are unwarned and slow to react. The ships drift inexorably into their neighbors, hulls grinding painfully together.

At the center of the tangle of vessels, the great black hulk of the *Dauntless* lurches into motion. The ropes lashing it to surrounding vessels tear free and the juggernaut escapes ponderously seawards. No one knows how to stop it now. It bears down on an elegant barquentine from Akash. All hands stand on both ships' decks, yelling and helplessly gesturing. A passenger on the Akashic ship fumbles with a flintlock, firing a shot that smacks pointlessly into the *Dauntless*'s hull.

But the Bird has passed on already, following the River Urgos up from the harbor. It coasts between the parliaments and anti-parliaments that stamp their marbled presences along the river's banks: a strange and clumsy blend of colors and forms, shapes and styles, gentle curves next to angular pillars and pediments, ornament rubbing up against austerity, all grown warily accustomed to each other over the centuries, all stained alike by the city's smoke. The city below stretches out from the river, rising endlessly north into the blue slopes of Ar-Mount. Sunlight glints off copper and brass domes, steel girders, white stone spires; many thousands of temples, and many thousands more things that *might* be temples. Perhaps everything here is sacred. From this soaring elevation, it all gleams. The dust in the ancient city's air glitters in the sun and rising wind. The wind smells electric. The city stands ready to be changed and remade.

The Bird turns from the River Urgos to circle the spire of Monan's seminary, standing alone on the muddy ground by the river's banks. A cloud of pigeons bursts from the ragged spire and joins the wheeling seabird chorus. The motleyed flock chases the object of their adoration in a squabbling mass as the great Bird veers west toward the massive warehouses of Barbary Ward.

By now, the procession of flares has alerted much of the city. Abandoning their midday meals, people are climbing onto Barbary's square roofs. Docksmen mix with the bohemians of the artists' lofts. When the Bird passes over, small but growing crowds cheer it, running wildly after it until the edge of the roof brings them up short. A few throw tributes of white cloth and silk in the Bird's wake.

Countless painters decide to capture the Bird's image. It'll test their art. It's impossible to make out its details—before the eye can fix on it, it's moved on. It's huge, yes, but it's impossible to say *how* huge. It seems to be unthinkably distant even as it thunders immediately overhead—perhaps it's vastly farther away and larger than it seems. Later, no one will even be able to agree what *kind* of bird it is. Some see a storm of bright feathers, others only the graceful motion of its wings. Little more than a sense of easy, invincible speed remains. A dozen minds conceive abstract new schools of painting to capture the moment.

The rooftops are already a painting, though, made an olive-white impasto by the shit-shower of the bird chorus above. One of the artists, a young man called Mochai, will later say drunkenly to his lover Olympia, shortly before she leaves him for someone less needy, that "what the gods *are* is what they leave behind in the city. Isn't that what Holbach says? That that's their real substance? So that's how I'll capture it!" And he'll go out onto the rooftops, chisel in hand, to chip up stuff to spackle his canvases with; he'll have to fight over it with the street urchins collecting for the night-soil merchants, and with the Bird's worshippers, who'll want it to burn on their private attic altars; and then in the end, a mob of shaven-headed youths in white robes will tell him his shit-paintings are blasphemous and obscene, and burn down his exhibition. But that's all much later, of course, and the Bird is here *now.*

The Bird has no church: its interventions into the city are too occasional and unpredictable, and it is utterly antithetical to order and structure in any case. But a handful of eccentric self-ordained devotees are here, wrapped in contraptions of linen and silk and balsa, ready among the sparse crowds, and as the presence rushes by, they run to the chasm between roofs, fling out homemade wings, and plunge. In the moment of its passage, their wings catch flight, the Bird's power passing briefly into them, and they wheel up to join it, tears of joy and terror on their faces. Those who miss the moment fall to be broken in the alleys below. Down there, the city's no gleaming, gauzy thing; down there it's hard and bruise-dark and stinking.

Jack Sheppard stands on the roof of the Barbotin House, legs tensed. His hands are occupied with his work, but his mind and eyes scan the sky. "Come on," he mutters. "Come on. *Come.*"

Beneath his tensed feet is an unthinkable weight of windowless iron and stone. He's been buried under it for too long. A moment of crisis is coming, a fulcrum around which he can pull himself up and out of the earth and across the sky. He can feel it starting already. Or is he imagining it? He's so young, still. (Fifteen, sixteen? He doesn't know exactly.)

He's pale, sharp, and a little ratlike, like all those raised in the House. He is accustomed to opening his eyes very wide to see in the darkness of the House's halls, and, on the rare occasions when he is out in open daylight—as he is now, working on the roof, on the laundry detail—he squints, making him look harder and fiercer than he really is. Like many of those who grew up working the House's silk mills, he is missing a finger, and has other scars. He wears a grey cap, and a grey wool jacket, itchy in the summer heat.

He is standing on top of Barbotin House. It occupies the length of Plessy Street at the edge of Barbary and Fourth Ward. Other work-houses in the city look like plain prisons; this one looks like a tomb, or like an iron puzzle box with no solution. Heavy-riveted panels of gunmetal are plated over the concrete and stone, sullenly sealing all windows. Within, there are no lamps or torches or even candles. Desperate children might turn fire into a weapon against the House; and besides, the Masters explain, this is a House of Tiber: fire is sacred here, and these boys are not worthy. Generations of dust accrete in every corner, unseen. The House's silk mills must be worked in the gloom. It's a dreary, dangerous business, and Jack's sick of it.

The House is set far back from the surrounding buildings, across a field of high barbed fences. It looks like something only a lunatic would design, and indeed, Jack knows its history and knows that to be the case. No boy has ever escaped.

Jack's pinning a dirty grey sheet to the line when he feels it whip slightly in his hands. He is intensely ready; he has schemed and fought to be here, at this time. When he sees the red flare, he knows what it must mean.

There is one special sheet in the bundle in his laundry basket. He snatches the bundle up and tenses himself.

If he's wrong now, he'll never have another chance—he could have four, five more years here before they spit him back out onto the streets, exhausted. It does not occur to him that he might die in the attempt. He has not thought what he will do with himself in the city outside, if he does get free.

Now, then: he launches himself into a mad run for the edge. He hurdles Carswell, who kneels obediently on the floor, folding a pile of grey cloth jackets. He bursts through a white line of sheets, thinking for a moment of the way the comedians at the Palace Cabaret, in his childhood in the days before the House, would come bursting through the velvet curtain and into the brassy stage light. He starts laughing. This is a *show.* *"Laaaadeeeez an' gennelmennnn!"* he shouts.

Mr. Tar starts up and shouts, "What's this? Stop that boy!" Hutton, trying to curry favor with Tar, grabs Jack's arm. The older boy could hold Jack easily if he really tried, but he has no idea how desperate Jack is, so he stupidly turns his back and looks smiling for approval at the Master. He stumbles away a second later holding his bitten and bloodied ear. Jack swerves around a chimney and drops onto the slate slope of the lower roof. He stops for a second. When another boy comes up to the edge, Jack levers up a tile and throws it at his head. With a bark of triumph, he spins his rough cloth cap after it.

He scans the sky anxiously. Nothing there, no speck in any direction. "Oh no. Come on. Come on. Come *on.*"

When it comes, it comes tremendously and all at once. Pigeons, rooks, gannets, and gulls burst over the roof and scatter the sky. Unbelievably, men and women wheel among them. In the center, the object of all attention, is the Bird.

Jack shakes out the bundle of laundry and draws out a bedsheet. It used to be as grey and mottled as every other sheet in Barbotin, but Jack has stolen some silk-dyes and bleached it white. He understands that to be an important gesture. Into the sheet are stitched stolen rags and filaments of silk. He shucks off his jacket, quickly, roughly. Beneath it, his shirt is also bleached white, and ornamented with long, brightly colored threads of stolen silk. He whips the sheet around his shoulders. He looks as comical and pathetic as a flightless bird.

Mr. Tar has climbed down onto the slope now. Jack salutes him, and runs to the edge. He slips on the steep slope for a second as a tile gives way under his feet, then rights himself. Jack's foot connects with the guttering under the eaves, and he kicks himself off into the air and throws his arms out.

It works, Praise Be, it works, but not well. His magic is crude and makeshift: he had to do the best he could with the materials to hand. He imagined flying like a bird, like *the* Bird. Instead, it's as if, for a second, he's free of gravity and with each step he can kick off again higher, so beautifully poised is he; but in the next second gravity returns like a blow across his back and he loses his balance. He falls hard and scrapes his knees. He looks back in sudden despair. But Praise Be! He's on the next roof, separated from Barbotin House by a wide chasm. Behind him, Mr. Tar is on all fours at the edge of the House's roof. Tar is clutching the guttering with one hand to steady himself, and with the other holding Jack's talismanic silk-shot bedsheet, torn from his back.

Jack's standing on the bare roof of another warehouse. There is a door in a square brick extrusion in the corner of the roof, but it's locked. There's no other way down. Tar yells and blows a whistle. There are answering yells from within the House. They'll find their way into this new building soon.

Jack runs to the edge and looks over the abyss to the next roof. There's another door there, this one open, *propped* open, with a brick. A group of women stands on the roof waving after the departing Bird and its flock. One of the young ones turns and sees Jack run. She gives a quick little clap of excitement.

He can't get to her. It's a whole street away and three stories down. His makeshift wings are gone. The Bird's presence is dwindling in the distance, drifting up over the escarpment that divides Shutlow from Mass How, and everything is very heavy again. The ritual is broken. There is no power left to call on.

The Fire with it anyway. He runs to the edge, closes his eyes, and reaches out, snatching at the last threads of potentiality drifting in the air, and leaps, praying.

How very gratifying it is, madam, to know It's coming. To be proved right. I've never seen anything quite so lovely as those flares. I'd be lying if I said I'd been entirely confident."

The Countess Ilona raises an eyebrow; it's a thin black line in a sharp face that's painted china-white, above a gilt gem-studded collar. The thick paint *almost* makes her ageless. No one would dare tell her it doesn't.

"You appeared confident. I should hope you *were* confident, Professor. I put a great deal of trust in you."

Holbach smiles blandly and curses himself. "A figure of speech, madam. A little joke. My predictions were very sound. I would not have had you, um, expose yourself in this manner had I not been perfectly confident..."

"*Expose* myself? Is my position that vulnerable, Professor?"

Holbach offers a mutter of conciliation, *didn't mean to say aha of course no um no oh I'm sure no,* and a submissive half-stoop; and, begging her pardon, he excuses himself to oversee the final preparations. A velvet-frogged footman steadies his arm as he steps off the dais and onto the grass. Holbach rewards the servant with a smile of thanks, full of confidence and, he's sure, quite without condescension. He heads off over the Heath, inspecting the line of men stretched out before him.

Smooth, plump, and genial; scholar, augur, and courtier; a man of affairs, of dignified age: Holbach knows better than that by now how to talk to the city's potentates. The excitement is getting to him, placing, he thinks, let's say, sharp burrs in the, ah, velvet of his blandishments. No, a terrible metaphor, awful: he can do better. Let's say...

Holbach stops before a man in the middle of the line sweating from the exertion of holding his rope. Holbach straightens the golden silk of the man's robe where it has bunched over his shoulder, smoothing it so the silver trim falls straight. The man starts and shifts, but doesn't let go of his rope. The Countess's man knows what's good for him.

"No, no: nothing wrong. Don't concern yourself. The Countess appreciates your efforts, of course. Good man."

The Countess's dais stands at the edge of the West Meadow of Laud Heath, against the bosky shade of the Widow's Bower. Before it, the grass rolls out east and slopes down gently to the river's bank. Two lines of golden-robed men stand in front of the dais. Each man holds in both hands a rope. Between them they tether a huge balloon. The gas-filled sphere, patched with azure and argent, strains against their arms' strength.

They raised it an hour ago, the dashing Captain Arlandes, pride of the Countess's forces, leading the men in their battle against gravity in fine style: Arlandes on the back of a black charger, uniformed in sapphire-blue parade-jacket, gold-trimmed, gold-medaled, one hand—one dueling-scarred hand—on the pommel of his golden saber, barking orders to the men, who fear the Countess, but love Arlandes.

The honor of being the first person to ride in the balloon went to Arlandes' young bride, Lucia—Arlandes himself and Holbach being indispensable on the ground, and the Countess not being so inclined.

She sits now delicately on the wicker floor of the basket, dressed in a froth of white lace. In the basket with her are an eagle, a parrot, a rooster, and a duck, all with clipped wings. The birds are carefully chosen, an integral part of the ritual. Lucia's just a passenger, an ornament; she is, as Holbach put it, a part that does nothing in the machine, which was not very considerate of her feelings, but not intended maliciously. "Perhaps, Professor," she'd offered, "I might exercise a calming influence on the poor animals," and he had of course agreed eagerly, but somewhat insincerely. In earlier controlled experiments, the birds had been quite frantic and in no way safe to touch or pet, and he thought Lucia's charms unlikely to change that. She herself was bright-eyed and rapt with excitement, at the honor, at the adventure, at the change they were about to work in the city. "Hush now, precious," she'd soothed at the duck as Arlandes helped her into the basket. "The Professor is *very* wise. You'll be free soon." She'd blushed a little to be seen talking to the birds, but Arlandes kissed her hand and Holbach beamed at her in what he calculated was a fatherly but not inappropriate manner. Then the balloon lifted and she was gone from sight.

Flanking the golden-robed men, two columns of riflemen keep the mob at bay. The city has been expectant all morning, whispering rumors of the Bird's return. When word went out that the Countess Ilona was carrying out some mysterious project on the Heath, a scattering of curiosity-seekers came to watch. And when the wonderful air-filled globe ascended, the crowd exploded.

It seems like the whole city is here now, mobbing the Heath and choking all the narrow streets around it. The city hasn't seen a balloon flight in living memory. Carriages are left empty in the street, and children climb on their roofs for a better view. Workmen's rough cloth rubs against velvet. Bottles are passed around. A thousand boots ruck the lawns' green into black mud. And, of course, agents of the Gerent, the Chairman Cimenti, and all Ilona's countless other rivals drift among the crowd, watching suspiciously.

Holbach paces the line. He's dressed formally for the occasion, in a tailed gold-buttoned coat of thick red velvet, and a weighty ringletted wig, sweating slightly under his clothes, what with the summer sun and the tension and the crowd's heavy heat. He knows what the crowd's thinking: that this is something different from the city's usual run of spectacles, from all the gods and ghosts and monsters that thrum across its lines of power. This is a *machine*. *Hands* built this and raised it with deliberate, cunning purpose. The power of flight, under human mastery. What other powers—the crowd must be thinking—could these people arrogate to themselves? The balloon is the more beautiful for being a little blasphemous.

And, Holbach thinks, he was only telling the truth: the Countess *has* exposed herself. If today's venture succeeds, the people will adore them, will praise their triumph to the skies; but if nothing comes of it, after all this spectacle, they'll forget how wonderful the balloon is; they'll just remember the failure. She'll never outlive the humiliation.

Holbach has exposed himself, too, no less than her. He is a scientist; he has a reputation. And he has risked it in print, something he does not do lightly.

Nineteen years ago he published his *Critique,* his first monograph on the Bird, the one that made his name. And earlier this year, in a dense, technical paper that was nevertheless widely read— a point of pride for Holbach, who would like to be a man of the people—he set out to predict the Bird's next return. He did it by reference to the complex massing of the city's signs—a chaotic, organic weaving of almost infinite threads of potential. A fashion for silks; a new verse inserting itself in an old children's rhyme, *the bird is on the steeple/high above the people;* a rage amongst new-minted aristocrats for heraldic designs featuring birds; the roaring success of the Eagle and Kingfisher in Toulmin Street; a day on which all the grubbing, deformed pigeons of Kanker Market were replaced by doves. Certain graffiti around the city, and many other, less obvious signs. Dreams of flight, of course, not least his own.

It is by such signs as these that the symbiosis between our city and its gods is revealed, he'd written, in one of his entries for the Atlas; *so the gods shape the city, and the city shapes the gods, and our lives are hammered out between the two.*

The research was difficult. It has been decades since the Bird last appeared, and the divided and disordered city has never been good at keeping its records. And, of course, Ararat *teems* with divinities; it would be easy to attribute a sign to the Bird that was really a harbinger of, say, the Key, also a power of freedom, or Monan, also a power of sharp winds and the open sky. But despite the uncertainties, Holbach dared to commit himself to a date for the Bird's return. *Today.* His rivals are circling, hoping for him to be proved wrong.

And, privately, Holbach had approached the Countess Ilona with his plan. Today's work is dreadfully expensive, and he needed powerful patronage to make his dream come to life.

If his predictions had been wrong, after all this, she would not let him live. But he knows that he's not wrong. He felt the Bird's return even before the first flare went up. It's somewhere out there now. The city feels like a great wheel about to turn. With the right lever, some of that power can be put to useful work. Changes can be made. The maps can be redrawn.

He has passed beyond the lines of robed men. Someone has left a copy of some broadsheet on an iron bench. Tilting his head a little, he sees that it's the *Sentinel*. He tries to read the headline. These things are often portents; the city speaks through them. A drift of wind ruffles the paper's pages. Then a redoubled wind lifts it and it opens its broad pages and hurls itself at Holbach's face. He can read

Bird and *Today* and *Coming* and *?* before it wraps itself inkily around his head, and he flails it away. *It's here,* he thinks. He should be on the dais, of course. Puffing and red-faced, he sets out back to his place.

The Bird's coming up from the southwest. It circles the dun tower of the Mass How Parliament, turns sharply, a knife twist, as if with malice, and veers north and up Cere House Hill. The turn's too sharp for many of its human flock to keep pace. They find themselves alone in the sky for a horrific moment too long. Without the Bird to fill them and lift them, their ersatz wings are just a stupid joke, and they are prey for gravity again.

Indifferent, the Bird slows again and gently climbs the Hill, every inch of which is scabbed with a great crust of buildings grown together. Where the structures have not simply been built into each other over the years, the builders have covered what used to be open squares and streets with great swathes of grey waxcloth, pinned tightly between domes and peaks: an ancient depth of cobweb. Tall curling spires rise from it. Ugly blackbirds lurch from their roosts in the spires, and they join the flock. The waxcloth shrouds of the Cere House whip in the wind and open the gloom below to shafts of light.

The sky over the Heath is full of wings and motion now. The crowd screams and cheers. The trees explode with gusts of avian life. Sparrows and pigeons flutter up to join the Bird. Little bright larks flit around the throng's edge. The great white Bird soars over the Heath toward the Countess's men.

Holbach pulls himself up onto the dais, and, gasping, says, "It's . . . here! What're you . . . *doing?* White! Come . . . on!"

A footman raises a white flag. At the signal, the white-robed men square their shoulders against the dragging ropes and run for the river, heavy boots gouging at the lawn. (*The Parks and Gardens Committee will be furious,* Holbach frets for an absurd instant.) The ropes pull taut and drag the leaning and wobbling balloon with them.

Today's work is part worship, part science. It demands both ceremony and precision. Holbach counts under his breath, then croaks, "Blue!" A blue flag comes up, and two more rows of white-robed men run after the first, trailing kites, overtaking them.

"Gold!" and down the Heath toward the river, there's a crack and a hiss and a cloud of stinking smoke. Another flare scores into the sky and bursts. Stars iris out lazily from the explosion. Holbach's team crafted the fireworks to pattern, for an instant, the loose outlines of a swooping dragon. Against the bright blue midday sky, the shape is indistinct, suggestive, a ghostly afterimage. Another firework, and another, raise a procession of ghost-creatures in the sky: swan, moth, bat, owl; all in faded pastels, in jade, heather, coral. The quartet at the foot of the dais begins to saw away at Barnave's Opus 131 (*The Eagle's Morning*). The crowd cheers frantically for all this new activity, whatever it is.

The Bird curves itself in space toward the balloon, leisurely, as if curious about this bright clumsy challenger. Then it rushes suddenly forward, its presence sharpening into a line across the sky. The balloon leaps and the Countess's men are dragged from their feet and let the ropes slip from burnt and bloody hands. Lucia shrieks. The Bird soars close past the balloon and the feathered cloud following the Bird engulfs it for a second. Half obscured by the flock, the balloon seems to turn itself inside out, and for a moment it becomes a great pair of wings, sixty feet of azure taffeta spread out on the wind. The wings beat once, then the fabric falls slowly to the ground, curling smokily in the air. The basket drops, not slowly. The little menagerie of birds in the basket takes flight, their wings whole again, and joins the god's flock.

The kite-holders reach the river, where a flotilla of small boats cluster against the jetty's black timbers. The men tie their kites to prow and stern of the waiting boats, then push them off. The boats row out into the river, the kites tugging lightly into the air, whipping and diving in the excited breeze.

In the middle of the river sits the frigate *Thunderer*, pride of the Countess's small fleet and veteran of a decade's campaigning against the pirates out in the far reaches of the Peaceful Sea (and sometimes against the fleets of the Countess's rival lords, in incidents that it's safest to forget). It carries thirty-two long guns, and more than one hundred crewmen wait nervously on its decks: not the largest ship in Ararat's navies, but famed for its speed and grace, and speed and grace are of the essence for Holbach's experiment. Its figurehead is a robed amazon, lunging from the prow, carved lightning bolts in her hands, freshly repainted. The wood below is rich and dark.

Before dawn, without fanfare, the Countess's men brought it in from the sea, and up the Urgos into the city, forcing aside the river's regular traffic of garbage barges and coal barges. The Urgos is broad and deep, but the warship is incongruously huge in it, like some abyssal leviathan heaving onto land.

They've taken down its sails. Holbach supervised the work, up on the forecastle, watching a forest of masts and rigging topple noisily around him—the crew shouting and cursing and straining, Holbach wincing to see such a beautiful machine torn apart. Then Holbach's team brought onboard the second and larger balloon, dragging its deflated jellyfish body up the planks and onto the deck: now where the mainmast should be is a tumbled heap of golden cloth, waiting for air and life to be breathed into it.

Holbach had tried to explain it to a skeptical Arlandes as they stood on the denuded deck: "Of course the balloon won't lift it, not of its own force; it would have to be, oh, a *hundred* times bigger; but it's a sign the Bird will recognize."

Arlandes had arched one eyebrow. He had distractingly beautiful blue eyes. "You think the god will do as you command it, Professor?" Holbach had shrugged plump shoulders and looked away from those eyes and that cold smile and said yes. "Yes. Yes and no. The ship's a *sign,* like the fireworks and the kites and all the rest. Imagine it—well, imagine it as a great big bright floating cathedral dome, to be filled with the Bird's blessing. It'll *work,* Captain."

Gods, he hopes that's true. But it's too late to worry now. The moment's come; and at once it's gone, and Holbach watches the Bird pass over the river and glide off north toward Faugère and Hood Hill. The Countess grips his shoulder with an elegant, bony hand, and she *squeezes.* Her nails are very sharp indeed.

Holbach watches. It works so smoothly. A loose, then rapidly tautening, golden sphere swells up from the *Thunderer*'s deck. The balloon's inflating. Thick ropes (not visible at this distance) will be tightening, tethering the balloon to prow and stern. Sailors like little black ants swarm on its decks.

Then the small pointed several shapes of the kite-boats rise into the air, in a darting, uncertain ascension, halting and lurching. And in their midst, the *Thunderer* rises, too.

Its hull is deep below the surface, deeper than Holbach realized. It pulls slowly from the water, which rises with it in a lingering kiss, then opens and falls back in curtains of rain. It climbs against the backdrop of the buildings on the river's right bank; higher than the dome of Hoffman's Academy, than the bell tower of the Temple of the Crawling Stone, higher finally than the rusty cranes over the Brattle Bros. warehouse. It's so massive, even at this distance, the vector of its motion so improbable, that for a moment it seems to Holbach that the ship is still, and the city and the blue sky are opening back and falling away behind it. He grabs the rail to steady himself.

Holbach starts to count, "One, two, three..." The Bird has gone. The warship remains, impossibly airborne. "...sixty-one..." Still airborne, the impossibility compounding with every moment. The naked hull's like a swollen black belly, quite grotesquely unsuited to its new element, and yet it hangs there, defiant. "...one hundred and twenty." The men in the kite-boats toss out ropes to the *Thunderer*'s deck. The frigate's crew lash their satellites in radial position, forming the fleet into a crown, suspended over the city. In triumph, the *Thunderer* drifts up over the Heath. Its guns fire in salute, again and again, frighteningly loud.

The crowd cheers and screams and stamps, louder even than the guns. Holbach claps, and smiles and smiles and smiles. His experiment is a success. All these mad gestures, all this manipulation of signs and portents, balloons and fireworks and so forth—which Holbach thinks of as a science, and the mob thinks of as worship—has trapped the Bird's gift in the *Thunderer*'s hull. It need never come down again. No one has ever done anything like this before.

But now politics calls; a different sort of science is necessary if he is to harness this moment to his own fortune. So he bounces around the dais, pumping the hands of every man there, congratulating them, and himself. "Excellent work ... Your contributions were invaluable, Minister. . . . I hope we can count on your support for future ventures, Your Grace. . . ."

As her peacock courtiers puff each other's plumage, the Countess steps to the front of the dais. Her white face is expressionless. Her footmen scream for silence; then, as the reporters for the *Era* and the *Herald* and the *Intelligencer* cluster at her feet, she offers a cascade of half-threatening reassurances: *This is a gift to the city, to be used only in the interests of all of Ararat, as she sees them*; and *This ship is an act of worship, a living temple to the Bird, there's nothing impious or sorcerous in this, and it would be irresponsible even to suggest that there is, she hopes there'll be none of that. . . .*

Behind her, Captain Arlandes stares at the crumpled mess in the middle of the West Meadow: an unraveling wicker basket, and a little broken figure in a white dress. For some reason, he's drawn his saber, and he's holding it in a weakly shaking hand.

Holbach's glad-handing rounds bring him in front of Arlandes, and he offers his hand to shake. "Grand work, Captain. Are you looking forward to your new command?" Arlandes doesn't take Holbach's hand. He seems frozen. Holbach, too, just stands there, hand out, an awkward smile fading slowly from his face.

It seems there has been an incalculable interval of timelessness and weightlessness. Then Jack lands hard on hands and feet, on rough brick. He can't think what he called upon to cross that abyss. Yet here he is.

One of the watching women on the roof approaches him, her hand outstretched. Maybe she means to help him, but maybe she means to hold him. He spits at her face, snarls and bites the air at her. As she recoils, he's running for the door, and down the stairs, and down through ranks of rattling looms and out a broken window and *out* into the alleys.

✳   ✳   ✳

The Bird drifts north. Beneath it, the city rises steadily into the slopes of Ar-Mount. The Bird's flock has dispersed now. The river is a silver-blue ribbon below and to the west. It would take many days to follow the river this far, and you would pass through many dangerous parts of the city. And you might meet other gods on the way and forget where you were going: not all the city's powers are so gentle as the Bird, and the river in particular is something of which one should be very, very wary.

Here, dense, reeking streets and markets are woven around a maze of colossal stone walls, left here in some ancient age of the city. The Bird circles listlessly and settles on a high crumbling arch at the corner of two walls. It folds its wings and shuffles clawed feet, dislodging chips of stone. It looks very much like a bird now—a bird, not merely the suggestion of a bird. Its flat feathers are the dull shade of the stone; its huge eyes are yellow and blank.

The Bird has spent almost all the potential it brought with it. It has scattered its gift across the city, sometimes compelled by arcane science, sometimes freely. It has made changes to the city's matter, to its sacred and shifting topography, that the cartographers and city-scientists will notice over the weeks to come: changing the course of the river, very subtly, shaping elegant new curves; raising a daring crest of high towers over the hills. No less important, it has redrawn the territories of the city's avian life. It is neither pleased nor displeased with its work. Now it's ready to move on, to open the way from this part of the city to another, to begin again.

It leans slowly forward, stretching and turning its neck. It relaxes, then slowly stiffens, craning out to the facing wall. Then it isn't a bird anymore, only a steep flying arch of yellow stone. A tiny last mark on the city's map.

A presence leaves the city. The city's summer gives way to autumn. A thin, cold rain starts to fall.

TWO

The never-published fourth edition of Nicolas Maine's infamous Atlas would have described Ararat thusly:

> *ARARAT: The sacred city, the gods' great perpetual work, the city of a thousand lords; but you know this. It's everything you may see from your window, and much that's beyond your sight, and more that is cruelly buried. Everything written here was written first in its streets, but here it is given meaning and order.*
>
> *Everything that is true of Ararat somewhere is a lie somewhere else. We shall try to do it justice in the pages before and behind us, but we crave your indulgence for our errors. If it's truth that angers you, we are not sorry.*

. . . which entry, penned partly by Holbach, partly by the playwright Liancourt, was of course a little joke, for Ararat was the subject of the entire Atlas, and even all its many volumes couldn't hope to capture it: it was as absurd as trying to contain the Atlas itself within a single one of its entries.

Ararat's poets and votaries, the boosters of its business and the toadies to its rulers, struck a less ambivalent tone. This was *Ararat,* they hymned: blessed, haunted Ararat! First among cities, heart and also summit of the world; ancient beyond reckoning, but rebuilding itself a million times a day, stone and brick and iron, flesh and dreams, all of it woven, unpicked, and rewoven by the crisscrossing paths of a thousand divinities: a condensation of meaning into city-stuff, gleaming and proud. How very pale and thin the rest of the world seems next to Ararat! Let those who can sing its praises; but at the docks, on Gies Landing, Arjun just sat on his pack in the rain, between two stinking fish stalls and a juggling clown in smearing snakeskin facepaint, and he asked himself what the *fuck,* a crude and dissonant curse he had picked up at sea and disliked, but some dissonance was, he felt, required here, what the *fuck* he was doing.

His mission had propelled him over the sea, and across half the world, but now he thought he had never, throughout his long journey, allowed himself to look directly at that mission, never seen how vague and obscure of implementation it really was. Now he was in the city, and it was time to begin, and he did not know how. *And what if I'm wrong? What if it simply isn't here?* He had only a little money left and no place to stay.

The people who surged and jostled him and bellowed and tried to sell him things were mostly light-skinned; almost eerily pale, some of them. City-folk did not get enough sun. Others were dark or at least grime-blackened. The golden-brown of Arjun's skin appeared unique, and he attracted curious and possibly hostile stares, which he met with a polite smile and a sinking heart.

After a little while, the rain drove the clown off. Sheltered under a green awning, Arjun took his pen from his pack and unfolded a sheet of paper. Resting it on the hard back of his copy of Girolamo's *Techniques,* he started to write: *Fathers, Mothers, I have come to the city, at the end of summer, over the sea, bringing our hopes with me.*

Like Ararat, Gad sat in the shadow of mountains. It was far to the south, almost at the other end of the world. Its farms were on stony earth, under dark moss and purple heather. The air in Gad was very clear and cold. Sound carried far there. Perhaps that was why the first settlers had been able to hear the Voice.

The Choristry was the only building of any size in Gad, or for miles around. It stood in the middle of town. It was built like a wheel, topped by a shallow dome. Four spires rose at the compass points. A fifth rose from the dome's center, higher than the others.

Its walls were made of a dark mountain stone, carved and silvered in somber and abstract designs. Ample windows opened its contemplative silence to the mountain light.

The town of Gad sloped out down the hill, under curving roofs of thatch and clay, bowed as if in worship around the Choristry. Its roads were narrow and tangled, the widest of them barely enough for the carts that came in from the farms. There was no other traffic. Gad had only one market, and it had no particular name.

Gad had no neighbors in the mountains. A single road led down onto the warmth and noise of the plains. Winter's snow made it impassible, but in the summer, Gad did a little trade with the towns of the plains, sending down its small surplus on ox-drawn carts.

Sometimes, a Choirman went down onto the plains with the carts. The dusty, drunken cow towns of the plains could be rough places, but Choirmen traveled unmolested: any idiot who laid hands on a Choirman's black robes would soon face justice—or what passed for justice in the heat and noise of the world down there. And the towns were eager to house the Choirmen, for their medicine, or their skills with animals, or their patience in resolving disputes; but above all, the plainspeople—whose daily lives were dry, tough, and practical—wanted the Choirmen for their song, and for the intimations the song could bring them of Gad's sacred Voice.

In dusty bowls out back of the town, or in clearings in the scrabbly woods, the Choirman, or more often woman, would sing until night fell over the plains, then slip away. At dawn, she would wait where she sang the night before, cross-legged on the ground, black robes pooling around her feet, waiting for the town's children to come to her. She would test them all day, helping the shy children to improvise a clumsy descant upon her plainsong. She listened closely to their voices as nervous parents waited at home. Most often, she would pack up and leave town alone. Only a few children had the gift of song, and those she brought with her.

Arjun was very young when Mother Abayla tested him and brought him up into Gad. He soon forgot his previous life, except for a few scattered images. He remembered horses; cows; a piano banging away over a warm drone and shimmer of sitars and the drunken beat of hand-drums, in a room full of towering, twirling legs in dusty brown leather and bright lace and silk; the smell of dust and cows and cheap rum. Nothing much else. The Choirmen disdained piano and sitar and drums, but still, when he composed, he imagined that cheap piano and the peasant drums and drone, and the memory gave his music a thumping liveliness entirely unlike the other students' exercises. Otherwise, he never thought much about what his life might have been like before Gad.

They let him keep his birth-name. They added *Dvanda* to it—a word that referred, in their scheme of thinking, to an augmentation of chords through doubling and repetition, but that they chose for its sound, not its meaning: so that he was *Arjun Dvanda* at the chanting of the roll. It fitted the meter better.

The Choristry's floors were made of cool grey stone. The Choirmen's feet brushed it gently. The first thing he learned was to walk quietly, and listen closely.

Arjun's voice broke early, and fatally. It was not terrible, only pedestrian and a little flat. Good enough to belt out a sing-along at some peasant feast day down on the plains; better, in fact, than anything one could hear anywhere else in the world; but not good enough for the Choir. The Choir existed to echo the Voice. Only the purest singers were fit for that task. Those boys whose promise went sour were sent back sadly onto the plains.

Arjun was allowed to stay only because of an exceptional gift for composition. That was his earliest real memory: sitting in Mother Abelia's lacquer-paneled office while she and Mother Jessica and Father Julah explained this to him. They gave him a choice: he could stay, or he could leave the Choristry and go into Gad, where he would be taken in. He was very small on the hard wooden chair. The Mothers and Fathers were not cruel, unless it was perhaps cruel to offer a child that choice, but they were very honest.

Arjun chose to stay. When the Choir practiced at noon, he was permitted to take tiny parts, so long as he stood with stronger singers. When the Choir sang at twilight, in the hall in the central spire, chanting their measured adoration of the Voice, he was permitted to stand in the outer circles, where the less gifted students listened in silence.

Sourly he cultivated other talents.

The Choirmen were masters of many delicate arts. One school within the Choir specialized in clockwork, in workrooms in the south spire. They built precise clocks, and clever toys. A wind-up man walking; a dancer curling into a dying fall, then uncoiling up again; racing horses with tricky hooves that never quite touched the painted grass. There was a big Headman from the plains who had been a friend to Gad, who had sent two sons and a daughter to the Choir, but who had never himself been able to come to the mountains. They made a diorama of Gad for him, with little tin figures on tracks orbiting the Choristry through intricate carved streets. The plains demanded music boxes, too, and they got them, though the Choirmen found their noise tinny and false.

In the Choristry's gardens and greenhouses, another school cultivated herbs, medicines, and spices. Other Choirmen brewed beers and rum and liquors in the tunnels. Others made musical instruments, most of which they kept for themselves; the plainspeople had little use for the finer instruments. Arjun threw himself into composition. Every student composed music as an occasional exercise—it was a way to come closer to the Voice's song—but Arjun did it constantly, obsessively. By the time he was fourteen, his desk in the library was stuffed with densely scrawled notebooks. He made the other students perform his compositions. His pieces became increasingly difficult and angular. They had such strong and pure voices. He lacked their grace. It got awkward and painful.

They elevated him from the outer circle of the students into the second circle. He was now, they told him, a closer echo of the Voice; and with time he would become closer and closer until he reverberated with it perfectly. He was allowed small parts in the song, on the less significant days of the calendar. They added *Atyava* to his name, and moved his quarters to the east spire.

✻　✻　✻

In Father Julah's office high in the east spire, Arjun discovered a rare gift for languages.

He had gone there to discuss a problem with a piece he was composing. Fingers steepled, head lowered, black-bearded Julah listened patiently to the precocious child's problem. When Arjun was done, Julah thought for a while and dug through his shelves.

"Here. Father Nayaren's *Principles.* It used to be a basic part of the regular syllabus when I was your age. Keep it. I want you to read his second chapter. And—aha!"

Julah held up a book bound in deep red leather, stamped on front and back with a thin snaking dragon in gold foil. He opened it at a random page and held it up to Arjun. Instead of any letters Arjun recognized, it had rows—no, columns—of intricate designs. Like diagrams of one of Father Anias's clockwork engines; like musical notes, or the tangled roots of herbs.

"It's Akashic. I do not know the author. The book purports to have been written by the Petal Rain Dragon of the Heavenly Parliament, though I rather expect a human hand had to hold the pen for him. The let-us-say *difficulty* with which he deals is not dissimilar to yours. You can't read it, of course, but I can, though not as well as I'd like. I'll read to you. *'Gakusei'*—that's 'students'— 'listen...'"

Arjun came back the next day, and the next, to listen to Julah read. It went slowly because Arjun wanted to know the Akashic for every word Julah spoke. And when that book was finished, Arjun found other Akashic books. He found dictionaries and grammatologies, and began to teach himself the language.

Over the centuries, the old building had amassed a huge and startlingly diverse library, scattered among the Choirmen's offices, the vaults, the storerooms and workrooms. Arjun scoured the shelves and dug his way into hidden troves of strange words. He learned with preternatural quickness. It was just another kind of music, and it was easy to learn music, there in the echoes of the Voice. Within a year, he had mastered Akashic, and was teaching himself Tuvar and Mali.

There was no one to speak most of the words with him, and he had to guess how the words were pronounced. Even Father Julah had no real idea. Arjun hunted out books of poetry, and tried to guess how the strange vowels were spoken from the rhymes and meters. Alone in his room, he practiced a dialogue of a dozen languages. The sound of things was very important to him. But he had stopped composing, and hardly ever sang anymore.

When he was fifteen, he ran away, following a girl. Later, he wouldn't remember why, exactly. Nor could he remember her face.

Tsuritsa was an outsider. Her family came up with the carts, to buy clockwork tricks to sell on the plains. They set up their wagon outside Gad, on a patch of ground too rocky to farm, and stayed for a week. At night, they kept up a fire.

Tsuritsa was at least a year or two older than Arjun. She wore a red dress; she was black-eyed and her skin was strikingly pale. Arjun came to watch her dancing around the fire with her brothers. Two other boys came with him. He sat cross-legged, hands folded, at the edge of the firelight. After a while, Tsuritsa stopped dancing, and took the fiddle from her brother, playing while the others danced. Arjun stayed put as the other boys slipped away.

When Tsuritsa was done, Arjun called out from the shadows. "You're fouling the music's structure. At the end, the feeling should build, but you let it die. I don't know if you know any of the technical terms, but I can help you make it better."

Her brother told him to get lost, but Arjun kept sitting patiently, until she said, "All right. Show me then, choirboy."

Over the next few nights, she let him teach her a few tricks with the fiddle, standing behind her as she held the instrument, his hands over hers. She taught him a few words of her traveler's patois, and she let him take off her ruched and dirty dress, out in the fields away from Gad and the caravan.

When her family left, he followed them on foot. He could never remember making the decision to set out after them; when he thought about it later, which he did rarely, he remembered a sensation of confinement, of drowning, of clawing up out of weeds, and a dreadful urge to run. He could not keep pace with the wagon, and he had not brought enough food or water. The Choristry's servants found him a few days later lying under a farmer's fence by the side of the road, half frozen.

They put him to bed, where he lay with a fever. It felt as though the clutching weeds were dragging him back under foul water. He could see green waving weeds in the candle's shadows. His body was a dull weight. His breath fouled and revolted against him. His future was a dark river. He hated every aspect of himself and his body and his room and his world, and his graceless, honking voice, with an exhausted, passionless, but minutely detailed hate.

The herbalists kept the fever from killing him. A clear morning came when they told him he would soon be well again. And when he could walk, they said, he would be ready to mount the stairs in the central spire and to come within the presence of the Voice.

The Choir had no histories of its own founding. The Choirmen were skilled with their hands and voices, but incurious about their history. They thought of themselves as timeless.

The children made up stories, imagining a lonely goatherd looking for a missing animal, following an obscure path through the rocks up the mountain to find a silvery stream where he bent down to drink, and stopped, hand cupped, hearing a divine wordless song from the spring; or someone from the plains, like, say, a great leader, or a boy everyone laughed at, haunted by dreams of music, leading their people up to find the music's source. Something like that might have been true.

The Voice had a number of other names; sometimes they called it the Great Music, or the Chord of Chords, or the Immaculate Chime or the Golden Drone or the First or the Final or the Seven-Fold or the Thousand-Fold or the Constant Echo. The names of the god were as multiplicitous as its nature was simple, but that was a deficiency in the men who'd named it, not in the god itself. Arjun always favored *Voice*. Why not? It *spoke* to him.

The Choir, the Mothers and Fathers said, was an echo of the Voice. They devoted their lives to that echo, bringing it out into Gad and down onto the plains. And in the Choir's corridors, or out in Gad, you could sometimes hear a tiny pure fragment of the Voice itself, as if it was carried on the wind, or as if it unfolded itself out of silent space within you.

(Years later, as they lay in bed together in her flat in Ebon Fields, Arjun would try to describe it to Olympia: "Sometimes, you could be talking to someone right next to you, and they would hear it, though you couldn't. They'd tilt their hands to one side and fall silent. Smiling. Or sometimes they cried, but with relief. Or both. We'd wait for it to pass: we knew what it was like. It was very important. I don't think I can explain." She didn't quite understand; he didn't mind.)

The Voice was present in this intermittent and reflected way everywhere in Gad, but there was only one place where it was perpetual and pure. The Voice was alone, high in the central spire, above the hall where the Choir sang at twilight. When a student was ready to be elevated, it would communicate an obscure signal to the Choirmen, and they would bring the student into its presence, to be sounded.

Arjun should have felt pride, but he was hollowed out by fever. When Mother Abayla and Father Julah came for him at dawn, two days later, he went with them quietly.

They led Arjun up the winding stair in the central spire. His legs were still unsteady. They climbed into the round hall where the Choir would meet that evening.

The stairs wound up around the outside of the hall into the rafters. Silver bells hung in the darkness beside them, ascending in a stately spiral. The heaviest and deepest tones, known as the Oxen, were the lowest-hanging; at the peak of the spiral the highest were delicate as little silver birds. Father Julah flicked dust from the highest bell with his sleeve and a shiver of sound ran down the spiral, plunging down the octaves into the shadows. Mother Abayla clucked at him and he hung his bearded head, shamefaced.

Mother Abayla unlocked a door under the shadow of the eaves and they walked through a dim attic. A wrought-iron staircase at the end of the attic spiraled up into the roof. At the top of the stair, Arjun opened a hatch and climbed up into the Chamber.

It occupied the pinnacle of the spire. It was impossible to see the

Chamber from the ground; Arjun was surprised to learn that it was made of glass. The sheets of clear glass were supported by a frame of black iron girders and beams and struts of dark wood. The sky outside was the pale grey of dawn.

Arjun sat cross-legged and waited. He heard no music, only the quiet creaking of the glass and iron and wood of the frame around him. The wind whistled through the cracks. The room swayed slightly, barely perceptibly, there at the spire's tip.

He sat in silence, listening to the wood's tense creaking. At the edge of hearing, the glass panes produced a shrill, silvery, drawn-out screech as the frame stretched and squeezed and swayed in the wind. His mind was very clear and empty.

He focused on the creaking of the wood for a long time. The sound was senseless and shapeless. So he adjusted his attention and brought the sound of the wind within his grasp as well. The two sounds worked quietly against each other. There was the echo of a melody, and the beginnings of a rhythm, so slow and quiet that a less well-trained ear could never detect it.

He let his head hang down and expanded his attention again to encompass the sounds of the glass and the iron, then the silent sounds of the stone; then the sounds of the birds outside, the building, the quiet paths worn by the robed Choirmen; the sounds of the town and the river. He felt for a shape, a structure in the drifting susurrus.

At the edge of his focus, he found it. It was so quiet and slow and simple that it was barely there at all. Music came from the walls and from the sky, and from beyond and behind the sky. The edge of a vast presence was reaching gently into the Chamber. If he reached out, he could touch it. It worked a transfiguration on all the sounds it entered into; it played an impossibly beautiful music on the strings of the Chamber, and on the dome of the world. Arjun felt the clutching weeds retreat. He felt very clear and pure. He felt sad, but capable of great goodness and strength. The Voice whispered to him and held him.

He came down in the evening with tears dried on his face. Mother Abayla and Father Julah helped him down in respectful silence, holding his thin arms, locking the door behind them.

The next day, Arjun took the tonsure and put on the black robe.

He moved into a journeyman's office, on the second floor. He took on students in the evening, teaching them languages. Some of them were his age, or older. None of them shared his talent, but he tried to be patient and kind with them. For a long time, he felt reconciled to everything, and gladly so.

Arjun was not the last person to hear the Voice, but he was nearly the last. In the months after he left its presence, it called for only two more students, two girls a little older than him. They were the last students to be elevated.

No one knew exactly when the Voice started to withdraw. That made it harder. Four months after Arjun heard it, Father Pulli returned from the Chamber confused and frightened, and confessed to Mother Abayla that he had listened for a whole day and heard nothing. The Mothers and Fathers assembled to discuss his problem. They were very concerned. Was he too impatient? Was he distracted, somehow? They let him know that they loved him and wanted to help him.

Later, they realized that Father Pulli was surely not the first to come back from the Chamber without hearing the Voice, but only the first to admit it. They remembered how many of their colleagues had seemed distant, irritable, and confused. How many had been lying, perhaps for weeks? Mother Kinnaka came back from the Chamber claiming to have heard the Voice when no one else could, but said that it was dwindling, losing its way, falling into mere noise. No one knew whether to believe her.

They could only conceal it from the students for so long. Their fear and confusion were too obvious to hide. And it was no longer possible to hear the Voice drifting on the air. The absence was hardly noticed at first—it had never happened very often, anyway—but it became more painful as the months went by.

The Choir was like a fading echo. Without the Voice reverberating through its walls, the Choristry was just a big ugly black building, cold and shadowy and cluttered. What was its point? There was no music in it. Quite literally there was no music in it: the walls and spires had been carved artfully with flutes and runnels and chines, molded and mouthed with reeds of steel and silver and glass so that, while the Voice was present, the whole structure whistled and murmured a soft constant chant that rose and fell with the wind; now the noise alternated shrill and flat, and arrhythmic and senseless like the whine of mosquito wings, and it kept everyone awake at night. During the day, their rituals seemed empty and pedantic. The children became like any other children who had been taken from their parents and set to work hard in dark rooms. They became nervous, angry, bitter. The Voice wasn't there to comfort them. The Mothers and Fathers were hard teachers, unsympathetic masters.

(Years later, Arjun would try to tell the city how it felt; Olympia would be polite, while others, many others, laughed or rolled their eyes, but no one understood; Ararat was too rich in gods to understand poverty.)

Fewer and fewer students came to Arjun's office to study. The words came much harder without the Voice. Most gave up.

Every evening, Arjun passed by the workshops on his way to dinner. They grew emptier as the Voice's absence stretched out. The wires and springs twisted out of the students' hands; they lost their patience and dashed their work against the wall.

Two years went by. Some of the older students realized that the Voice would never call on them now, and walked out into Gad, or onto the plains. Two of the apostates found work in the office of Gad's Headman, where they raised bitter, pointed questions about the Choristry's tax status. The Choirmen created a committee to handle negotiations with Gad. Then there was fighting in the market, between some students and the boys from the town. The debate over who should punish them was tense.

Three years after he last came back from the Chamber, Father Pulli hung himself in his office. It was days before they found him. Others followed, as if Pulli's death had finally given them license.

They still went down onto the plains sometimes, and the plainsmen were still grateful for their medicines, but it was hard to find any song to sing them. And the plainsmen kept their children back, if they were elder sons or useful on the farm or in the business; they brought only surplus children to be tested. The Choirmen couldn't bring themselves to take the sniveling, distrustful infants, even if they showed promise. They couldn't see the point.

Gad was no longer willing to supply the Choristry, and the Choristry was no longer willing to share with Gad, so they started to trade. They put Arjun to work on the accounts, with Father Uttar's group, for a couple of years. He believed the Headman's office was cheating them. He made a report to the committee, and negotations went on over his head. The graft continued and his next report was ignored. He supposed they got something in exchange for turning a blind eye, but he never knew what it was. He couldn't see the purpose of what he was doing.

The Voice kept him going. He held it close as long as he could, but it grew pale and thin and brittle, slipping away like any other childhood memory.

Working in the archives, digging through forgotten texts, Arjun conceived a plan. He went to Father Julah first. He sat on the edge of the sofa and thought about how to make his point.

There was a mirror sitting behind Julah's head. Sometimes, while he conducted tutorials, Julah would look into it and groom his beard (greying now) with a pair of tiny gold scissors; he seemed to enjoy company for the act—though he did that less often these days. Arjun could see his own reflection in it. Thin, dark, and intense. Perhaps too intense. He tried to compose his face into a persuasive compromise between reason and passion. But this was no time for too much tact, and he spoke firmly.

"Father. The Voice is gone. We are like an unstrung harp. There is no breath in us. It will not come back."

Julah was silent for a moment. "Arjun, I've always tried to help you. I think you know that. But all I can counsel now is patience. These are hard times."

"Patience? What are we waiting for? Without the Voice, we have no purpose. We can't go on. Another decade, maybe, no more. Gad will swallow us. The plains will turn their back. We can't take any more students. It wouldn't be right. What do we have to offer them? The Voice is not coming back. It's been too long. I don't know whether it can't reach us anymore, or whether we drove it away, or it tired of us . . . but it is not coming back."

"Do you remember Leb? He came to me, talking like this, not long ago. He left us, Arjun. I don't want you to do that. Are you asking me whether you should leave?"

Arjun looked Julah in the eye. "Yes. I am asking you for permission to leave. Wait; listen: I ran away, once. You brought me back, and up into the presence of the Voice. Now I need to go away again. This time, I'll bring the Voice back to you."

He told Julah, and he told Abayla, and then he told various subcommittees, and finally, standing in the great shadowy hall, he told all the Choirmen assembled in council, like big black crows in their robes. He asked them if they had heard of a city called Ararat, to the north, on the other side of the world.

They'd heard the stories. A city of unthinkable size and age, marking a line across the northernmost edge of all the Choristry's maps; beyond that line was nothing but the city, borderless, uncharted, a great question mark. A hundred counts and dukes and parliaments and churches fought over those mazy streets.

They had heard the stories about the gods in Ararat. Everyone had: in Ararat, a thousand gods walked the streets. The city itself gave birth to gods, they said, and was half fevered with their worship. The Choirmen had heard that a great bird visited the city's skies; that a haunt of smoke and mirrors slipped through the theaters, behind the red curtains, crazing the city's dreams; that there was a hunger in the canals. In Ararat, their own dear Voice would be just one presence of many. It was painful to think of that.

Arjun dug out texts scavenged from the vaults, works of theology and science by Ararat's scholars, and read the relevant passages to the Choirmen. He made his case to them. *First,* the Voice had removed its presence from Gad. They could sit in the Chamber straining their ears until they starved and they would not hear it. Gad was dying. *Second,* Ararat was alive, its streets were fertile soil for divinity; and *third,* Ararat, he told them—jabbing his finger at the relevant sections of Kamisar's *Discourse on Theogeny* (*Consider the city not as a spider in the center of her web, but as a ball sitting on a sheet of gum-rubber; consider the depression it causes in the stuff of the world*)—drew the world's divine presences to it. Hungry for gods, it stole them from the rest of the world. He offered examples drawn from history books and scribblings in the margins of old scrolls. Where else but Ararat could the Voice have gone? Perhaps it was lost in Ararat's streets now, or sounding in some empty steeple; and *finally, therefore* it could be followed. Arjun could follow it, find it, bring it back to them. At the very least, if he searched the streets of the city of gods, he could find some clue as to where the Voice had come from and where it had gone.

The Council was skeptical. He thought they wouldn't have let him go if Julah had not persuaded them, and he thought Julah had only done that because otherwise Arjun would slip away like a thief in the night, and Julah wanted to spare him the disgrace.

Arjun himself had little hope that he could bring the Voice back to Gad. In fact, he couldn't even imagine how that could be done: he was glad they didn't ask too many questions. He just couldn't bear to *wait* anymore; he thought that if he could find the Voice for himself, in some alley, and hear it one more time, that would be enough for him, and it was all he could do.

By the time Arjun finally secured the Choir's blessing, snows blocked the path down from the mountain. He passed the time in his room reading about Ararat and the route there.

He knew the journey would be dangerous. He found a copy of the soldier-courtier-seducer Anian Girolamo's *Techniques—Military and Amatory,* and practiced Girolamo's instructions for handling a blade, trying to follow the illustrations. He had no way of knowing whether he was getting better.

He went down in the new year. The Choirmen provided well for him. He had money, and a supply of toys and medicines to trade in places that didn't recognize money. He took the Girolamo, the Kamisar, and a few other texts, and a knife. Down on the plains, in an alley behind a dance-hall, he bought a pistol.

He went north slowly over the dry plains. For a while, he traveled with a caravan much like Tsuritsa's. Later, he rode with a group of cattle hands, lying to them that he was handy with his pistol and on a horse, but he slowed them down and they left him behind.

The rainy season came and the heavens turned on their axis and poured the seas down over the plains, and the world turned to mud and white floodwater. He stayed in a town called Happal, where he tended the oxen. He slept in the barn and sang at night to the huge odorous beasts. When the rains lifted, he left the plains; he bought passage downriver on a flat-bottomed barge, which took him north through stinking swamps. Skirting the mountains, he crossed the hills on the back of an ass he bought in a town in the valleys. Winter fell again; he lived in pine-timbered Hokkbur with Ama, the village doctor's daughter, where they found him exotic and fascinating; he taught her children the piano until it was safe to go on. He paid his way over the vast northern desert on a great machine that roared black smoke and ran on iron tracks over the sand. He had never seen or heard of such a machine. He suspected that the fierce, dark men who claimed to own it understood its workings no better than he did.

His tonsure grew out. In the desert his skin grew darker and harder, going from brass to stewed tea to old teak, under a gathering black storm of beard. He got used to hunger. He'd always been slight, and delicate; he grew wiry. He had occasion to practice with his gun.

He crossed the Peaceful Sea on a trading ship out of Ghent. Arjun asked what cargo the small ship carried. With a gap-toothed grin, the captain explained that larger, slower ships might take timber or food, but the real riches and risks in trade with Ararat lay with more esoteric cargoes. That year, his hold was full of animal teeth. Various species. If his intelligence was good, the order of Uktena was flush with money and still persuaded of the sacred significance of these little fetishes. A big *if:* two years ago, he had brought a cargo of double-backed mirrors for sale to the followers of Lavilokan, only to find that they now considered double-backed mirrors blasphemous for some fool reason. It had nearly ruined him.

He touched the mast for luck and shrugged: the city was crazy, what could you do?

The ship came into the Bay on a bright morning. Arjun barely saw the passing of the Bird. All he saw was a rush of white that lost itself in the city's skyline. The captain fell to his knees, moaning. Arjun waited tactfully, pleased to find that it didn't frighten him at all. Perhaps it was an auspicious sign.

The crew took the ship into the harbor in awed, nervous silence. They passed easily through the chaos there. They had been ready to be stopped, questioned, held up for bribes, but in the shifting, slopping, splintering mess that the Bird's passage made of the harbor, no one cared to stop a little trading ship.

They tied off at Gies Landing. Arjun reached out for a dull black bollard, and hauled himself up and onto land. He shook the captain's hand once, firmly, and slipped into the crowds.

Arjun stopped a man for directions, some sort of trading-company official, who fidgeted and looked over Arjun's shoulder at the wreckage behind him, but pointed the way.

He pushed through the crowds, holding his pack close, wary of thieves. He passed under an ornate wooden arch and left the docks by a broad paved road leading northeast, curving up and around stately Stable Hill. From the side of the road, through a green curtain of tall lindens, he could look down on the river, and on the square, brutal warehouses and sunken alleys of the docks. The road was clogged with traffic: carriages painted with the livery of a dozen lords, gilded palanquins, rude wooden carts hauling produce from the docks. Passengers the length of the road had dismounted to stare into the sky. As he passed, the traffic slowly wound itself into motion again. It began to rain.

Cato Road ran north under another arch, this one squarely built of white stone, topped by two rearing horses, and dedicated, according to the plaque, to one Chairman Cimenti. North of the arch loomed a row of grand marble buildings. Broad steps stretched down from colonnaded facades to the tree-lined street; ranks of anonymous office windows towered into the sky. The steeples and domes of vast temples rose in the background.

Clarion Street cut off south from Cimenti's arch. It took Arjun, as he had been told it would, into the dignified red-brick houses of Foyle's Ward. He turned onto Mullen Dial, where a ring of discreet professional offices marked off a small open space in the heart of the Ward. The cobbles shone slick and black in the rain. Arjun walked clockwise around the Dial, counting off numbers on the brass plaques. Seventeen was his contact.

The week after Arjun went before the Council, Father Julah had handed him a yellowing letter. It came from some vault to which Arjun did not yet have access. Nearly one hundred years ago, Julah explained, the letter's author, Father Alai, had gone north to Ararat. The Choirmen of the time kept no record of his reasons. Kindly, Julah did not say the obvious: that they had considered Alai's travels to be a shameful vanity.

Three years later they had received a letter. The Voice alone knew how it had crossed that unthinkable distance. It was clearly not the first letter Alai had tried to send. Alai boasted cheerfully that he had founded a small choir in Ararat, that he was well on his way to adding the Voice to Ararat's crowded pantheon. He had reported that Ararat's people were very friendly, and very kind, and very generous. He left an address.

Arjun frankly doubted Alai's sanity. Who would leave the Voice behind to go preach in a distant city? What did the Choir care what Ararat worshipped? What was the point of another Choir in another place, a world away from the Voice? Still, this was his only contact. This man's successors would surely help him. Perhaps they had even found the Voice themselves. Perhaps, even, it was they it had come to. It was at least a place to start.

He banged the brass clapper, and waited.

Afterward, he walked back down Cato Road in the rain. *Of course* there was nothing left of Alai's hundred-year-old outpost.

It had been reconsecrated to some local Power, then reconsecrated again, then turned into lawyers' offices. *How fast things change here!* The woman behind the door had been intrigued to meet him and hear his story: she'd wondered what former owner had installed the huge organ that occupied the third floor and could not, she said, be removed without bringing down the structure. There was no other trace of the man.

He walked back to the docks, and sat down back at Gies Landing. He wondered how he had come this far without thinking past this point. There was no one to help him, and no place to start. He could not think what to do next or where to go.

He wrote his letter. He filled it with tinny, false confidence—very much like Alai's letter, he thought. He folded it and put it in his pack between the covers of the Girolamo, and wondered if he would ever be able to send it, and whether the Choirmen were waiting to receive it.

The sun went down behind the jutting roofs of Barbary Ward. Thick fog came in off the water, muffling the sounds of the docks as they wound down for the evening. The boy from the bar behind him came out and lit the streetlamp's flame. Arjun sat alone in a ghostly halo. The streets were like tunnel mouths.

He stood up. He looked at the broad uphill sweep of Cato Road, rising up out of the grey, and into the black mouths that swallowed the docksmen going home into Barbary Ward. He tossed a coin.

THREE

In the first hours after his escape, Jack ran frantically through the streets, trying to put as much distance as possible between himself and the House, keeping to the alleys and the shadows, flinching from passersby.

After a while, it started to rain, a chilly drizzle becoming a downpour that bent the trees and flooded from the gutters. Jack's thin silk-shot shirt quickly soaked through. Real fear seized him. In Barbotin, when it rained, it drummed on the outer walls and made the interior echo distantly—and frequently, gods knew, the damp seeped in through cracks—but nothing like this. Jack found that he feared the falling sky.

He found the first shelter he could: a brick overhang at the back of a brewery, next to the drays' stables. The nearness of animal bodies was comforting; it was a thing from his childhood. The rain washed thickly over the courtyard. He held his hand out to catch it; after a while, he leaned his head out and forced himself to look up into the vortex of falling water. He blinked and gagged and his eyes stung; he looked up again, and again, until the rain slackened. Then he ran his hand through his slick black hair, scraping the water from his face.

He knew where he was. These drab grey streets; this place was called Shutlow. The locals pronounced the *-low* with a cat's-meow whine. That was how you knew them. He was born there. In the north was the grey slope of the escarpment, with Mass How at the top; Shutlow lay below it, like something not-quite-satisfactory left on the doorsteps for the charitable societies.

He knew his way home, although his memory's map was more moth-eaten than he had hoped. And so many things had changed, and many more of the old places were dead and vacant, boarded or bricked up. Shutlow had never been a thriving neighborhood, but now it looked smaller and grubbier than ever. The people looked nervous and put-upon, in their petty offices. He wandered for a while, too scared to ask for directions, painfully aware of his bizarre clothes.

The house he'd been born in was still there, but it was no one's home now. They'd converted it into offices. The street-level shingle advertised the Gies Mercantile, Import & Export; oversized script painted in the upper windows promised the services of a dentist and a notary public.

His family was gone, then. Perhaps his parents were dead. They were the drunken, distant sire and dam of a feral litter: he wouldn't miss them much. He had grown without them. What about his siblings? Locked up somewhere? Dead? Moved all around the city, perhaps? He could think of no way of tracking them down. He wasn't sentimental, anyway.

The house, though: he was sentimental about that. That hurt. He walked round the side, tracing the wall with his fingers. He remembered its cracks and marks. There, under the window, was a crude scratching, a foot high, of a man bearing what was meant to be a hammer. He remembered it fondly. Its edges had been rubbed smooth by generations of tracing fingers. Figures like that were all over Shutlow, and probably all over the whole city, in amongst the gang markings and the advertisements and the beggars' marks and all the rest of the city's graffiti and glyphs. There had been another one scratched into the wall of the house opposite, in the form (more or less) of a cat.

If you saw a god manifest itself in the stuff of the city—and if the experience left you untouched, or at least unscarred—you scratched one of these into that sacred fabric. *Theophany* was the word the House's Masters used. Normal people might say *wonder* or *miracle* or *unveiling;* or *show* if they wanted to appear tough-minded, cool, indifferent. To see such a thing was either very lucky or very unlucky. You carved to mark the event, and to remind everyone whose work the city really was.

The one under his finger was Atenu, the Laborer. The one over the street was Yemaya, Sphinx-Mother. If he'd had a knife, he'd have carved wings into the soft wet wood under his hand. They'd be etched all over the city by morning, he thought.

No god had visited them in the corridors of the House. Even Tiber, the Fire, in whose name the House was run, had kept Its distance. Maybe that was for the best: there was no one to blame for the House but the men who'd made it. Too painful to think otherwise.

He found the Sphinx's mark after poking around for a few minutes. It was behind a straggly plant that had not been there before. He sat by it and looked across the street into the window of the Mercantile's office until the young man at the desk came to stand in the doorway and watch him suspiciously, and Jack recoiled into an alley.

He slept that night on hard earth, curled around a scraggly tree in an empty lot: the cold nearly broke him.

He dreamt of the Barbotin House. It was a shadowy dream.

What little light there was in Barbotin came from a narrow central shaft open to the sky. There was only one door out, on the ground, and one only passed through it once as a child. On the floors above, he had worked the silk in half-light, winding and twisting the thread, serving the machines. Encased in windowless iron walls, the nights were lightless and savage. In summer, the House was an oven, and in winter, it froze.

Who would build something like that? Jack knew the story; parts of it the Masters taught, and parts were rumor. The building was once a warehouse operated by the Ergamot Mercantile, a formerly powerful concern that was bankrupted by its last president's paranoia; the structure on Plessy Street was a minor manifestation of that illness.

To spite his creditors, as the Mercantile sank, its ruinous president gifted the building to the Church of Tiber. When the Church tore itself, victorious, from the resulting mire of litigation, it had no idea what to do with the monstrosity it had won. The structure sat idle for some years, before Father Barbotin conceived a vision: that huge safe-box, inescapable and impregnable, was surely made by the city's gods to be a *school*.

Father Barbotin's first plan was that the building could keep the flower of the Church's own youth locked away from the city's temptations, held to their studies, but his colleagues were unwilling to see their own sons locked under iron in the grime of Barbary Ward. So he was forced to propose—Jack pictured him saying it; he had a very vivid image of the long-dead Father, its clarity sharpened by hate—that the place be used as a workhouse, to trap and tame the masterless youth of the docks. And that way, it could pay for itself: those boys could be put to character-building, productive, *marketable* work. Properly adjusted, the plan caught on quickly. Tiber was a power of justice, of punishing and purifying flame; it was natural for its church to branch out into the workhouse business.

Barbotin's bust stood on the center of every floor, in the narrow well of light. It turned an enigmatic smile on the House's occupants, neither cruel nor sympathetic. Did he hate them for the shabby corruption of his dream—what he had hoped would be a retreat for the city's finest young men, turned into little more than another workhouse for its scum? *They* certainly hated *him*.

The House never entirely lost Barbotin's commitment to education. The boys worked the machines all day, but in the evenings, they were herded randomly into dark rooms for their lessons. The Masters were no great scholars—only the most pathetic of the Church's men would consent to grind out their days in that place—but before the boys were turned back out onto the streets, they were given a haphazard but intense theological training. Jack was a scholar of a weird and narrow sort. He was equipped to give the catechism like a priest or argue doctrine with the theologians. Though of course he would never be either; the stain of Barbotin could not be forgiven.

So Jack listened intently when Mr. Garond—a spindly half-seen shade hunching over his desk—read to the class from the pages of the *Sentinel* about the predicted return of the Great Bird. Later, he took books from the House's little library into the lightwell and studied them. He palmed scissors and thread from the workrooms, stole silk from the storerooms, and worked on his ritual. Soon after, he fought Dallow.

In the Barbotin House, laundry work was something to be fought for. It was hard work even for the oldest boys to turn the great mangles, but it was safe enough. Safer than the silk machines. More important, though, was the fact that the House had too few mangles for the volume of laundry it produced. There were days when excess laundry was taken to the roof to be dried in the light and wind, and the laundry detail, too, were allowed to take their pale and scrawny bodies up into the air for a moment. They fought over it: it was pathetic, and they knew it, but they had little else worth fighting for.

Jack picked on unpopular, brutish, bearded Dallow, once a ship's boy from Aysuluk run wild on shore leave in the city. It was to protect little Simon from Dallow's demands, Jack said, and that was partly true, but he would have done it anyway. He took Dallow by surprise, downing him with a foot to the back of his knee, and stamping on his fingers, breaking them.

When he was done, Jack leaned in to Dallow's bawling, snotty face and whispered, "Sorry, mate. But you would have done the same." Dallow was quite old, he had thought. Eighteen, perhaps; the two, perhaps three years that separated him from Jack were a wide, dark gulf. They might let him go early, now that he was unfit for work. It was almost a kindness, really. Turning to the watching boys, he'd said, "I get his billet, all right? Anyone else want to try for it?"

Four nights ago, he removed some critical pins and bolts from three of the mangles. A dozen boys were chosen to be whipped for that outrage. He was not among them, but he could see no way to offer himself in their place and still keep his plan. And every day after that, the Masters had to lead the laundry workers up into the light on the roof, and so he was in place at the right moment.

He began to dream of the Bird's coming. White wings filled his mind for a moment; then he was wide awake, and it was morning.

✹   ✹   ✹

Children darted in and out of the alleys around Moore Street. Children like himself: he could see they were nervous and hiding, too. Some of them were wearing the coarse grey wool jackets that marked them as workhouse escapees. Filthy and torn, as if their wearers had been free and wild for months.

He followed some of them, and watched them come and go from the abandoned shell of a pub at the south end of the street. The sign still hung, naming it the Black Moon, but the windows were boarded up, marking its death. (Jack recalled the Masters' lectures: the faithful of Dloan placed coins over the eyes of the dead.) Three stories of wet black timber. The whole building seemed to be leaning over the pawnshop next door, like a slow-moving giant looking for support. One day the two might touch.

The children came and went in twos and threes, or alone, slipping around a gate in the collapsing fence at the building's side, and into the back garden. Some were brazen, some furtive. Some were tiny little animals, no older than eight or nine; others were Jack's age, fourteen, fifteen, sixteen: rangy street-thieves, with underfed frames and the beginnings of thin beards. Jack watched them all day. He was hungry and cold, but wary of making a mistake. He took sips of stale rainwater from a barrel in the alley.

That evening, he crept in, around the gate and into the weed-strangled garden, and through a window at the back. The Moon's downstairs bar, stripped of its former furnishings, sunken slightly below the road, was full of children sleeping in corners on stolen rags, or on the bare boards. The windows were broken but sealed with newspaper or blankets. There was a weak fire in the corner, crawling around a couple of old chair legs in a pile of ash.

The place was cold, and it smelled, but it was sheltered from the rain. Jack sat himself in an empty corner.

A dozen pairs of distrustful eyes were looking at him. Jack looked around, and met the eyes of what he judged to be the oldest boy, a tall, slim, blond-haired creature, with a spark of curiosity in his gaze.

"I'm staying for the night," Jack said. "I'm not going to be any trouble, but I'm staying."

A smaller boy, his face scarred by some sort of pox, hooted out, "What's that supposed to mean?"

Jack kept his bloodshot eyes fixed on the blond boy. Hungry and weak though he was, he steadied his gaze.

"Ah, leave it," the blond boy said. "Look at him. He's too tired to do any harm."

A red-haired boy nodded. "Stay, then. Touch nothing and keep to your corner. We'll see about you in the morning."

FOUR

I very much regret to..."

Arlandes stood stiff-backed in the drawing room of Mr. Hildebrand's mansion, stuttering and staring down at his feet, at the shiny oily black of his boots and at the rug, which was the dusty green of mold or grave-moss. Mr. Hildebrand himself—Lucia's father, and Arlandes' own father-in-law, even still, death apparently not being enough in law to annul the relationship—sat in a red leather armchair, arms neatly folded in his lap, nodding his grey head solemnly. Arlandes had chosen to stand.

Both men wore black.

The mansion stood in the smog and noise and industrial reek of Agdon, and though the building was on a hill, and well-surrounded by trees and lawns, the curtains were drawn at midday to keep out bad airs.

"That is, sir, I regret that..."

He halted and his voice cracked and he began again.

The men of the Countess's navy—Arlandes' men—were mostly the scum of the city, press-ganged wharf-rats, and Arlandes typically mourned their deaths no more, at most, than one would mourn the loss of a well-trained dog; but the officers were of course drawn from the ranks of better men, from among young men of breeding, and sometimes in the course of events those young men met their deaths, and Arlandes had always made it his business to extend his condolences to their parents. The Countess encouraged the practice, on the grounds that the Captain's noble grieving presence might nip bitterness and blood-feud in the bud.

But he had no language suitable for the occasion of dear Lucia's death.

"Your daughter, sir . . ."

The old man continued to nod, apparently in time with the clock's heavy tick. On the table between them the maid had placed a tea set on a silver tray. The tea smelled pungently of aniseed and wet moss; it was a concoction boiled up from some root dug up from damp roadside ditches in the northern district of Dog-Bellow, and it had recently come into fashion for occasions of mourning and grief.

"Sir, I regret the events of the funeral. I regret very much the events of the funeral."

The old man raised his head and looked Arlandes in the eye. One of the old man's eyes was blind and milky. The other was sharp—blue-green and bright and dry. The old man's face was lined and pallid, spade-bearded. There was no trace of Lucia's beauty or innocence in his face. He was every inch the man of business, every inch the stern overseer. He looked Arlandes in the eye and shrugged and offered an awkward stiff smile.

The funeral had not been conducted with the dignity the girl deserved.

Arlandes had done his best. He had planned as diligently as always. Through the good graces of the Countess, they had been permitted to hold Lucia's funeral deep in the inner precincts of the Cere House, as if the girl had been a hero or lord of the city. Arlandes had attended the funeral flanked by his most loyal officers; they had walked the Cere House's dark corridors together in silence, boots clacking on the paving stones, all in jet-black of a tight military cut, black-braided, sabers clanking dully against black boots. An attendant of the House had led them through its corridors with silent gestures. They had gathered in the Seventh Precinct under the rustling shadow of the waxcloth, where the body was to be slowly and reverently dismembered.

The Cere House catered to a variety of rites of ending. Mr.

Hildebrand was a follower of austere and incandescent Tiber; his fortune, Lucia's fortune, the fortune into which Arlandes had married and which was now no more than ashes and dirt to him, came from his interests in a number of the Church of Tiber's mills and workhouses, including Harmony, Merry Vale, Barbotin, and Broadway. Accordingly, Mr. Hildebrand had demanded that his daughter be burned. Arlandes, like most military men, preferred not to play favorites among powers. Lucia herself had had a fondness for Lavilokan, of the mirrors—which was hardly surprising: she had been an only child, and a shy girl, and a pretty one. She'd believed she'd seen the god's shimmering face more than once in the glitter, in the shadows, in the corner of her dressing-mirror, and perhaps she had. Accordingly, Arlandes had insisted that the Observants of Lavilokan conduct the proceedings. Mr. Hildebrand had shrugged and let him have his way. Hildebrand wasn't a pious man. It would look bad in front of his business associates, but it was safer to cross them than to cross the Captain.

There had been three Observants, in velvet robes sewn with tiny glinting mirrors that clinked and rattled as they slowly crisscrossed the floor in front of and behind Lucia's bier. When they came up close to Arlandes, the mirrors caught his reflection like a scattering flock of ravens. They read the service from heavy books with blank silver pages, in which it was said they could read their god's words in the lines and angles of the infinite refractions.

Arlandes' mind had been as blank and as brittle as the Observants' mirror-masks.

Arlandes and his officers had stood stiffly on the left of the bier. When Lieutenant Duncan had tried to rest a hand on Arlandes' shaking shoulder, the Captain had wrestled away as if assaulted. Duncan had stood with Arlandes on the deck of the *Vanguard* at the Lion's Mouth when the air was black with powder and smoke, and Arlandes loved him dearly, but his touch—any touch but hers— was unbearable.

Mr. Hildebrand had stood on the right, surrounded by what appeared to be business associates. The mother was long dead; there was an ancient, wizened, weeping servant-thing there that might have been a nanny.

The Countess had not attended; affairs of the city made it impracticable. Holbach was present—whether as the Countess's envoy or on his own behalf Arlandes had not known or cared. The fat scholar's face had been sickly green with well-deserved guilt. One of his *intellectuals*—some girlish young man, or some girl disrespectfully in men's mourning attire—had held his plump left arm and whispered to him. He'd had more sense than to approach Arlandes.

One of the attendants of the House—a Mr. Lemuel, a wiry little black-robed functionary, who had made the broken body presentable, who had placed the lilies and brought out the blades on a steel tray, who had presumed to shake Arlandes' stiff hand—stood on Holbach's right side, and made inappropriate remarks, too loudly, as if he were watching some play-act staged for his private amusement, and poorly staged at that. When the Observants started to read from their blank books, Lemuel had stage-whispered: *I'll bet you they've just memorized the words. How much for one of the books, do you reckon?* Holbach at least had the common decency to recoil and blush but had sheepishly suffered Lemuel to continue speaking to him. When the Observants each took up one of the sharp glittering blades and began carefully, methodically, to divide and subdivide Lucia's body, slice by slice, joint by joint, until no piece could be distinguished from any other bright bloody piece, until the body was lost in a blank haze of its own reflections of itself—a procedure that was much less elegant in practice than in theory, and that made even Arlandes' veteran officers blanch and retch—Lemuel had chuckled and snorted: *Nasty. Oh, this is a nasty part of the city.* Numbly Arlandes had clutched the hilt of his saber. Lieutenant Duncan steadied Arlandes' hand again and he left the weapon sheathed and remained stiffly frozen.

In hindsight Arlandes doubted that Lucia would really have chosen such an ending. She'd been a gentle creature—their consummation, all too recent, had been a thing she had faced with a becoming trepidation and a wonderful, charming courage. She'd have wanted a softer and gentler passing. But of course all endings were terrible things. All divinities and their rites and the sacrifices they demanded were terrible things.

It had not been possible to keep the proceedings private; also present were numerous gossips and gawkers and several of the Countess's idle cousins pressing their handkerchiefs to their faces in horror and a trio of shabby-suited hacks from the broadsheets taking notes.

And also belatedly present, arriving just as the Observants, their mirrors dulled by gore, were finishing up their work, were seven men and three women in white and off-white robes or long loose smocks, each of them wild-haired and dirty, each whining and pleading and moaning as they shoved forward through the crowd. One skinny white-haired woman staggered into Holbach and knocked him to the floor. One of the men slammed into an Observant and they both went down with a great crash of breaking glass. The others—crying out, *She was touched by the Bird! She was touched by the Bird-God!*—stretched out and dabbled their dirty fingers in the blood of Lucia's body. One of the women touched her fingers to her lips and let her wild eyes roll back in her head. One of the men seemed to be trying to paint his face with bloody wings. Several attendants of the House came running up after them and tried to wrestle them away; the Bird-worshippers scattered and hopped and leaped madly, legs in the air. Mr. Lemuel started to laugh. That was the point at which Arlandes drew his saber.

Before the chill and the numbness left his mind and a great and desperate futility and shame took their place, and he collapsed weeping on the bier, the blood soaking his clothes, he had run four of the worshippers through, one by one, with the quick lunging foot-forward motion in which he had been drilled. Three of the four, pierced in throat or breastbone, expired on the spot, though not quickly. The strikes were neat but the deaths were not. All that sacred decorum and mystery turned to the floor of a butcher's shop! One of the Observants took off his mirror-mask to vomit, revealing his yellowing sweaty terrified mutton-chopped face, cursing in shock and disgust.

Three were dead; the fourth twisted to take the blade in the shoulder and was likely to live. But they were not persons of any consequence—they were only the last pathetic lunatic surge of a mania that was now passing from the city—and the Countess had been able to ensure that no consequences would follow from their slaughter. Because of the embarrassment of the incident, however, Arlandes had not lodged any complaint with the House regarding Mr. Lemuel's conduct.

I cannot tell you how deeply I regret . . ."

"Think nothing of it, Captain."

"Sir, I am most deeply ashamed . . ."

"An understandable incident."

"Sir. I do not refer only to the incident at the funeral. Sir, the circumstances of . . . of her passing, sir . . ."

He kept thinking of her body; of turning over the body broken on the grass, in the bloodstained white dress.

The old man sipped his tea. "Nonsense, Captain. Nonsense. She was a brave girl, wasn't she? We were very proud." He set the cup down and lifted his eyes to Arlandes' own for the first time. His eyes studied Arlandes' face carefully, cautiously, almost pleadingly. "Very proud. An accident; it's always a risk, that sort of thing, isn't it, Captain. We bear no grudge. Will you be sure to tell the Countess we bear no grudge?"

Arlandes was unable to speak; he nodded.

"Will you assure her that it was an honor—an honor to be associated with her great work? We were very proud to enter into that relationship with your Countess. Very proud, Captain. I told you how proud I was when you asked me for, for Lucia's hand. This doesn't change that, not as far as I'm concerned. I'm glad you came here today, Captain. This tragedy doesn't change that."

Arlandes remained still.

"How is the—the ship? Your new command? Wonderful thing. Exciting new days ahead, right? Could be a whole new order. Just what this city needs: a strong hand to knock things into shape. I see a city full of new opportunities in this thing. I hope the Countess won't forget those of us who sacrificed for it, though you'll tell her we bear no grudge, won't you? Though if she were minded to offer some sort of compensation, we'd not say no. That's all I'll say on that front. But I hope we won't be forgotten. I hope my dear Lucia won't be forgotten. That's all."

Arlandes nodded, gestured to the door, wordlessly excused himself.

In the hallway mirror—dusty, vulgarly ornate—he caught his own reflection. His black clothes, his bloodshot eyes, his pallor on which the old dueling scar over his eye stuck out sore and livid: he was a stranger to his own reflection. There was nothing sacred in that mirror, no trace of whatever Lucia had seen in the glass's silvery depths. Only a tired and sick man, looking older by the day.

It would be a relief to return to the sky. He was painfully sick already of the earth.

FIVE

A rjun found lodgings in the Golden Cypress, on the cheap end of Moore Street, where Shutlow drained down into Barbary Ward.

The Cypress was a strange survival. Its name dated back to an older cycle in the life of Moore Street, when the docks were further up-River, and sailors from warm seas came to drink on the Street. Those crowds were long gone, and the name was sadly out of place on this dark cobbled street. The beer garden out back was shadowed at all times by the warehouses on either side. Chill fog off the canals gathered there.

Moore Street had still had a sort of rough life only a few years ago, but some of the trading companies had closed, and others had moved their facilities, and the docksmen went elsewhere to drink, and Moore Street's pubs started closing. Somehow the Cypress had kept going while the Black Moon and the Harrow and Red-Beard's folded and were boarded up and given over to the desperate and wretched squatters of the city. The pub stayed afloat on the hunched backs of a few scowling old men, who sat and drank stiffly and apart from each other.

Madam Defour kept a cheap boardinghouse behind the beer garden. A piece of card-stock glued in the Cypress's smeared window promised BED & BOARD REASONABLE WEEKLY RATES, in a crabbed hand; in rather larger and more vigorous script it warned NO TIMEWASTERS NO DRUNKARDS NO KAT-CHEWERS NO "FREE-

THINKERS." Inside, it smelled of cabbage, aniseed, and peeling paint, and the stale smells of Defour's lodgers, all aging bachelors or vague and helpless widowers.

Defour herself was a sharp birdlike little woman. She interviewed Arjun in her tiny office, clutching her grey woolly shawl about her and complaining of the cold. She pronounced him "Acceptable. Younger than I'd like. But new to the city. You'll be looking for work. That should keep you quiet enough."

Arjun thought it as good a place as any other, and it was cheap. And there was a dangerous city outside, full of over-reaching towers, crazed constricting alleys, strange gods. It scared him to think that the maps in the Choristry's library had not been able to place any borders around it. Shutlow was a dusty little corner of that vastness; a place for tiresome, ill-paid office jobs, for eking out one's retirement on a small pension, for a sad kind of nervous respectability. The escarpment to the north cast a constant grey shadow. It was hard to imagine coming face-to-face with some maddening god in such a place. It was somewhere safe to begin.

He took a room on the second floor, an awkward little yellow box. A shelf over the bed was cluttered with tarnished pewter icons and idols, left behind by previous lodgers. Their postures and expressions were utterly inscrutable to him.

He started to tell her his story. Not the truth, but entirely a lie; that he'd come to the city "as a representative of my order, my Choir, in the hope that there might be trade between our..." But she made no pretense of interest, and he let the subject drop.

In the daytime he went walking in the city. Every morning, he would set out in a different direction, charting out courses at random, walking until the light began to fade and he had to turn back to Moore Street. He struck out north, through drab Shutlow up into Mass How, where he admired the great kilns of the terra-cotta works. The border between the districts was clear even to an alien; the sad litter and muck of Shutlow's streets ended sharply when it met the bounds of Mass How's fussy street-sweepers. He made it as far as Laud Heath, and climbed the hill to the old Observatory and looked down across the meadow and over the river. The next day, he went under Cimenti's arch into Goshen Tor, and looked up past the grand facades into the close-packed windows, trying to imagine the engines of commerce at work behind them, the lives locked within.

One day he went as far as the cafés and theaters and pleasure gardens of Faugère, where he spent more than he could afford on coffee, a new experience he found both repulsive and compelling. He spent the evening drifting among the jewelers of the Arcades, where constellations of lights hung smokily under a canopy of mirrorglass and silver. Barmaids dressed like princesses beckoned passersby into bars and cafés. They did not look at Arjun; his poverty must have been obvious. He spent too long there, and had to walk home nervously in the darkness. He envied those who passed him in carriages.

He bought a blank loose-bound journal from a printer's workshop on Janus Street, and he made notes, methodically, charting the streets as he went. Inky trees grew on every page, sprouting every day from the kernel of Moore Street to encompass North Shutlow, South Shutlow, Mass How. He marked off the streets one by one as they disappointed him. His pockets filled with scraps of scribbled paper, snapped pencil stubs, the dust of dried ink.

He got filthy looks from passersby who saw him sketching out his maps. He wasn't sure why; it seemed they took it as an insult or an intrusion. One day, a fat red-faced man slapped the journal out of his hand and spat on it. He tried committing the streets to memory as he walked, and marking them down in his room at night, alone. He couldn't do it; he couldn't hold it all in his mind. He could recall, quite perfectly, each note and accent and tricky ghost note of Julah's notorious Opus 21, but the streets defeated his memory. Sometimes he suspected they changed from day to day. After a while he gave up; he let the streets take him where they wanted.

He followed the streets south, too, into the slums and shanties and hacked-about concrete blocks of the Fourth Ward. He kept his blade prominent as he stepped carefully through the cracks and filth of the narrow streets, weaving around the stick-and-daub huts that sprouted in every street or ditch or scrap of empty space. He stepped over bodies sprawled on the mud that were either dead-drunk or dead. He followed the canals to the brutal mills of Barbary. He

stopped outside a huge concrete building under a sign that read
POULTRY TERMINAL 7. The sounds and stench drove him home.

There were temples and churches everywhere. He didn't go into
them. He wasn't ready. He tried to steer clear of the cloisters and
ghettos the various cults carved out of the city, where strange and
sacred laws applied. Whenever he saw an efflorescence of bright-
robed men in the street, or a sprouting of strange statues, he would
take a sharp turn and keep walking.

For an afternoon, he sat across the street from one of Tiber's
churches, a high-arched building in the Third Ward. He sat on the
edge of a dried-up stone horse trough and watched the crowds flow
in and out of the church's doors. The stained-glass windows showed
a pillar of fire towering over stylized golden rooftops. He stopped a
woman leaving the church and asked her what it stood for. She
looked at him oddly, and explained that it was not a *symbol* of anything. Tiber *was* the Fire, she told him; it burned to the north, in a
plaza full of courthouses and prisons; on a clear night you could see
the glow from Third Ward, if you found a high place to stand. He
thanked her, thinking that the Voice seemed very insubstantial and
remote next to the city's brash wonders.

In the evening, Arjun went back to the Cypress. He nodded to the
barman, who stood in the dark clutter of brass and glassware behind
his bar, swabbing out a dirty glass with a grey rag and grey water.
He received a curt nod in response; then it was down the steps at
the back of the bar, into the murky garden, and through into the
house.

Defour was sitting in the dining room, playing cards by candlelight with Heady, one of her lodgers. Her shoulders, hunched over
her cards, were draped with layers of dust-grey shawls. She leaned
back, holding her cards to her chest, and called out to Arjun as he
went by in the hall.

"Are you joining us tonight?"

"Not likely," Heady said. His scurfy white hair was slicked
greasily back over his head. He wore a shabby suit, with an incongruously bright and smart red handkerchief in the buttonhole. "A

solitary type." He flicked a card down. "Above our simple pleasures. No offense."

"Well, he's new here. I expect things were different in Ged. I dare say the city is overwhelming for him."

"Gad," Arjun corrected her.

"Certainly," she said. She put an answering card down with a firm smack, and smirked, scrutinizing her remaining cards. She wore too much makeup for a woman of her age: it crumbled around her eyes when she squinted. Heady was leaning back and looking up at Arjun.

"I suppose it *is* overwhelming," Arjun offered. "I walked across Mourner's Bridge today. I could see all the way up the river. The banks were built up as far as I could see, even up on the slopes of the mountain. It seemed unreal. I wondered if anyone had ever mapped the city all the way up the river."

"Watch it. None of that talk here," Defour snapped. "That sort of thing'll get you in trouble. The city isn't to be mapped by the likes of us. I don't know how you did things out *there,* but this is sacred earth." She arranged her cards and smiled condescendingly. "Still, it must be nice to have so much time just to *drift* about."

"Very *grand,*" Heady sneered. "A fine use of a gentleman's leisure. *Aristocratic,* one might say."

"One wonders if it is really as fulfilling as a solid day's work, though, Mr. Heady."

"A man should work, I've always thought. But it's not my place to question."

"Should we be worried, do you think? Are his means of support ... *improper?* Will he bring shame on my house?"

"Well, you've put up with Norris all these years."

Defour put down her cards and glared. "Now, Mr. Heady, don't say that. Mr. Norris has had a hard life. We should all be very grateful for him." Heady looked uncomfortable.

"Well, good night," Arjun said into the silence.

Defour rounded on him. "*Rent* tomorrow, I believe. I hope we don't have to expect any problems. Though I don't see how you can pay it, the way you live."

"Certainly. Good night." Arjun forced a polite smile as he left, reminding himself that the Cypress was *very* cheap, and he was too poor for pride.

A string quartet was playing in a glass dome in the Arcades. It was a cold autumn day outside, but the Arcades were warm and bright under strings of gas-lamps hanging from arch to arch. The lamps made a dizzying miasma in the air, on which floated spices, incense, and perfumes from the shops and stalls.

Arjun stood at the back of the crowd, trying not to stand out. The crowd was well dressed, the men in velvet coats of rich green and red, the women in elaborate cascading dresses. Arjun's clothes were lined and beaten, ingrained with trail-dust from the plains and deserts he had crossed; so, he feared, was his face. He had scrubbed and shaved in the tub down in the Cypress's scullery, but he did not feel he was clean. He thought he probably looked like a brigand, or some kind of horse-thief. The quartet was playing a sentimental piece. The aristocratic young man next to Arjun was making a great show of dabbing tears from his eyes. Occasionally he gave a shuddering, theatrical sigh. There were several like him in the crowd. Clearly, deep feeling was in fashion here, Arjun thought.

The quartet was quite competent, and the piece was effective, although surely not sufficiently to explain the audience's wetly welling emotion. If it had been the work of a student at the Choristry, it would have been judged workmanlike.

No, that was unfair, Arjun thought, unkind and petty. There was an occasional grace to it. He came back the next day, and the next, and listened to the quartet cycle through their repertoire. There were fewer flashes of grace after the first day. There was never any echo of the music he was looking for.

In one of the narrow streets that wound under and into the Arcades, Arjun spent an afternoon watching a street musician, a flautist. He tossed a small coin into his hat every hour. There was a blind man in Barlow Street who blasted out martial themes on a cracked trumpet. He was dressed in a faded and filthy soldier's uniform; perhaps it had been his own, perhaps not. In Faugère, girls in rags walked by the cafés, stopping by crowds to sing, in hopes of selling flowers, matches, or icons—pathetic songs romanticizing the hardness of their own lives and deaths. Arjun followed a group of them on their rounds, until they stopped and stared warily at him. He was frightening them, he realized, with his attention. They were probably used to being preyed on by strange men. He left them alone.

An old man on the corner of Moore Street played a hurdy-gurdy in the evening, weakly stamping his foot and singing in a broken voice. Arjun listened, then came back with a notebook, and took down the names of all the songs the man knew. He visited Miller's Row, where the printers displayed song-sheets on the walls along the length of the street. Cheap as they were, they were beyond his means, so he walked slowly up and down the street sounding them out in his mind, committing them to memory.

The city was full of sacred music, too. Robed choirs dedicated to a variety of powers proceeded through the streets. Churches rang their bells and wailed their calls to prayer. Organ music spilled from their doors. Lunatics, broken by divine visions, howled out hymns from the gutter. He avoided all self-consciously sacred music; he imagined he would find what he was looking for unexpectedly, by sudden grace, in the city's profane and commercial clamor. Somewhere in it he hoped to hear an echo of the Voice, some trace of its spare rhythm, some snatch of its sad melody, some subtle harmony that might bring it to mind. He felt like it was always on the edge of his hearing, but he never heard it.

Defour liked to host her lodgers in the boardinghouse's dining room. It was dark and stale, and the fading music-hall posters around the walls did little to enliven it. But her lodgers were all single men, and poor, and could not refuse a free dinner. They sat around a lace-draped table in the middle of the room. Two black-crusted tureens held a stew made of the blubbery salty meat of some beast hooked up from the harbor. The candles were fat, smoky, and greenish. A few dusty moths circled them stubbornly.

Fat schoolmasterly Mr. Drabble sliced off a small piece of his meat and held it to the candle until it singed. "For Tiber," he explained, answering Arjun's curious stare. "A sacrifice. And just in case, why not for Lavilokan, and Bladud, and..." He rattled off a rapid list of names; others around the table suggested others, casually, as if they were gossiping about old school-friends. They cut it short and dug in before the food had cooled too much.

Defour started the conversation: "Perhaps our new guest could tell us where he's been today? How does our fair city strike him today, I wonder?"

"I went to the Optical Cabaret," Arjun said. "Standing room was half price for the day. I wanted to hear a song they call 'The Rat-Catcher's Daughter.'"

"The Palace!" Defour said. "What did you think?"

Arjun had not been impressed. "It was interesting," he said. Into the silence, he added, "I think the singers were men, dressed as women. It was quite surprising."

Mr. Haycock snorted. "That's all that place is now since that swishy defrocked curate bought it. Mind you, I'd not say no to landing him as a customer. Expensive taste in filth, I hear."

"You should have seen it in its day," Defour said. She gestured with her grey head at the posters on the wall.

"Art Checken out of Hood Hill sells to him. *Filth*."

"You used to go there often?" Arjun asked.

"I *headlined* 'em, didn't I? See? Gracie Defour. That's me."

"They say he tries to pretend it's for the sake of classical learning," Haycock offered. "One of *those*. All the better: you can charge extra for the intellectual pretensions."

Haycock—a dwarfish man, a fierce and twisted pug-snout upturned fiercely at the world under a bald head—was a dealer in rare books and curios: not only pornographic texts, but also sermons, codexes, works of science and art; piles of remaindered journals, banned or merely forgotten. His clients were sometimes shady, sometimes illustrious, sometimes both; he loathed them all equally. He carried out his business from no fixed place, operating a number of stalls and lockups, or by post; therefore, he was never off the clock. He rattled out this sort of business-chatter almost constantly. Arjun thought he meant it aggressively. Him and Heady both; conversations between the two men were like peculiarly lead-footed fencing bouts. Arjun ignored him, asking Defour, "So you bought this place when you retired? You must miss the stage."

She glared, then shrugged. "I suppose you don't know. You don't say that. Not to one who took her ticket."

Arjun felt the sting of a frustration that was becoming familiar. He was at sea in this city, constantly wrong-footed by inexplicable shifts in the conversation. ". . . ticket?" he asked.

She fluttered an eight-pointed gesture over her heart, and said, "The Spider." She indicated the little black-legged brooch at her throat. Then she explained (while Haycock described some of the perversions available to his customers for the benefit of the rest of the table, who had heard Defour's story before).

She had been a milliner's girl, who had turned to the stage. Most of the others she had known failed and some of them starved. She was the lucky one. She headlined the Chymic, until the Palace out-bid it. Did Arjun know "What Will You Do, Love?" Or "Lero, Lero"? In her day, those were *her* songs. The crowds roared for them; they loved her even more when she teased and *didn't* sing them. Anything she did could only make them love her more.

Then a letter came for her, backstage. A plain brown envelope, addressed in a shaky child's hand, placed under her mirror. She knew what it was, and could have chosen not to read it, but she did.

She followed the letter's instructions and went to a small fenced-in park in Foyle's Ward, where a motley crowd waited. Beggars and gentlemen jostled each other to get to a plain wooden box sitting on a bench. Each of them reached in blindly and took a ticket, then slunk home without talking.

Her ticket told her to release a dove on stage during her act. It made her shiver: she had taken a ticket at random—how could it be so perfectly targeted to her? But of course she knew how. She obeyed the instruction; how could she not?

And she obeyed every other instruction that came to her on the little tickets, over the years. Many of them made small, arbitrary changes to her act. Her fans adored her all the more: her performance was out of her control now, and stranger and wilder by the week. One of them ordered her to marry a certain weaver from Salt Marsh—her first husband, dead now, let him rest. Sometimes she was told to write her own tickets, and leave them at the Spider's obscure churches, for some stranger to draw. *Take in a girl from a workhouse and educate her,* she wrote on the first one, when she felt she should do good; *Steal gold from a temple,* she wrote later, when she dared to be bad.

She was afraid at first, but as the lottery played on she threw herself into each change with utter determination. The tickets and letters were a chain linking her to something impossible, transcendent; a power that lurked at the center of its web and pulled obscure strings, changing lives. No one ever saw the Spider with their own eyes, they said, or knew where it lived, but when she took a ticket, she was on the end of its line. She was connected to it and to all the other people throughout the city who took its tickets and wrote them, whoever they were, whatever lots they held. That was how the god manifested. Sometimes she dreamed the Spider's glittering black presence in her room at night, its cold mirror-eyes on her, its clicking mechanical legs. Its magnificent complex *indifference.*

Perhaps she opened the letter because she feared it was only meaningless fortune that had put her where she was, and another roll of the dice could throw her back down; the Spider's lottery gave a purpose to chance, made the arbitrary sacred. But perhaps it was just to feel the god's tug in her soul.

Her final ticket told her, *Change lives with the first person you see from your window. Never draw another ticket.* So she swapped with the fat man who owned the Cypress; nervously they exchanged identical tickets between their shy hands. It was the most intimate thing; then they forgot each other. The Spider only knew what he was supposed to do with *her* life. She knew that some idle gossips—and she most *certainly* meant to include Mr. Haycock, and Mr. Clement, and Mr. Drabble—liked to spin stories about the fortune she'd squirreled away somewhere from her days on the stage; she advised Arjun to get no funny ideas on that account. Oh, at her final performance, her fans moaned as if at a sacred wounding! But that was years ago. They forgot her quickly. "As they should," she said, "as they should." Her ticket was what it was. There were many better but many worse. She missed nothing. It was a *vocation.* She looked both defiant and sad. Arjun looked away.

✽ ✽ ✽

At night, Arjun reread his small store of books, by the light of the candle Defour had provided (making a note in her rentbook).

He had marked certain passages in Varady's *Speculations*. One concerned the disappearance of a priest—*an eccentric figure, with his feathered dress and his habit of issuing inappropriate challenges*—who had come from the jungles of Luahl in pursuit of a jaguar god that had vanished from Luahl's treetop temples. *He told me he was tracking the god,* Varady wrote, *and his manner was such that I believed him, although I would be hard-pressed to explain why: his methods, sniffing after trails on all fours in the streets, tasting tree bark, and so on, were very odd and irreligious to my way of thinking. I believe he found what he was seeking; regrettably, he vanished before I could question him. I will have more to say on this later.* But maddeningly, Varady never came back to the story.

And Arjun reread Girolamo's *Techniques*. In his capacity as courtier, Girolamo advised the traveler to the city, or the city native who had business in some unfamiliar district, to make a presentation of themselves to whatever local powers or Estates held sway there. In his capacity as a soldier, Girolamo had traveled widely in other countries, and it was his view that the squabbling rulers of Ararat were far more jealous of the proper gestures of respect than the rulers of more unified polities.

That advice struck Arjun as reasonable. Best to observe the city's traditions, if he wanted its help. Of course, Girolamo's information regarding the particular rulers he had dealt with was many decades out of date. Arjun needed advice from the living. But his circle of acquaintances was narrow. After a little thought, he went to Heady's door and knocked softly.

Heady was one of the city's jurors. A professional. A small living, but it was his. He had explained it to Arjun on their first meeting, with great pride and in minute detail. Ararat had such a multiplicity of courts and laws that there was always a demand for a reliable juror, one who could be trusted not to give a disobliging verdict. He sat in whatever causes were going, wherever they didn't check the property qualifications or would let them slide. Every morning, he would go down to the courthouses to make himself available. He never paid much attention to the facts; they would only distract him. And he certainly never learned much about the law of any of the courts. Who could? There were so many; woe betide any man who committed a crime over which two or more courts claimed jurisdiction; his trials would be a longer and worse ordeal than his punishments. However, he learned to determine with perfect accuracy how the judge wanted him to vote, which was the more important qualification anyway.

Not always a "judge," of course: in Ilona's courts they called him the Inquisitor, and Mensonge's courts were run by priests; in Mad Ananias's courts they let a horse stamp out the judgments, but it was the official who chose which questions to feed to the horse who really counted. All the same sort of people, in Heady's professional experience: they just wanted to deal with reliable people who knew not to make trouble, how to show respect for their betters. So they called him back, time after time. He had a little reputation, if he did say so himself.

He especially liked criminal cases (preferably sexual matters), but a good long family-estate dispute was a source of reliable income for months—not that he was in a position to be picky. Best of all, though, was when they got some dissident or heretic on the hooks. "Not the loonies, the pathetic street-howlers. Those are just sad. I mean the smart-arses. The *fancy* ones, you see?" It was his great pride to have been the thirty-first juror, back when he was young and keen, in the famous trial of the blasphemer Nicolas Maine, and to have done his part to help the censors and the Chairman to stand up for the decencies of ordinary folk, returning a richly deserved sentence of exile.

Arjun doubted whether Heady's profession was honorable, but it was clear that the man knew who was who and where to go. And Heady was happy to help. He was very proud. He was glad to give advice; the price was that Arjun had to listen to it.

"You're a good listener, you know," Heady told him. "No back talk. Eager to learn."

"I was raised to listen."

"Don't sound so smug. No one makes a living that way."

Arjun followed him one morning to Chairman Cimenti's walled compound in Goshen Tor. They set out while it was still dark, heading down to the river. Dawn came while they were crossing the Jaw. They went up the hill to the Tor. Heady lectured Arjun on his need to make something of himself, pointing at all the monumental offices around them by way of illustration.

When they got closer to the compound, Heady told Arjun what he knew about the Chairman. "First, he's one of the Estates that claims authority over Shutlow. I suppose officially he's only involved there as a charitable venture; but he's a big man in these parts, and don't you forget it. Second, he's a banker. The Chairman is the big man at the top of the Cimenti concerns, which own, well, most things you can see from where you're standing. *Very* rich. Pays good rates, too. Not that that matters to you, who's above that sort of thing. Very nice, it must be. And third, then, he doesn't keep a horde of do-nothing thugs in uniforms around like most of the rest of the big Estates. Not that I mean to say that they don't do good work, because they do. Keeping the peace. Keeping things *straight*. It's the gods' work. What was I saying? The Chairman, yes. Spends his money on agents and spies. So watch what you say about him. Fourth, he's a banker, like I said. Likes professional people. Businesslike. Go-getters. Ha! Good luck to you, young man."

"I understand he's a great patron of the arts. I've seen his crest at a number of concerts."

"Yeah, well, if you say so. That way. Go on, then." Heady pointed him toward the Chairman's offices and walked off to wait outside the courthouse in hope of work.

Arjun spoke through a copper grille to a smart young woman. "Good morning. I am Arjun Dvanda Atyava, of Gad. I represent the Choir, from far to the south. I am here to pay my respects to the Chairman."

He repeated this again and again, making his name a chant, to many different smiling faces. The receptionist took him through a marbled foyer, through a door behind the desk and into a high-windowed hall filled with rows and rows of clerks sitting poring over columns of figures in heavy books. She handed him off to a clerk who took him upstairs at the back of the hall and through a room of women tapping away at strange devices, like little square harpsichords, that rattled and choked out paper marked with heavy black print. Arjun realized that the clockwork bird he had brought as a gift was less impressive than he had hoped. The clerk passed him on to a hard-faced overseer who took him along a walkway past the vaults. And so on, up and around the building, until a bewildered secretary brought him into a gilded office occupied by a blond, neat, smiling young man, who was happy to accept Arjun's respects on behalf of the Chairman, as one of his *personal* secretaries, and expressed the Chairman's best wishes, and ushered Arjun out through some back passage onto the street before Arjun could explain his purpose in Ararat or ask for help. The way out was so much quicker than the way in. So that door into the city was closed, then.

SIX

In the morning, the children formed into clusters and left the Black Moon. Jack watched them patiently, wondering how best to insert himself into their society.

Most of the smaller children there were scavengers, mudlarks; they went down to the river at low tide, to the sewers or canals, to gather the leavings of the city: firewood, coal, metal, scraps of clothing, scraps of food, anything the ragmen could take. They scavenged filth and ashes and bones. Horseshit and dogshit for the tanners. Jack couldn't enter their business. You needed a basket, a bucket, a scuttle, something to hold the scraps you found. He wished he hadn't thrown away his cap.

Two of the boys sold newspapers; they picked up bundles of the *Era* or the *Sentinel* from a cart in the market and they stood in the streets all day shouting and waving the papers, which they could not read. Too public, too noisy; Jack didn't dare. He might be seen. And besides, he was too old for it; he was no longer fresh-faced.

Instead he followed the two boys his age—the tall blond boy was Fiss and his red-haired friend was Aiden, they said, and they seemed to be in charge—and watched them steal food in Seven Wheels Market, where the stalls sprawled in the shadow of the great wide wheels of grey stone. (Each was the size of a mill wheel; whatever ancient people had carved them and brought them up from the river had, everyone said, used them for sacrifice.)

He watched them cut two rabbits from a pole in Coney Wheel, and lift a box of matches from a barrel in Chandler Wheel, and slip

grey linens from the secondhand clothing heaps in Saddler Wheel.
He watched them buzz the pockets of the clerks as they came out of
their rickety grey brick offices in Sunder Square. He watched as,
inviting damnation, they slid the smooth carved prayer beads from
the back-pockets of the men who came out of Atenu's temple.

He watched their subtle walk, but he couldn't replicate it. He
was too awkward. He stood out. His brightly threaded shirt didn't
help. Hands went to purse strings when he came close; merchants
leaned protectively over their stalls and fingered their clubs. The
first day, he went hungry.

In the evening, Fiss tossed him a hairy sliver of dried fish, and
said, "Eat. Look: if you won't leave us alone, at least stay out of the
way, all right? You don't know what you're doing. You'll get us all
caught."

The second day, he followed Fiss and Aiden anyway, though at a
distance. Back to Seven Wheels again, where he remembered a few
things; how the market's ragged western edge ran down into Fourth
Ward, and how brave he'd felt as a child when he'd gone into that
western sprawl, where they said that gangs up from the Ward held
sway. And he recalled that Seven Wheels, though it looked rich
enough to him after the workhouse, was where Shutlow's poor fed
and clothed themselves; the better sort went north and east to the
tall department stores of Hoeg Street. He supposed, though, that it
was too hard to steal from those places, and he told himself to remain patient and watch Fiss closely. And quickly enough it all
started to come back to him. He sauntered up to the butcher's slab,
his eyes and his apparent attention elsewhere, arousing no suspicion, snatched a fistful of sausage, and bolted. The shout went up,
but he forced his way through the crowds and away. He ate down by
the canal.

That evening, Fiss shook his head to see Jack come back to the
Moon. "We saw them chasing you. Never thought you'd get away.
You won't last a week, Jack, if you keep that up."

Jack just smiled. He remembered the trick of it. Now he was
free, and fed, he felt faster and more confident. By the third day, he
was quicker still. By the fourth, he was quicker than Fiss or Aiden
had ever seen, moving lightly, with an innocent smile. He could

take whatever he wanted. He moved in on Fiss and Aiden's marks while the other boys were still just standing there. He snatched a purse from under a priest's red robes; two handkerchiefs, one monogrammed, from pin-striped clerks at lunch in the market; a plain craftsman's knife from the belt of a hard-looking man on his way to the Ward; other bits and pieces. Volume came easy. Quality might need practice.

As they sat around the floor of the Black Moon's bar that night, he made a show of graciousness: he gave Fiss and Aiden the lion's share of the takings, saying, "This was yours. No offense. I just couldn't wait. Thought I'd save you some time."

Fiss looked him up and down. A couple of days ago, he had looked at Jack with an exasperated mother-hen pity. Now he appraised him sharply, sizing him up. Jack smirked back.

"Why are you wearing that shirt?" Fiss asked. "You look like a clown, with all that silk."

"Like a *tart*," Aiden said. "Who's a pretty boy, then?"

That got a laugh. Jack didn't rise to it. Instead, he told the story of his escape, explaining the magic he had worked with the shirt, the blanket-wings, and the bright silk.

"No one gets out of Barbotin," Fiss said. "Bird or not."

"Not till they're old," a boy called Riley agreed. "They let you out when they've squeezed you dry. Old man Lagger from the corner was in there, and look at him now."

(*No he wasn't. Yeah he was. How do you know?*)

Aiden asked him about some boys he knew who'd ended up there. Riley knew another. Jack was able to describe them both.

A murmur went round the room. "My sister knew a lad who came out of there," Fiss said. "Head full of book-learning, but sick, and no useful trade. So talk like him, then, if you can."

Jack recited Tiber's catechism; when that wasn't impressive enough, he summarized and criticized the thesis of Lagrange's *Ordination and Incarnation*.

"That's the stuff, all right," Fiss said, "whatever it means. Barbotin, broken out from. Who would have thought it?"

Some of the smaller children came to Jack that night. He was a godly man, they said: they had heard him. They never got to hear any such talk, not in the kind of lives they had. Could they listen to him some more? They asked him about Tiber, and he told them that that god was very distant, and wouldn't warm them. They looked heartbroken. They asked him about the Spirit of the Lights, and he said he'd never seen it; it wasn't welcome in Barbotin. They asked: *They say there's a golden god that walks round in the north somewhere, comes down from the mountain, and it makes the streets all gold where it walks.* Jack named it for them, and told them: *If it's real, it's far to the north. You'll never see it.* But they kept asking; they were hungry for something wonderful. He couldn't say no to them, so he talked to them about the Bird, and how it had been to fly. Fiss listened, too, pretending to sleep, Jack noticed.

Fiss woke Jack, digging his grubby patched boot into Jack's ribs, firmly but not ungently; when Jack started, shocked to see that it was already morning outside, and that he had slept later and deeper than he had allowed himself to for years, Fiss said, "So the others are out earning their keep. You're fast, and you're clever; you can come with me, take a look, see what you think."

Jack followed Fiss down to the docks, through lunchtime crowds. The lanky blond boy was much too tall for his ragged grey trousers, but he carried the absurdity gracefully. He kept up a running commentary on the passersby, the contents of whose pockets he claimed to be able to tell at a glance; when they sensed him looking too closely, and turned to stare back, Jack tensed to strike or run, but Fiss just smiled confidently and wished them the blessings of the god of their choice, which seemed enough to set them at ease. It was a good trick.

Fiss led them up the stairs at the back of the Cup-Bearer's little chapel, perched on the edge of the Jaw, the great crowded bridge that joined the two halves of Ar-Mouth harbor.

"That's the place," he said, pointing down over the Jaw's edge to a small square building of red brick. "It's a storehouse and countinghouse for one of the shipping companies. I come down here and watch sometimes. It used to have just one guard out the front; now, see, there's a team of them pacing up and down. But look—no one around the back. If you could get in . . ."

Jack watched a stream of young men, dockhands, move in and out of Fiss's warehouse and the others in the street, loading and unloading sacks and crates. A young brown-smocked preacher of Atenu, the Simple Laborer, stood on an upturned crate, offering them an extended sermon on the virtue of their exertions. His words were only half audible over the noise of the docks, but the gist was clear. Jack thought that he could do the preacher's job, or that of his audience, if only he knew where to start. He asked Fiss, "What's in there?"

"I don't know. But they must think it's worth protecting. It has to be something better than wallets and handkerchiefs. I think maybe we could do it. But I don't know how. And then there's another problem. I've seen other people watching it. A serious gang, from the Ward, I think they are. I've seen some of them around at the place I sometimes go to, you know, unload what we take. I don't want to cross them. We're not anything like as dangerous as them. So then. Any ideas?"

Fiss was looking at him intently, hopefully, but Jack had nothing to offer. All he could think was that the preacher was barely older than him, and some of the dockhands were younger. He didn't know what to do with himself; his years in the House had not prepared him for any kind of adulthood. Everything they were doing down there looked both absurd and intimidating, in equal measure. But he was surely too old for Fiss's way of life; so, too, was Fiss, of course. It couldn't last.

Fiss shrugged. "Never mind. Don't feel like flying down through their windows? Maybe later." He laughed, and walked away. Jack stayed, for a while, watching the crowds; when he closed his eyes and let the noise rush around him, he could imagine he was flying.

If any of them still doubted his story, they believed it when Mr. Tar and Mr. Shunt came asking round about him. Two black-suited, dirty-bearded men, pale and red-eyed, of uncertain age. They were overheard everywhere, asking bartenders, shopkeepers, whores, old Lagger, the crone at the Cypress. A boy had escaped them, and they wanted him back. "Defn'tly you they was asking about," Fiss said. "And they were from *Barbotin.* They said so."

Any other House might let a boy slip back into the streets, one who was more trouble than he was worth, knowing they were all the same and another House would snatch him up again soon enough, or the cold, or hunger, or fever. Not so Barbotin, it seemed.

So he slipped away from Shutlow's shabby streets. He told no one where he was going; he didn't know himself. At first he chose streets at random. He quickly decided that, between any two possible streets, he would always choose the richer one, with the grander and cleaner buildings, and he would always try to seek higher ground. He was looking for somewhere as unlike his native ground as possible, somewhere they would never think to look for him.

He ended up across the river, in Goshen Tor, than which he could imagine nothing stranger. He marveled at the towering offices of the banks, the endless grids of blind windows. Multifaceted, like the eyes of the Spider were said to be.

It was not safe for him in the streets around the banks; the watch was always there in force and he felt sorely out of place. It was no safer in the temple prefectures. The Tor's temples were rich, and old, and paranoid, and he stood out dreadfully there, too. But he could not go back, so he went up.

The temples were massings of ancient stone, marble and steel and glass. Not one of them was still consecrated to the god for which it had been erected, in ancient and unrecorded time. Spires were thrust up proudly, then abandoned when the gods to which they were sacred fell from favor and the rituals for which they were constructed were forgotten. The city's builders would stretch out bright domes over the roofs, then leave them to turn green and mossy and cracked a century later. Temples grew together and divided violently, cannibalizing each other's bricks for new towers and arches. The banks were almost as ancient, and transformed themselves almost as riotously. From the streets, everything was ordered, marmoreal grandeur; from the sky, the Tor was chaos.

It was easy to hide on those roofs, and Jack did. He found his way up the fire escape at the back of the Latimer Museum, up from a backstreet that was not like the dark and dirty back-alleys he knew, being instead lamp-lit and lined with discreet gentlemen's tailors and clubs. From the Museum's high gables he balanced across a narrow beam to the mazy roof of a temple of Tiber. He hid in an abandoned office clinging to the side of what had once been an observatory dome. At twilight, he crept down to steal food from the kitchens, hopping over uncertain, rotted floorboards, sneaking through dusty halls and down into the temple's living parts. He ate out in the air on the roof.

He was on the edge of the dome, chewing a rind of bacon, when a great shadow swept over the roof, rising behind him. There was a throb, a drone, and a sense of great pressure. The air rushed past, followed by a great curve of wood, like a falling moon. He was frozen with dread. It passed overhead, seeming close enough to touch, and he dropped to the floor, but as it went past, he saw that it was in fact far, far above him. Impossibly, the shape resolved itself into a ship: a deep, stretched curve of a hull, a heavy hump of rear decks. As a child, he'd seen such ships (with sails, though, where this had a great gibbous balloon instead) painted on theater backdrops, in pirate romances. Such things had no business here in the city, or even, he thought, in the real world, much less in the city's sky. He couldn't believe it; had the city changed so much while he was locked away?

It dwindled in the darkness to the north. He watched it go. After a while, there was a distant sound of thunder and a flash of fire on the horizon. And another.

A few days later, he stole a newspaper from one of the offices below. The *Era* reported that the Countess Ilona's miraculous warship, the *Thunderer,* had destroyed the fortress of the Urbomachy's notorious crimelord Jack Bull. A glorious day, the *Era*'s editors rhapsodized; a promise of the bright future to come. *Perhaps one day the city entire may be lifted into the sky. No borders to spark conflict; and no shadows in which crime can hide and disease breed! And for this miracle we must thank the Countess Ilona*—some previous reader had scrawled "whore" in the margin—*and the scholarship and vision of Professor*

Holbach, who in a remarkable ritual on the banks of the Urgos, on Tisday, Cabriel 14th . . . Jack tapped his finger on the date.

The story was accompanied by a blocky, awkward print of the warship. Jack thought it looked beautiful.

The rest of the page was taken up with a column under the heading "THE THUNDERER" but, to Jack's disappointment, it wasn't about the marvelous ship; THUNDERER seemed to be the pen name of whatever loudmouth boss owned the paper. It was a pompous, blustery rant, attacking some merchant named Shay, who had, in some manner too horrible for the *Era* to describe clearly, transgressed against the city's gods. *Reader, you are rightly angry,* it said: *This man's disrespect for Our City may be tolerated no longer. Because The Gods themselves may not strike him, the responsibility falls to those charged with Rulership of Our City, and it is to them that we address our Plea. We certainly would not wish to be forced to suspect that Shay is suffered to go about his Business freely because his offerings are of interest to some man of Power* . . .

Good for Shay, whoever he was, to have annoyed that pompous fool. Jack tore off the ugly verbiage and kept the print of the warship. He folded up the sheet and slipped it into his pocket.

Not long after, he snuck into the sumptuous bedroom of some bishop or prelate, where he washed his face in a golden bowl, and looked at it in a silver mirror. There'd been no mirrors in Barbotin. He was thinner than he had thought, and less strong-jawed. Still no growth of beard yet, which he knew, of course, but it was still somehow surprising to see.

From a glass cabinet on the wall, he stole a beautiful curved knife. It had a dancer's balance. A small but satisfying revenge. A *first* revenge.

He quickly regretted it, though. The priests soon put a watch out at night, pacing the halls with blazing torches. He could slip past them easily enough in the shadowed empty halls, but it wasn't long before they turned their attention to the roofscape. They sent up patrols of young seminarians, armed with sticks, poking around the derelict huts and abandoned towers.

They came close to Jack one night. The sound of them outside woke him. He gathered his belongings under one arm, and slipped out of the window, and ran across the open roof to hide in a dark corner behind a pile of rotted planks. He knew that they would find the corner he had used as a toilet.

They were closing in. He couldn't ever sleep safely, he realized, with no one to stand watch for him. He could not survive for long on his own. Sooner or later, his luck would fail. The city was too vast; he was lost in it, alone. He went back to Shutlow, and the Black Moon, where they might take him in again. Perhaps it was safer now.

SEVEN

Arlandes woke from a dream of Lucia, dancing. In all of his dreams she was either dancing or falling, or sometimes both.

His valet had laid out his uniform on the walnut dressing table of his quarters. He still wore the black—he saw no reason yet to stop.

He dressed himself without thinking, his eyes half-closed, as if still in a dream. He slid a brown leather briefcase from under his bunk. He sat on his bunk with the case in his lap for some minutes. It was time; it was surely time; in his dream without thinking or being able to think he had decided it was time. Then he stepped out into the brilliant blue sky of morning.

His quarters were in the stern. He crossed the bare deck toward the prow, passing briefly under the cool shifting shadow of the air-balloon. His feet felt light as air; everything on the great ship felt light as air.

There was no roll or yaw, no heave or pitch, only a steady imperious stately drift, and his legs were not used to it.

There were no tides. When the wind blew—and the wind blew fiercely up there—the crew clutched at their hats, but the *Thunderer* did not sway. Whatever powered it was not dependent on the wind.

The sounds were strange. There was none of the creak or slosh or slop of a true ship. The rustle and snap of the great balloon overhead—that was passably similar to sails. Chains clanked and the wood creaked but somehow did not *settle;* it was weightless. Or not weightless, quite; there were no words yet for what it was.

Arlandes was no poet to coin new words for it. It was a weapon and it went where he pointed it—where the Countess ordered him to point it.

Whenever they docked—the dock being a kind of scaffold, like a scaffold for the hanging of giants, built on the hillside on the Countess's estates, overlooking the palace, in a place where six months ago there had been a stand of beautiful oaks—Holbach was there, hanging around, rubbing his fat hands together and asking to be let on board. He yearned to study his device in operation. Holbach consorted with poets and playwrights and various kinds of degenerates and perhaps one of them could name the sounds the ship made; but Arlandes had resolved that the fat scholar and his cronies would never set foot on the ship's boards unless and until the Countess *personally* ordered otherwise.

"We followed the river north overnight, Captain, and now we're tacking west over Grafton and..." Arlandes waved Lieutenant Duncan away and proceeded alone across the deck.

The ship would go where it was ordered. No storms would impede it, no waves drown it. Arlandes doubted that his presence was even necessary.

Where the masts had stood were stumps of oak bound in brass. Gibson and Dautry were polishing the bindings. They saluted and went quickly back to their sweeping—they knew better than to wish Arlandes a good morning; they knew very well that he frowned on familiarity.

Otherwise Arlandes was alone. The *Thunderer* was undercrewed; it went of its own incomprehensible power, and there was little to man but the guns.

No salt spray to sting the skin and redden the eyes. But the light somehow was colder and brighter and the wind harsher than on the ground.

The men were different, too. A kind of spring in their step. They laughed more. One-eyed scar-faced grizzled old hands suddenly catching themselves laughing, giddy as serving maids on carnival. Perhaps it was the lightness of the air, or the nearness of the sun. Perhaps it was that the city they inhabited was so different: no alleys, no filth, no beggars, no shadows; only rustling flags, and weather vanes, and high glittering windows, and the golden spear-tips of the spires; and more often there were only clouds, and birds. Only Arlandes remained solemn.

They talked about him behind his back, of course.

He leaned over the lightning-carved prow. He was alone out there—the helm, that complex arcane machinery that he did not understand or care to understand, was down belowdecks. No doubt Lieutenant Duncan or someone was down there tending to it.

The sprawl of brick houses and tanneries and mills below him must have been Grafton. Not a district with which Arlandes was familiar.

There was to be a trade conference that day between the Burghers of Grafton and the Stross End mercantile—the Gerent's drab-suited bunch. Chairman Cimenti's bankers were to be present, too. The *Thunderer's* mission was simply to be there; to hang in the sky, over the delegates' heads; to be *seen*.

And Arlandes—what would Arlandes do with himself all day, as the ship hung idle? Sometimes he itched to spark the thing's heavy black guns.

Tiny throats piping, wings snapping and chattering, a flock of blackbirds came wheeling around the prow, scattering and circling around the intruder in their space. They passed away to starboard. One tiny creature circled the deck for a moment, alone and frantic, before returning to its flock.

Arlandes leaned the briefcase against the prow's rail and snapped it open. Folded neatly inside it was a white dress, bloodstained.

The city spread out beneath him. Grafton's tallest buildings were its jute-mills, chimneys craning up toward him, their smoke-belching mouths distant black specks. On the western edge of Grafton a tributary of the river wallowed into unhealthy marshland and fen, scattered with shacks among the thorntrees and the scratches of wooden bridges over the slime. The hills west of that were capped and crusted by tower blocks. They looked somehow uninhabited; Arlandes wasn't sure what gave him that impression. It was something about the windows—no sun glinted from the distant tiny panes. A dead zone, perhaps. Miles of deep valley behind those hills; then further hills, on the edge of Arlandes' vision, sprouted domes and minarets like mushrooms. A storm flared over the domed hill, and the sky in the distance was hazy with rain, and Arlandes could see no further.

And if he turned north he could see all the way to the Mountain; he could almost see the clouds around the Mountain's peak, and the towers around its slopes, and the *density* of it. The crew all avoided looking at it; they'd all picked up the same habit of dropping their eyes when they had to turn that way. If he turned the helm north he could be there in only a few days. They said the streets that carved the Mountain were strange, and dangerous.

If am lucky, the Mountain might make an end of me.

He'd once imagined that the city would seem smaller from the air. Holbach had told him to *imagine it, Captain: the whole city laid out before us, to be comprehended as one perfect whole.* He and Holbach had both been wrong. The city's far walls were invisible, still mere rumors, far beyond every hazy horizon.

And it *shifted*. The streets below him that curled and twisted like warped timbers also *shifted* like waves. Like the folds and bloody lace of her dress, falling. So they said, of course. So they said. *The gods shape us for their ends,* as they said. *They are always weaving.* But to see it, to see it clear and cold from above, was terrifying and disgusting beyond all reason.

Two nights ago, for instance, they'd passed low over Carvalho Street, and they'd seen the lights come on in the Rookeries—the gaslights and torches coruscating in gold and purple and green, hung all around the doors and windows of the bars and brothels and playhouses and teahouses and wrestling-pits. The lights had formed a twinkling aurora in the night sky. And Arlandes—unable to sleep, pacing the deck—had watched that aurora spread and climb and reach into the sky; had watched it drift down Carvalho Street like smoke, like a tide, watched the tide cascade down through the crowds in the street, who raised their hands and shook ecstatically as the crawling shimmering god passed through them. Some would go blind; others might never see anything again but colors and glitter and star-blaze. It changed what it touched. The Spirit of the Lights, of course; Arlandes, distracted by the glory of the incandescence below, and by his fear, forgot its proper name. When the Light suddenly winked away, it was like blindness; the sky seemed suddenly dreadfully black. All of that Arlandes might have seen from the ground, but he would have been *within* it, and not seen it clear and cold. It was only from the air that he could see how the street was changed with the god's passing; how the Rookeries burned brighter and higher, in new stained-glass colors, deep fleshy reds and icy blues; how Carvalho was wider and deeper and straighter; how the Rookeries' light spilled down the new boulevard; how the shadows in the drunken alleys off Carvalho were deeper and blacker than ever.

What sacrifice had the god taken for its work? Blindness would only be the beginning of it. He'd gone below and ordered the helmsman: *Take us away from here.* It still chilled him to think of it.

Lucia had not been well-traveled. She was an only child and her father kept her close to the hearth. She'd not know how cruel the city could be. He reached into the case and stroked his finger down the white lace of the dress until he came to a blotch where the lace was brittle with dried blood.

Beneath him Grafton was riven with darkness and shadows. Under the mills' fumes, slums spread like oil slicks. Grafton's mill-workers were all at their employment, and the streets were still and quiet, but it was a false stillness, like the surface of a pond; something dark and heavy might rise from it at any moment.

Turning and leaning over the starboard rail, he could see the river behind him, thick and green and turbid, clogged with barges and black coal scows. In the old days, he recalled, sailors would not launch a ship of any consequence down the river without a sacrifice of a child—a sailor's child, or an orphan dragged from the streets, bound and fed to the River. Things were more civilized now. But he thought of Lucia's death, falling as the *Thunderer* rose, as if the two masses were turning around some grotesque invisible fulcrum, working some horrible machine. The gods were always hungry. His gut lurched and he clenched the bloody lace in his fist. The city sickened him. If he could, he would never come down from the air. It suddenly occurred to him that he need not come down. He could take the ship and simply *go*. Duncan would follow him, if it came to it; so would some of the others, *enough* of the others. Why should he use the miracle for which Lucia had given her life to bully and threaten for the Countess? He could *go*. The Countess would never catch him, never be able to bring him back. But where would he go? What would he do? Fear and guilt and anger boiled in him.

With a low growling moan he pulled the dress from the case. He lifted it to his face and breathed deeply; there was no smell but the sour metal of blood. He was vaguely aware of Gibson and Dautry, behind him, leaning idly on their brooms, watching him. He waited for a long, long moment until a strong wind blew across the deck, whipping the dress out streaming in the air, and then he let go.

The wind carried it up at first, up into the glaring sun and silver-bright clouds; then it fell, changing its shape, curling and twisting. He thought of how he had first seen her: she'd been dancing then, too. The falling whiteness billowed open, then snapped closed. *It's time*, Arlandes had thought, *to let her go:* but he'd made a terrible mistake. He couldn't bear it. He lunged out over the prow as if to snatch her back. The rail thumped hard into his chest and he gave a hollow bark and he suddenly remembered how the romantic notion of casting the dress onto the winds had come to him, who was not naturally a romantic man; it had come from the musical play *Hare and Isabel,* where the prince scattered the cuttings of his beloved's golden hair from the highest parapet it had been possible to construct on stage, and swore an oath to her memory. Arlandes could not remember the playwright's words, and he had none of his own, and the moment had passed anyway because now the dress was spiraling down out of sight. He hadn't watched the play; he had watched *her,* leaning over the brass rail of their high box, out over the tense darkness of the theater, laughing and crying. He couldn't let her go. He lunged so recklessly for the dress that he nearly tipped himself over the edge after it. But it was too late, and Grafton's factories' grey smoke swallowed her.

EIGHT

Jack watched the Black Moon from the roof opposite for a day before concluding that it was still safe. He saw Fiss and Aiden come back from a day's work, and followed them in a few minutes later. He was surprised by the warmth of their welcome.

"Thought they got you," Fiss said. "Where'd you go?"

"Uptown. The Tor."

"You mad? It's crawling with the watch."

"Yeah. I know that *now*."

"You got away with it, though," Aiden said.

"Better than *got away*. While they were chasing me around down here, I was hiding in their own stupid temple. Look what I took." Jack pulled the bright stolen blade out of his jacket and twirled it in his wrist. They crowded in appreciatively.

"So are they still looking?" Jack asked.

"You got lucky. Haven't seen them in days."

A black-haired boy shouldered past Fiss, and stood in front of Jack. He was Jack's age, probably, but larger, with a grown man's set to his shoulders already, and heavy black brows. Jack didn't recognize him. "This him?" the boy asked.

A girl in a blue dress called out, "He doesn't look like much." Jack didn't recognize her either; in fact, he thought, the room was full of children he didn't recognize.

"That's the lad," Fiss said. "Believe it or not. They've been dying to see you, Jack."

The black-haired boy grinned and slapped Jack on the shoulder. "Barbotin House. Fuck me. Tell us about it."

The large boy's name was Namdi. He had escaped from the work-house at 34 Lime Street. "Took this lot with me," he said, gesturing at a handful of scruffy boys. "We were all out in the yard, breaking up rocks. It wasn't the worst place I'd ever been in. I mean, it was cushy, really. I was in Dagger Row, once: the Master there was a fucking *madman*. But when that thing came overhead, I just felt . . . I dunno. I felt *light,* sort of; couldn't take it anymore. I felt like I wanted to be *free.* I just had to *run.*"

"Did you . . ." Jack began.

"Not the way you did. Nothing like that. I just knocked the Master on the head and we legged it over the wall."

The girl in the blue dress said, "My name's Beth. These girls here are with me. Don't get any ideas, they're not here for you boys's pleasure. They're here for shelter. Fiss said we could stay. So: we got out of Ma Fossett's house. Same story as Namdi, more or less. It was hard, but it was all right, until that day. The *god.* That, it was like, I had to be like it. Free."

"That's right," Namdi said, "that's what it was like."

"So we snuck out the window that night," Beth said. "Hid until they stopped looking for us."

"There's a lot more like them out there, Jack," Aiden said. "All over town. Started turning up just after you did. All broke out of this hole or that, or run away from their masters."

"It was a busy day round these parts," Fiss said. "These two strays turned up and wouldn't leave. We told them about you. They thought we were making it up. Who breaks out of Barbotin?"

"Never mind Barbotin. You *flew,*" Beth said. "With the Bird. Tell us what it was like again."

How could he tell them? There weren't the words. When it happened, it felt like nothing that could be named. It could never be repeated or shared, so what use were words?

Except that ship, that amazing ship: that rose at will, and took its crew with it. Was that possible?

Instead, Jack said, "Later, maybe," and turned to Fiss. "They must be looking for them, too," Jack said. "If there's that many of them—us—out there, they must be looking."

"Course," Beth said. "They took a girl just yesterday. She was stealing food down in Brand Market, and the watch took her. Caitlin here saw it. They're on the lookout, all right. There's too many of us now. *The citizenry is terribly concerned,*" she simpered mockingly.

"They'll get us again soon," Namdi said. "They always do. Put us right back. It's worth a whipping to get out, though, even if it's only for a bit."

"No," Jack said. "I'm not having that. No one goes back."

They were hard to organize. They were only children, after all—Jack was almost the oldest—and unruly, and disobedient. The trick was, Jack had to explain again and again, that they couldn't all go out at once. Not anymore. Not if they were all going to stay free. No more running wild. The watch would take them one by one. "Someone has to keep the workhouses running, don't they?" Fiss told them. "That's what you're all for, boys and girls. They'll take you back in a second."

"That's right," Jack said. "Are you listening? You have to be careful now. So you lot stay here for the day. We'll share what we bring back, I swear. And you lot are lookouts. You have to stay, and keep looking, right? This is important."

It took a while to make them disciplined, to make them understand that they had roles to play, duties to perform, if they were to stay in the Black Moon. One or two were caught in the meantime. The change happened, though, in time.

Fiss was amazed by how thoroughly they were transformed. He came up to find Jack sitting on the roof, as was his habit in the evenings, and said, "They don't even complain anymore. The boys we sent down to Seven Wheels Market are back. The lookouts are out for the night. And no complaints." He sighed. "I tried to tell them the same things, you know. They just forgot, or said no, and got caught again. They never used to listen to me."

They listened to Jack. He was the hero who had broken out of the impregnable Barbotin House. He was touched by the Bird-God. He was the one who talked to them at night, telling them stories about the Bird, and the Nessene, and Lavilokan, like he was a priest or something; like he was a missionary, except that he was the best thief they had. And he could *fly*. He couldn't really, he told them, but the little ones never listened. They thought he was waiting for his moment to take wing.

The children listened to Jack, and Jack listened to Fiss. Jack had been so young when they locked him away; every day, something reminded him of all that he didn't know about the city. He needed Fiss. It was Fiss, for instance, who knew how to fence what they stole. Jack went along once or twice, and watched Fiss deal with the hard men who bought and sold at the back of pubs in Ar-Mouth, or in dingy back-parlors of haberdashers in the Ward. Fiss had an easy, confident, joking manner with those men, respectful but unafraid; it was, Jack thought, very adult. It was more than Jack knew how to do.

It was Fiss around whom the whole group had formed. Fiss was first—and Aiden, who was always with him, and who it seemed had escaped with him, although neither of them was willing to say where from, or why. Certainly they were not ordinary street-children. Aiden was quiet, thoughtful; Fiss was kind, funny, sensible. Those were rare traits in the sort of lives they lived. They were able to make the Black Moon into a refuge, a shelter for whatever children wandered by, but they lacked the strength and the hardness to discipline them. Jack had that strength, so long as he had their help.

And it was Fiss who started calling him Jack Silk, because of his strange bright-threaded shirt. The name stuck. It was all right, Jack supposed. At first, he thought it was a joke at his expense, because Fiss made everything sound like a joke. But that wasn't how the others took it. They took it seriously, like he was a hero, a myth. He knew that he had to be worthy of it.

✶ ✶ ✶

Word spread: Silk's lot were doing well. They had food, and blankets, and even money. They could offer protection. More children came. They wanted shelter, and they all wanted to see the miracle boy for themselves. Most had broken out of their workhouses, or run from their apprenticeships, or their families, or their panders, on the same strange day as Jack.

There were Martin and Ayer, two more from Lime Street, who had followed Namdi out over the fence, but then got separated in the streets. Namdi at once proudly took responsibility and charge of them, speaking for them. They didn't seem to mind; they were grateful enough for a place to stay.

Turyk had run away from an apprenticeship to a carpenter in Mass How. He had not been chained, not physically: all he had to do was to look out the window at the Bird dwindling in the blue distance among the clouds, and throw down his tools, snatch up the day's takings, and run out the door. "He's mad," Namdi said. "That's a good job. Who'd run from that?"

"He pulls his weight," Jack said. "Mind your business."

Laura and Elsie came from a whorehouse in the Ward. They couldn't be more than twelve or thirteen. It made Jack feel guilty to look at their skinny bodies. He asked Beth to look out for them. "What do you think I'm doing?" she said. "You just make sure nobody troubles them."

Jack heard many other stories of escape, but none as strange as his own. He had to tell his story again and again. All those who had run away on the day of the Bird believed him instinctively. They felt like they'd done it themselves.

Once, the watch came poking through the abandoned shells of Moore Street. They hopped over the fence and hid down by the canal. The lookouts were sound, then. *Good.*

Not all of them were escapees. Some came who had been accustomed to begging. Shutlow was a poor place for it; it held its purse strings tightly. They were weak and covered in sores. They were taken in, but Jack would not permit begging. They had to be taught to steal. Jack wanted them to be proud.

Then there were those who had been in other gangs, who came

to the Black Moon for protection from their enemies. The first came from Fourth Ward, where his lot had lived in the sewer, scavenging the city's filth, until they got driven out by the Chaste Flame. The Flame smashed their stuff, and beat them bloody, day after day, until they joined up or ran away. Others came with the same story, up from the Ward, over from Barbary.

"The Flame?" Jack asked Fiss.

"Don't you know? I know you don't know much, but you should know this, from your books. They're Tiber's mad boys."

"In the House, they taught us about a Chaste Flame. They were a counter-church of Tiber. A kind of cult, but all children, like a gang. There was a mad monk, Vilar, Volar, I think, who founded them. They wore white robes and carried torches. The Church pronounced them anathema, and put them down. But they keep coming back. Always children: it was one of the heresies they were protecting us from in the House, they said."

"If you say so. The important thing is, they're not just in books. They're all over the city, the last couple of years."

"I heard they started up this time in the 'Machy," Aiden said. "Down in the warrens."

"But you see them all over," Fiss said. "They burn things. Whorehouses, playhouses. Pubs, cafés. Books, music, pleasures. Making things pure. Never seen them myself. But they say they're like angry ghosts. They say it's like they're on fire."

"There's a lot of children want to join them," Aiden said. "There's a lot in this city want to see others' pleasures burn."

Busy days passed, but the children kept talking about the Flame. They said the Flame shaved their heads so you couldn't tell boys from girls. They said they came on you like phantoms, bearing fire, and killed and beat and burned. They said they could pass through walls, drift on the smoke, that they could not be killed. Some of the children spoke of the Flame with terror and tears, others with envy. All the stories of their own escapes, their own daring, their hopes for their freedom, gave way to an endless chewing-over of the fear the white robes inspired.

It made Jack sick to see them shut in their own fear like that. He sat out on the roof trying to think how to break its bars: there was a lesson to be learned from the way the Flame did things, he thought.

He called them all up into the Moon's loft one evening, and stood by the window, framed by the street's dying light.

"I hear you talking. Flame this, Flame that. I know some of you are thinking about joining them. And I know some of you are just here to hide from them. Like the Flame *owns* this city. Well, what are we? Are we nothing?"

They shouted that they were not.

"We broke out from all over. We were all given the signal, and we took it, and we broke out from everything, all over. No one can take us back, if we don't want to go. We can take whatever we want. Who's scared of the Flame?" No one was. "They got a uniform and they got a name, and that makes you think they're something special. *We're* special. Not them."

The little ones cheered. The older ones looked skeptical. It was all so much grander and better and more obviously *right* in his head than he had words to express. His mouth was dry. But they sensed his excitement, and watched him intently.

"So what I think is, I think we need a name, too."

He unfolded the *Era*'s print of the flying warship, and held it up against the light. "Know what this is?"

Several hands shot up among the little ones. "That's the Countess's ship," Namdi said. "I saw it."

"Wrong. That's our sign. *Ours.* Namdi, you remember the day you got out from Lime Street? Beth, you remember? Turyk, you remember when you told that Master of yours where to stick it? That's the same day this thing went up. The same thing that made us free, made this thing free. I saw it, too, up in the Tor. It's incredible. It can go anywhere. No one can stop it or touch it. Like they can't touch us or stop us, not if we keep moving."

Namdi nodded, grinning. "It's amazing."

"Same day as we all escaped. Same thing that brought us all together. It *is* amazing. It's the future. It's going to be our sign."

They were all looking at him. Bright faces in the attic's shadows.

He was unsure what to say next, so he said again, but louder, "This is our sign."

He handed the print to Fiss, who looked at him curiously and passed it wordlessly to Aiden, who shared it with Beth; then they all gathered in, looking at it and at Jack. The *Thunderer:* the Thunderers. No mere thieves or vagrants. It would be their name and their strength: they, too, would amaze. He was very excited; he thought they liked it. It was a start.

NINE

Arjun spent the day on Fraction Street, up on Mass How, in the instrument-makers' shops and workshops, in dark spaces full of jangling wires and strings and clanking brass and the cacophony of poorly made instruments being tuned, of untutored would-be musicians banging away. All of the city's tunes, few of which he liked, none of which was the music he hoped to hear, all sounding at once, and mostly badly played. He was ejected from one shop after another when it became clear that he had no money. It crossed his mind to apply for work, but he did not wish to be tied down there, to be caught in those dusty webs of catgut and piano-wire. Perhaps when his money ran out he would reconsider.

He came back to Shutlow in the evening to find the streets full of bunting. Clotheslines were hung with red flags, and, if flags weren't available, with cloth or rags dyed red. Red banners flew over Seven Wheels Market, stitched in black with the image of a ship, lightning at its prow, lifted by a swelling balloon. Moore Street's evening shadows glittered with broken glass and scattered flags. Off in the distance there was still cheering and the honking of a brass band. On the horizon—north, over on the Heath—there was the faint spark of fireworks against the black sky.

He sat in the guests' room in the unraveling green armchair in the corner. Haycock was there warming his feet by the fire, jotting down sales and prices in a crabbed hand in an overstuffed ledger-book.

"Was there a festival, Mr. Haycock? Or a parade?"

"Too bloody right there was. Bloody awful racket. Where've you been? Don't you read the papers?"

"Hardly ever, Mr. Haycock."

"Ignorance is bliss, ain't it? There's been a famous victory, they say. Or the Countess says, and so everyone else says. With that bastard ugly ship of hers. Over pirates. Or what the Countess is pleased to call pirates. The distinction between our city's glorious leaders and a bunch of pirates being a subtle one that's probably beyond a foreigner such as youself. We're all so very bloody excited, waving our little banners. Though what good it's going to do me is beyond me. Don't talk to that puffed-up bootlicker Heady, that's my advice. He's insufferable tonight."

Down on the Heath it was dark, lit only by firework flashes. The great ship *Thunderer* hung darkly far overhead, fixed and frozen in the night.

From the *Thunderer*'s prow Arlandes could still see the sunset burning sullenly down behind the cranes and factory towers of Agdon Deep.

The crowds on the Heath had screamed and cheered loud enough for the *Thunderer*'s crew to hear them. They were dispersing now; it was a cold evening. It was colder still up on the deck, and Arlandes hugged his thick black wax-coat tightly around himself.

They had taken the *Thunderer* down through Goshen Tor, hanging so low they were level with the tops of the tallest buildings, and the bankers came running close to the windows to stare, shouting silently and banging their fists on the thick glass. The crew had saluted back at them and laughed. It was enough, probably, to have driven the Chairman to a blind fury: to have that weapon parading itself through his territory, his own people cheering it . . . But the Countess had ordered it, so Arlandes obeyed.

She smiled all the time now. Her painted jeweled face, her white skin and red lips, curled into a constant sly smile. She was full of plans.

The battle—if you could call it a battle—had been fought that morning, at dawn, as the sun rose over the Bay so that the water seemed stained with blood. There was an island in the Bay, a rocky island, crowned with a fort: Sleutel's Island and Sleutel's Fort. The rocks and the reefs made it almost unapproachable by unfriendly ships, so Sleutel and Sleutel's predecessors had generally been left alone. They seized the occasional ship; it had always been seen as a kind of tax.

The Fort crumbled at the first volley from the *Thunderer*'s guns. It was built of some soft yellow sandstone and it turned back to sand. There had been riflemen on the turrets firing pointlessly at the *Thunderer*'s side; when the walls burst into powder and smoke they'd fallen screaming. The inner structures of the Fort were made of wood, and burned. The *Thunderer*'s bombards had sprayed oil and powder and flame wherever they struck. It had been a resoundingly successful test.

There had been perhaps two hundred people in the Fort. Not all of them had been men, though Arlandes did not know their exact numbers, and had not cared to descend into the rubble to count.

Arlandes was neither proud nor ashamed. The fireworks exploded over the Heath and lit his face violent reds and greens and he still stared blankly at the sunset.

What crowd there still was, was still cheering. They couldn't see him, of course; only the great black hull blocking out the stars.

He knew what they said about him. He rarely went anywhere these days except the Countess's estates and the *Thunderer* itself, but he'd overheard the gossip: the Mourning Captain, all clad in black. There were stories in the papers and ballads sung in the streets. The *Era*'s editorials called him a throwback to a nobler, more sensitive age, which sat poorly with their claims that he and his wonderful ship were heralds of the city's future; but it sold papers either way. He'd caught the popular imagination. Romantics pictured him grieving at the prow of his ship; he'd confiscated a chapbook from one of the men on which, under the words GRIEF'S LONELY WARRIOR, he was pictured in black, a single tear on his chiseled cheek, gazing at the horizon, hand on his sword. It was a publication of disgraceful and dispiriting stupidity. Young women wrote him letters by the sackful; after reading a few—perfumed, appallingly florid—he'd ordered his valet to burn them and all similar missives.

Less-romantic gossip pictured him going mad in his quarters, clutching the bloody dress to himself in the darkness, weeping and pleading. That was possibly closer to the truth; though he'd let the dress go, he clutched it close in his dreams. And certainly he saw nothing romantic in his situation. Every day it was harder to rouse himself from his bunk. There was a constant numb ache in his head. His men avoided him; he snarled and swore at them, and had found himself more than once gripping the hilt of his sword with half-formed intent. He was not sleeping; his dreams were waking dreams, and cold, and repetitive, and pointless. But when the guns fired—when the walls burst and those tiny, fragile figures had scattered and fallen—well, that was something. That was a sort of feeling. The flash and the thunder were like a kind of joy.

TEN

The next morning, Arjun followed Heady to the fortress of the Marquis Mensonge, which crowned the arc of the Diorite Bridge like a helmet's plumes. There were flags everywhere, purple and silver. A soldier at the gate, in purple and silver, too, planted his mailed fist in Arjun's ribs and shoved him back into the street, telling him to waste someone else's time, if he must.

The day after, Heady gave Arjun directions to the Mass How Parliament, and he queued all day outside its stolid bronze-red bulk. The queue seemed to move no faster than the dead dignitaries carved into the walls. The police turned them all away in the evening. Arjun began to doubt Girolamo's advice.

He went walking down to the Fourth Ward. He leaned over the edge of a dry canal and listened to a group of children down in the mud. They formed a circle to sing together. Something about a plague; one by one, they clapped hands and fell laughing out of the circle onto their backs. Arjun recognized the tune: it was a simplified form of a hymn the cantors of Lavilokan sang, up on Goshen Tor. They scattered when they saw him watching.

In the evening, he joined the crowds up on Laud Heath, for a carnival thrown by the Countess Ilona. Clowns and fire-eaters entertained the jostling crowds. Fireworks exploded overhead. At the west end of the Heath, the Countess's orchestra played for a quieter audience. Arjun slipped in at the back to listen.

As the last light drained from the sky, the orchestra came to the final, jubilant crescendo of Karpinsky's *Sacred Dance,* a crashing of cymbals and a banging of drums; and up over the hill, across the sky from behind the Observatory, the *Thunderer* came in ominous progress, a black shape limned by fireworks, hanging over the Heath. Arjun felt for a moment that he and the crowds down on the dark Heath were all underwater, looking up. The orchestra went silent as the great ship's guns took up a slow, pounding rhythm, both celebratory and threatening.

On his return, he found that Madam Defour had cajoled all her lodgers out into the garden, where, in the weak candlelight, she conducted a strained flirtation with Heady. The other lodgers sat around the table making desultory conversation. Arjun had no choice but to join them. He asked Haycock about his day.

"Fucking awful. I hike all the way up to Tyn Wald and I sit myself in some godsawful café all afternoon until the pervert running it wants to know whether sir will be ordering anything further and I'm out on my arse, my purchasing options being limited, which ain't surprising given that I have waited all day to meet a man to purchase a copy of *Arcana Caelestia,* which perhaps I might sell, keep me in food and drink for long enough to eke out the whole horrible business a little longer, were it not that the bastard did not show up, all bastard day."

"*Arcana Caelestia?*"

"You interested?"

"I don't think so. I've never heard of it. I was wondering about the language. *Arcana* sounds like—"

"Not interested. What *are* you interested in? Heady says you just drift around like a fart listening to music all day."

"As I've said, I'm here to represent my order to Ararat's Estates, in hope of commerce between our—"

"*Balls.* You're looking for something. You're no kind of merchant-trader; I mean *look* at you. And from what I hear, you haven't 'represented your order' to anyone but a lot of buskers and other street filth, who are, I can tell you, one rung down on Ararat's great ladder from book-dealers, which I can say from experience is a rung that is sunk deep indeed in the shit. Heady believes your story 'cause he's a creature whose senses are highly specialized to detect the tiniest *quivering* motions of power, which you've not got, so he can barely see you. But *I* see. It's my business. Tell me and maybe I can find it for you."

Arjun told him. He was relieved to get it out. He had not told anyone the truth about his mission; it was too private. But this was the first time he had been pressed, and why not?

Haycock then changed the subject, starting an argument with Norris and Clement about some sporting event; a team sponsored by the Countess had pulled off a surprise win against a team sponsored by the Agdon Worker's Combine, up at the Urgos-Eye Stadium. Some game with balls, it seemed, and spikes; Arjun couldn't follow the rules. Nor, it seemed, could old Norris, quite, though he tried; and whenever the poor enfeebled man tried to agree with Haycock, which he did with doglike eagerness to please, stuttering and tongue-tied, Haycock would take a sharp turn, vehemently denying whatever he had asserted with equal vehemence the second earlier, until Norris's blotchy face dripped with tears and snot, and Clement was snorting with nasty laughter.

In the morning, Haycock accosted Arjun in the hallway and presented him with a list of books that might shed light on his problem. Anything and everything that had been written on the relation of the city to its gods: *The Detective of Dreams; The Gutter and the Stars;* Lodwick's *Extrapolations;* Varady's *Speculations; Riddles and Their Riddlers; Those Whom We Cannot at Present Name but Are Possessed of Animal Heads.* "What languages can you read?" Haycock asked. "Tuvar; really? Akashic, too? What a lot of hard work; aren't we eager? Then there's a lot more I can get you. Let me think."

Arjun was sorry, but he had no money. He really didn't, he told Haycock, he was sorry. He was sorry. He looked down at Haycock's bald head. It was lined, like a thumb. The deep grooves seemed to pulse with irritation. Haycock stamped off, thinking.

Haycock stamped all the way up Cato Road, and into Foyle's Ward, dragging his heavy weather-beaten case behind him, snarling and spitting at anyone who got in his way or slowed him down. It was the end of the month and he had an appointment with Professor Holbach. Holbach provided Haycock with a generous allowance for transport by carriage. As was his usual practice, Haycock had opted to pocket the money and walk, and by the time he'd crested the hill he was, as was his usual practice, in a foul mood.

He met Holbach in the garden of Holbach's mansion; they sat by the fishpond. The mansion and the grounds bustled—thin, pale scholars; artists, fashionably disheveled; various young women. Clever and elegant people. Haycock stuck out like a bruise. The whole pile, and all Holbach's other airs and graces, including expecting household visits from professionals like Haycock, who had other pressing commitments and had their own professional dignity to consider, was all paid for by the Countess for services rendered. That was what one or two clever ideas could do for a man. That was what a man could do for himself if only—if only!—he could get himself off the grinding wheel of business for a few short days so that he could think deep thoughts and plan big plans. Some men had good fortune and others never did; but Haycock swallowed his resentment and offered a smile that was close enough to pleasant that the fat professor had to pretend not to be offended. Haycock lit a cigarette and opened the case.

"So there's a distinct nautical theme to this week's haul, Professor. Nautical and riverine. Everything smells of moss and weed and coal-dust this month. There's mildew on 'em, more than usual, but it scrapes right off."

"Do you have the books I asked you to find? Do you have the Ferdomas or the Celyn?"

"Hold on, Professor. The river flows where it flows, you know? I've brought a lot of bloody heavy stuff up here, for your eyes only, out of the goodness of my aching thumping heart, so let's have a look. Here!" He produced a thin folio volume, rough-edged, cheaply printed, and waved it under Holbach's chin (which withdrew, like a turtle's head, into Holbach's coat's folds of velvet and lace). "First printing of *The Captain Unmoored: A Play in Three Acts,* featuring the tragedy and *et cetera* of your friend what's-his-name. The notorious *mis*printing, the one where the printer's boy got drunk and inserted that dirty joke at the Countess's expense. Not all were destroyed. I know a boy works at the censor's office. Interested?"

"Gods, Haycock, get that thing away from me."

Haycock tossed it back into the case with a grunt and a smirk.
He'd only brought it to annoy Holbach—to start him off guilty and
wrong-footed. He knew how the fat man moped over the girl's
death. "How about this, then? An account of the famous sinking of
the *Duchess Marina* back in '04, as told by a survivor, a serving maid.
Last of the pleasure-cruises in these parts, that was. A slice of history. Not a lot of survivors; not many of 'em ever put pen to paper
about it. Not much of a market for it. Black water and grinding
hulls. Screams from the riverbanks, drunk men from the bars
throwing ropes that won't reach. Watching her poor old mother going down for the last time, bony old hand clutching sinking drift-
wood. It'll give you nightmares. Up your alley?"

"Haycock, did you manage to find anything that I actually
asked for?"

"Old Pastor Crane from the Candlers died and left behind a nice
collection. Here's a rare one. A compendium of nautical diseases;
illustrated plates by the famous Dr. Van Duers. Diseases of both
sailors' flesh and ships' timbers. Take a look at that! You'd shoot
yourself if something like that started growing on your face, you'd
think."

"Oh dear. Oh goodness. I don't think so."

"Well then, these illustrations may be more to your taste. From
the library of a client who'll go unnamed; Galliatin's *Erotica of the
Sea-Kingdoms*. Beautiful, isn't it? Lovely fucking economy of line.
Pretty little mermaids. Strapping young sailor-lads. Miracle it's
never been burned—the publisher was. Shame to let it go to someone who won't appreciate its many virtues."

"Hmm."

"Or Dr. Montagu's *The River and Its Economy: An Historical
Account*. Found this one in a lot they were selling off at the Malvern."
Haycock flipped through pages and pages of statistics and ledgers,
past technical illustrations of barges and cranes and mill wheels and
steam saws, before coming to rest on a map of the river. "Dull, yes?
But look at this: look where the river runs."

"It appears to run through Agdon, rather than Barbary, and
northwest through, ah, that's odd, is that Grafton?"

"Exactly. Not much like *our* river, is it? So what do we have,

Professor: Dr. Montagu methodically going mad, counting every last penny of business up and down the river, and he's not noticed where the river fucking *is,* or is this one of *those* books, from one of *those* places, that's found its way here? Now *that's* up your alley, Holbach, and you know it."

"Yes, yes, all right. What do you want for it?"

"And then there's this." The little red book had no apparent title. "Also from Pastor Crane's collection. Collected papers from the trial of one John Harrifon, barge-hand, strangler, hanged man. Did for a dozen little children before they caught him. Wrapped 'em in sacks, weighed 'em with bricks, threw 'em in the river, like a less ambitious artist might with cats."

"This is disgusting, Haycock. You really do have the most depraved taste."

"Is that right? Don't think I haven't noticed that you meet me in the garden, Professor." Haycock jabbed his finger under Holbach's nose. "Don't think I haven't noticed that you won't have me in your fucking house. Don't think your money's so good you can treat me like dirt. I'll throw your retainer right back in your face, Professor. Don't forget I know things about you, Professor, Professor Loyal-Servant-of-the-bloody-Countess, Mr. Bloody *Atlas*."

Holbach's pink face went white. Haycock, who had risen to his feet, settled back into his chair. He spat into the pond and startled the fish. Holbach said, "My apologies. I continue to trust to your discretion, Mr. Haycock."

Haycock grunted. They sat for a while in silence. Haycock lit a cigarette.

"Anyway, Professor, the point is the man, old John Harrifon, swore blind all the way to the hangman's scaffold that he'd killed those little buggers as sacrifices for the river-god. Or one of the river-gods. And he had a lot to say about it. Mad stuff. Your sort of thing, right? God stuff."

"I suppose so. I suppose I'll take it."

"I suppose you bloody well will."

"Haycock, did you for some strange reason make a deliberate *effort* to seek out books of an aquatic nature? I'm sure I never asked you to do so. I'm sure I asked for the Ferdomas, and the Celyn."

"I bring you what I find, Professor."

"That's interesting, of course. The city speaks to us in signs of all kinds, you know."

"So you always say, Professor. Me, I've got a business to run. We can't all be pet geniuses for the Countess."

"Signs and portents. Potential shifting and reweighting. Certain energies subside and others rise to prominence. Certain threads thicken in the weave. A shifting toward *water*, perhaps? Perhaps, ah, perhaps in response to the raising of the *Thunderer*. Water reasserting itself. Reclaiming its primacy over air in the city's life. Though perhaps I flatter myself. Perhaps I flatter myself to think the city notices my efforts. Hmm. I'm just thinking aloud, of course, Haycock. Your trawl is hardly a sufficient source of data from which to work. The calculations of this science are very complex. But still. But still."

"Yeah, well. Let's talk about what you owe me for the Harrifon, and the Montagu. And while we're at it, Professor, there's another bit of business. A young man of my acquaintance is looking for work. You're always looking for translators, right? You name it, he speaks it. Chirps away all singsong like a little brown parrot. Funny little foreign bugger, but clever in his way. *Gad,* he's from. Got that · in your Atlas, Professor?"

"Hmm. Outside the city, you say? No, Haycock, no, we probably don't. Bring him to me and I'll see if I can use him. You'll get your commission."

Haycock took a grubby nub of pencil from behind his ear and prepared his bill. "So, what you said about water. Is that good or bad?"

"I expect it can be turned to advantage. Perhaps it means fluid times. Times of change and growth and rebirth. Hmm. I feel quite optimistic. I'll tell you what, Haycock, tell me more about Galliatin's *Erotica,* would you?"

ELEVEN

In the evening, Madam Defour took her guests for a promenade through the streets of Shutlow. She thought it would be nice, she said, to take the air. Her guests couldn't really refuse, though the sky was cold and grey. Defour held up a pale green umbrella to ward off the autumnal drizzle. She stepped high, holding her skirts, along the line of flat stones that ran along the middle of Moore Street, lifting the fussy pedestrian out of the street's wet filth. She gave her umbrella the occasional stagy twirl. Her guests trudged along behind, shoulders hunched against the rain.

Apart from Defour's umbrella, they were a drab and monkish procession. The city's autumn was weather for waxy black rain-cloaks or long grey coats. Arjun had picked his own coat from a musty pile in the basement of Klozny & Klozny's on Many Street.

Klozny's had been an adventure in itself; he was still turning over in his mind the strangeness of it. He'd wandered for what seemed like hours through the corridors, half-lit by shuttered candles, smelling of dust, old perfume, sweat, wax, spices, a thick grey soporific funk of heaped wool. His first time in a department store, of course: he'd startled at mannequins, he'd touched things he shouldn't have touched, he'd gotten lost, he'd attracted stares. He spluttered in the dark stinking tobacco-shop on the second floor; in a bright cold hall on the third floor he nearly knocked over a glass table piled with ices and chocolates; somewhere in the basement he scuttled through an appalling room whose walls were oak-paneled and lined with plaques bearing a variety of mangy animal heads, trying to avoid eye-to-glassy-eye contact with either the living or the dead. In low corridors there were shelves and shelves of tiny lacquered sculptures of pretty little street-children, of noblewomen in ballgowns, and of stranger things that were presumably gods. He picked up a china noblewoman in a china ballgown: when he figured out what the numbers black-penciled on her base were he fumbled in shock and almost dropped her. Who had that kind of money? And of course Klozny & Klozny wasn't even that smart, even Arjun could see that, there on dirty crowded Many Street, up on the outskirts of Mass How, on the hillside, so the floorboards subsided at sad angles—the *smart* folk, the truly rich folk, shopped elsewhere. Goods came to them, perhaps. Arjun wasn't sure how it worked. But in K & K there was, wonderfully, eerily, *music,* piped through the corridors somehow, low repetitive strains of violins that always seemed to be going somewhere but never did. He never found the source, though he pressed further and further into the shadows, though he pressed his ears up against the walls and peered into the corners, though he even got down on his hands and knees to inspect the wainscoting, risking a trampling by crowds of middle-aged ladies. By that point the suspicious attentions of the store's staff were quite pointed; they followed him flexing their knuckles, ready if necessary for violence in defense of Klozny's tight profit margins. He finally found himself in the discount basement, and he purchased an old coat mostly because he felt he had no choice. He brought it back home oddly proud of his achievement. Madam Defour pronounced it *rather shabby,* and Heady, who professed to know about clothes, agreed: *shoddy goods.* But the coat was now a *done deal,* as Mr. Haycock might say.

It let in the rain, though.

All the rainy way down Moore Street, they kept their hands in their pockets and their heads hunched. Arjun hung near the back of the group, among Defour's disfavored.

Clement and Ewan walked in front of him. Both were little men. Clement had brought a copy of the *Era* with him. Ewan held it, Clement stretched out the wings of his raincoat over it, and they read it together by the light of Clement's cigarette, jabbing their fingers at things that annoyed them. They craned their heads together and whispered. *Disgusting,* Arjun heard, and *makes you sick,* and *blasphemy* and *should be strung up* and *no way to show respect for the powers* and *bloody outsiders* and *shame. Shame shame shame.* Or possibly *Shay.*

Clement turned his head back. With his glasses, in the dark, he looked like an owl. "What are *you* looking at? Mind your business." Arjun shrugged and took a step back.

He walked by himself for a while as they crossed Nancy Street. Defour signaled with her umbrella and the line turned sharply left down Capric Street—sharply away from the whorehouse on the corner of Nancy, where the girls stood out under the gaslights and whistled after the lodgers' retreating backs and Haycock whistled back.

The rain was not unpleasant. The city hissed and sighed and breathed deep with it.

Norris tapped him on the shoulder. Arjun turned. Norris was smiling, so Arjun attempted to smile in return.

Norris's smile was a shy, silly thing. His thin neck and arms were scarred with ugly, fading tattoos, but his eyes were wide and weak, like a sick child's. He was an old drunk, nothing more, Haycock had said, sneering, but Arjun thought there was some deeper deficiency in the man.

Defour had a way of talking to Norris; she humored him kindly. He was the only person she treated that way. Something in Norris invited pity. Arjun tried to mimic Defour's manner.

"Haycock says you're looking for something that ran away from you," Norris said.

"He told you that, did he?"

"He says you're mad."

"There was a Voice that sang in a high room above my home. My home was made of its echoes. It left us alone, and without a purpose. I suppose I feel its loss very deeply, and that makes me strange. But this city seems full of equal strangeness."

"He says everybody's mad."

"Well. Good. They probably are."

Norris leaned up to Arjun's ear again and whispered. "I went looking for something once." Arjun stopped and turned to listen.

"It was '47, '48. I worked for Butcher Mose. Bad boy, see?

Younger, then. Flush. Money rolled in for Mose's men. Knew me in all the Wards. Legbreaker. Hit women. Fathers and children. Not like it was at first. I'm talking later, now, see?"

"Slow down. I'm listening. It's all right."

"At first. I get confused. Later it got hard. At first, '42, '43 maybe. I was a new boy. I went into a place, all the women knew me. Money to flash around. I was on the up. Broke out of gaol, once or twice. Daring, that's what it was. Ran with Greeley the Barber. Went up to Goshen, stole from the temples and the nobs. Brought it back and threw it around."

"I've heard the ballads about Greeley. He was much loved, for a crimelord."

"They were about all of us. Used to pay the girls to sing them to us in the bars. Welcome everywhere. This is still before. Drank all around town. Smart boy. Joe, Bill, Hod, Owney, all with me. All over the city, place to place, every night. Lights and smoke and drink and singing. Like you, see? Singing."

"Perhaps. I suppose so."

"Owney got killed on business in Goshen. Greeley died locked up in the Iron Rose. I got married, but the girl died in childbed. A fever hit the Ward in '44. They closed all the places I knew. Sailor, Star 'n Garter. The Howling Wolf."

"And then you worked for Mose?"

"Not the same. Still on top, I was, mind you. Under Mose. That Haycock thinks he's so hard. I was the real thing. Hurt people. Made them afraid. Point is, it was harder. Colder. Lonely. Too much competition, had to get nasty. Not the dashing young rogue anymore. Older. A bully. Hated and feared. No more drinking and singing. That's it. That's what it was. So we went looking. Me and Hod. Down where the Howling Wolf used to be."

"What were you looking for?"

"The Horned Man. Red-Beard. Do you know what I mean?"

"I've read about it. A power of drink and revel."

"That's right. They said he was twenty feet tall. They said he drank out on the Heath or on the Wilding Moor or down in Garhide or the 'Machy's warrens. Crew of mad wild women. Dangerous. Loud. No one ever saw him themselves, but they knew a man who knew a man who had. They said you might, maybe, see him anywhere, any boozer in the city, he could come barreling on through, no warning, cloud of music and shouting with him."

"You wanted to find it. To get back what you had, even if it was only for a moment."

"They said he'd come through like a blast of wild wind and everyone would go with him. Taken. Who knows where?"

"Is that what happened to you?"

"No. Yes. Me and Hod, we knew how to look. Found a man in Stammer Gate. A scholar. Lived in a tower up over the square. Kept bats and birds. Paid him what we got from Mose. He told us how. We went down to where the Wolf used to be and we started there, 'cause that's where we last saw Owney, and he was one of us when it was good. We went up to the Star. Then the Whistler. Every place we went, we threw more money at the crowd."

"Did they forgive you?"

"No. I mean, maybe. Not at first. To the Compass and the Lion. The Mineshaft. They hated me there in them days. Good reason, too. But they were cheering for me that night. But they were all blurry; wasn't just the drink. Up to the Hesperus. To Shecky's place, as never had no name, even in the good days. We took the door out the back, I remember, and we went up these stairs between two, two . . ." He gestured oddly, steepling his hands sharply against each other, "See? And we went into this place where it was like the old crowd was there. It was like they were all young again. I swear Owney was there. Danced with a woman I'd have sworn was my wife."

"Could I follow this route, to find this god?"

"No. The gentleman made it special for us. It was places that meant something to *us,* see? Wouldn't do nothing for you. Anyway, we went out that place through a back door when the bell rang. There was another place under the arches. And another, when the bells rang again. Must have been days, but it was still dark. The places we were in, I don't know, there was one that was lit so *bright,* but not by fire. There was a place with the strangest damn music, and clothes. There was a time when I think we was out on the moor, but it was so dark, you couldn't see nothing but the fire. And women dancing round it, all bare. Sounds nice, son, I know, but it wasn't."

"You were getting closer to the god. Did you see it?"

"I saw *Him*. On a stone bench. Just in a place, looked like the Compasses, a bit. He looked like—so *big,* but not tall or wide, or . . . All these people with him, and they were all like me. Following. I wasn't special. They loved Him so much."

Arjun waited. Eventually, Norris spoke again, emphatically, as if sick of talking.

"I don't have a way with words. Haycock could tell you what it was like. But *I* saw Him. I was with Him for a long night, a bloody good night, as good as it ever was; couldn't ever be the same after-wards. And Hod never came back, and *I* came back in the end, woke up out in the 'Machy in some trash heap, in '58, '59. I know I haven't been right since. I *know*. The god took all my strength with Him. We shouldn't have tried to *use* Him; He wasn't *safe*. Nothing's right since. No point in anything now, right? Came to this fucking place to wait it all out."

He picked up a stone from the street, and turned it over in his grubby fingers. "None of it's the same anymore. None of it's real, ei-ther; when we were with Red-Beard, everything changed around us and everything was new all the time. Now I know none of it's *real*." Without warning, Norris flailed back his arm and threw the stone across the street. A window broke loudly. "See?" he said.

Heady and Clement came running back. Heady held Norris's arm while Clement asked him, "What did you do that for?" Norris babbled incoherently; his brief articulacy had vanished. Arjun hung back.

When Arjun went back to his room that night, he struck a match in the dark and lit the candle on his shelf. There was an envelope tucked underneath. He picked it up and turned it over in his hands. It was plain, thin, and brown. His own name was written on it, in a round, characterless, childish hand.

There was a tingle in his chest and at the back of his head. A faint tugging. He felt a black weight at the other end of a quivering silvery line. The Spider, or one of its agents, had sent this. A strange sort of welcome to the city.

He looked at it for a long time. He knew that if he opened it, he would do what it told him. Would it put him on the path to finding the Voice? Probably not. From what Defour had said, it would be something utterly arbitrary. That was the *point*.

If he opened the letter, he would most likely be giving up the search for the Voice. But it was tempting. That search felt stillborn, hopeless; the Spider would set him on another path. Any path, any purpose. Perhaps one that could replace the Voice.

Behind him, there was a knock on the open door and Haycock walked in. Arjun clutched the envelope in both hands and made as if to hide it behind his back, like a child caught stealing, before getting control of himself.

"It's midnight, Mr. Haycock. What do you want?"

"It's morning," Haycock said. And he was right: Arjun looked at dawn light on the dome of Haycock's head. He began to speak, but Haycock interrupted, "Put that nonsense away," and snatched the envelope out of Arjun's hands and skimmed it away across the floor into the dust under the bed. Arjun felt a presence leaving the room. "Got a man I want you to meet. Make yourself useful, see if we can't do something with you yet. Get your coat."

They trudged across the Heath in the cold morning light, Haycock stamping muddy footprints into the dewy grass, and scaring the birds out of the trees with bouts of snarling, calling curses upon the names of all his competitors and customers. They followed the path that ran around the base of the hill and then up through a high fence of trees to the walls of the Countess Ilona's estate.

Arjun had been unsure he wanted to go with Haycock, until the little man had told him they were visiting the Countess's estate, and that he might be able to get Arjun into the Countess's presence. Haycock wouldn't say who it was he wanted Arjun to meet; when Arjun asked, he just tapped his nose and said, "Trade secret, for now. See how it all works out, won't we?" All he would say was that he had an appointment with a customer.

"This is my boy," Haycock told the man at the gate. "Too old for an apprentice, I know, but he's simple. Can't be picky in my position. Ambitious young lads do not queue up for this post, you may be surprised to hear. Let us through, then."

"My friend is joking. My name is Arjun, of Gad. I represent the Choristry, a power from far to the south. I am here to pay my respects to the Countess. I bring gifts from the Choristry."

The guard put down his pike and searched them. Arjun was wearing his black Choirman's robe for the occasion. When the guard was satisfied, a footman walked with them across the gardens and courtyards and into the Countess's sprawling mansion. They passed through the mirrored halls and climbed the broad stairs into the tower. The footman slipped through the doors to the Countess's room, leaving them waiting outside.

A man in uniform emerged. A drawn, miserable face and a black armband clashed with his medals and rich brocade.

"That's Captain Arlandes," Haycock said. "See the mourning-clothes? Funny story there . . ."

The footman emerged. "Mr. Arjun, of Gad, the Countess will see you now. Mr. Haycock, Professor Holbach is with her."

A man who must be Holbach stood by the window, looking through a golden telescope out over the Heath. The *Thunderer* hung outside, over the estate. A richly dressed white-faced woman who could only be the Countess was stretched out on the sofa like a jeweled snake, smoking a cigarette.

Haycock sidled over to Holbach, trying to bow to Ilona and avoid drawing her attention in the same sideways motion. Arjun bowed low before Ilona's sofa. There were little flakes and creases in the white around her lips; he tried not to notice.

Holbach took Haycock aside and hissed at him. "Mr. Haycock, I told you not to interrupt when I'm with the Countess. I will see you in my office later."

Craning up close to Holbach's ear, Haycock whispered, "There's someone I want you to see. A business prospect." He jerked a thumb at Arjun, then flinched to see the Countess glaring at him from her disturbed repose. A belated awareness of monstrous faux pas crept across his face.

"Haycock? Is that your name, creature? I can and will have you flensed, literally *flensed,* if you bring your business in here again. What were you thinking? What was my *guard* thinking? This is not the place. I stay my hand now only as a favor to the Professor, who seems to find you useful."

Both Holbach and Haycock showered the Countess with fulsome gratitude, Haycock managing to have slipped out of the room at the end of his performance. Holbach went back to his telescope.

Arjun kneeled before the sofa, and began. He praised Ararat; he praised the Countess's mansion and beauty and leadership. Ilona rolled her eyes. "You are not required to kneel. Please stand." Arjun hurriedly stood.

He told her of the Choristry's skill in medicine and science, the respect in which it was held over all the broad plains, its great wealth. He carefully made no definite promises, but he tried to hint that he could make it worth her while to help him. Ilona gave him a look to indicate that her interest was piqued, if only in the tiniest degree.

Arjun praised her power: clearly, he said, she was the foremost of the city's potentates. Her territories were very great and rich, and here in the heart of the city, by the Bay; an enviable position, one the Choristry respected. He gestured widely with his hand. Out of the window, his eye caught the floating bulk of the *Thunderer.* "Your ship is a miracle. I have stood below it; it hangs over the city like a loving and angry god. You have put a new god into the city's sky."

"That's an interesting way to put—" Holbach said.

Ilona cut him off with a snap of her fingers. "What do you *want,* man?"

Hastily, Arjun rushed into his story. "I have come in search of a Voice that sang high above our Choir. . . ."

Ilona sat through his story. When he was finished, she threw herself back into the sofa and held a pale hand to her head. "You bore me after all. How disappointing. Our city is already adequately supplied with lunatics, thank you. Good day to you. Go trudge the streets with the other broken, god-addled wretches. Professor, please call the guard."

*　*　*

No one was going to help him. The city was closed to him, and he was without friends. Perhaps he could make his own path into the city; and he could light that path, so that he might draw the Voice to him.

Arjun stopped in Moore Street that evening, and listened to the broken old man on the corner play his hurdy-gurdy and stamp his foot. Arjun did not give him money. Instead, he sat down with him and hummed a tune to him. It was a simple tune, adapted for the clumsy wheezing machine the man played, but it had a trace of the Voice in its melody, a distant echo. Arjun showed him where to put his fingers and sat with him until he could play it. He left him playing it over and over again.

Arjun watched as a grey-suited clerk came out of a pub and passed the hurdy-gurdy, reeling slightly, threw the old man a coin, and walked on humming a fragment of the tune.

TWELVE

A ragged child ran down Moore Street, rattling a stick along the railings and drumming it on the hollow boards. He stopped for a moment by old Lagger, the hurdy-gurdy man, and listened to his tune, rapping his stick in time with the rhythm. It was nice. Then on again, counting down the buildings. Third one down from what's left of the Black Moon, round the back, into the garden.

A shape formed out of the shadows behind him and grabbed his arm. There was a moment of struggle, then a knife appeared in the larger boy's hand. It was a tiny, sharp fishmonger's knife. The child went limp and still.

"I'm here for Silk. I'm not here to steal nothing."

"What's your name? What do you want? Who told you?"

"Een. Lads down at the docks. From the Nessene's shelter down there. Hagley, Bill, Shutter? They said you had food? I'm not useless. I used to steal for Thin Mag. I was in the Tallow House, and I got out, all on my own."

"Who's Thin Mag? Why're you here, if she's so great?"

"Why d'yer think?"

The larger boy put his knife into his jacket pocket and let go of Een's arm. "Namdi," he said, gesturing to himself. "So is it true about them, then? Are they as bad as they say?"

"Dunno. Prob'ly. Is it true what they say about your boss?"

Namdi smiled. "Maybe. We'll see."

✦ ✦ ✦

Fiss came up and joined Jack on the roof, where he sat watching the first stars come out. There had been no stars in the House.

"All right, Silk?" Jack shrugged, and Fiss went on, "There's a new boy downstairs. Namdi found him skulking about. Name of Een. Looks all right. Wants to see the amazing flying lad. From some lot down at the docks. Forced out by the white robes."

"All right. I'll see him later."

"Catch," Fiss said, tossing a package to Jack, who caught it without looking. "He brought these with him. Not bad, eh?"

It was a bundle of cigarettes, held together by a red ribbon. Each dun tube was stamped with a gilt seal in a foreign script. Een must have stolen them from a ship down at the docks.

"Are we collecting tribute now, then?" Jack said.

"Well, the boy wanted to trade something for his shelter. To show he's not useless. Can't see the harm in taking them. And it's not bad, is it?"

"It's not bad," Jack said, throwing the bundle back. "If he's good, and he knows his way around the docks, we can use him. I'll talk to him tomorrow."

"Right then." Fiss lit up one of the cigarettes and leaned against the chimney. They looked out over the roofs in silence as the evening sky darkened.

"Fiss? You still there? You smell burning?"

There was a muffled crash of breaking glass. A stink of burning wood. A crest of flame flared up from the roofs at the other end of the street. Jack ran to the other side of the roof and looked out over Moore Street, watching intently.

Fiss stood behind him. "That's the place on the corner. The baby-killer woman, the 'bortionist."

The wind took the greasy smoke down the street. Just ahead of the smoke came a group of small figures in ghostly white. Jack counted them by the torches in their hands: fifteen, perhaps twenty. He watched them stop a few doors away. Old Lagger was frantically trying to put his hurdy-gurdy away and gather up his hat and coins. One of the white figures rushed up to him and pushed him over and started kicking and kicking.

"Fiss," Jack said. "Get the lads."

By the time they made it downstairs and outside, the white-robed youths were at the Cypress. Some of them had gone inside, Jack saw. There were about ten of them in the street. Their heads were shaved and their faces were streaked with soot. He thought they were no older than him, but it was hard to tell.

One of them stepped forward. A red burn stained his stubbled head. "Who are you?"

"Who are *you*? This is our street."

Burn-mark looked confused and upset. He wasn't expecting resistance, Jack could see. Burn-mark started saying something stupid, something conciliatory. Jack wasn't listening. Burn-mark wasn't in control here. The white robes behind Burn-mark weren't listening either. They were steadying their brands and preparing to rush, whatever Burn-mark said. Jack drew his beautiful knife. He had no idea how to hold a knife for fighting. He held it point up, in front of his face, and hoped for the best.

They came at him, surging past Burn-mark, who stood there stupidly for a moment before joining the rush.

Fiss, Aiden, Namdi, all of them, hung back. Of *course* they did, he thought. None of them were fighters, were they, not really? Not even Namdi, though he liked to think so. Nor was Jack, but here he was. It was too late to back away without disgrace. He had no choice but to stand his ground. No, more: he had to move forward, to face it willingly. He ran at them.

A heavy brand fell at his face. It was slow, and he stepped back easily. Another came down over his shoulder, and he twisted away. Burn-mark was there, lifting his brand in both hands. Jack watched them thoughtfully. He reached out casually with his knife and flicked a scar across Burn-mark's blotched face. He watched Burn-mark stagger back, raising his hand to his face, dropping his brand. Jack reached over and made the same lazy mark on the face of the white robe next to him, along a shaven jaw that was slowly opening in a bellow of outrage. A hand slowly approached, reaching to seize his shirt. He leaned away, and drew the knife along the grasping arm, opening the folds of the robe. For what seemed like a very long time, he watched bright blood well from the wound.

Then he stepped back out of the knot of tense bodies. The white robes lurched into motion again, staggering back. They looked to Jack like statues coming to slow life; no, *puppets,* strings jerking them clumsily. Jack staggered too for a moment. Fiss and Aiden ran up to steady him. He was all right, just stunned. Did he say that or think it? " 'M 'righ'," he repeated.

More of the white robes came out of the Cypress to see what the noise was. They ran into their dazed comrades and started shouting and shoving. They raised their brands over their heads and came on at a run. Jack stepped forward to meet them. His feet felt light as air. The white robes were all moving so slowly. And now, this time, Fiss and Aiden and Namdi and all the others came up behind him, all shouting and proud.

The savage children came into the Cypress during the evening meal. The lodgers were all sitting at the table when Norris came staggering in, reeking of booze, and threw himself sobbing into a corner. The white robes swaggered in after him. One of them pointed at Norris. "Sickening. Look at him. The *stink* of him."

The guests sat there, scared and humiliated, as the white robes paced around the room. One of them rapped his unlit brand against one of Defour's old posters. "What whore is this?"

Arjun ran upstairs and came back holding his flintlock. Standing across the room, he leveled it at the boy who had first spoken, and told him to leave. They stood facing each other for what seemed like a very long time. It sickened Arjun to point the weapon at a child, but he held it steady. The boys glared at him. Only one shot, and they were trying to get behind him.

There were sounds of fighting outside. The white robes looked at each other and slipped out into the street, spitting on the floor as they went. Arjun followed them a minute later, holding the gun out stiffly.

Outside, the white robes were running away to the north. Another group of boys staggered south, supporting by his thin shoulders a boy in a strange and gaudy silk-ribboned shirt.

Arjun lowered the gun and ran down the street to the fire.

Sparks drifted on the smoke. Men and women were out in the light of the blaze passing buckets up from the canal. Arjun put his shoulder to the work. He felt better than he had for weeks. He saw Heady there, working with him. Later, he went back down the street and picked up the old hurdy-gurdy man and his battered case and helped him into the Cypress's dining room. They sat together in silence. Defour brought them something to eat.

THIRTEEN

"T hen walk with me, Captain."

The Countess set aside her work—she had been carefully prun-
ing and shaping her roses—and rose from the bench. She stood with
a sigh of stiffness and removed her thick-cuffed gardening gloves.
Arlandes took her arm.

Light streamed in through the glass of the greenhouse. The air
was hazy with dust and pollen and with thick smells of loam and
night soil. Arlandes walked arm-in-arm with the Countess past the
roses, the tulips, past petals and pistils in reds and yellows, purples
and blues, and in subtler shades than he could name, past thorns
and glistening grasping swellings of orchids. The Countess paused
twice to snip away some imperfection or to gently straighten a failing stalk with wire and twine. She pointed out a kind of creeping
vine that grew, she said, in street-side ditches on refuse and offal, in
the north, near the Mountain; it was very rare. It was gorgeously
purple and it quivered and wavered its fronds. Arlandes attempted
to admire it.

Two servants stood at the door. She waved them away. "I will be
quite safe with my Captain, thank you."

The Countess was not in her finery. She wore plain overalls,
loose and dirt-stained. She wore no wig; her hair was grey and wiry
and pulled back stiffly from her scalp. Her face was unpainted;
stripped of her usual smooth whiteness, her face was deeply lined
and brittle-boned. Even her eyes were different: the glittering
emerald of her eyes was the product of delicate and exotic gels

purchased from distant eastern districts. Without her lenses her eyes were brown and almost soft.

It was a rare honor to be permitted to see her like that. Which meant, Arlandes had always thought, that the jewels and paint and lace that she presented to the outside city were gestures not of respect, but contempt.

The greenhouse stood at the top of the hill, where the light was best. The estate spread out below, red flags fluttering and high windows flashing gold in the sun. Beyond that were stands of ash and oak (in the shadows of which were spring-guns and mantraps) and the spiked walls of the estate. Below that was Laud Heath, rolling out green down to the river. Crowds milled back and forth over the Heath: the women's brightly colored parasols were like a haze of distant flowers.

The Countess steered Arlandes' arm toward a path through the trees. He went passively, silently. Her arm was bird-thin and her grey head no higher than his shoulder.

She stroked the silk of his sleeve.

"You still wear black, Captain."

He nodded.

"It speaks well of you, Captain. Sacrifices must be made for the city. But we do not forget them. Some of our peers, Captain, for instance the Gerent of Stross Mercantile, may treat the lives of ordinary folk as if they are currency, to be spent and forgotten. But he is a vulgar man. We feel more finely."

"She was not ordinary to me, my lady."

"Of course not. Captain, I have never been married, as you well know. But I have mourned my father. And I have mourned four brothers, dead of plague, or murder, or war. I have mourned more nephews than I care to count. Do not presume to instruct me in grief, Captain."

"I apologize. My grief spoke for me."

She smiled and touched his sallow cheek. "I understand."

The path divided and they took the more shadowed route, beneath the oaks.

"They love you, Captain. In your grief. Our people in all our districts mourn with you. Do you know that? They love you perhaps more than me."

"No, my lady."

"But of course they do! It is different for men and women, my Captain. You carry a sword. You command men in battle. You take to the sea, or to the skies, as it may be now, and destroy their enemies, while I remain here. Tending my garden. You are a hero. They will never love me the way they love you. I will plan and scheme for them and bring order to the chaos of their lives, and they will only fear me. You'll rain down fire on them and slash your sword around and they will love you for it."

"This is politics, my lady. I will not presume to disagree with you on that subject."

"Very wise, Captain. I have buried four brothers; I know these things."

She stooped to inspect a twining plant, a dull green thing that crept up the trunk of one of the oaks. She curled it round her thin fingers. "When spring comes round again, this will flower the most beautiful blue, Captain." She let it go and stood again. "Why have you come to see me?"

"I wished to discuss my orders. My lady, you have ordered me . . ."

"It's good that you've come down again to earth. Do not forget whom you serve as you flit around up there."

"I do not forget."

"Good." She took his arm again. "Since you've come to me, I have a new task for you. Shh, Captain. My prior orders stand, and you will do as I command. We will speak no more of it. Let me explain what else I want from you."

They emerged from the copse. She gestured down over the Heath, where the distant crowds shifted.

"Captain, these are uneasy times. Although aren't they always? Unrest and strange passions. There was an incident not far from the docks last night. A number of buildings were burned. Buildings of no account, but still: it is an affront to my order. My people tell me it was the cult of the Flame. Those *nasty* boys."

"The *Thunderer* cannot strike against street-children with torches and clubs, my lady. If I turn the ship's guns on the city—well, the cure will be far worse than the disease."

"I know, Captain. I know. It's too early for that. Those boys will burn themselves out soon enough. They are only a sign of the times. And soon enough, if it's violence they want, I'll make room for them in my armies."

"My lady?"

"Don't be naïve, my Captain." She smiled and pressed a finger to his lips. Her nails were short, chewed-down and ragged, not the jeweled painted curling things she wore in public. Her skin was thin and brittle. "Back to the challenge of the present moment. This present unrest makes us look weak. Did we not promise that the *Thunderer* would be a swift sure hammer of order? Yes, we did. I think that we did. There is a man—one Mr. *Shay*—who has been troubling us. He conducts a very blasphemous business."

"Blasphemous?"

"Sorcerous. Tampering with the gods and powers of the city."

"Like our own Professor Holbach?"

"He differs from Holbach in that Holbach has my protection, and Shay does not. Shay comes into my territory without my permission. And he *angers* my people. He disgusts them. There have been protests. The priests come to my palace to complain. I bid them be patient, and they nod, and they go back to their temples regardless and whip their congregations into a fury. This is not the first time he's come through these parts; he was here ten years ago, and he was heard of in Mass How twenty years ago. It always leads to riots in the end. Have you not heard of his name?"

"I have not."

"You have not been paying attention to the city. Don't forget us, Captain, in your grief. Don't forget us up there in the blue skies. Are they very blue?"

"You should come up with us one day, my lady."

"Ha! Can you imagine me climbing your rope-ladders, Captain? Besides, women are bad luck on warships, are they not?"

"So they say. I think an exception could be made in your case, my lady."

"You think my position allows me to escape from the burdens of

my sex? Quite the opposite is true, Captain. Ssh now, Captain. If
you do not know of Shay, there are many people in my employ who
can inform you. Talk to Holbach. This is a matter of blasphemy.
This is god business. This is Holbach's business. I want this man removed; talk to Holbach first."

Arlandes bowed. They walked in silence, following the path
down across the lawns toward the mansion.

"My lady? The *Thunderer* has spent the last week patrolling
Stross End. At your orders. We are not welcome there. The mercantile, the Gerent: they do not want us there. They have started to
place riflemen on the towers of their factories. They are moving in
cannon and arming their towers. Every day we anger them more."

"Are you afraid of the cannon? Can they harm you?"

"I am afraid of nothing, my lady. I do not believe they can harm
us. What good will it do if they hole our hull? We can hardly sink;
we have no business floating in the first place."

"If they fire on you, will you shrink from returning fire? Are you
too softhearted in your grief?"

"If you order me to fire, I will fire. If you do not, I will not. I
would only ask that you tell me why; if you fear unrest, why anger
the Gerent in this way?"

"And if I do not answer, will you refuse to serve me?"

Arlandes did not answer. Soon they were walking up the steps to
the mansion's west wing. The Countess sighed. She let go of
Arlandes' arm as her courtiers poured out around her, bowing and
pleading for her attention, holding out her robes for her.

"Oh, my beautiful Captain. It would sadden me greatly if one
day I had to doubt your loyalty. Go talk to Holbach."

In the Observatory?"

"Yes, Captain."

"Right under our noses? Are you quite certain?"

"Quite certain, Captain. He's not hiding, after all; he's in business. He *advertises.*"

Holbach shrugged. The chairs in Arlandes' office were hard
wooden things, and his soft plump backside shifted uncomfortably.

Arlandes sifted through the papers on his desk: the pamphlets, the news rags, Holbach's own notes and jottings. He sighed and pushed them all aside.

"This is disgusting, Professor."

Holbach shifted again, and plucked at the brocade of his coat. He looked nervous; he looked as if Arlandes made him nervous. That strange bitch Holbach dragged around with him—the girl who wore a man's tailcoat, who carried a heavy silver-tipped stick like a man, whose manner was altogether so arrogant and offensive that Arlandes refused even to remember her name—stood behind him, arms folded behind her back. She claimed to be a lawyer, which did nothing to endear her to Arlandes.

"*Shay*. Can he do what he promises, Professor?"

"I would say that I'm almost entirely sure he cannot. No one I've ever heard can do it. But the city's a very big place. There are a great many wonders in the Atlas. Last year no one thought men could take to the skies. But here we both are, eh?"

"It's disgusting whether it's real or fraud. It's causing unrest. Disorder. Disrupting our precious peace. The Countess wants me to do something about him."

"You, meaning the *Thunderer*?"

"What else would I mean, Professor?"

"You'll destroy him with your cannons? Blast the old Observatory to rubble?"

"I imagine so."

Holbach turned and looked back at the girl, who shrugged.

"Captain, may I suggest that you leave him to me? Discretion and circumspection may be the better way to approach this man."

Arlandes, running his thumb's flesh firmly up and down his letter-opener's dull blade, studied Holbach closely. And the woman. "You want to question him?"

"Well, not me personally. I expect he's only a fraud, a con-man. I am far too old and fat to go confronting criminals in their lairs. But my curiosity is piqued."

"Some people say you have too much curiosity, Professor."

This plump oily pervert, libertine, freethinker, coming into Arlandes' office and dropping sly hints about the Atlas, as if

Arlandes didn't know, was too stupid a soldier to suspect that Holbach was involved up to his fat neck in that vicious and subversive publication. The woman too, probably.

Holbach looked nervous and pale. Arlandes turned his sneer into a half-smile and Holbach relaxed visibly.

Arlandes leafed through the papers again. The Countess had given him an order. And it would be a pleasure to thwart Holbach. But—but—*but*. This man Shay. This was nasty business. This was blasphemy. This was sorcery. Unless it was fraud, in which case it was simply beneath his dignity. This was god business, as the Countess had put it. This was the sort of thing that had killed Lucia. It disgusted him.

No; it *scared* him. That sickness in his gut was *fear*. And he was too weak, too tired, too lonely to fight that fear. With a great surge of relief he folded and sank back in his chair.

"I'll give you two days, Professor. Then the guns."

"Thank you." Holbach rose from his chair, grunting a little. Then he stood awkwardly, rubbing his hands together, clinking his finger-rings nervously.

Finally Arlandes raised an eyebrow and Holbach spoke. "How are you faring with your command, Captain?"

"The *Thunderer* performs ably. I don't know or care to know how, but it performs ably."

"I meant to ask after your own well-being, Captain. In light of your loss. I meant to express again my—"

"I spend my days and nights servicing a great machine, of your making, Professor, the fuel for which is my wife's life. The fuel that it burns is her memory. That is my state of mind, if you must inquire after it."

Holbach flinched and sagged. The woman touched his arm, and then spoke. Her voice was strong and clear and cool. There was a complacent self-confidence in it that made Arlandes itch to strike her. "If I may, Captain: perhaps you can think of it this way. Your wife was touched by a god. She was taken up by it. There's something holy about that. Perhaps the ship is an altar and you're honoring her sacrifice when you fly it."

"Madam, you don't mean what you say. Your sort never say what

you mean or mean what you say. It's unwise to make sport of simpler folk." She shifted so that her head was cocked, her eyebrow
raised slightly. "It's unwise to make sport of me." The woman took
a half-step back. He rose and she took a full step back and dropped
her eyes away from his. Holbach took her arm and they backed out
together.

They thought he was ridiculous, but they feared him, too.
Holbach and all his queers and intellectuals and subversives. And
quite rightly. The crowds and the common folk still cheered for
him, still cheered for the *Thunderer,* but the smart set knew better.
They knew that the *Thunderer* was a terrible weapon, and so was he.
He expected the common folk would learn that soon enough, too.

He spent the afternoon in the gymnasium of the barracks, spar-
ring. He sparred with dull blades with the cowards, and with raw
edges with the brave ones, with his favorites among the men. He
opened a new scar on Duncan's cheek, for which badge of honor and
courage Duncan thanked him manfully. For his own part, Arlandes
took a dull-bladed slap to the ribs that ached splendidly, and made
him quite forget his grief for an hour or two.

FOURTEEN

The next day, Arjun went down to Gies Landing. He listened to the sailors' songs as they stumbled, arms over each other's shoulders, grown together like root knots, in and out of the dives of the docks. Some of them held on to their own songs, in exotic tongues; others took on the city's songs, laughing as they stumbled over the city's rhymes.

He sat on the jetty and watched the ships leave. *I can't go back now,* he thought, *even if I were to despair: I couldn't begin to pay my passage back.*

There was a child waiting for him outside the Cypress that afternoon, who jumped up to say, "Mr. Arjun, sir? Letter for you." He pressed an envelope into Arjun's hand, and left, looking sincerely aggrieved at Arjun's meager tip.

> *May I presume upon your time, Arjun of Gad? I believe we may be of assistance to each other. Please come promptly. I will be at home to guests this evening. 122 Fallon Circle, Foyle's Ward. Our previous meeting was a pleasure and I look forward to renewing our acquaintance.*
>
> *Gracien Holbach.*
>
> *P.S.—If the boy is honest, you will find money for a carriage, with my compliments.*

Arjun shook four green notes out of the envelope. Rials, the Countess's currency. How did Holbach know where to find him?

Haycock, of course. Haycock knew Holbach, did business with him. Arjun knocked on the book-dealer's door, but he wasn't in.

Back down at Gies Landing, he found a carriage rank. "I don't take rials," the coachman said. "See the crest on the side of the cab? Belongs to the Gerent. Dollars only." Arjun shook his head in exasperation and looked around for another carriage.

"Never mind," the driver called. "I'll stretch a point."

The driver flicked the horse into motion with his stick and they went forward under the arches and banners, up the hill toward the Tor. Arjun had walked this route many times, but it was very different from the inside of a carriage, lifted up out of the filth of the streets. No one shouldered into him cursing, or grabbed his sleeve to beg or preach at him. And it was so much faster than walking that it redrew his map of the city, changing his sense of scale and time: it was still quite early in the evening when they turned into Foyle's Ward.

Fallon Circle was quiet and elegant, its houses set back behind gardens. The round tower of 122 was visible from the end of the street. Evening lights in the windows, all the way up. The building beneath it was a huge and dusty sprawl, stately yet disheveled. A butler met Arjun at the door and led him through what seemed like a maze of libraries and cluttered reading-rooms and up into the tower, then gestured him through into an office.

Holbach was leaning against the window. A woman lay on the sofa, smoking a cigarette. Déjà vu seized Arjun for a moment, and he forgot what he was going to say. But the woman was not the Countess. She was much younger—the flesh of her face was still soft—and she wore her dark hair plain and short and scraped back. She was wearing a man's suit of well-tailored silk. She looked intelligent; not beautiful, but compelling. She met Arjun's eye and smiled, tapping out her ash into a copper bowl.

"I'm so glad you came," Holbach said.

"I was curious, Professor. I expected nothing to come of our last meeting. I recall it less fondly than it seems you do."

"Few people would dare speak quite so dismissively of an opportunity to meet our glorious Countess."

"I intended no offense. It was simply . . . frustrating."

"I took no offense, Arjun. May I call you Arjun? No other title? Arjun, this is Olympia Autun. This is Dr. Joseph Liancourt." Holbach gestured at a stocky man with unkempt black hair, who hunched over a table, scribbling. Liancourt grunted.

"Miss Autun," Arjun said, "are you also in the Countess's service?" She laughed.

"Olympia is a lawyer. She is in no one's service. Liancourt you may know. The playwright? *The Sign of Winter? The Fourth Temple? Hare and Isabel?*"

"*Hare* was a potboiler. Please, remember me for *Sign,* or not at all."

Arjun shrugged. Liancourt shook his head sadly.

"Ah well," Holbach said. "So, I was intrigued by your story, at our previous meeting. Have you had any success?"

"I'm afraid I haven't. I'm trying to be patient."

"Well, we'll see what we can do."

Olympia stubbed out her cigarette. "This doesn't concern me. Professor, we'll talk later. Liancourt. Arjun, a pleasure."

She left. Holbach gestured for Arjun to take her place on the sofa. "Intrigued. Yes, very much so. We will talk at length, later. A lost god. Insubstantial. A *Voice,* as you put it. Where did it go? Perhaps you are wondering if it was ever really there. Intriguing questions."

"I rather suspect he's just a lunatic," Liancourt said. "Look at his eyes. An obsessive. One encounters them, in the theater. Best to humor them, yes, but not to employ them."

Arjun felt a sudden stab of panic. He stood up and moved to stand between Liancourt and Holbach. "Professor, I don't want to repeat our previous conversation. I am tired of being turned away. Can you help me? Will you?"

"All right. Shall we get to the point, then?" Holbach said. "Our mutual friend Mr. Haycock tells me you are looking for work. He says that *you* say you can read certain languages that are almost lost in this city. I can use that skill."

"Mr. Haycock would like to sell me certain books. I had to decline his business; I have little money left. I think he would like you to pay me, in hopes that the money will find its way through me to his pockets. But I'm not interested in money. I have enough for my food and shelter for the time being. You know what I *am* interested in. Can you help?"

"Please, sit down, Arjun. Sit. We have time to talk. Perhaps things were simpler in your distant mountain hermitage; here in Ararat, we need to talk things through." Arjun sat and held his tongue.

They began with testing, Holbach opening books at random and asking him for the meaning of certain passages. Arjun tolerated it as patiently as he could. Some of them he could read fluently. Others he had never seen. When Arjun offered a halting translation of a yellowed Tuvar scroll, Holbach clapped his meaty hands and laughed. "Hear that, Liancourt? I'd despaired of finding anyone who could unscramble this text. The ancient languages must be re-markably well-preserved in Gad."

Arjun shook his head. "The language is forgotten, but we pre-serve many books. I found grammatologies and dictionaries that translated between Tuvar and Asi and Kael. I taught it to myself. I do not know how the words should sound."

"Remarkable. Now"—Holbach raised a finger—"I can see your questions working to the surface again. Why would you work for me? How can I help your purpose? Well, I expect you are aware of my reputation. I am the man who predicted the Bird's return, and harnessed its power. Some of my, ah, *projects,* may be relevant to your search. In fact, I have an opportunity for you right now. Something I hope you will pursue this very evening."

Arjun remained silent. "It's a small matter," Holbach began, "but the Countess is displeased. There is a man whose activities *dis-please* her. His name is Shay. We know where he can be found. He has advertised his presence, through unsavory channels. No, no, that doesn't concern you: she has brutes for that sort of work. You're not the type. What should interest you is this: Shay claims to have certain, ah, *powers,* a certain unusual *science.* He's probably a fraud or a maniac. But if he's the real thing, you of all people will want to know what he knows. I think you should visit him, talk to him. And quickly. Before the Countess's brutes kill him or drive him un-derground."

"You want to know what he says to me."

"Oh, certainly. I couldn't claim to be disinterested. I would eagerly await your report. And, if you do this for me, I promise you I will help you find your Voice. I am, I think I can honestly say, the greatest theologian in this city. I will help you, if you come work for me. Now tell me: are you armed?"

Holbach had a carriage waiting outside the tower. *He was confident that I would take his offer,* Arjun thought.

The carriage took Arjun across the river and onto Laud Heath. Arjun had the coachman stop on the lawn at the base of Observatory Hill, and walked up the hill alone. Lanterns hung in the trees, marking out the path in the gathering dusk.

After a few minutes, the path rose up out of the trees. Arjun stopped halfway up the hill and looked out across the dark city. The streets were traced out in fire. Arjun picked out the places he knew: a tiny circle carved out of the city's vast map. With his finger in front of his eye, he traced the circle's circumference. *Everything within a day's walk of the Cypress,* he thought. *If I had money for carriages, or horses, or boats, I could expand that circle, bring more of the city within my map.*

Gad, and all the towns he had passed in his travels, would easily fit into the space marked out by his finger. Ararat extended seemingly infinitely beyond. The high, high walls in the north—that must be the Urbomachy. Was that the Iron Rose? Those must be the factories of Garhide. That scar of red light could only be the pillar of fire: Tiber. What would it be like to be near it? He knew that there were courthouses all around the fire's plaza, tempering themselves in the light of its justice. It must drive their inhabitants quite mad.

He could see no walls, no borders; the city's lights were a haze on the horizon. How did this endless sprawl feed itself? It seemed impossible. No profusion of gods could take the place of honest farmland. Could it? He made a note to ask Holbach for books on the city's economy, and moved on. No time to waste.

There were fires on the hilltop, surrounded by clusters of dark man-shapes. There was a banner strung between the trees over their heads—TO THE FIRE WITH THE BLASFEEMER!—and the squat dome of the Observatory Orphée rose behind them. They were between Arjun and the gate in the derelict building's fence.

Holbach had warned him to expect something like this. Shay's peculiar business infuriated the churches, the pious, the mob. The *Sentinel* and the *Burgher-Gazette* were competing with each other to see who could denounce Shay's blasphemies more furiously. There were protests in the streets—Arjun thought he had passed one a few days earlier, but the protest songs were uninteresting and he had paid no attention. Hence the Countess's concern: Shay was an irritant, a source of unrest in her territory.

While Arjun stood there, one of the men left the fire and came toward him, calling out, "What's your business here?"

Arjun took a deep breath and stepped forward into the firelight, saying, "I heard about the scum in there," jabbing his fist at the Observatory, feigning rage. "The blasphemer. What are we going to do about it, friend?"

The figures around the fire turned to him, with the heads of black-eyed eagles and boars, lions and snakes. Then Eagle-head took his eagle-mask off to reveal the face of a bearded young man, and handed Arjun a jug. "Come sit with us, friend."

There were about thirty of them. There were signs—rubbish strewn on the grass, dead fires—that there had been many more during the day. Only the diehards had stayed into the night.

"It's evil," said a woman who had been wearing a spider mask, dozens of blank glass bead-eyes on a bristling black brow.

"It's against the order of things," Eagle-head agreed. "The gods won't allow it."

"We read about it in the *Herald*," Spider-head said. "They said he'd been here for weeks, doing his filthy business. Our own neighbors could have been coming here."

What were they going to do about it? They showed him. They took their last swigs from the jug, and put their masks back on—not just animal heads, but clocks, locks, flames, horns, mirrors, a ring of blades, a scribbled page—transforming themselves into the avatars of their various gods. They picked up pots, pans, and sticks and proceeded around the fence, banging out a rough, mocking music. They kicked their legs out high in an ugly parody of dance. Huge paste-and-paper heads wobbled loosely. Eagle-head went at the front carrying a torch and chanting, *Out, out, out, hang 'im high, cut 'im down, ride 'im out.* They went off around the corner of the fence into the dark.

Arjun waited, and they came back a few minutes later from the other side. Clearly, their anger was up; they went for another lap, disappearing again behind the trees.

He had at least a few minutes before they came back round again. He ran up to the gate and tried it: locked, of course. He looked at the spiked fence. He passed his gun and his lantern through the fence, then his jacket, then grabbed the railings tightly in both hands and pulled himself up and over the spikes. He fell to the ground on the other side, with a long rip in his trouser leg but nothing worse. *Better than I expected.*

The front door was boarded up. Arjun found a broken window and pulled himself through into darkness. He struck the lantern's flame. A dusty corridor ran around the circumference of the abandoned building, curving away in either direction.

Arjun checked his flintlock. It was loaded with a single shot. Shay might be dangerous, Holbach had said: either he was a fraud, in which case he might be a hardened criminal, or he could really do what he claimed, which might be worse.

Arjun set out clockwise. The corridor rose and spiraled inward, the turns getting sharper, until he took one last turn and he was under the dome. A shaft of moonlight came in through the dome's aperture. The huge telescope was fallen at an angle, the gears and struts on one side rusted and rotted through. It was like a great golden beetle, legs smashed, body bent.

There was light coming from an open door. Arjun made his way around the wreckage and stepped through into the next room, which was dominated by a large brass orrery: an expensive arrangement the height of a man, of loops and whorls of burnished metal, describing complex and implicate arcs around a golden solar sphere.

Across the room, through the long shadows of the brass loops, Arjun could see a man sitting in a chair, reading a newspaper by candlelight. The man wore round glasses and a neat black suit, well-tailored, though the shoulders were dusted with dandruff. He had long, dirty white hair. He rose, and folded the paper. He was very short and thin.

"I am Mr. Shay." He spoke with a cold dry rasp, with an unpleasant rise to his voice, as if daring Arjun to find him repellent. "Well. Are you here for business, or to vent your outrage?" He pointed to the paper. "The *Era* is terribly full of outrage. Apparently the soul-health of the city's children requires that I be hanged forthwith. Or has some lord decided I am a nuisance, and sent you here to put a stop to me?"

"I don't entirely know yet."

"A good answer. An honest man."

Arjun put his lantern down and took a step closer. Shay moved around so that the orrery was still between them. Its outer loops had broken and fallen to the floor. There were worlds underfoot. Shay asked Arjun's name, and Arjun gave it to him.

Shay circled the orrery as Arjun stepped closer. "You have an unusual accent, Arjun. Where are you from?"

"A place called Gad. Far to the south."

"There are still places outside Ararat, then. Sometimes I wonder. I am strangely relieved."

"You are from the city, then, Mr. Shay?"

"In a manner of speaking." He stopped circling by an open door. "Let's see what I can offer you, then." He darted through.

Arjun followed. At first, he couldn't see where Shay had gone. The room was dark, and full of moldy chairs, arranged in circles around a circle of tables in the well of the room.

The door shut behind Arjun and the roof opened and stars splashed overhead, more than he had ever seen, even on the clearest mountain nights. The wheel of the galaxy spun across the sky, rushing in. A single point of light gleamed brighter and sharper, came closer and larger. A second star overtook it, rushing down, growing red and angry, blotched with orange. It was whipped away and another point of light expanded to fill the sky with a huge purple sphere, belted by a vast plane of smashed dust. Arjun stumbled back and fell. The planets paraded before him. A peaceful blue orb expanded across the heavens, and was gone. Darkness for a moment, then stars again, turning.

It was not really the sky, or the stars; the images were running across the ceiling somehow. He tried to reach up and touch them, but it was too far overhead. Pale white light ran over his reaching fingers, then red, then green. Shay came down the steps toward the center of the room. "My apologies, Arjun. I find it amusing, and it creates an appropriate atmosphere."

"How are you doing it?"

"I'm not doing anything. What do you think I am? Don't answer that. The machinery is in the ceiling. It was a mess. Hasn't been maintained in gods only know how long. No one in this part of the city would know how. It's most likely from elsewhere, like yours truly, fallen through, from some less fusty district. I know a few tricks, though. I found a way to get it working. Do you like it?"

"Less so than the real sky. It casts a false light."

"Not such a good answer," Shay sneered. He stood by a table, on which were arranged a number of small glass cases. There was a faint glow from within them. "Here they are, then," Shay said. "Ararat's divine presences. Caged and for sale. This is my business; this my merchandise. Interested, appalled, or both? What brings you here?"

Arjun walked up and down, looking in the cases. Their dusty plates were seamed with black gum. The glass was thick and grimy, like the windows of old charity-shops on empty streets. Inside each one, phosphor ghost light sparked, in dragonfly green-gold, occluded jellyfish purple and blue. An uncanny plasm. A shimmering slick, which shifted and coiled and scratched the glass. A soft electric crepitation. The light made his eyes feel shadowed and grainy.

He turned away from them, and said, "I'm not here on my own account, but as an agent for Professor Holbach."

"Is *he* a purchaser?"

"I don't know yet. He tells me you trap the faint and forgotten gods. Or you *say* you do. The presences the city has left behind. He says you catch them, cage them, and sell them, like animals, or slaves, or toys. Is that what these are?"

"Faint? Lean in close. You'll see just how faint they are."

"Who would buy these?"

"Who wouldn't? To hold the powers of the city in your hand. As you love them, to possess them. As you hate them, to revenge yourself upon them. I don't give a shit what you do. Sit it on your lap, hold it, let it sing to you, tell yourself it loves you and it gives you meaning, to possess such a wonderful thing. Spit at it. As you please. You would be surprised how much business I do. Rich and powerful men come sneaking in at night. They all try to cover their faces, do you know that? As if I know or care who they are. You don't seem ashamed, though. I like that, Arjun. Go on. Lean in closer; feel their presences."

Slowly, Arjun approached one of the cases and leaned down close to it. A buzzing filled his head. He felt drunk, dizzy, glorious, young, surrounded by friends and lovers. He laughed and cried. He pulled back and his head emptied out and was cold again. Laughing, Shay said, "That's the *god* in it. See?"

Arjun leaned in over another, touching the case with his palm. A shock ran up his arm and he felt his muscle tense. His head pulsed like a raw wound. His lips curled back and he bared his teeth. A thrill of violence went through him. A noise halfway between bark and howl tore out past his grinding jaw. He pulled away, shaking his head, and went down the line of cases, through clouds of love and lust, hatred and pity, and more complex sensations: a complacent certainty of justice done, a craving for glory. When he was close to them, the cases radiated wonder. When he stepped back—which was hard to do—the sensation faded and left him feeling empty and soiled. They were ugly things. The glow in each of them seemed to be pressing at the glass, trying to escape. Surging and breaking, weakly.

"Are they aware in there? Do they feel?"

"An interesting question. If they have minds, they are—this is my view, Arjun—they are nothing like ours. Despite the delusions of the idiots outside, they do not love you, Arjun, or this city. Not in any way you could understand."

Nevertheless, Arjun thought the things wanted to be free. He could feel it. Was that what the Voice was? Was the Chamber a cage? Had they held it prisoner? Maybe it hadn't abandoned them;

maybe it had *escaped* them. He went round the cases again, listening for its song. It was not there.

"Are you disgusted, Arjun? Many people are. You must have passed by a number of them on the way in here."

"I don't know. I still don't know."

"They call it blasphemy. Sacrilege. Some other words they can't really explain. They'll try to run me off soon, I expect."

"Yes. The Countess's men are coming for you soon."

"Someone always does. I'll take myself elsewhere for a time, and come back, soon, soon enough. I always do."

"I'm here to ask you some questions. About your work."

"Oh dear. I suppose I won't be making a sale tonight."

"I have no money, Mr. Shay. And the prices of these must be . . . extraordinary. Besides, they are not real."

"Didn't you *feel* them, Arjun?"

"I felt *something*. But I once felt the touch of the real thing. These are . . . false. Shoddy goods. A cheat. They're only shadows of gods. What are they really?"

Shay shook his dirty white mane. "Oh no. I'm not here to answer your questions."

"I can pay for your answers. I have nothing, but Holbach can make it worth your while to answer me."

"I doubt it. My methods are my living; why would I share my secrets? And who is this Holbach, anyway?"

"You haven't heard of him? I gather he's famous."

"I spend my time elsewhere. Other parts of the city."

"He's the creator of the *Thunderer*."

"Isn't that some local newspaper?"

"What? No. The warship. The flying warship?"

Shay stared at Arjun. "That changes things. I've seen it; it's a remarkable achievement. I don't care about the money, boy. But tell me how the ship works, and I'll give you answers."

Arjun thought quickly. He knew nothing about the ship, nothing at all. He took a gamble, and said, "The charm isn't permanent. Holbach has to renew it each morning. He makes sacrifices of birds, down by the Bay. He burns the feathers."

"Aha! There's always a trick to it. It's always both a true miracle *and* a sham. Now, you were honest with me, so I'll be honest with you. They're not gods. They're mere traces, sloughings-off; reflections, you might say. Good enough for most of my customers; perhaps they lack sensitivity. Now, how was the ship raised? He used the Bird, that I know. But how?"

"Ah. The ship itself is made from pine taken from trees swept by the wind on mountain peaks. That's part of it. How do you capture these reflections?"

"Well, not so much reflections as afterimages. I catch 'em on glass. There's a trick. That's part of it. Tell me more."

Arjun kept lying. Shay swallowed every wild lie he could conceive. Or it seemed he did. Perhaps Shay was lying, too. It was hard for Arjun to remember everything Shay said, while still keeping track of his own fabrications; many of the details of Shay's science escaped him. But he remembered that Shay reached under the table and snapped open a big black briefcase, and pulled out an odd little box, a bit like an accordion with a glass eye. Shay called it a heliotype. They had them, and better, in other parts of the city, Shay said. "Or they will. Some streets'll take you there, if you walk 'em right."

They captured light on glass. And, if properly treated, the glass could capture these afterimages of the gods, these ghostly trails of glory. Did the heliotype *make* these spectral energies, or *steal* them? Shay didn't know or care.

"I've never seen anything like this. And I've crossed this whole world. What do you mean when you say 'other parts of the city'? When you go into hiding, where do you go, Mr. Shay?"

"How will you pay for that information?"

Arjun tried to think of something else to say about the ship. Where was there a gap in his web of fabrications, some space he could fill with more lies?

In the silence, he realized, he could hear noises below. A window breaking. The chants of the crowd echoed distantly up the spiral corridor. *Hang 'im high!* They had got their courage up. Arjun wondered whether they had noticed he was missing, and followed him over the railings. They were coming. *Ride 'im out!*

Grunting, Shay started packing the strange cages away in his briefcase. Arjun said, "Mr. Shay, you can't leave yet. I don't care how you capture the images. I need to know how you find the *gods*. Do you track them? Summon them? How is it done?"

"Oh? Used yer time poorly, didn't you? Can't you hear 'em?"

"Those questions were for Holbach. This is for me. I can't let you leave."

"Oh dear. We don't have time for this, boy." Shay abandoned his packing and put down the case he was holding.

"Take me with you, then."

"You can't follow. You don't have the trick of it."

The mob sounds were still some way below. Arjun drew his pistol and moved to stand between Shay and the door.

"It's like that, is it, boy?" Shay put down the briefcase.

"You don't have time to argue, Mr. Shay. You have to take me with you. We'll go together."

"Haven't you been listening? There's more to this city than you know. Than you or them below'll ever see. Paths, places that open up only to the one who walks 'em right, and that's me, and not you. You're not even city-born. The city you see's a curtain before your eyes. Where I go, you can't come."

"Show me how, then. Show me and I'll follow. You won't leave here without me. *Please,* Mr. Shay, be reasonable."

"What'll they do to you, do you think, if they find you doing business with me?"

"They may kill me. They *will* kill you. I can chance it."

Shay's sharp teeth smiled. "Very well, then. There's a trick to it. Listen." He started to whistle tunelessly.

The light in the case at his feet grew and pulsed and scratched at the glass. Arjun felt the throbbing at the back of his head. A great thrill rose in him. The walls stretched away. He could hear applause. All around him were people calling his name. He had never been prouder; there was nothing he couldn't do with all this love, and he loved them back. . . .

He stood there looking wide-eyed down the rows of empty chairs. He didn't see Shay rushing him until the last second. The little man's hair was wild and he was snarling. There was a knife in his hand, stabbing up. Arjun jumped back. Flailing his arm out in panic, he struck Shay's knife with his pistol, knocking it aside. Shay staggered back, shocked. Arjun lost his own footing and fell back into a chair. Shay came at him again, the knife held high to stab down, and Arjun, his head clear, raised the pistol and fired. The bullet smashed Shay's skull bloodily open. The flintlock's dirty powder-flash lit his brittle white hair, and a wave of fire circled the orb of his head like dawn rising over the red planets above. Shay's twitching leg gave way and his body fell back.

Arjun breathed out. The mob would be here soon. There was no time to think about what he had done. But he couldn't leave the things in the cases. Gods or reflections, aware and suffering or not, they were grotesque, pathetic—lies, told without love. There were miracles in the city, that were perhaps no less sacred in their way than his own beloved Voice: they deserved better than to be reduced in this way. He supposed he did find Shay's work blasphemous, after all.

With the butt of his gun, he broke open the cases. As he cracked each one, the lights took on a greasy liquidity, and flowed out and away. A few did not just dissipate, as one might expect; instead, the lights gathered across the floor, clutching in tight knots of radiance. Some took on tiny forms. Glowing homunculi drifted away into the room's shadows. Something soft and blue and nearly-not-there, the height of a man's knees, crept over the dusty floorboards; something the size of a man's fist formed itself from throbbing red light and knuckled away into the dark. When Arjun blinked again, they were gone.

When he was sure he was alone, he knelt and looked at the device Shay had called a heliotype. The big black briefcase was full of plates, boxes, and chemical-jars that seemed to be integral parts of the device. There was no time to take it all with him; it was far too heavy to run with.

Taking the steps two at a time, he ran back out into the observatory dome. The chanting of the mob was very close now. He was very frightened. Who knew what they might do to him?

There were no other doors, but far over his head, the dome was split open to the sky, where the smashed and slumped telescope still protruded. Arjun put a foot on the telescope's broad, gleaming back. It wobbled, but did not collapse; it was braced against the hole in the roof. On hands and knees, he shinned up the ruined column and out onto the dome's curving roof, where he collapsed and let the cold night wind clear his mind.

The mob came into the room below. He listened to them smashing what was left of the machines, and thought about what he had done to Shay. His mind kept running again and again down two tracks. He was disgusted with himself: he had blundered, he had killed, he had broken open a remarkable mind and left a bloody ruin. He was excited, proud: he had survived Shay's uncanny attack, emerged unscathed. It was pure luck, though, he told himself; *nothing but a panicked instinct, and besides, he was half your size and twice your age, and you had a gun to his knife;* and he fell again into self-disgust.

The mob went away after a while. He wondered if they felt satisfied or cheated. He stayed out on the roof, looking out over the dark Heath, until something below caught his eye.

A movement down in the Observatory's grounds: a mote in the dark, glowing pale green. It was shaped like a dwarf or a child, tottering awkwardly on little legs. It leaned its wan body against the fence, and slowly oozed through, and staggered on down the hill. One of the afterimages, Arjun realized. The stolen shadow of a god. He had thought they had all vanished. This one was stronger than the others. Where was it going?

Arjun slid down the dome's roof on his back, bracing himself with his hands on the cold metal, going as fast as he dared. He dropped the final distance, landing heavily but unharmed. Then he climbed over the fence again. On the other side, he could see the faint, flickering glow, drifting down the hill.

At first he tried to keep his distance, but when it entered the trees, he had to come closer to avoid losing it. It didn't react. He got closer and closer, until he could see it clearly. It was no taller than his waist, and featureless, but its stumbling movement put him in mind of a crippled child. He kept a few arms' lengths away, out of wariness. Which one was it?

They left the trees and the homunculus drifted and fell across the lawns. Arjun followed. The little circle of pale corpse-light moved across the dark grass.

The Heath was empty and silent, but it was said to be dangerous at night. Desperate vagrants camped out here. He stopped to reload his pistol, fumbling powder and shot out of his pouch, nearly
spilling it in the dark.

The glow flickered; it ebbed, then seeped softly out again. The
little thing inside it continued down along the path around the
reservoir, its light reflecting out over the water, until it came to
an ivied fence at the Heath's edge. There the homunculus passed
through, its pale form seeming to snag on the obstruction for a moment. Arjun followed over the fence.

They were in a narrow cobbled street adjoining the Heath. They
turned left, then right, always going downhill. The thing slumped
down the middle of the empty streets, its glow too weak to illumi-
nate the buildings on either side, and Arjun could see nothing
except the cold light ahead of him. Sometimes they passed a turn
to some lit street, friendly windows and illuminations inviting
into the night; but the thing would always lurch away down a dark
alley instead. At other times, Arjun heard the sounds of crowds,
drinking and shouting, buying and selling, away over the rooftops.
It sounded like a theater crowd, once, though he thought they were
going down to the warehouses of Barbary, far from any playhouse.
The thing walked clumsily, but with a purpose, as if it was going
home.

It pushed through a bowed and broken wire fence. Arjun stepped
through a ragged hole a few feet away, and they crossed a vacant lot.
Dogs or foxes lived here, leaving dry white spoor and gnawed bones
among the weeds. Past a rotting boathouse, they came to the edge of
a canal, where the water sat low and dark.

The canal split in two and they followed the smaller course. A
sheer wall of slimy stone dropped down to the cold green surface.
These were, Arjun thought, the grimy industrial canals that ran
through Barbary and Shutlow, and out to the factories of Agdon
Deep. He had seen a painting of the canals of Ebon Fields, in the
north, with their elegant curves, pleasure boats, and delicate, arching bridges. This was very different.

Not far ahead, a great black warehouse sat squarely across the path and the canal. Its cracked windows reflected the pale glow. The canal ran into a tunnel under the building.

The thing stopped in a patch of weeds. It remained still for a long time, then began to stoop and pick around, reminding Arjun of the children who went down to the riverbanks to pick over the city's refuse. He sat down on the damp stones to watch.

Another figure came out of a dark alley along by the warehouse. Arjun tensed and began to get to his feet; he felt a sudden urge to proclaim his innocence, to say *I am not involved, I didn't do this, I saw nothing.* But the new figure ignored him, and Arjun bit the words back and sat in silence to watch.

The new thing looked like a man, but Arjun couldn't see its features. A long coat? A hat? Its lines were unclear. It ebbed and seeped shadow and a soft stagnant light.

It came slowly toward the spectral thing in the weeds.

Neither figure made a sound.

As they came closer together the two figures resembled distorted reflections of each other, glimpsed through dark water. When they touched—when the larger figure, that was like a man, reached out a shadowy arm and seized the childlike homunculus by its shoulder, and leaned predatorily in—they were like two aspects of the same troubling thing. The two figures bathed together in the sad, ugly glow, until it seemed to flicker from them both, and from the whole unpleasant scene.

Whatever Arjun was seeing, he thought, was not in either figure, but in both, or in the space between them. Or in the repetition of the scene—something about the set of the larger figure's shoulders suggested pointless, grinding repetition: as if this was a ritual, or a tiresome duty; as if this was something that happened here again and again, and would happen forever.

The thing in its tiny and vulnerable aspect struggled like a child, and shook. In its murderous aspect it tightened its grip.

The thing—the *god*—was in the ritual. It was in the vision. It was in the bitter sense of futility that choked Arjun's throat and weighed down his limbs so that he said nothing, did nothing, as the vision enacted itself.

This *ugliness*—it was what this god had in place of music.

The child-thing shuddered, then went still. The man took the child up in its arms and walked down the slimy stone steps to the narrow path by the water's edge. It stopped in the mouth of the tunnel and stepped down into the dark water. There was a faint, hungry glow from the tunnel's mouth. Then it went out.

Arjun was more frightened than he could say; he felt it as a physical cold.

But he couldn't just run. He needed to know what was in the canal. He had come to the city to search among its divinities. This was surely one. It was frightening, but how could he have thought strange gods would be otherwise? And it was more than that: the tunnel mouth called to him. It was all he could do not to lower himself at once into the water. He knew he should turn back, but he couldn't. He drew the gun for comfort and walked carefully down to the water's edge, and into the tunnel.

The tunnel was empty and silent. There was no light at its end. Mud and weeds sucked at his feet. Arjun's steps echoed. Nothing came rushing out at him. He ran a hand along the slick, mossy wall.

"Is this your home?" His voice was weak and strained.

Finding a firmer voice, he said, "What are you?" And, "Are you here at all?" And, "Was that thing a part of you, or only an image, a shadow? I was the one who set it free."

He said, "What was that I saw, outside? Was that something that happened here? Is that how you show yourself, in murder? Is it a part of you, too? Is it some ritual you demand?"

There was no answer. Whatever presence there had been was gone. He was so relieved that he nearly laughed out loud. He had tried. He had done his best, he could go back. He turned around.

The tunnel stretched out behind him. The light at its end was tiny and distant—a grey scratch of moonlight. Impossible: he had taken no more than few steps inside. Hadn't he?

Arjun set out walking toward the light, moving as quickly as he dared on the slimy stone, with his stiff, nerveless legs. He got no closer to the exit. As he walked, he bargained. "I am not one of your worshippers. That's true. But I meant no disrespect. I have done you a service. I freed your image. I spared you that indignity. I can be of service to you.

"I have some training in music," he said. "I can sing your praises." But he knew that was pointless: the thing did not care for song.

He thought of Ama, from back in the hills so far to the south. When he spoke of the city's gods and miracles, she corrected him, gravely: *hauntings,* she called them. Should he have kept her talisman?

The light dwindled, until he wasn't sure whether it was still there, or was just an afterimage scratched on his straining eyes. Then it was gone. He ran. Underfoot was deep, clutching mud. He stumbled and fell. The weeds and mud took him.

Arjun hung suspended in the dark and the cold. His head burned and throbbed, but that was all right. He could not move, but there was nowhere to go. So many people came here in the end. Why not him? It hurt very much, but the city had to be fed. He felt all the lives that had been broken along the rivers and canals of the city, by the weight of the city's industry, by the black water, by cruelty and thoughtlessness. Children above all; the water demanded sacrifice. The malice of empty places. The city's dark and primitive past, always sucking back down.

He felt all this, and it felt right and necessary. There was nothing to fight. This was the way it was. The presence was there with him, and there was nothing else. The magnificent and terrible hunger of the god filled the tunnel and the world. The burning in his head was a hymn. He hung there, in the void of that presence, accepting, worshipping.

He opened his throat and It rushed in.

He had no name for It. He needed no name for It. It occupied all his thoughts. It was the River; It was all the city's waters and It touched everything, It seeped into everything. All weeds and rot in the city were nourished in it. In summer every black fly in the city's skies would hatch there; Arjun *felt* them unfurling sticky wings. It fed all the city's factories; Arjun's body spasmed and shook and he *felt* the engines groan and roar.

And in the end everything in the city would rot and feed the River.

In the west he *felt* a bloated strangled body rise on the tide into suddenly foul night air by a café on the banks, and well-heeled patrons retched and dropped their drinks and saw, in that pale rotting face, the face of the god.

This was a hard and terrible fact about the world. It was something Arjun had always known but no one had ever dared to say. There was a deep bitter joy in facing It, in knowing It.

This is how everything ends.

He shook again, and he opened his throat to the blackness again, and It began to swallow him from the inside out, and he *felt*, in the north, a storm rising over the River where It coiled into the slopes of the Mountain. A black acrid rain drowned the night. He felt Its cruel will bearing down over the city. He felt the rain crash down the streets and shake the trees and drive the birds from the sky.

Abruptly the vision was snatched from him.

He fell back into the meaningless pain of his body, blind and helpless and insignificant in the dark.

The god was gone. He was alone.

For a moment he was able to wonder: *what happened?* In the last instants of the revelation there had been something he had hardly noticed, some wrongness, some *flaw;* an imperfection that echoed and grew so huge, so suddenly, that the whole vision shattered. Some *division.* If he could only remember . . .

First the loathing distracted him, then the pain. Now that he was alone he felt the purest, most sickening revulsion for that murderous god and its false revelation and everything about it and everything *touched* by it. He could not stand to be in its waters a moment longer. In the next moment a burning agony gripped his throat and he understood that he was drowning, and all he cared about was survival.

✳   ✳   ✳

Arjun struggled in the freezing, stinking water of the canal, kicking and flailing and thrashing his head, casting about for the surface and the air. He broke the surface before his brain gave in to the crushing and the poison. He went under again.

Then somehow he was clutching a slimy post in the rushing water.

And some time later, he pulled himself up onto the path and vomited out foul liquid. He fell back, panting and looking up at the stars, and lay there in the cold night.

The last thing he was able to think was: *I remember.*

At the last moment the god had *noticed* him. The shock had sent it recoiling in something like terror.

FIFTEEN

Fiss and Aiden brought Jack back from the fight, reverently, each holding a trembling arm. Namdi walked alongside, pumping his fist. "Right across his face, Jack, his fucking face! He won't forget you. So *fast.* Who taught you that? His face!"

They laid him down on a coarse, filthy blanket, in one of the hollow upstairs rooms of the Black Moon. His limbs shivered, and his head was full of light and wind. It was impossible for him to rope his darting thoughts together and bring them back down to earth, so he lay staring silently on his back.

After a while, Namdi came to sit with him. "You're going to get up again, Jack. You took *ten* of them on, and they never touched you. You're going to be all right."

Fiss came, and held up his head and made him drink water from a cracked mug, then sat back against the wall and said, "We're all worried about you, Jack. I saw you fight them. I was closer than Namdi, and I watch closer, too. That wasn't skill. I don't think you've ever even held a knife before, have you? You weren't just quick. You were *too* quick. You cut them all before they could even move. How did you do it? You don't know, do you?

"You know, we never had a leader. There was never anything to be led, just a few children who passed through. But they used to listen to me and Aiden. We were here first. We made this place."

Fiss wrapped his arms around his thin legs. "Now they're all talking about you downstairs. Silk this, Silk that. The fight. The escape, and the thieving. Your speed. How you *named* them. Aiden and me, we could keep them out of trouble, if we were lucky, and help them find food, and a place to sleep. Not this.

"Which is all right. I don't mind. You need us, though. Because, *look* at you. You don't know where you are, do you? You're only half in the world, half the time. You need us to get things done. Don't forget that."

Sometime after midnight, Jack brought himself down and pulled himself together and descended into the cavernous dark bar. Those who were awake and those who were soon awoken cheered for Jack Silk. He felt like he was only halfway down.

When Jack was much younger, a monster haunted Laud Heath and the wilds of scrub and weed down by the river. A monster, not one of the gods before which his parents prostrated themselves, not the sort of thing that would earn a child a slap across the face if you spoke of it without reverence. Just a beast. A *wild* beast.

Some people said it had fought its way out of the sewers. Others said it had escaped from Chairman Cimenti's menagerie. All agreed that it looked like a dog, but one of monstrous size and ugliness, with eyes that burned like a plague pit put to the torch, snakelike tongue, twisted shoulders. They called it *hyena*. They said that it stole children, that it had brought down a dray horse, that it followed women home, slavering. They said it went to ground in the day and went ravening at night.

Men came through the streets and pasted up crude renderings of the beast. Jack couldn't yet read the words underneath the caricatures, but he knew that the posters were promising a reward. The militia went hunting for it every night, their torches blazing. His father and his two eldest brothers went out on the Heath with their friends and neighbors. The fishermen brought their nets with them, Jack remembered. All of Shutlow and Ar-Mouth and Barbary were wild with loathing. The pubs spilled out at closing time in a fighting mood, and went roaring up to the Heath in the dark. It was no god, and they owed it no reverence; they were free to indulge their hate.

The watch couldn't catch it. Nor could the mobs, or the citizen committees. Drunken brawls, near-riots, broke out on the Heath at night. After sundown, the amateur hunters were easy prey for thieves. There were stabbings; Jack's father came back one morning with his eye blackened and his scalp bleeding. The Countess declared a strict curfew on the Heath.

None of them could catch it. It had gone to ground somewhere. It was too clever and wild. It made fools of them.

Jack fell in love with the monster. His heart beat in sympathy with it. He tore down the posters in his street and burned them in an empty lot, feeling like he was sharing in the beast's splendid defiance. He got into a fight with some of the older boys in his street when he told them the beast would never be caught. Their fathers were out there every night, they said, protecting him: how *dare* he say that?

There were other boys who shared Jack's fascination, and they would lead each other through the barrens and onto the Heath, hoping to meet the creature face to snarling face. They hid in the bushes on the Heath; they crept through the thorntrees of the Widow's Bower. They went down to the wasteground banks of the river, where sometimes children drowned or were murdered, and poked through the rusted hulks and the empty rotting boat-sheds, always expecting to see the creature at any moment. They never thought what they would do if they met it. They ranged off far afield into the side streets, the weed-grown lots, the graveyards overgrown with ivy and briars; places where it was ridiculous to expect the beast. Jack mapped out the secret places of his city.

That was how Jack got taken into the custody of Barbotin House: the watch caught him after curfew. Jack's friends were processed to some place in Fourth Ward, and Jack was sent to Barbotin. The reasoning behind those differing sentences was never clear to Jack. And a few months later, a new inmate told Jack that the Laud Heath Beast had been taken by the militia, and carried through the streets in triumph, lashed between two stout rods. It just looked like a yellow dog, the boy said, like a scrawny twist of bloody fur: no kind of monster at all.

Now Jack was chasing a different kind of beast. In his dreams, the *Thunderer* was wild in the city's sky, far out of reach of the grasping spires. It was their secret sign.

The lads stitched the image of the ship into the pockets of their jackets, using a bolt of blue silk Aiden had stolen from the tables in Seven Wheels Market. Beth's girls laughed at them. "Look at you," Beth said. "Like the crests the boys at the church schools wear. Aren't you fancy now."

Fiss stuck his chest out and tilted his nose comically in the air. "You jealous? We look splendid and you know it. You shouldn't even be talking to us." Fiss and Beth both laughed.

"It's not like schoolboys, anyway," Namdi said, seriously. "It's like soldiers, with medals."

With stolen paint, they painted a huge image of the ship on the mold-ridden wall of the Moon's empty bar. Then they painted it in corners and cracks all over Shutlow.

The younger boys liked to play at being Arlandes, the great ship's captain. From the chatter in the streets and the markets, they picked up that there was bad blood between the Countess and the Gerent of Stross End, and they acted out battles between the warship and the Gerent's guns. On other days, they imagined Arlandes directing his mighty forces against their enemies in white robes. They knew that Arlandes was famously in mourning, for a young bride tragically lost in the ship's raising, but they found it hard to act out that aspect of his character.

Occasionally, the warship went overhead on some unknowable mission. Then the Thunderers took to the roofs and yelled after it. If it was moving slowly, they might try to chase it.

Shutlow's buildings were all tumbled together, falling on each other's shoulders like huddled refugees. Its streets were narrow and dark; few were more than alleys. No one had thought it a virtue before. Jack was proud to prove them wrong: if you were fast and fearless, you could leap from rooftop to rooftop, scrambling on hands and knees up sloped tiles, catching just barely onto rusted fire escapes, climbing hand-over-hand to find a flat roof where you could run full tilt between chimneys and water towers, scaring up pigeons, to throw yourself across the next alley (its contents irrelevant,

depressing; don't look down) to continue the chase. He thought—
he hoped—that no one before him had discovered that property of
Shutlow, that saving grace.

Someone probably had, he knew, but none of the Thunderers
had discovered the sport. He had to teach them. He had to dare
them into it.

He knew he'd never catch the great warship that way. But so
what? The chase was its own prize.

One by one, they would draw up before a jump that defeated
their nerve, and stop, clapping for those brave enough to go on. Jack
always went furthest, but reckless, forceful Namdi was close behind.

SIXTEEN

Holbach was trying to work through a problem in his mind, regarding certain anomalies in the recent manifestations of Lavilokan. The mathematics were difficult, and it was hard with people talking. With a sigh, he put down his pen.

He sat at one end of a long table, covered with a fine white cloth, on which the Countess's insignia was stitched in gold, over and over. The Countess sat in the center of the table, of course, and around her were all her various advisors. Captain Arlandes sat at the other end of the table. They were splendid: the advisors in laced and ruffed doublets, Arlandes in medal-hung crimson, the Countess a riot of diamonds and gold, her face as perfect and white as marble.

A second table faced them across the empty floor, a plain shape of machined steel. The Gerent of Stross End hunched in the middle, dressed in dark business-suit and tie. He was surrounded by his senior executives, all dressed the same way.

They were sitting out in the open air, on the sandy floor of the Danaen Amphitheater. Gulls went by overhead. Stepped rows of stone seats swept out and back in all directions. It was the only structure, apart from a small ferry station, on the wooded Isle of Wine, in the middle of the river. Neutral ground.

The Countess's advisors passed bits of paper around. One leaned in and whispered to her, for a very long time. Then she spoke, formally and sonorously. "Gerent. I regret to say that your proposal is not acceptable. The issue in Ar-Mouth is not one of tribute, but of *jurisdiction.* Your generous offer cannot compensate us for the encroachment on our authority."

The Gerent conferred with his advisors, then responded, enunciating firmly, "It appears I must clarify my words. Neither *tribute* nor *compensation* were offered. However, if you are not willing to consider a *sharing* of the harbor's *profits,* then we are of course willing to discuss issues of jurisdiction."

Holbach was not there to offer his opinions, only so that he could be *seen* to be there. A subtle reminder of the *Thunderer's* power; something to keep it in the Gerent's mind, and to let him know that it was in the Countess's mind too. All he had to do was stay awake and try not to look foolish.

Presumably Arlandes was there for the same reason. Even if they didn't recognize Holbach, which was unlikely but possible, everyone could recognize the *Thunderer's* tragic captain. There was even a play, *The Captain Unmoored;* posters all over the city bore his mournful countenance. Holbach couldn't bring himself to see the play. He feared he might be the villain of the piece. Holbach could not look at Arlandes without guilt. The man was still shadowed by the death of his wife on the day of the *Thunderer's* launch: that absurd, pathetic death. Poor gentle young Lucia. She'd been a mere afterthought, a decorative touch. The Countess had wanted someone to go up with the balloon, for the look of the thing, for the benefit of the crowds. Why hadn't he said no? *Because the girl was neither here nor there to your experiment,* he thought. *She canceled out. So you gave her no thought. You selfish, silly man. Nicolas would be ashamed of you.*

And that young man was on his conscience, too. Arjun. No word for days. And he did not seem to be the kind to just vanish, distracted by some girl or wager or exciting new theory, as Holbach might have when he was that age. It was troubling.

But Shay really *might* have been able to help Arjun. It had not been a wholly selfish gesture to send Arjun in his direction, had it? Perhaps he *had* helped: perhaps Arjun had vanished because Shay had been able to point him toward that Voice of his. They said Shay had secret paths; perhaps Arjun was on them now. That lifted his mood, but then he was annoyed to think that he might never hear what Arjun had learned of Shay's secrets.

The Countess spoke. "We should not be limiting our discussions to Ar-Mouth. Our grievances, I fear, are inextricably linked to the issue of Kanker Market."

The Gerent locked shocked. His advisors turned to each other, whispering, and huddled in around their lord. They didn't seem to have a response prepared.

Holbach began to worry. The Countess had been so aggressive lately. This was the third such conference of the week. She had made stiff demands of the Mass How Parliament, which they had referred nervously to committee for further consideration. She had taken a frighteningly high-handed and demanding tone with the Chairman Cimenti, who had acquiesced to her demands with a smiling grace that had left the Countess infuriated and Holbach quite terrified. He would take revenge, Holbach thought; would he still be smiling when he did it?

It was the *Thunderer,* of course. She was making the most of her new weapon. It certainly wasn't what he had created the damn thing for. It was supposed to be the great triumph of the Atlas-makers: he had dreamed that it could carry his cartographers all over the city, perhaps as far as the rumored walls in the east and west, which the Atlas had never so far reached; perhaps even over the mountain in the north. It would lay everything bare.

Not for this. Never for this.

Someone tossed a copy of the *Sentinel* across the table and the sudden motion made Holbach snap to attention with a grunt. One of the Gerent's men was yelling about libels and threats published in that rag, that lying rag. *Oh,* Holbach thought, *is the* Sentinel *one of ours, then?*

His mind wandered; he let the newspaper remind him again of Arjun. The *Sentinel* had reported—*gloated*—that the Observatory Orphée had been sacked by the mob, and the body of the blasphemer Shay paraded down Laud Heath and cast into the river. So where was Arjun? Had he gone on to find his god, or had Shay killed him? Or the mob? Was he lying in some hospital?

Yes. Hospitals. That was how best to proceed. He could have someone search the hospitals. Olympia, perhaps. She could take care of that, as she took care of so much else.

But enough of that. He looked around. The conference was heated now. The Countess and the Gerent were both talking as fast as their advisors could hand them paper. Numbers, commodities, place names, dates, old treaties, obscure laws, ancient battles.

Having decided what to do about Arjun, Holbach put the problem out of his mind and tried to go back to his work. He took a silver fountain pen out of his pocket and began to sketch the angle of Harp Street from memory, plotting the points of the theaters along it, and the intersecting arcs of Foss Row and Monmouth Street. He marked the points of two fires reported in last week's *Sentinel,* and a murder. He pondered the possible sacred forms that could be composed from these points.

He lost patience again. It was too hard, without his tables, maps, and books, and with all this shouting. He rested his head on his hands and ran his fingers through his beard. He hummed a tune inside his head—a pretty, sad melody that he had first heard a few days ago, sung by a flower girl in Faugère.

The shouting had stopped for a while before Holbach noticed. He looked around. The Countess and the Gerent were glaring at each other. Under the Countess's stiff white facepaint, a faint flush of blood was visible. The Gerent was squeezing the edge of his table in a liver-spotted claw.

The Countess spoke first. "I regret the failure of this conference. I'm sorry you were not prepared to listen to reason." She stood in a sweep of golden skirts. Her entourage quickly gathered up their papers and followed, and together, they passed under the arch and into the cool tunnels below.

The Countess's anger vanished as soon as she was out of sight of the Gerent's men. As they walked through the tunnel, she reached out and stroked Arlandes' stiff impassive cheek with the backs of her fingers. She was smiling. "My beautiful, sad Captain. It seems we will have need of your *services.*"

SEVENTEEN

The Thunderers stole whatever they wanted. Now that Jack was with them, to dart in doors and dart out windows like a shaft of light, they could take anything. They all seemed faster when they were around him. Suddenly they had money.

When they had more than they knew what to do with, Jack went into Fourth Ward to buy a whore. Fiss smiled and said that he had more important business to take care of, but Namdi went with Jack eagerly. All the way there, Namdi talked about his various conquests. Some of the stories were probably true. Jack had no stories of his own, so he kept quiet.

They found a place upstairs from a seedy bar on a street that was really just a cut between two tangled masses of crumbling brick. Jack and Namdi went to their separate rooms.

At first, the girl reminded Jack uncomfortably of his sister, who had worked in a place probably much like this—although his sister would be older than this now, he thought. He put it out of his mind quickly, and soon it didn't matter at all. He lay there shortly afterwards, feeling both proud and oddly sad. The whore took a swig of some piss-looking booze from a lipsticked glass and said, "What else do you want, then? Fuck off now, will you, chicken?"

Namdi met him outside. They both opened their jackets a little and smiled; they'd both stolen a bottle from the bar on their way out. They found a churchyard a couple of roads over, dedicated to a god neither recognized, and hopped the fence and sat on the gravestones drinking, telling each other lies. Weathered statues of the god, or perhaps its priests, stood between the stones. They looked like spry old men, knees half bent, right foot forward, shoulders rounded and arms up. Namdi suggested that they were boxers; Jack thought they were making gestures of benediction. There was no way to be sure: someone, or generations of someones, had broken off the statues' hands. A tinny trumpet-blast heralded a group of men in red uniforms, marching down the middle of the street outside. Behind the trumpeter, two standard-bearers marched abreast of each other, carrying flags on their pikes. One flag bore the Countess's insignia. The second flag bore an image of the *Thunderer*. Two short lines of red followed.

It was a recruiting party for the Countess's militia. Both boys froze against the stones, making themselves inconspicuous. They'd both known people scarcely older than them who had been pressed into the Countess's forces, or the Parliament's, or the Council's, or the Agdon Deep Worker's Combine, or whoever.

When they were gone, Namdi took another swig and said, "Maybe I will, though."

"Will what?"

"I mean join 'em. You're not thinking about it?"

"*Fire* no. What do you mean, join the redcoats?"

"You know about the Gerent. How he's been threatening the Countess. Cutting off her ports, refusing her taxes, stealing cases from her courts, paying her no respect."

"So what?"

"You know the Gerent works children to death in his factories?"

"They work children to death down *here*. This is Fourth Ward, idiot. And you can't tell me Lime Street was any easier."

"Everyone says there's going to be a fight, and it's time to settle who's in charge. We've got to stand up for ourselves."

"What do you care who's in charge? And what do you mean, 'ourselves'? The Countess isn't *us*. I hope they both kill each other. Who've you been listening to?"

Namdi shrugged. "I don't know. Just everyone."

"She sends her men through here shouting about the Gerent, or whoever it is, and you believe them?"

Namdi leaned back against the stone and turned his head away. "Not really. I don't know. I thought you'd want to, too."

"Why?"

"You know. The ship. We're the Thunderers, like you said. We have these," Namdi said, tapping the crest on his jacket, "and everything else. And the *Thunderer* is the strongest thing in the city. Who wouldn't want to be on it? And it's hers."

Jack stood up and stretched his arm back and threw the bottle in a high arc so that it brushed through the branches overhead and smashed against the roof of the nameless church. "No. It's not hers. It's ours. That's what it's all about. Come on, then. It's getting late; they'll be missing us at the Moon."

The next day, Jack took Namdi and some of the other boys down to Gies Landing at Ar-Mouth. He told them they were going to steal dried fruits from the ships that came in from Aysuluk.

They found a group of young sailors with spiked hair and tattooed faces, staring around, dismayed by the crowds. "They look stupid enough," Jack said. "They'll do." Namdi, Tull, and David ran after them, taunting them, cursing in all the languages they knew, until the sailors lost their patience and gave chase. The boys dodged through the crowds, ducking under stalls and benches covered in wet fish and bowls of spices and a hanging curtain of exotic, recurved blades, and the sailors came after them, knocking people aside. Jack and Frawney and Nef rushed in through the confusion and lifted their lunch from the brimming stalls, while Beth and the others stood watch.

They slipped out from the disturbance easily, dispersing into the crowd to coalesce again at the other end of the Landing, past all the crowds and the beer-tents and the groaning cranes. They sat on the stone steps at the foot of the lighthouse and ate, looking out over the bay and the tall masts cautiously threading their way around each other. The spray in the air was cold and bright. Jack watched the crowd intently.

After a while, Jack saw what he had brought them here for: a slow line of red, the crowds parting nervously around it. Another recruiting party for the Countess.

"Come on," he said. "Put all that away and follow me."

It was a longer column than the one in Fourth Ward. Their uniforms were brighter and in better repair. A drummer marched alongside the trumpeter. Two men at the front and two in the back carried the Countess's insignia on their pikes, while a pair in the middle shared the flag of the *Thunderer,* slung between their weapons. By the time Jack reached them, they were marching round and round in a circle, inside a ring of market stalls, beating out a trumpery rhythm, pressing their pamphlets into the hands of passersby.

Jack signaled to the rest of them to stop following him. They climbed up onto the low wall around a money changer's office and watched as Jack went round the circle's edge and hopped up on a pile of wooden crates by a fishmonger's stall. Calling on the gift he had been given, he put his hand lightly on the swaying pole supporting the canopy and vaulted up. The fabric tightened for an instant under his feet as he broke into a run and threw himself onto the slick canvas over the next stall. He came round the edge of the circle at a run, over the heads of the crowds and the shopkeepers, gathering speed, weightless.

The men in red uniforms were marching toward him. The lead man was shouting some rubbish not worth listening to, something about *duty* and *honor*. When he saw Jack coming, he stopped with his mouth hanging open, and the drummer behind him bumped into his back. Jack launched himself off the tightly bowed edge of a black canvas and across the yard, to land lightly on the man's shoulder. Between the waving pike-points, he stepped from head to shoulder to capped head along the column. He leaped over the banner and, turning, snatched it neatly away. Waving the thick fabric over his head, he launched himself off the back of the man at the tail of the column and onto a butcher's awning, then across the market's canopies and *up* onto the low sloped roof of a countinghouse. He ran up to the peak of the roof, high over the market, and turned back, and lifted his trophy in his left hand. One of the soldiers, recovered from his shock, fired on

Jack, but the shot went wild and shattered the roof tiles twenty feet away. Jack turned and ran down the other side of the roof.

Back in the Moon that evening, Jack held the banner in his fist and thrust it at Namdi's face, saying, "See? The *Thunderer*'s not theirs. It's ours. We don't owe them anything."

They nailed it up on the wall behind the bar.

EIGHTEEN

Arjun lay on the stone through the night. All of his strength was drained. His wet clothes entombed him. As the foul water left his lungs, fever set in and wracked his bones. A hundred hideous false dawns colored the sky. A group of children found him in the morning, twisted up against a lamppost, and took his money.

For a time in the afternoon, he was able to stand. He stumbled through the alley to a street with sounds of life, and fell down again. A face came and spoke to him, and he was aware that he was speaking back, but he had no sense of the words.

Later, two men in brown uniforms came for him. He spent some time on a stone floor, then he was taken to a place where he was given something strong and pungent to drink, and slept.

His bed was in a small room with plain walls. They had taken away his sodden clothes and dressed him in a white gown. There were bars on the window. A wall of iron bars opened onto the corridor. People came and watched him through it. At first he thought they were phantoms of his imagination. There were other cells like his there, full of screaming and ranting and raving.

There was a family outside his cell, watching him solemnly. A mother and a father, two small daughters. Father wore a dark suit and blue tie. The girls were in pink dresses and curls.

He grabbed the nurse's arm with a weak hand, and asked, "Who are they? What do they want from me?"

She drew a warm wet cloth across his forehead. "Shush. You've not got yer strength back. Rest. They'll do you no harm. You've been blessed. Just let 'em share it."

One of the little girls waved shyly at Arjun. He turned against the wall and sunk back into sleep.

When he woke up, afternoon sun was coming in through the window. He recognized the sounds of the bay outside: rough voices shouting in sailor's cant, the cries of the gulls.

Two young women came to see him. Like the family before, they were dressed well. They looked like the wives of lawyers or doctors from Foyle's Ward. They stared at him through the bars.

"What was it like?" one of them asked, nervously. Arjun had no answer. He curled his body against the wall.

"Which one was it?" her friend asked. "That touched you? They said they found you by a canal. Was it the Typhon?"

Arjun didn't answer. When the nurse came, hours later, he asked her, "What is the Typhon?"

"The Typhon. The Vodya. The Nix. The Nöckan. One of the gods of the river. *You* can tell *me* what it is, I think."

"Nix. It means 'nothing' in Kael," he muttered.

"That's nice. Now try to sleep."

He lay awake, drifting in and out of fever. In a lucid moment, he thought: *Typhon. It has a name.* Water-spirit. Nothing-spirit. Haunter of rivers and canals. So, what *was* it like? What should he tell these people, these voyeurs? It was hungry. It took sacrifices. It was a god of the sucking ooze and the brutal past, rot and foulness. It was a thing to be loathed.

But they *knew* that. It was *ancient*. He had hung dying inside it; he had *felt* its age. The Typhon had been in the River before the city's busy little people first chained it with bridges. It was there before the first life they ever fed to it. Of *course* they knew about it. Their mothers must have told them: *Never go near the river alone.*

And they drank from the River, and they let the canals cut their way into the city's veins, and they let their economy rest on it in a hundred ways. They had reached an accommodation with it. It was in their blood.

Three middle-aged men in business suits came to see him. They knocked rudely on the bars. They appeared to be drunk. The breweries were all poisoned with River-water, and these men were, too. They asked, "What's your story?" and he lifted himself from his bed long enough to spit at them. They laughed and seemed to find that entirely satisfactory.

The nurse gave him something sickly sweet to drink. Was it night? It was night.

"It noticed me," he said.

"What did? Drink up."

"The Typhon. It saw me. It hated me and it was afraid."

The nurse shook her head and gave a little businesslike laugh. "That's a new one."

He disliked the nurse more than he had ever disliked anyone in his life. "No," he said, "there's something wrong with it. It's broken." She nodded without listening. Her refusal to understand was intensely irritating, not least because he did not understand what he meant himself.

He couldn't keep the sickly sweet stuff down. The nurse deftly caught the vomit in a metal bowl, in which Arjun's reflection bulged and lurched monstrously.

The nurse came again the next morning to change his bedpan. He was able to sit up to ask her, "What is this place?"

"You sound stronger. That's nice. But rest now."

"I *am* resting. But where am I? It sounds like Ar-Mouth."

She sized him up. "That it is. Under the Jaw."

"And what is this place?"

"I am Sister Judith."

"Thank you for your care, Judith. But I asked, what is this place?"

She busied herself with his bedding. "One of the Houses of the

Nessene, of course." Seeing his blank look, she said, "The Healer. Our Lord of the Ocean. Haven't you heard of him?"

"Oh," he said, "another one of your gods."

"The watch found you. You was half-drowned and half-froze, and you'd no money, so they brought you here. You're safe now."

"I'm stronger now, Judith, and I'll be ready to leave soon. I don't think I'll be able to repay you for your services."

"Just a little longer," she said, and gripped his weak shoulders and pushed him firmly down onto the mattress. "Until you're well again." She left.

After a while, he got up and tried the door; it was locked. Across the corridor and down a little was another cage much like his. A shaven-headed man sat in the corner of the cage, curled over on himself like a dry dead spider.

"Are they treating you, too, friend?" Arjun called.

The man jerked and spoke, his voice ecstatic. "Water-thing, tendrils *gripping,* you're *marked,* you *glow.* Between two mirrors, smoke stung my eyes: a *wounding.* Many eyes' fire, all round . . ."

The man raved on. It sounded like he had been touched by some god. Like Norris, only more so. Like himself, too, Arjun supposed. The man's ranting was an ugly tangle of empty words.

Arjun felt weak, but clearheaded. He would *not* go mad. *Just another fever,* he thought. *The fever of my childhood lifted when I heard the Voice. I came across the world hoping to find it again. Now a second fever . . . and what now?*

The touch of that ghoul in the canal was maddening, evil, filthy. But was the Voice any better? There'd been a moment when the river-god's embrace had been like that of the Voice, and he would have gone willingly with it. Had the Voice driven him mad, stolen his soul, *scarred* him the way the Typhon nearly had? And the way that poor man in the next cell had been scarred? He couldn't be sure that it hadn't. His quest seemed insane. To have spent his life pining for the Voice seemed like madness. Perhaps the Voice was a thief of adoration the way the Typhon was a thief of lives. There were sirens in the seas, they said; why not in the mountains? He slept again, uneasily, guiltily.

The next morning, when Judith passed his food and water through the bars, he asked, "My clothes, Sister?"

"We burned 'em. I'm sorry. They was full of fever-water."

"I see. I thank you, Sister, but I'm ready to leave now."

"Just a little longer. There's a lot of people in this city would be glad of a good bed!" She fussed quickly away.

In the afternoon, a group of young men came to watch him. They were thin and unshaven. Two of them wore glasses. They looked like seminary students, or perhaps poets. Arjun sat on his bed and shouted, "What? What do you want? What is it you think I can tell you? The thing in your canals is a *monster*. A *vampire*. Go feed *yourselves* to it, if you want to know what it's like. It's sick. This whole city is sick. Who would worship something like that? You should be *ashamed.* Go away. Go *away.*"

They kept watching him, smiling eagerly at each other. *That was all they wanted,* he thought. *Any kind of raving will do.* He turned against the wall and waited for them to leave him alone.

A young woman woke him, rattling a silver cane across the bars of his cage. A long black coat of masculine cut, and pin-striped trousers, but certainly a woman. He remembered her from the meeting with Holbach. Olympia Autun, wasn't it? Sister Judith hung back, staring at the eccentric visitor resentfully.

"Mr. *Arjun* of Gad! Good morning!"

"Good morning, Miss Autun. Are you here on behalf of Professor Holbach, or for your own entertainment?"

"The former. Arjun—may I call you just plain Arjun? I feel you're part of the family now—Holbach has been very concerned about you. He's said nothing to me for days except, 'Olympia'— please do call me Olympia, Arjun—'Olympia, where *is* that bright young man? What *did* I send him into?' He blames himself."

"How did you find me?"

"Hard work, persistent questioning, and rather a lot of money."

"Is this really a hospital, Olympia?"

"Of course. Why wouldn't it be? You were raving in the streets. From what I hear, you were bloody lucky to be alive."

"Can I leave?"

"Ah now. That's not so clear. The watch of the Mass How Parliament picked you up, and charged you—you were present physically, though perhaps not mentally—as a danger to the peace. Then they handed you over to the Nessenes, who—this is your story, right, Sister?—locked you up in this cage because you wouldn't stop ranting about some river-monster."

"He was god-touched," Judith said. "Sometimes they're dangerous, to themselves or others. It was for everyone's good."

"I am not dangerous, and no longer ill," Arjun said.

Judith started to speak, but Olympia silenced her with a swish of her cane. "But you're on display, Arjun! You're an object of adoration. You lucky fellow!"

Most people in the city, she explained, never came into the presence of the gods. Not *personally,* mortal mind to divine presence. They heard about them from others. They went to churches and temples and listened to the stories. Sometimes they might see something far off in the distance, like when the Bird passed over a couple of months ago, or like the Fire you could see in the north. Some of them would enter into the Spider's lottery, just to feel the touch, however remote. So whenever the Nessenes took in a man wounded by the direct touch of a god, raving and moaning about his experience, there was always an eager public to come and share in it. "They want to be close to you, Arjun. You and all the other poor wretches in here," Olympia said, waving an arm at the other cells. "And they'll pay for the privilege! And hardly anyone comes away from seeing the thing you saw, looking as bright and healthy and cheery as you do. So the Nessenes will hold on to you for as long as they can, won't they, Sister?"

"Only until we're sure he's stronger," Judith said.

"Yes, Sister, of *course.* Arjun, this is what they do. I suppose one can't complain—it pays for the hospital."

"I am very tired of this city and its gods, Olympia. This is madness. There was nothing in my experience a sane man would wish to share. Can you get me out?"

"Not easily. They're holding you under the authority of the Mass How Parliament, by treaty with the Countess. They *do* have the power to keep you, at their reasonable discretion."

"Tell Holbach: Shay's dead. And he was no fraud. But I won't tell you anything unless you get me out of here."

Olympia looked amused. "There's no need to play tough. Holbach is *paying* me to get you out of here. Arjun, Ararat is a city of many prisons. I have seen many of them, in my practice: this may be the gentlest of confinements, irritating though I'm sure it is. I'll be back. In the meantime, try to make yourself boring; maybe they'll let you go. Sister, show me out, please."

Arjun stayed in the cell for nearly two weeks, waiting for Olympia's rescue. Sister Judith opened his cell every day to lead him to the bathroom, accompanied by a hulking male nurse. He didn't talk to them. After a few days, he was strong enough to exercise in his cell, which lifted his spirits a little.

When the voyeurs came, he turned his back on them. A few of them kept staring anyway, as if some mystery would reveal itself in the folds of his gown, but most quickly moved on to the next cell, where a woman who had broken her back following the Bird lay helpless, whipping her head from side to side and crying.

He thought of Norris, from the Cypress, who had chased down Red-Beard in the maze of the city's pubs and brothels, and left all his strength and youth with him. Was that why Defour was so protective of Norris? For the glamour of his sacred wounding?

They brought him paper and a pen. To relieve the loneliness, he spent his time composing another letter to the Choirmen (though the first still sat in a drawer in his room). He wrote to explain that he despaired of finding the Voice, that in fact he no longer knew whether he cared whether he found it or not, that he had been wounded in such a way that his love was poisoned by doubt, that he wondered if the whole thing was not madness, sickness—that he thought perhaps he hated the Voice, now, as much as he loved it. He tried to say that perhaps he was wrong to come, but he kept saying instead that he hated them for letting him go. That wasn't what he wanted to say, he thought; he didn't know. He tore up his drafts and threw them in the corner, until the sisters told him that paper was expensive, and that he had used up his ration.

One of his voyeurs, a young man in a cassock, was eyeing the crumpled drafts as if they contained some secret wisdom. Arjun swept them under the cot, for spite's sake.

NINETEEN

After Jack's theatrics with the press-gang's banner, Namdi kept his silence, but the talk about the Countess and the Gerent went on among the other boys. Some of them started to say that they sided with the Gerent against the Countess. That wasn't the point either, Fiss explained, patiently. "The ship is our symbol 'cause it's free, do you see? Not 'cause it's powerful; because it's *free*. It's up there over the heads of all the people. It can go anywhere. Like us. You shouldn't follow the Countess because of it, or the Gerent because we say you shouldn't follow the Countess. They just want to turn it into a weapon, and beat and break things down here on the ground, so they can shut everyone up in prisons. That's not what Silk wants. Do you see?"

Jack found it disgusting. He sat on the roof, looking down at the garden, watching the younger children play. They formed themselves into teams and fought with sticks—the Countess's men, led by the boy who won the fight to play Arlandes, against the Gerent's men, who always lost. It infuriated him.

He tried to keep himself and everyone else busy with work. He took three of the worst offenders—boys who he caught holding sticks like rifles over their shoulders, aping the press-gang's march—and ordered them to go out to Seven Wheels Market, to patrol for incursions of the white robes into Shutlow. "If you *must* be soldiers, you can work it off that way," he told them.

He went out alone a lot in the evenings, avoiding the ritual—at some point, it had gone from a habit to a ritual—of playing priest

for the younger children. Anything they said would only be a disappointment to him.

Fiss could talk to them, even when they didn't listen, and make
jokes so that it was all right. Jack couldn't do that. He had no patience for talk, and his *coup de théâtre* with the banner had been less
effective than he had hoped. He could feel what he wanted for them,
like a tug in his chest, always pulling forward and out, but he didn't
know how to say it. They were getting away from him. He made
himself remote and forbidding, willing them to feel his displeasure.
But that wasn't enough either.

He went out walking every evening, down to the docks, across into
Fourth Ward, all through Shutlow and Barbary. Over the rooftop
ways, or down in the shadows of the streets. He got as far as he could
go in an evening, and stopped. There was always one more turning
that would carry him further into unexplored parts of the city, but
he was not ready to walk out on them yet. So he crisscrossed the
same streets again and again, his thoughts a maddening, futile spiral: what should he do, what *could* he do, with these children for
whom he had somehow taken responsibility? How could he make
himself, and them, worthy of the gift they had received?

He thought they didn't see him go. He would sit up on the roof
of the Black Moon as the sun began to sink toward the square towers in the west of the city. When the mood took him, he would
jump across to the roof of the pawnshop next door, and then over to
the boardinghouse. He would return by the same route, coming in
through the window.

Namdi came out onto the roof on the evening of River-day. He
had Martin and Ayer (his boys from Lime Street) in his tow. He
rapped his knuckles on the tiles for Jack's attention. He had a gift;
at his instruction, Martin and Ayer reached into their jackets and
pulled out bright tangles of silk thread in blue and crimson and
gold, which they held out to Jack in cupped hands.

"Well done," Jack said hesistantly.

"It's for you," Namdi said. "A gift, if you like. Peace offering."
He looked uncomfortable saying it.

River-day was an ill-omened day for gifts and treaties, but no one would have taught Namdi that, and Jack saw no reason to mention it. He took a handful of the thread, curiously. Namdi reached out and tugged at the loose shoulder of Jack's shirt.

"No offense," Namdi said, confident again, "but look at you. Jack Silk, you're looking grey these days."

Jack looked down at himself. The threads of his shirt were ragged and sparse. It had been a long time since the escape from Barbotin, and he'd never meant the shirt to last for longer than the moment's magic required. What threads were left were dirty and faded and grey.

Namdi looked at him expectantly. Behind him, Martin and Ayer were nervous. Jack shook Namdi's hand, firmly, and said, "Thank you." Then, when Namdi and the boys had gone, he shoved the threads into his pocket and forgot about them until Bell-day, when he came back from one of his long walks to see Martin and Ayer, sat down by the small fire in the bar, sneaking nervous looks at him; their faces asked, had they displeased him?

Moved more by guilt than by any desire of his own, he took needle and thread (they always had uses for needles; they never bothered to dispose of thread) and went up onto the roof to work on his uniform. His hands were practiced and very quick at the work, and he grew quickly bright again.

While he was working on that, Fiss came out to join him on the roof. Aiden followed, leaning silently against the chimney.

"They don't understand," Fiss said.

"I know that."

"I mean they don't understand why you're angry."

"I know that, too."

"We all know you go away every night," Fiss said.

"You know?" Jack asked.

"We're not stupid. Are you always going to come back?"

"Maybe."

"What is it you need, to stay?"

"I don't know. They don't understand anything."

"They're young. And not well-schooled, you may've noticed."

"It's like it's just another prison. Do you understand?"

"No. I don't understand. This is our *escape*."

"I can't stay here, in this place, every night, until we all get taken by the watch again. I need to *do* something with it, with the freedom. This *speed*, that the Bird gave me. To be worthy of it, of keeping it. Or I'll have to go."

They were both silent. Then Fiss said, "So you don't know what you want. But we're not good enough, is that right? You can fuck off, then, can't you? Better now than later."

Jack looked back at him, stung. Before he could say anything (*How dare you?* crossed his mind, and also *I'm sorry*) the window slammed open and Namdi reached out and slapped the tiles for attention. "It's coming. Look—out over the Jaw."

Jack looked east. There was a black shape in front of the clouds in the distance: the warship, moving over the city. The fleet of sharp little boats flocked around it like crows.

"It's moving slowly," Namdi said. "We can catch it. Come on, then." Namdi ran for the edge and threw himself across onto the roof of the pawnshop. He ran on without stopping, with a long, confident stride. Brushing past Jack, Fiss followed after Namdi, checking himself as he landed, and then starting the run for the next jump. Aiden came, too, and others followed from out of the window, whooping. Jack ran after them.

Fiss fell back before the end of Moore Street, balking at the gap between 47 and 49. Aiden stopped in Shymie Mews, before a sharp drop down from the gables of Anansi's temple to the old Ghentian butcher's place. The others all reached their limit before they left Shutlow. Jack drew level with Namdi near Allen Street, atop the houses running like a row of yellow teeth.

Namdi was panting, red-faced, the veins standing out on his neck. For Jack it was easy. It was good to move straight ahead, gathering speed, in wordless rushing air. Gently, he slowed to keep pace with Namdi, who threw himself violently from building to building, landing heavily, sweating despite the cold.

The shape of the ship grew larger, then smaller again, its course taking it past them, up from Ar-Mouth and northwest. They turned in its wake and followed it.

Namdi finally fell behind at Sunder Square, on the edge of

Shutlow, where he missed his footing on a loose tile and slid, scrabbling, down the sloped roof; by the time he had checked his fall, he
was far below the path. Jack kept going, gathering speed. Under his
rushing feet, vaulting up the little houses on the escarpment,
Shutlow gave way to the terra-cotta buildings of Mass How. The
streets were wider here, full of evening life and music. The buildings were taller and their architecture more varied. It made the
puzzle of Mass How's rooftops more challenging. Jack took an eccentric, zigzag route north. Through all his changes of direction and
elevation, he kept the ship steady in his sight. He crossed Mass How
in no time at all.

He went up Cere House Hill, his feet soundless on the shrouded
roofs. He crossed a span of temples and towerblocks for which he
had no name, west of the Heath. The turrets of some great estate
rose on his right. He recognized the Countess's flags. He crossed
some place where the houses were round and built of white stone,
and poles stood on every corner, with men sitting cross-legged on
top of them, up above the city, staring at the sky. They turned and
watched him as he streaked by. Factories; slums; then a wide, curving street full of theaters and music halls, in exotic forms; the air
smelled of spice, then smoke, then sewage, then fruiting trees. A
row of parapets rose before him, and a strip of low hovels fell behind, like waves thrown up in the ship's wake. He was far from any
part of the city he had ever known. Impossible for a man on foot to
go so far in one night, even at street-level, doubly so by roofscape.
He was closing in. The city was a blur under his feet.

He knew Stross End when he saw it. There was a slim pamphlet
being passed around Shutlow, *Our Cause against the Tyrant of Stross
End*. On the frontispiece, in the foreground, a lizard-like man with
a hooked nose and a stained business-suit clutched at a pile of
money with clawed hands. Behind him there was a dehumanizing
mass of towers, some belching smoke, others lined with narrow office windows and topped with huge clockfaces and bell towers. In
the background, under the towers, in vulgar, forceful denial of per-
spective, the artist had rendered shadowed courtyards full of

hunched, frail-looking men in shapeless smocks, scuttling from factory to office to mill. To Jack's surprise, the rendering of Stross End was not unfair.

Stross End was lit by fires from the smelting-towers. The *Thunderer* slowed as it came over the courtyards and into what appeared to be the central plaza. Jack found a route up onto the top of a block of office towers on the far side of the plaza and sat on a ledge above a great clockface. He watched expectantly. Now that he was close, he could see the fleet of smaller boats around the *Thunderer,* each carrying a group of riflemen.

He tried to ask himself how he had come so far, so fast; how was it possible? But the immense warship hanging above the courtyard commanded all his attention. Was it his imagination, or could he see a man on the *Thunderer*'s foredeck, holding a saber over his head? Was that the Widower Arlandes?

The courtyard emptied.

At the north end of the plaza, one tower was taller than the others, and bore the Gerent's crest in place of a clock. Men in black armor came rushing out of the tower's tall iron doors, filling the courtyard in ranks. They pointed their rifles in the air and fired up at the *Thunderer*'s hull, without effect.

Arlandes—if it was Arlandes—slashed his saber down. At his signal, the *Thunderer*'s guns fired, shaking the sky. Two shells exploded in the ranks below, sending broken bodies flying. A second struck the Gerent's tower, and the twisted metal of the Gerent's crest fell into the courtyard, followed by a shower of bricks and dust. Black smoke covered everything.

There was an answering flash from the top of the Gerent's tower, and then another, from the other end of the plaza. *Not rifles,* Jack thought: *artillery. They were prepared for this.*

A constant, rolling thunder filled the air. A shell from the Gerent's guns struck one of the kite-boats, and it fell in flames. One of the towers slumped sideways and disintegrated across the courtyard, its structure gone, its matter loosed to spill and burst. There was fire and dust everywhere.

The kite-boats flocked around the *Thunderer,* and hovered over and among the towers. The tiny men in a boat below Jack's perch staggered to the side of their vessel, and heaved a box over it; flame flowered where it landed on the courtyard below.

A shell punctured the golden balloon above the *Thunderer,* and tore out the other side of the deflating fabric. The ship listed and fell at an angle. Jack held his breath. It righted itself. A second shell tore open a hole in the *Thunderer*'s wooden side, without any noticeable effect on the warship's functioning. Whatever powered it, such wounds clearly meant nothing to it. Of course, Jack thought: how could one expect to sink it, when it already defied gravity? Ignoring the fires on its dark decks and the scrambling and screaming of its crew, the *Thunderer* revolved slowly above the courtyard, a mandala of war, and fired again and again at the Gerent's guns.

The ground under Jack's feet shook and tilted. There was fire below. A shell had struck the tower he was standing on. The floor dropped as something below gave way. He panicked, looking around for somewhere to run or jump to. All around was fallen or in flames. He had let the battle hypnotize him, and now it was too late. The ground slid and dissolved beneath him. He leaped wildly into the air. He did not come down.

He hung in the night air, drifting slightly in the wind, above the smoke and the flames. Tears ran down his face, tilted to the sky. *Of course. Of course. Why did I wait so long?* The gift was still in him. *Praise Be.* He felt dizzy.

Everything below was in fire and ruin. Distant screams and moans floated up on the wind. He heard a terrible crashing sound as the flaming skeletons of two buildings slid into each other.

The *Thunderer* and its fleet were moving slowly back to the south, their hideous work done. Jack angled his body into the sharp wind and followed, far above and behind the ship.

TWENTY

The *Thunderer* hung low over the Stross End courtyard, beneath the jagged accusing shadows of the ruined towers. Despite the cold morning drizzle, fires were still burning somewhere; smoke made thin black stains on the grey air. The stink of charred wood and brick-dust blew across the deck. Arlandes looked down over his work.

Below him—under his watchful shadow—the Countess's red-coated men went to and fro, dragging bodies from the rubble and making two tidy heaps at the north and south of the courtyard. Dragging stragglers from the Gerent's forces struggling out of their hidey-holes and making a tidy corral of them beneath the clock-tower. Setting up, beneath red flags, a breadline for the displaced factory-hands. Restoring order and peace and quiet. An occasional shot rang out.

At that moment, Arlandes knew, the Countess would be making her speeches. On her podium on Laud Heath, or by the docks. Her face a jeweled mask of white, her voice dripping concern. *Regretting the necessity of violence.* She would probably make a visit to the ruins soon.

By which time the redcoats below would have cleared away the rubble. Put out the fires. Carted away the broken bodies, each one of which reminded him agonizingly of *her*. Torn down the buildings, for no building around the courtyard was altogether intact, and their towers sagged and trembled dangerously. Swept the blood off the flagstones.

Or perhaps they'd simply leave it. Leave it like a raw wound in the city's flesh. As a reminder.

Arlandes shivered and was numb. His men were grim and cold and sick and almost speechless.

He didn't delude himself; he'd do it again if she ordered it.

He looked at the ruins around him. He turned his head left to right, and everything he saw was in ruins. He'd never seen anything like it in all of Ararat. A new kind of death had come to the city.

TWENTY-ONE

It was early in the morning when Olympia next came. Cold morning sunlight made the hospital's white walls icy and ethereal. There'd been no guests, no voyeurs, no audience nor supplicants all morning, or the day before or the day before that, so Arjun sat in silence on his bunk, alone with uncomfortable thoughts, wondering if perhaps he was no longer of interest, if perhaps whatever strange information he'd carried back from that terrible place had been assimilated by the city's buzzing mind, was no longer news. . . . It also occurred to him that perhaps it was simply too cold out for sightseeing.

Olympia's voice preceded her. It carried down the chill corridors and rang confidently off the iron bars. There was an approaching echo of curt orders and arch mockery, interspersed with the defeated resentful mumbling of the Sisters, always a step behind the beat. Arjun watched silently as they turned onto his hallway. Olympia, striding, sent Sister Judith and Sister Margaret scurrying before her. Without further objection, Sister Judith unlocked the door to Arjun's cage. Olympia stepped in. Arjun plucked at his too-small robes.

"Good morning, Arjun. My apologies for the delay."

"You have a way for me to get out of here?"

"They've already agreed to release you. Oh, don't look so surprised. You expected a midnight rescue, pistols blazing? That may be how things are done in the mountains, but this is Ararat. I took the matter to court, Arjun. I had an appointment to argue your case before a judge in Mass How tomorrow. I made it not worth their while to fight for you. Frankly, I think they found you disappointing anyway. Now pack up and come with me."

She had a coach waiting outside, an elegant two-seater. The driver sat reading a newspaper. He wore no coachman's uniform; he was wrapped instead in a long coat of rough brown wool, draped heavily over ursine shoulders. His spade-broad face carried a thick black beard. Casually, he asked, "No trouble then, Miss O.?"

"No trouble, Hoxton. The Sisters had no stomach for a fight. Here he is. Hoxton, Arjun; Arjun, Hoxton."

"If only it was always that easy, eh?"

"If only, Hoxton, if only. After you, Arjun."

Where else did he have to go, what else did he have to do? Arjun stepped up onto the coach. The driver had a heavy knife—more of a machete—strapped behind his seat, and it knocked against Arjun's knees whenever the coach bounced. "You must tell me everything, absolutely everything," Olympia said. "As soon as we see the Professor," she added, burying herself in a book. The words *Bambridge's Conflict of Laws* were stamped on its spine.

Arjun leaned forward. "Mr. Hoxton, am I right to think that, if Olympia *had* been forced to stage a daring rescue, guns blazing, the guns would have been yours?"

"Ah. Well, everyone likes to be useful, Mr. Arjun."

The air was sharp; Arjun was very cold in his thin hospital gown. As they passed through Ar-Mouth, he was surprised to see old drifts of dirty snow by the side of the street. "It snowed a couple of days ago," Olympia said. "And before that rain, and *rain,* and the most *awful* hail. The weather took a turn for the worse while you were in your cell."

"That's not the only thing, Miss O.," Hoxton said.

"No," Olympia agreed. "No, I'm afraid it wasn't."

They rode gently up Cato Road, under the triumphal arches. The statues were topped with snow, fresh, white snow, raised above the dirt of the streets. It formed a virginal blanket over the backs of the embracing lovers on the Diamond Queen's Arch.

There was a small garden of bare trees by the side of the road, at the base of a sweeping black wall carved with names. A string quartet played slow, mournful music. Old men in dark winter coats stood around them, heads bowed, hands in pockets.

"Stop a moment," Arjun said. He got down and stood by the railings, looking into the garden. Snow collected at the base of the wall, shrouding the flowers left there.

Olympia pointed to the wall's inscription: *The Battle of Mantle Court,* and underneath, *The City Will Always Bear Their Mark.* "Two Estates clashed in the north of the city, when these men were young," she said. "It was stupid. You don't need to know why; it looks like you will watch us suffer it all again."

"I was interested in the music."

"Oh, that. I've heard it before somewhere. It's been all over the city these last few weeks. Actually, I think I heard some girl singing 'Lero, Lero' to its tune. It's very pretty."

"Yes, it is. It's gone through many translations to get here. Much has been lost. But I suppose it is, even still."

"Does it mean something to you?"

The music changed, segueing into a triumphal, upward-slashing piece. Arjun turned away and got back on the coach. He wasn't sure how to answer that question anymore.

Fallon Circle was no longer quiet or peaceful. There were men in red uniforms out in the street in front of Holbach's mansion, marching up and down the street, or gathered around camp tables playing cards and smoking bituminous roll-ups. The soldiers checked their names, and let Arjun and Olympia through. There were more soldiers in the wood-paneled entry hall.

Holbach emerged from a door and waved them in. He led them through the deep shelves of his library to a table at the back, under an arched window, where they sat down. "This may be the only place in my own home where I can speak freely," he said.

"What is all this?"

"You haven't heard? Olympia, you didn't tell him? I see. Arjun, I suspect she wants to make me tell you, just to make me suffer. She blames me, you know. As perhaps she should. You've been missing for a long time, Arjun. Almost a month, and a month is a very long time in politics. The Countess's grievances with the Gerent of Stross End came to a head."

"Her grievances were imaginary," Olympia said. "She wanted to make an example. To display her new weapon to full effect."

"Yes, yes. The weapon *I* built for her. So, Arjun, two days ago, she sent it north to Stross End, and turned its guns on the Gerent's tower. It brought down half the offices of the Stross Mercantile. And I am under constant guard for fear of reprisal."

"I told you how she would use it, Professor. Nicolas would have told you, if he were still with us."

To fill the silence, Arjun asked, "Were many people killed?"

"Dozens, maybe hundreds. No one knows whether the Gerent was among them. The Countess has been too busy to talk to me since it happened; I don't know whether she has him imprisoned somewhere, or perhaps even let him go. But he's a spent force. He gambled all the strength he had in the defense of his tower."

Arjun found it hard to feel strongly about the deaths in Stross End. He had barely heard of the place before today; it sounded so far away, separated from him by a dense unmappable urban vastness, all full of people he would never know or even see. But these natives of the city, they had found a way to expand their sympathies to encompass its reaches. Perhaps, he thought, he should learn how to do the same.

"We should get a move on," Holbach said. "I have a lunch appointment. So then, tell us *all* about it."

Olympia leaned forward, steepling her fingers, Holbach leaned back in his chair, and Arjun began. Holbach's eyebrows raised, and he said, "*Not* a fraud. You're sure? He couldn't have used lights, mirrors? Hypnosis? He couldn't have drugged you?"

Holbach quizzed Arjun on his conversation with Shay for what seemed like hours. Arjun found that he remembered very little, after the horror of the Typhon and his weeks of fever and confinement, but he did his best to answer.

"We'll have to ask Branken whether he knows of this 'heliotype' device," Holbach said. "More his field than mine."

To Arjun's relief, whatever anger Holbach might have felt at Shay's needless demise was outweighed by his own guilt. "I was thoughtless, Arjun. My curiosity got the better of me; I didn't think of the risks. There were others I should have sent instead, perhaps. I hope you'll accept my apology."

Warily, Arjun told them about the Typhon. When he was done, he said, "I had expected you to react differently. I was afraid you would fall all over yourselves in reverence for that, that *thing*. I couldn't have stomached that."

"You needn't have worried," Olympia said.

"We rather tend to share your estimation of the creature," Holbach said. "The Typhon is a great power, but not, shall we say, a *useful* one. To be feared, yes, but not, ah, admired."

"Frankly, you're lucky you're still alive," Olympia said. "You're lucky you didn't drown, and what a waste *that* would have been."

Holbach nodded. "He probably, I don't know, washed up on the bank? Snagged on a bank? Do the canals have banks? I'm afraid my studies rarely take me to those parts of the city. So many little mysteries! Olympia, you know, since Brindley died, sad business, *ugly* business, we've had no canal engineer. Is his work still current, do you think?"

Something uncertain and nervous must have been visible on Arjun's face, because Olympia, ignoring Holbach, looked sharply at him and said, "Yes?"

"I do not wish to describe the vision."

"Quite fair," she said. "Horrible. But?"

"But at the last moment I felt the creature recoil. I did not drown because it turned away from me."

"Ah, now." Holbach tapped a plump pink finger on the table for attention. "Not a creature, please. You are a foreigner and may not understand. Who knows what kind of low people you've been living with while you're here, and what sort of unsophisticated and irrational notions you've picked up. But Ararat's powers and presences and gods, whatever you may wish to call them, are not creatures. Like some big animal!"

"It *saw* me, Professor, and—"

"No, no, you see, that's impossible, that's what Wayneflete calls a confusion of categories; you might as well—"

"It *hated* me, Professor. It meant to hurt me."

"You might as well say the night intends darkness, or gravity means you to fall, or, ha, that—"

"Then there's something broken in it, Professor, something sick..."

"Or, yes, quite, that the sunset's broken, or eleven o'clock is sick, do you see?"

"It was scared, Professor, it will *never* forgive me."

"What?"

Arjun realized he was standing; he thought he might have been shouting. Olympia, embarrassed, was averting her eyes; Holbach looked damp-eyed with pity.

Arjun sat down.

Holbach and Olympia entered into an urgent communication of raised eyebrows and significant glances and discreet head-shaking.

Arjun was suddenly very keen to remain, and very afraid that he was about to be ejected from the mansion, from the company of these people who, eccentric and infuriating though they were, might at least be able to shed some light on the events and visions of that horrible night.

And besides, he needed money.

Mr. Haycock had a kind of smile and laugh that he used whenever he'd said something so offensive that Defour looked ready to expel him from the dining-table. That laugh somehow worked to render everything that had gone before it harmless and quickly forgotten. Arjun attempted the same trick now.

Holbach sighed. "Again," he said, "I'm most terribly sorry. Oh dear. I hope at least you found something that might help you with your own search?"

Arjun realized that in his dread of the Typhon, he had forgotten his own god. He shook his head. "I don't know if I'm still looking. No—please don't ask."

There was silence.

Holbach went on. "Well. My offer stands. I need a translator who knows Tuvar. And I want to repay you for the injury I feel I have done you. Are you interested?"

"I lost the last of my money. Perhaps in the water, or perhaps the

Sisters took it. I have to eat. I need new clothes. I may need to pay
for my passage back to Gad; I haven't decided yet. So, yes, I am.
What is it you do, exactly, Professor?"

Holbach loved to hear himself expatiate on his work; that was obvious from his eyes, his gestures, the rolling cadences of his well-
rehearsed discourse, his enthusiastic digressions from it.

"I think of myself as a scientist, not a mystic, or a priest, or a
wizard, although I have been called all of those things. A scientist.
No less than, say, Dr. Branken, whom you may meet soon, whose
specialty is optics, or our colleague Marchant, the jurist. _I_ am a scientist of the _holy_. You might say that I am a geographer; a cartogra-
pher of the sacred city, a student of the forces beneath its surface
that buckle and shape it. Forces that, if I may adopt Dr. Kamff's
term, though hardly in his intended sense, as you may know if you
know his work—no?—which I would call _tectonic_: our makers, our
architects. _Demiurgic,_ it's sometimes said, but I prefer my word.

"Much nonsense is spoken about these forces. Indeed, the city is
in a sense built out of that nonsense. Out of an absurd reverence. As
I think you're aware. Now, true, our gods are very strange, and hard
to understand, just as the city they build is full of secrets and
strangeness. But, for all that they are obscure, there is no reason to
see them as fundamentally _mysterious_. No more so than the forces
that lay the course of the river, or shape the coastline, or sculpt the
mountain. They may be mapped, plotted, brought under reason."

A housekeeper brought in coffee on a silver tray. Arjun accepted
gratefully. He stirred thick honey into it, and swigged it eagerly. It
was better than any of the Nessenes' cures.

"I can understand my fellow citizens' knee-bending tenden-
cies, of course. I was present, as you are no doubt aware, for the recent return of the Bird. I was otherwise occupied, of course, and it
was very far away, but . . . And then, once, I was in the Arcades, I believe purchasing perfume for a young lady who is sadly no longer
with us, and Orillia—the spirit of the lights? The god of the
Illuminations?—manifested; all the glass of the Arcades, and the
lamps hanging in chains from arch to arch, all became brilliantly

deep and, ah, *brilliant*. I found myself bending the knee and tearing at my hair with all the rest of the crowd. So I *do* understand.

"But, now, that's the problem; my fellow citizens, and too many of my fellow scholars, try to understand these forces by entering within them, within their manifestations. You might as well study hornets by sticking your head in the nest. It makes us mad. We must study them at one remove, through their traces. A science of signs. It takes patience, but it's the only way."

Olympia affixed a thin black cigarette to her holder. Without looking, Holbach skidded a brass ashtray toward her.

"For example. You must be aware of my success in predicting the Bird's return to our city. There were many significant signs: for instance, white doves appearing in Kanker Market, in place of its usual pigeons. A sign of pressures within the city, welling up; the very same pressures that form and *are* the Bird itself. Prefigurations and intimations of its return. You might do something similar with, say, Lavilokan, whose signs often manifest on the stage, as befits a mirror-god.

"So, I might see myself as a natural geographer. One might also see the city as a machine, the tectonic forces within being like the pressures or charges that build up in an engine and move its parts. I have even, at times, believed that they may be more by-products than essential forces, like the heat the engine gives off. An engine, I do not dispute, of *enormous* complexity. I have been accused," he said, warming to a digression, "of *simplifying* the complexity of the city and its, ah, *presences*. *Nothing* could be further from the truth. Consider my rivals' schools: take Dr. Lodwick, for example, and his *Extrapolations*. What I have described as tectonic forces, he persists in seeing as *gods*. He sees them as *meaning* something, you see, as having something to *say* to us. So he reads as *signs* things that are only, ah, happenings. Events. Eructations. It makes him see simple rules and regularities where there are none. Do you see?"

"Ah . . ."

"To him it's a conversation, like we're having now. He thinks that *they* mean to mean something to *him,* to *us*. To me it is a matter of natural processes, which, not being *intended* for our understanding, are immensely obscure in their operation. Prediction and con-

trol of such forces is an art as well as a science." Holbach slapped the
table. "And *that* is my *point,* you see. A man who understands the
operation of the engine and the placement of its levers may put it to
work, harness its forces. As I did with the *Thunderer.* Whatever may
become of it, however it may be used, I'm afraid I can't regret its
creation. It represents the promise of science. An all-seeing, all-
mapping eye. My promise to posterity, to our future."

It sounded like an applause-line. Arjun tried to look impressed.
It was very foreign to his way of thinking: the Choir had never worried about the future, or sought to harness the Voice, only to echo it
back and forth until the end of time. He supposed they were not
great thinkers.

"So you see why I was interested in *you*. Your, ah, *Voice*. A god
from *outside* the city, one that you believe may have been drawn
here. Is that possible? I'd like to know. And I know nothing of the
gods outside these walls. I should learn more. It's all an intriguing
problem. We *must* talk, soon, perhaps."

In the pause that followed, Arjun said, "I would think the city
would hate you, Professor. The mob outside the Observatory, for example. Would they love you any better than Shay? Wouldn't they
call this talk of forces and engines blasphemy?"

"Certainly, if they heard it. Though many others would cheer
me on. As always, we of the city are complexly divided against ourselves. In any case, I don't publish this sort of talk where the mob
can see it, or the censors. At least not under my own name."

"Nicolas did," Olympia said.

"And look where it got him! Silenced and exiled; lucky to escape with his ears uncropped. Braver than me, yes, but gone, while
I am still here. No, *this* talk is for the enlightened. I can adequately
publish my research without betraying my deeper thinking. I can
translate my work into the language of the knee-benders. I let them
call the *Thunderer* a blessing from the gods, rather than a triumph of
human reason. It is safest." He deflated. "I suppose, for the time being, the *Thunderer* is only a promise to myself, one that cannot safely
be shared."

Arjun rubbed his brow. He tried to ask whether any of this mattered; if everything Holbach had to say could be equally well said in

the language of worship or in the language of science, was the difference real? He wasn't sure. He stumbled over his own sentences and Holbach, he thought, missed his meaning.

"Well," Holbach said, "not to worry. You don't need much of a grasp of theory for the work I have in mind. At least you're not *shocked*, which is promising. Your work: let's discuss it."

Holbach led Arjun round the shelves, stopping to pick up a variety of books: a pamphlet the color of dead skin, two thick tomes bound with black leather, a twine-stitched bundle of typed papers. He heaped them into Arjun's arms. "Your work is to translate these for me. Now, you know what I'm interested in. The Tuvar were, by all accounts, great or at least prolific theological scholars. Together let's bring their science back into the light! Ah yes, take this, too. And, ah, yes, this.

"These are all very old, of course—nothing has been written in Tuvar in this city for, oh, gods only know—but it's surprising how little theological science has progressed. Now this," he said, slipping a slim journal onto the pile, "you should start with this. If the references to it in Varady's *Letters* are accurate, this records an important series of studies on the Black Bull. It should interest you; the Bull is a potency that no longer exists, a god that has abandoned its post. We'll talk later, see how you're doing. For now, my lunch appointment beckons. Then I'll be yours for the rest of the week; I'm afraid my other engagements have been canceled." He gestured sadly toward the door behind which the soldiers stood watch. "I rather think people are afraid to be seen with me. Olympia will talk to you about your salary. A pleasure, again."

Holbach tried to shake Arjun's burdened hands, then patted his shoulder instead. He turned and disappeared between the shelves. Arjun heard a trail of conversation start in the next room: "Good morning, Corporal. How is your boy's inflammation? . . . Oh dear, I *am* sorry, perhaps I know someone who may be able to help with that, let me think. . . . And your wife?"

In the hallway outside, Olympia leaned against a marble bust of a bushy-bearded thinker and said, "Congratulations. Welcome to the fold. You're not the *strangest* person ever to work for the Professor, but you should be interesting anyway." She drummed her fingers on the bust's bald head. "Holbach has no idea what money's worth these days, so he usually pays his translators—"

"What did Brindley die of? Holbach said there was a canal engineer who worked with you. Who wrote about the canals for you? What did he die of?"

"Oh, that's before my time. Some sort of disease. Black lung? Shudders? Langshaw's Disease? The canals are nasty places to go poking around."

"Can I read what he wrote for you?"

"Ah. Maybe. We'll see. Holbach may have been a bit indiscreet, actually. Do you mind if we don't discuss this further? I suggest you keep yourself busy and put the canals out of your mind. Nasty places! Now I have somewhere to be, so we should talk about your work. You'll be paid . . ."

A coach brought Arjun back to the Cypress.

"Not dead, then?" Haycock said. "Very fetching gown, though. Mad, is it?"

"I was sick for a while. Now I'm getting better."

His room was gone, rented to a Mr. Lovage, who opened the door only a crack and avoided eye contact. "How was I supposed to know you were coming back?" Defour snapped. "And you left owing a week's rent, I might add."

Haycock had sold Arjun's books. "An easy mistake to make," Haycock said. "Under the circumstances. I'll make it up to you. *Dis*count. We'll talk about it, all right?"

As an afterthought, Arjun asked after the envelope under the bed. "What envelope?" Lovage asked.

"Never mind," Arjun said.

The salary Holbach had promised was generous. With Holbach's letter of reference, Arjun rented a place in Stammer Gate, south of Foyle's Ward, not too far from Holbach's house. His new neighbors were students, scholars, priests of no particular denomination. His flat was in a stone tower, once the bell tower of some dismantled church. The windows overlooked a graveyard.

He made no effort to furnish the room. There was a bed and a desk and a chair; that was enough. He pushed the desk up against the window, where a cold draft reminded him of home. There was a chandler on the corner of his street, in a waxy little burrow of a shop. Arjun bought a crateful of candles. He emptied it out, and turned it upside down to make a side table on which he could rest a bottle of black ink and a jug of wine.

There was some dusty contraption hanging on the wall, a thing of mirrors turned on each other bound with wire and snakeskin, hung with bells and teeth and roof-tile. Was it one particular god's icon, or a mishmash of many? Whatever it was, he took it down and folded it over, then slid it under the bed.

He placed the book Holbach had told him to start with on the desk, piling the others at his feet. He opened out a sheet of paper next to the book, and dipped his quill. He spent the first evening staring out over the graveyard, probing the cold riverbed of his mind for what remained of the passion that had brought him to the city, the ink going dry on the pen's nub.

TWENTY-TWO

G ravity began pulling at Jack as he floated over a strange ghetto.
It was a close circle of tall, curved buildings, their spires curling in like a gently closing hand. He sank closer, accepting a compromise with gravity; he did not know how to fight it yet. He let
the ship dwindle in the distance.

As he got closer, he could see that the spires rippled with strange
valleys and ridges, like running wax. In the moonlight, the circle
was like the hand of a ragged corpse. He settled, and sat cross-
legged, his dirty hair falling into his face.

The surface was uncomfortable. The ridges he had seen from the
air repeated themselves on a smaller and then a smaller scale, finger-
tip etchings. He ran a tired hand over it, marveling at the work that
must have gone into it.

He'd flown. It was hard to look directly at the thought. There
was an unbridgeable shadow between the rational mind that was
sitting on the roof, wondering how to get home, and the entity that
had moved on the wind. The sensation was strange.

One night, he remembered—staring at the back of his hand, his
flexing fingers—one night when he was still quite new to the House,
he had been herded into the lecture-room on the fourth floor, and
sat in the shadows while Mr. Coil ranted.

"As for the presences: it is our solemn duty to be patient and
quiet and open to their messages for us; as my colleagues say, without them, we are without meaning. Tiber in particular, of course, of
course, *of course,* Praise Be. Without them, what would we be, what

would this city be, but little clockwork figures moving in our tracks to no purpose? So much is familiar. But now, ratlings, we are to discuss the latest scientific discoveries. As we once might have done in the salons of Nicolas Maine, for those are the heights from which I am fallen.

"The philosophers have opened the brain, rat-boys, cracked the skull with knives, broken the backbone and torn away all the bloody tissues that wrap you so snugly. Apes first, then *thieves,* such as your filthy selves. The brain is your thinking-meat. The way in which they have proved this is interesting, and again involves deviants and criminals, but I will spare your tender sensibilities, for am I not a gentle shepherd? A lump of matter in your sloped skulls does your thinking for you."

He'd gestured with his hands. "Roughly so big. Full of winding streets. They've found charges of electrical force running across and through it, prodding the meat into motion. Do you understand electricity, hatchlings? Imagine *fire;* how it crawled and sparked along the grain of the wood when your drunken, shiftless father was reduced to burning your furniture. The sparks run *here* and not *there,* and in consequence of that motion, the will forms in you to break *this* window or steal *that* purse, and on such motions our fates depend."

Coil had struck the table with the palm of his hand. "So! We may see the presences of the city's streets as being like the pulses of force that travel the paths of the brain. It is their motions that bring meaning to the city. We may see our city as an organ to house them, and to read their messages for us."

Coil developed the analogy at greater length, but Jack had stopped listening. The notion that his thoughts were the product of motions and twitching in the meat in the head disturbed him. Was he not the source of his own intentions? He spent several nights sitting on his cot, holding his hand out in the dark, flexing and unflexing his fingers, trying to feel the moment at which the decision to move was made; was he acted upon or acting? He couldn't tell.

It was something he had grown out of and stopped worrying about. Now he felt it all over again. It made him feel severed from himself. Flight was an impossible potential, which could not be under his will, but apparently was. He felt around inside himself for the power's trigger. He could not find it.

There was a dark plain in front of him, a few streets away. Fires burned out on it. He thought he could see beasts, moving in their pens, but perhaps they were just shadows.

He tried to figure out what he could be sure of. *First,* whatever power he had—and he could not pretend anymore that it was not some more-than-natural power—must be all of a piece with the speed and grace he had displayed in thieving, in fighting, in racing over the roofs. And *second,* it was obviously the result of the magic he had worked with the Bird. But he had expected only to borrow the Bird's flight for a moment, enough to escape. How had the power become fixed in him? Was it for some obscure purpose of the Bird's own?

As Coil would have put it, that was all that could be reasoned from first principles. The rest would have to be a matter of experiment. *Third,* then: the power had limits. Or he did. He could not remain in flight forever, at least not *yet.* It drained him; gravity could not be defied forever.

On hands and knees, Jack inched out on a carved ledge, thrust out like a formless fist. It was too dark to see the street below, which was probably for the best. He tried to remember what it had been like when he had launched himself off the roof of Barbotin. Holding that memory in his head, he leaped.

TWENTY-THREE

Arjun's work started slowly. It had been a long time since he had last tried to read Tuvar, and it was a difficult language. Of all the tongues he had learned when he was younger, he liked this one least: so much depended on subtle shifts of tone, and it troubled him that he had so little idea how it should sound. Its music was always beyond his grasp. Still, for the time being, he had no better notion of what to do with himself.

The thin red book Holbach had told him to start with was called *Journal of the Bull's Year*. It seemed to be the record of a series of—it was hard to know what to call them; Arjun was not sure whether they were experiments, in Holbach's sense, or religious rituals, or perhaps artistic statements. The word the journal's author used was related to the verb *to act*, so for the time being Arjun just wrote *activities*.

There were twenty-three such activities. The author, sometimes alone, sometimes with numerous associates, would go out walking in complex patterns across the city. Sometimes they fasted for days; sometimes they used drugs; in one case, if Arjun read right, they underwent some sort of skull-surgery. They made certain changes to the city: performed acts of petty vandalism or charity, played music, started fires, painted or moved things, took things away, left them behind. It was all aimed at encouraging or delaying or altering the manifestations of a god called the Black Bull.

It was hard to read. It was a private journal, full of abbreviations and cryptic, personal allusions. After a week's work, Arjun put the book to one side and started on another; he would come back to it when he knew more about the Tuvar. When he went round to Holbach's study to explain, Holbach distractedly told him, "That seems reasonable," and "Of course, I'm hugely grateful for your efforts," and ushered him out.

He decided to start with one of the volumes bound in black leather. From the look of the page, it was an epic poem, the work of many hands, annotated by what seemed to be a generation of scholars. It told of the diaspora of the Tuvar people.

They were from cold and rainy plains to the north. An empire had fallen, to their west, following the failure of a royal marriage, loosing barbarians across the plains. The Tuvar took down their tents and folded them across the backs of their oxen, and set out in every direction where the barbarians were not. After many adventures, including a period of slavery, working the giant wheels of some great steel machine, and an incident of temptation by nymph-spirits as they passed the shore, a group of them came to Ararat.

This was all centuries before the poem was written, and the poem itself was centuries old, and even the paper on which the book was printed was yellow and brittle with age. Arjun copied it out, copied great tranches of it out, in journals and scrap-paper; he carried it around to cafés to work on it; his desk and his floor and his pockets filled with scribbled paper.

It seemed that the Tuvar had settled in a northern quarter of the city, near the slopes of the mountain. They had found a place that had been burned over after a plague and returned to the weeds, and set about cultivating it. Then, in the second volume, the poem shifted from stories of the heroic trek, and began to describe endless legal and economic conflicts with their neighbors in the city. Prophets and explorers gave way to a succession of priests and mayors. Some of them made a lot of money in the fabric trade. And then there was a long, strange episode involving a conflict between their first leader and a native of the city, who was his mirror image and shared his fate and tried to steal his life. They had to fight for the one soul, they believed; they could not share the city. One of them died. It was not certain which one. The poem's authors described that incident as a typical example of the city's mazy treachery.

But above all, the second volume was about the Black Bull. That, finally, was what Holbach wanted.

In their homeland, the Tuvar had had one god, an ox-headed, priapic power of the rains and mists, which fertilized their plains and sired their livestock. It seemed to have no name: they referred to it variously as the Father, or the Son, or the Land. They had suffered terribly when they left it behind—food not grown from the Father's seed seemed tasteless to them, and earth not watered by it seemed dry and brittle beneath their feet—but they could not induce it to follow them by any sacrifice or ritual they could devise. Arjun felt their pain.

In Ararat, they found the Black Bull, a creature that stormed across the parks and heaths of the city, and thundered through the alleys, bowing and shaking the walls. It was found in old and wild places, like the blasted ground the Tuvar had settled on. Its horned head and broad shoulders reminded them of the Father. The steam that roiled from its snout reminded them of the mists of their home. It was a power of the city's rich ancient ages. There were monsters' bones buried in the timber of the city, under its black earth; the Bull raised up those relics, promising the depth and darkness of the soil, fertile and endless return and rebirth. They thought it was Ararat's gift to them, the very image of their first Father, so they set about worshipping it and theorizing it in all manner of ways.

They were much luckier than I have been, Arjun thought. It cheered him to read that. But then again, it saddened him to think that they had vanished from the city in the centuries between the writing of the poem and his reading of it. And their Black Bull, too, as far as he knew, and any other trace of any of them except a few books, unreadable to almost everyone, moldering in libraries across this foreign city.

He realized that he had a lot of money; Holbach was a stupidly generous employer. Arjun could afford to pay for some assistance.

He went back to the Cypress. There was a carriage rank near his flat, where the horses waited, hooves clicking sharply on the cobbles. With a great sense of luxury, he rode into Shutlow. It seemed very poor and mean. Not just poor—there were parts of Stammer Gate where starving scholars and artists and mystics clustered, after all, and his own flat was a cheap little thing, by the standards of Ararat's richer quarters—but dismal. *Drab*.

He waited until Haycock came home. The little man smirked to see him. "Back again? *Now* are you ready to talk business?"

"It's nice to see you, too, Mr. Haycock. I am, yes."

They sat in the garden while Arjun explained what he needed. Books on the city's gods, those could wait. For now, he had a job, and he needed dictionaries, histories, anything that might help him perfect his command of the Tuvar's language.

Defour passed them. She was wearing black and held a handkerchief to her face. She didn't see Arjun, or didn't acknowledge him, as she went into the boardinghouse.

"It's a big show of pious mourning for what's-his-name," Haycock explained. "Norris. The drink or the lung-rot finally caught up to him, I hear. Turned him right inside out. Right where you're sitting, actually. Ha! Heady saw it and he says it was awful. Says the old man came home one last time in the pouring rain."

Haycock illustrated the scene by walking the yellow fingers of his left hand across the tabletop. "And the hail. Too drunk to know to wear a coat. Drunk enough to swallow anything if it's wet. Coughs, and coughs, and *bam*!"

Haycock struck his left hand flat with the fist of his right. "Coughed his black guts right up, says Heady, and the blood looked like black coal slag. Not funny, really. Mind you, there's a lot of that sort of thing in these parts lately. Old drunks don't all last the winter; sad, but there you go. So, back to business, then. Hey, are you all right?"

Arjun had not been friends with Norris. They had only spoken once or twice. More accurately, he had listened to a couple of the man's rambling monologues. Still, he had known him. So he asked Defour where Norris was buried, and went to pay his respects.

It was a pauper's grave on the outskirts of the Cere House, a dirt circle ringed by statues. Norris was not important enough to deserve the rituals and honors bestowed in the Cere House's inner precincts and tunnels. He had a little plaque on the seventy-seventh row. Under that plaque were his ashes.

Next to the plaque was a flat stone, with a corner of brown paper sticking out under it. Arjun moved the stone aside. Folded under it was the Spider's envelope, addressed to Arjun. Someone had left it for Norris, Arjun assumed. Defour, perhaps? What did it mean to her? Was it meant to symbolize the hope of some new path, new possibilities, rebirth? Or was it meant to say, *Be happy with where you have come; accept your fate, even this one?* There was no way of knowing. He supposed she meant well. He put it back.

What killed you?

Arjun wasn't sure what he'd expected. When Haycock told him his nasty story, Arjun had been so *sure* that the Typhon's poisonous· touch had killed Norris—so utterly sure that he'd almost been able to see the cold black fog gathering over the beer garden, that he'd almost been able to smell the stink of the thing creeping up out of the waters and into the street. Maybe he'd imagined that some sinister unholy aura would still hang over the old man's gravesite.

But there was nothing; only a neat functional plaque, and, shoved under that stone, someone's small sad gesture of kindness.

Arjun waited there for a while, nervous and disappointed.

There was a choir, of sorts, gathered around a plot a few rows down. The dead man below had been poor but popular. They sang a sad, slow song. They had weak, untrained voices, but the music forgave them. It was the song he had taught to the hurdy-gurdy man in Moore Street. It had an echo of the Voice in it. *It's still spreading,* he thought. That was good. It pleased him to realize that melody felt good, again. It meant he was healing.

"I suppose you can take this as my gift to you," he whispered to Norris's plot. "For what it's worth." Then he felt embarrassed, so he got up and left.

TWENTY-FOUR

Arlandes was no longer loved. It was something of a relief. After Stross End the newspapers and the gossip had turned cold to him, as he was to them. The city no longer found him fascinating. All that romantic humbug—the tributes to his flashing saber, his grief and his lonely devotion to duty, his courage and stern beauty— all that was over. The city regarded him with a chill wariness. A few papers dared to suggest that he was overworked. Some rabble-rousers with a printing press published accusations that he was insane; the Countess quickly had them packed off to the Rose in chains.

There'd been a play running on Harp Street for a month in which an actor, some limp-wristed invert with his face painted black-eyed in a pastiche of grief, had played Arlandes. (Lucia's fictional counterpart had been killed by pirates; in the fiction, Arlandes had taken revenge and thus made himself whole again.) Arlandes had refused all invitations to attend, but by all accounts it had been a huge success. Ticket sales froze and withered after Stross End and it closed two weeks later.

Mr. Hildebrand—Lucia's father—had finally stopped trying to visit Arlandes, finally stopped trying to talk business with him. The old man had come crawling round once a week every week, until Stross End: after Stross End, silence, at last. He'd been an investor in that travesty of a play; perhaps he was licking his wounds.

To be disliked gave Arlandes a dull satisfaction. Better that the mob despise him than that it affect, whorishly, greedily, to share his private pain. Better that it shunned him than that it dabble its dirty fingers in his soul.

Throughout that whole winter he hardly spoke to anyone, and hardly anyone spoke to him, save to give or take orders. He spent half his life on the *Thunderer,* adrift among the clouds and the spires, silently brooding in the dark womb of his quarters, as the great ship lurched back and forth over Stross End, asserting the Countess's authority over her new territories, as it hammered the city's redrawn borders into place. He spent the other half of his life in his office, hunched over his desk. His office was in the palace, in the east wing, only a few minutes' walk from the Countess's chambers, but even she avoided him. She sent him his orders through footmen and toadies and her private secretary and, on one awkward hem-hawing occasion, Holbach. She no longer adored him. He was no longer her favorite; he was, it was clear, only a tool. He drank grimly and with implacable purpose. He kept his silence like it was a bloody-minded vow. He therefore never told anyone about the strange visitation he received on the night of the Feast of the Crossing.

He'd attended the ball in his mourning-blacks, and stood alone, and danced with no one. The Countess had introduced him to a group of the Chairman's young favorites—clever bookkeepers with bloodless smiles, as was typical of the Chairman's favorites. His grim presence had put the fear of the gods into them. His duty done, he'd retired to his office, taking the back staircases to avoid the revelers.

He'd first set eyes on Lucia at the ball for the Feast of the Crossing, two years ago. No one remembered precisely what Crossing the Feast was supposed to commemorate, whether it was a tragedy or a victory, what the Feast was supposed to mean; but that was what it meant to him. It had been cruel of the Countess to make him attend.

He'd sat in his chair, lit the candle on his desk, and stared blankly into the shadows. He sat in silence, save when he started humming quietly to himself, the pretty, simple, sad little tune that he'd heard . . . he forgot where, exactly. Not at the ball; it wasn't music for a ball. It soothed him, and so he stopped doing it; instead he ground his jaw silently.

The man entered with no knock on the door, and with no sound of footsteps. One moment Arlandes was alone, and the next he was not. A man sat in the armchair in the corner of the office. A wiry little man, in a dark suit, with close-cropped white hair.

The man had a smell of chemicals about him, and that smell had preceded him slightly.

Arlandes took him at first for a palace servant. Without looking at him, Arlandes snarled, "Out of here, sir, at once."

"Captain Arlandes? You're a hard man to get in to see. It took me a while to find a path. I've heard a lot about you."

"How tiresome for you. If you're lost, sir, the ball is downstairs."

"You call that a ball? It's a pretty rustic performance, Captain, down there. You should see some of the balls I've seen. If that's the best ball they throw in these parts, I'm not impressed. On the other hand, I've heard a lot about that ship of yours, Captain, and that *does* intrigue me."

Arlandes stared at the man, inspecting him up and down, from his neatly shined shoes to his thin shoulders. The man wore round spectacles, and in the candlelight it was impossible to make out his eyes. "Do I know you? You seem familiar."

"I go by *Mr. Lemuel*. No first names, if you don't mind; it doesn't do to get friendly with the customers."

"I *do* know you. You are an attendant of the Cere House. You were at Miss Hildebrand's funeral. You were insolent then as you are tonight."

"So how does it work, then? The big ship. How was it made?"

"You're remarkably brazen for a spy, Mr. Lemuel."

"I'm a businessman, not a spy, Captain. I'm a scholar, an explorer, an archeologist, a collector of all the clever little things that make this city so intriguing, not a spy. Whatever second-rate local warlord you're imagining I work for, rest assured: I wouldn't be seen dead in their service. Just tell me how it works and you'll never see me again. I'll be gone. Think of it as an act of kindness to a poor mendicant, who's stopped here briefly out of the storm, and will be passing into the storm again."

Arlandes laughed. "You'd have to ask Professor Holbach how it works. I'm only the hand that steers it."

"This Holbach person sounds a bit tricky. A bit clever, for one of the natives. I don't know if I'm ready to speak to him yet. No offense to you, Captain; I have the highest respect for the military mind, within its proper sphere of operations."

"You will not speak to Holbach because you will not leave this place, except in chains, *spy*."

Arlandes reached across his desk for his saber and his hand found nothing. He stared around in confusion. He turned behind him to find that his pistol was not in its rack. He turned back again to see Lemuel cradling the pistol in his lap. He stood and made to dart for the door, but it seemed that there *was* no door. It was surely only a trick of the shadows, but there *was* no door.

"Will you listen, Captain? Sit and listen."

Arlandes sat.

"We'll haggle then, if you won't tell me from the kindness of your heart." Lemuel folded his hands on his lap—Arlandes couldn't quite see where the pistol had gone—and unfolded them. A tiny white glow formed between the palms of his hands. He raised up his left hand. A small glass cube sat on it. Within the glass there was the faintest suggestion of beating wings. Indeed it seemed the wings beat smoky trails of light through the glass, outside the glass, and into the corners of the room. Lemuel lowered his hand; the cube remained floating. "What do you think of this, then? Your Professor Holbach's not the only one who can steal the Bird's power. What do you think of this?"

"I think it disgusts me." In fact it did more than disgust Arlandes; it filled him with fear. The beating of white wings made him think of her, falling, and he could hardly stand to look at the thing's light. "There was a man called Shay; Holbach said he was dead. Were you in business with him, Lemuel?"

"Not the cages, then." Lemuel reached out and plucked the glass from the air with his finger and thumb. He put it back in his pocket, and the room filled with shadows again.

Lemuel scratched his chin. "I suppose you'd take an offer of money as an insult to your honor?"

Arlandes regarded Lemuel in silence. He froze his face into a mask of arrogant disdain. It was an expression he'd perfected for dueling; it made strong men tremble. It seemed to have no effect on Lemuel at all. In fact, beneath the mask, Arlandes was terrified. Quite terrified. Lemuel made his skin crawl. The casual way Lemuel spoke about the most horrible blasphemies; it would not have surprised Arlandes if they'd both been struck dead then and there. If the city had simply swallowed them both up. All he could think of was Lucia's death; he imagined himself falling in her place.

Lemuel clicked his fingers. "Of course! You're the one with the dead wife, right? See, I told you I'd heard about you. Hence, I suppose, the getup. Am I right in thinking this is a part of the city where you wear black for mourning? Don't look so shocked, Captain. You'll have to pardon my insensitivity. I'm well-traveled. I've seen a lot of little lives and deaths. You know how it is. I imagine when you're up there on your big floating ship, blasting away, you don't feel much for the lives below, do you?"

"You make me sick, Lemuel. I should kill you."

"There's a place where she's still alive, Captain. This is a big city, right? There's a thousand places where she's still alive. There's places where she's alive, but better, if that's what you want. I can *show* you."

"What do you mean?"

"What do you think I mean?" Lemuel stood. "Pull yourself up out of your chair and come with me. Stop sulking and open your eyes. You've lived in this city all your life, and you think it's so *small*. I'll never understand how people can be so blind. Talk about making me *sick*. Come on, Captain: what was she like, then? A nice posh girl, I'll bet. There's a ball somewhere where she's dancing right now. Was she bookish? There's a study where she's reading, right this moment, somewhere. I can show you. She won't be the girl you knew, not quite, but nearly, we'll find one who's very, very near, if we're patient. You'll hardly know the difference. I'll let you look. If you're very helpful, if you have some really good stuff to tell me, I'll let you touch. Maybe I'll let you bring one back. Maybe I'll let you have two, what do you say? Fuck, I'll let you have a dozen; what do I care? People are cheap. Do they keep harems in this part

of the city? Come on, Captain. Off your arse. You know you want
this."

Lemuel walked to the door (the shadows retreated; there was
a door again). He held it open. The door opened inward, blocking
Arlandes' view of the hallway—but the sounds that came through it
weren't the sounds of the hallway, the palace, the ball downstairs.
There was a sort of distant grinding and churning of engines. There
was a faint sound of unpleasant rough music—high-pitched and
whirling. There were the sounds of gulls. The light that came
through the door was a cold midday sunlight; the deep lines in
Lemuel's face were sharply visible. The lines around his sneering
mouth and eyes.

Arlandes remained frozen in his chair. The terror and loathing
that gripped him were the most dreadful things he'd ever felt.

He spat, "You make a mockery of her death, Lemuel."

"Oh dear. What a romantic sensibility you have, Captain."

Lemuel waited. He sighed. He scraped his dirty fingernails
clean with his thumbnail. He reached into his pocket, and Arlandes'
gut lurched, but Lemuel pulled out no further dreadful blasphemy,
only a small white business card. "When I'm in these parts, I keep
an office, Captain. Maybe I'll still be there if you change your mind
and maybe I won't." He flicked the card in Arlandes' direction; it
landed neatly on the desk.

It read simply EXOTIC GOODS and DISCREET SERVICE. It bore an
address in the Cere House, in the inner precincts.

Arlandes looked up from the card just as the door swung shut.

A few moments later he rose from his chair with a sudden heaving motion, like a man staggering on a storm-tossed deck. He threw
open the door and lunged out into the hallway, where he crashed
into a pair of drunken guests from the ball downstairs. He slapped
the man in his masked face and roared at him, and made the girl cry.
There was no sign of Lemuel.

He watched the couple scramble away down the stairs, the girl
weeping, the man blustering empty threats. Then he retreated into
his darkened office again, to hide, and pity himself, and sulk like a
ruined frightened beast. He turned the card over and over in his
sweating hands until it wrinkled soft and grey. There was an ad-

dress; he didn't dare destroy it, though nor did he dare visit it. If he ever saw Lucia again he didn't know what he'd say to her, how he'd face her.

In the morning, orders came, via messenger, that he was to return to the sky, and he was able to put the incident out of his mind and return, with relief, to his duty.

TWENTY-FIVE

At the end of another week, Arjun collected up his notes and went to pay a visit to Holbach. Outside, it was pouring rain, but it had been pouring all morning, and all the day before, and seemed unlikely ever to let up.

He had a new rain-cloak—the old one having suspiciously disappeared from his room at the Cypress, along with his books. He'd purchased the new one from a spacious and handsome store on the edge of Foyle's Ward, on the recommendation of Olympia's coachman Hoxton. It was apparently quite smart. "For a student," Hoxton had said. "Only for a *student,* mate."

Arjun held his notes under his arm, under the cloak, pulled up his hood, and stepped outside. He made it only halfway down the street.

First his foot landed in a puddle, and a dreadful damp cold squeezed him. The puddle seemed deeper than he would have thought possible; he was drenched almost up to the knee. He nearly dropped his notes. His leg went numb and heavy and he was suddenly afraid. He walked stiffly on.

Then, as he walked past the graveyard, his hood blew back and the rain drove into his face. He cried out in shock and annoyance, and swallowed water. There was suddenly something slimy and unimaginably foul-tasting in his mouth, something thick and weedlike that pressed down on his tongue and threatened to block his throat.

He choked and coughed up a wet black leaf.

Another leaf brushed past his face in a swirl of wind and rain. The air was thick with them. The trees over the graveyard shook and swayed and disintegrated in the downpour.

He thought about what fed those trees and felt sick. He could still taste the muck in his mouth.

When he looked to the end of the street, all he could see, framed by the vague shadows of two tall terraces, was the rain. Beyond that everything was grey mist and fog.

In the depths of the rain something moved, and Arjun turned and ran.

His hands numb with terror, he dropped his notes, and as he ran he trod them under, and the overflowing storm gutters swallowed them.

The day before, the trees had been cleanly bare of leaves. The next day they were bare again. But it rained that day, too, and Arjun preferred to go hungry indoors rather than brave the streets.

The day after, the rain abated. Arjun ventured out to the nearest greengrocer and purchased dried fruit, dried meat, in bulk supply, as if—as the grocer put it—he were traveling north through unfriendly districts.

"Rain's moved on," the grocer offered.

"It's hunting for me elsewhere," Arjun said. "Ah, that's just something we say where I come from," he lied, when he saw the grocer's dubious expression; and he took his groceries and hurried home. That night it rained again.

Two days later a messenger came with a note from Holbach. The note read simply:

Hmm? —H.

Arjun ignored it.

His notes would take *forever* to reconstruct, and he lacked the will even to begin. Increasingly he doubted that he would have the time to finish.

✻   ✻   ✻

Arjun wasn't sure when he had first begun to suspect that the Typhon was hunting him. After Norris's death, surely. That poor old man's death was Arjun's first clear and irrefutable piece of evidence that the monster was no longer content—as it had been, apparently, for a thousand years—to prey on whatever innocents the city happened to offer up: bargemen, fishermen, children, strangers to the city, or anyone else unwise enough to go too close to the water. The Cypress was nowhere near water. Norris's death was explicable only as *malice;* as a sign that the monster was following Arjun's trail.

Arjun had never quite reasoned the matter out. When he'd first set out, nearly three weeks ago, to bring his notes to Holbach, he'd already known it. That first time, he made it half a mile before coming to a street that ran east alongside the leafy and café-lined banks of the Quiller Canal. The thought—*If I go near the water, it will find me*—sprang fully formed into his mind, and he found that he had known all along that he was being hunted.

If he ever doubted it, the proof was in the hungry beating of the rain at his window; in the cold moan and laughter of the drainpipes; in the deathly stink that rose off the water, and that everyone else pretended not to notice.

On the first day after he'd moved into the new flat, Arjun had gone to Holbach. At the time, Arjun not yet been sure about the situation, and perhaps the Typhon had not yet found his scent, because he had been able to walk all the way to Holbach's mansion without incident.

Arjun found Holbach in conference with a thin pale man; the two of them were busy dissecting and slicing at the little flayed corpse of a pigeon. Arjun found the procedure repellent, and the two scientists' conversation utterly obscure. He followed Holbach when the Professor left the laboratory. "Professor," he said, "Professor, I have been thinking about the Typhon. I think you may misunderstand its nature. It *saw* me, Professor, and I think . . ."

Instead of offering help or information, Holbach gave him more metaphors. "Imagine," he said, that time, "that the gods are like reflections in a mirror." Holbach stopped before the mirror in the hall and waved his hand in front of it. "Now, there, my hand moves in the mirror. See, now, my mirror-hand takes my pipe from a mirror-pocket. You might think the mirror-pipe moves because of the action of the mirror-hand upon it; similarly you may ascribe the *intention of moving* to the mirror-hand. Yes? As these images are to us, so the gods are to the city. They can no more see you or hate you than mirror-Holbach here can. Which is not to slight the significance of the gods; what could be more potent than images? Here we are talking about them, after all. They do not care about us, but we care about them."

Holbach returned the pipe to his pocket and waved his hand one more time at his reflection. His fingernails were still stained with the pigeon's blood.

Holbach said that he hoped he'd helped set Arjun's mind at ease, and excused himself: he had an appointment with a man from the *Sentinel*.

The next time Arjun broached the subject, Holbach offered him a detailed and ingenious analogy between the gods and *memories*.

The day after Arjun first understood that the creature was hunting him, he set out again for Holbach's house. He refused to allow the...*thing* to terrify him. His disgust for it overwhelmed his fear. Besides, it was a bright, cold winter day, and the sky was clear.

He took a different route from the previous day, skirting east around the edges of Foyle's Ward, along broad, busy market-streets. He plunged north into backstreets only when he had to.

He quickly found himself confronted by water again.

A canal cut across the street. It was steep-sided and narrow as a ravine. It was wide enough, barely, for a single barge to pass. It smelled of moss and damp and rot.

There was no bridge; the street simply ended. The houses on either side of that unpleasant obstruction looked empty. Their windows were broken and their gardens rank with weeds.

To his surprise, Arjun was able to approach the canal. Looking west down it, he could see an arching iron footbridge some half a mile away, and beyond that the canal receding into the distance, straight and severe; to the east the canal curved and twisted only a couple of streets away and his view was blocked by a windowless wall of brown brick.

It was impossible—it was an impossible trick of geography. If the canal stretched west as far as it appeared, it should have crossed Arjun's path yesterday, but it had not.

The waters had shifted overnight, twisting like a snake.

There was no sign to indicate the name of the street, or the canal. Maybe they *had* no name yet; maybe their names had been forgotten. Arjun wondered whether the empty houses had been abandoned, or whether they had not yet been settled.

In the garden nearest the water's edge, he found a sort of answer. The fence around that garden had been torn down, and the garden opened to the street; but unlike the other gardens, someone cared for it.

The grass was long but not altogether wild. The garden was full of wooden totems—upright poles, with a second shorter strip of wood nailed lengthwise across. Arjun had no idea what creed, if any, the totems stood for; they resembled the Tuvar character for the syllables "on" or—depending on context—"loy," but he thought that was coincidental. He thought he was looking at a shrine for the dead.

There were names cut into the wood on the lengthwise beam of each totem. First names only; all the women seemed to be called Mary or Elizabeth, and the men were mostly John.

Thirteen totems.

Plague deaths? Perhaps some foul miasma of rot and stink crept up off the water, and rolled down the street like mist. Perhaps a barge sank here? Something about the absence of last names made Arjun think these might be the names of children.

The sky was shadowing over and a single drop of cold rain hit Arjun's cheek. Instantly his nerve broke and he ran.

He could never find that grave-site again, or that canal.

On wet days Arjun stayed indoors, trying not to listen to the rain hammering on the roof, or the hail clattering against the windows. He moved his desk into a corner, against a wall, so that he would not have to look out over the city, and tried to lose himself in his work. He began a heavy tome on Tuvar agricultural practices and their unhappy efforts to bring them to the city. It was dull reading; he *inched* through it.

On days when the sky was clear it was safe to go out.

Sometimes Arjun went down to the waterways. He never had to walk too far in any direction before coming to a canal, a reservoir, one of the ornamental lakes of Faugère, or one of the shallow marshy ponds that formed on condemned ground north of Fourth Ward— and the River itself, had he ever been brave enough to face it, would have been only a few hours' walk to the east.

Arjun set the Tuvar aside and began work on a map of nearby waterways. He placed his flat in Stammer Gate at the center of the page, and marked around it with dotted lines for what he judged to be industrial canal, unbroken lines for the prettified recreational waterways to his north, and so on. No dreadful pattern emerged. He disliked the tight and angular way those broken lines seemed to crowd around the vulnerable white heart of the page, but it was hardly *evidence*. To be sure of the significance of his map—to be sure that the convergence of waterways it seemed to show was unusual, anomalous, significant—he needed something to compare it to. He needed to venture further afield, to sample other districts of the city. The project far exceeded Arjun's meager resources.

He scraped together some notes and half-finished pages—just enough work to justify a visit to Holbach on the next clear dry day of winter. Arjun thrust the map into Holbach's hands and Holbach let his eyes politely and blankly drift over it, and said, "Yes, I see, if you'll excuse me..." Then Holbach glanced at the map again, suddenly attentive, and said, "Hmm." The Professor folded the map into the nearest drawer, and said that tomorrow he was meeting with the Countess, and the day after he had a lecture to give on certain improbable architectural survivals discovered in the reconstruction of Stross End, and the week after that he had an experiment to supervise that would take him north, and then east, to make comparative observations of the sunset rising behind the

Mountain, but the map was quite interesting, quite interesting, and he would give it more thought on his return.

Arjun went home in high spirits and worked vigorously on the Tuvar for a week. He translated fully half of the thick history of the Tuvar's agricultural practices, and the interminable controversy that arose when the Tuvar began purchasing and destroying local blighted property to turn streets into fields, and the riots that ensued. On the next clear dry day when Arjun was able to return to Holbach, he learned that the Professor had lost the map; had, in fact, forgotten ever seeing it. That night there was a burial in the graveyard outside Arjun's window for someone *snatched from us in the prime of her youth and beauty by such a terrible sickness,* and the muffled echo of the mourners' keening kept him awake long after they had all gone home.

Winter gripped the city. It rained more often than not and it was nearly always dark. Arjun let the Tuvar gather dust again, and began avidly reading the newspapers for reports of deaths.

He found the bigger, grander papers—the *Sentinel,* the *Era,* the *Commercial Intelligencer*—essentially useless for his purposes. They wrestled ponderously with the great issues of the city. The *Sentinel* and the *Era* were always full of stories about the wonderful progress of the reconstruction of Stross End. The *Commercial Intelligencer,* which was published somewhere in the north and available only rarely in the newsstands of Stammer Gate or Foyle's Ward, mused darkly and obsessively on the irresponsible menace of the Countess and her unholy *Thunderer.* They were above tallying the insignificant dead.

Fortunately, a dozen local rags did little else. Arjun found the *Stammerer* especially useful. Its editor had a fascination with the subject that rivaled Arjun's own, so that Arjun began to wonder if the man had shared his own vision of the thing that haunted the waterways—but Arjun's letters were never answered.

Arjun was interested in two classes of deaths: deaths (of any cause) in or near the water, or deaths (wherever located) from diseases similar to whatever claimed Norris—Black Lung, or Langshaw's

Disease, or the Shivering Greys, or other sicknesses of rot or damp or industry or poverty or desperation.

He kept two piles of clippings, on either side of his desk. Winter dragged on and the piles grew with unnerving speed. Foyle's Ward was full of students who seemed prone to falling, in the dark of the winter nights, into the canals on their drunken ways home; they accounted for a fair number of the dead. Black Lung claimed the elderly at an impressive rate. Three children disappeared; four the next week. The *Stammerer* lamented the plague of wild children in the streets, who were a danger to themselves and others, and deplored a recent rash of violence against the Houses of Correction. The next week, two children were found strangled in a pumphouse, and one more disappeared from a wealthy home in Foyle's Ward. In the same week, a barge disappeared en route between the Blake & Blake Brewery and Foyle's Ward, and the crew—father and son—were lost. After a while Arjun had to subdivide the pile of *deaths by the water* into *murders* and *drownings* and *other;* he could not decide how to subdivide *disease,* and that pile swelled enormously.

Was that normal for the time of year? Arjun had no way to be sure.

When Olympia first came to visit him—she'd happened to be passing on business—Arjun conceded that no, he had *not* been seen at Holbach's mansion lately. It seemed pointless to lie to her—her eyes were too sharp and clever—so he admitted that he had no work to show Holbach, and no particular prospect of producing anything in the immediate future.

She looked as if she was about to say something cutting and unkind, but thought better of it.

Anyway, he explained, his circumstances made it hard for him to come to the mansion at all. It was not only that he could only travel on dry days; he had to set out after the damp grey fog of morning had dissipated, but early enough that he could be sure of being back before dark. He had to take a circuitous route to avoid water. These were just some of the rules he'd developed as a defense against the monster; he wasn't sure that they *worked,* exactly, but he had nothing but instinct to guide him.

Olympia was dressed somewhat less outlandishly than usual, in a black winter cloak. She had brought with her a long-haired young man in an expensive fur coat, and introduced him as Mochai, a painter. As Arjun explained his situation, Mochai shook his head and consulted his pocketwatch. It appeared Mochai and Olympia were lovers, because when Arjun was finished, Mochai took Olympia's arm with an attitude of commanding familiarity, and said, "This poor fellow's mad. Why did you say you removed him from the hospital? We should leave him be." She pushed Mochai's hand away and told him to be quiet, and he rolled his eyes.

Olympia passed Mochai her cloak, under which she wore a dark velvet jacket, and leaned against the wall by the desk.

She said, "Arjun, I'm sorry. Have you spoken to Holbach about this? He'll tell you this doesn't make sense."

"He's explained his theories to me, yes. At great length."

"You see, whatever you may have felt or seen, the god isn't interested in *hunting* you. You care about it but it doesn't care about you. Imagine a mirror—"

"Let me tell you *my* theory."

She allowed him to interrupt her; she nodded slightly to say *Go on*.

"I won't argue with you about the normal operation of your city and its gods. You are all very clever and you have studied the matter more deeply than I. Of course. And you may think I am very simple, but we had our own god where I came from. There was only one, so we had nothing to compare it to, and perhaps we understood it less well than you understand yours. But we understood it well enough—until one day it surprised us."

"That's different. They come and go; they always have. Holbach always says he's half-historian."

"I think the Typhon is sick. Broken. I don't know what word to use. I think it is a process that has become corrupted."

"You've thought a lot about this."

"Of course. Will you understand if I say it makes me think of a piece of music, in which a theme is being worked out, developed,

elaborated upon, and one is still composing as one goes along, im-
provising it with every moment, if you can imagine that. Into that
piece of music is introduced an error, an imperfection in the theme.
An unexpected ugliness. One cannot ignore it; one cannot simply
begin again; one has to explore its implications. The imperfection
grows. Soon it threatens to swallow the music. One tries to work it
away but each correction only raises new imperfections. It defies all
your efforts to expunge it. Now you find yourself playing what *it*
demands of you, what *it* makes necessary. You are trapped. You cannot stop playing or the ugliness will be all that's left, but each moment you play causes you increasing pain. Wouldn't you call that
poisoned music your enemy?"

She scrutinized him with compassion and curiosity; she was not
persuaded. She said, "I'm not very musical."

"Shay poisoned the god. Shay broke it. Shay introduced an imperfection into it. When he stole a fragment of its power, and made
that fragment into a toy, a creature, a *pet*. For whatever kind of disgusting man might want to make something like that his play-
thing."

"Holbach has his doubts about that, now. Actually, he thinks
Shay was a fraud, that he tricked you. He told me not to tell you
this, because he still feels guilty about sending you there; but I
think it's better you hear it."

She put a hand on Arjun's arm. Behind her Mochai idly flicked
through the newspaper clippings. "He talked with Branken about
the heliotype, the machine you described. He's had people look into
it. It doesn't make any sense. Everything Shay said was only patter.
You have showmen and patter even out in the wilderness, don't
you?"

"Yes! I mean yes, I am not a fool, and no, it was quite real. This
is what *happened,* Olympia. Shay stole something from the god, and
changed it, molded it, made it into something *human*. Is it my fault
if that's impossible? The world is as it is. I was stupid enough to return that fragment to the god, and now the god is sick with it.
Poisoned with it. Full of imperfections. I felt that the moment
when it turned its eyes on me. I think I was the first thing it ever
saw, the first thing it ever *knew*. Now it knows how to hate. If I had

been torn away from perfection and made to see the world as people see it, I'd be full of hatred, too."

She looked at Arjun for a long time. Mochai, behind her, consulted his pocketwatch again, and sighed.

She asked, "Why don't you leave?"

"I'm sorry?"

"If you believe all this, why don't you leave the city?"

"I don't know."

"What happened to the Voice you came here to find?"

He realized that he had not thought about the Voice for weeks, not since he'd heard that echo of it in the music at Norris's gravesite. Olympia's eyes flashed—she'd scored a point.

"You're a great deal more charming when you talk about music," she said. "Instead of rivers and drowning and death."

"I imagine I am."

"It's a hard city, Arjun, life's easier if you're charming."

"I'm sure that's true. Olympia, I asked you if I could read Brindley's writings on the canals. You said you had to think about it."

She sighed, and stepped away from the desk. Mochai smoothly fastened her cloak around her shoulders.

"You're no danger," she said. "All right."

She stopped at the door. "Music that improvises as it goes along?"

"I only meant to illustrate a point."

"We *have* something like that. Something like that exists. One day if you have time you should go northwest up to Moricand and stop in the bars there. It might do you good."

She came round personally, two days later, to deliver the Brindley. She brought three slim volumes, wrapped in a red cloth. For obvious reasons, she said, she couldn't trust them to a messenger-boy. He had no idea what she meant.

Each volume was bound in white, and plainly printed, in a dense type that marched in blocks down the pages, crowded with wild enthusiasm around illustrations, diagrams, formulae, musical notation, and above all maps, maps, and more maps. The myriad subjects seemed to be organized by no principle Arjun could see; it was not alphabetical, or at least not in any alphabet he recognized. According to the stark white covers, he now possessed volumes three, nine, and thirty-one of the third edition of the *Atlas* of Nicolas Maine and company.

This time Olympia was accompanied by Hoxton, who impressed on Arjun, with a kind of genial menace, the importance of never being seen reading those volumes outside the flat; keeping them under wraps when visitors came; bringing them safely back to the mansion when he was done.

"I rarely go outside anyway," Arjun said, flipping through volume nine to find the bookmarks Olympia had placed at entries titled *Locks and Inclined Plane Engineering* and *Curiosities of the Canals of Our Forefathers,* both signed —*B.,* which Arjun took as standing for *Brindley.* "It rains too much," he explained.

"Get a cloak," Hoxton said.

"I had a cloak from the basement of Klozny & Klozny. It was stolen."

"Get a *decent* cloak," Hoxton said. "I get mine at Tito's, on Ashcroft Street."

"Well," Olympia said, "I hope this helps. I can't keep coming around here."

"Tell Tito I sent you."

Brindley's writings were no help at all.

Brindley had written in great and densely mathematical detail on the blasting of tunnels, the design of bridges, and the engineering of locks and planes; on the suitability of various kinds of soils and clays and bedrock, and what to do in the event that the area of the city through which one wished to drive a canal was one in which the earth below had long since been developed into sewers and cellars and catacombs; on towage and earthworks. Olympia had also marked Brindley's long, obscure analysis of the *Political Economics of Coal-Transportation,* which sat improbably between a wittily unkind entry on *Modern Melodrama* and a foul-mouthed tirade against *Corn*

Laws. Brindley's breezy little essay on *Curiosities of the Canals of Our Forefathers* appeared, for no particular reason Arjun could understand, in the annotations to a comprehensive map of the district of Grafton.

The technical entries were dry and incomprehensible and irrelevant. *Curiosities* seemed promising at first, but Brindley doggedly discussed only pleasant matters: boat-races, famous marriages on the pleasure-canals, the tremendous gentle swans that had supposedly existed in an age when it had been possible to engineer such creatures (which Brindley considered apocryphal but charming), the scattering of flowers on the waters in the summer in Abbagnano, *et cetera.* Brindley made no mention of sacrifice or death or tragedy. In fact Brindley's good cheer was so relentless that it became suspicious. There was something in it that seemed like nervous flattery. Slowly Arjun began to suspect that Brindley was deliberately concealing some horrible truth; that he was willfully refusing to name that dreadful Name, for fear of angering it. Brindley offered an aside on the failure of experiments, at the turn of the previous century, with steam-powered barges, and Arjun thought: *Of course. The god would not allow it.*

Brindley's entries cross-referenced other interesting discussions—notably *Rituals of the Old River,* and *Characteristic Diseases of the Bargemen*—but those seemed not to be contained in the volumes Olympia had given Arjun.

When she came around again, a few days later, on the way between urgent appointments, Arjun asked Olympia for those volumes and she promised *maybe.* She was still flushed with excitement after her court appearance of the morning, in which she had done something daring and brilliant that Arjun was unable to understand, but that had somehow resulted in the release from gaol of the scandalous advocate of free love, Mr. Brace-Bel; a triumph, apparently. She wanted to talk about Arjun's god. "Forget Shay. Forget the River. It's a big city. You have to learn to forget things." He told her that he remembered very little about it now. They talked instead about music, until Hoxton shouted up from the street to let Olympia know she was running late.

*   *   *

Arjun went back to Shutlow, again, to see Haycock, again.

It was an unnerving journey. Shutlow was close to the River, in the damp bend of the west bank; it lay in a depression where mist collected and stale water puddled in the streets. Arjun was able to face it only by leaving on an unusually clear afternoon, immediately after one of Olympia's visits. He had been able truthfully to tell Olympia that he had nearly a week's work to show for the past week. They had talked about music, again, and gods, and politics, which Arjun had not understood. His mood was good when he set out; by the time he reached Moore Street he felt nervous and hunted again, and he remembered: *It knows you were in the Cypress. It trailed you there. It took Norris there.*

Arjun paid a boy a quarter-rial to run down the street and ex-tract Haycock from the Cypress. The boy did not come back. Arjun did not panic—it would have been both irrational and pathetic to panic—but instead promised a grubby-faced girl a quarter-rial of her own *if* she came back with Haycock in tow. She came running back shouting, "The old lady Duffer says Haycock's at his stall in Seven Wheels that still counts you owe me my money you fucking owe me my money"—which Arjun thought fair.

He found Haycock at his stall in an empty and desolate part of Seven Wheels Market, in the shadow of one of the great stones, on what was turning into a drab and damp late-winter afternoon. Haycock's stall was heaped with moldering books, their paper yel-low, their covers fading to the shades of spoiled fruit.

"Holbach says he's worried about you," Haycock said.

"That's not important."

"Makes me look bad; that's not important?"

"I'm sorry. I have business for you." Before Haycock could say anything further, Arjun began his story. He told Haycock every-thing about his meeting with Shay, his vision in the canal-tunnel, his fears, his theories about the god's extraordinary condition. Haycock nodded and grunted, *huh, huh,* without great interest. Arjun tried to describe the dread; he said it was like drowning, it was like being held under by weeds, whenever one saw the face of the creature form out of the rain, or drift shifting in shapeless expressions of agony across the filthy surface of a puddle, whenever one felt, in the stink of the sewers and the stale water, the *pain* it was in, the *hate* it had . . .

"Then why aren't you dead already?" Haycock interrupted.

"I'm sorry?"

"If the god's hunting you, why aren't you dead already? If *I* wanted to kill you, I'd have bloody well done the job by now."

"It's not like that, Mr. Haycock. Part of it's poisoned by humanity, now; part of it is thousands of years old. Older than the city, maybe. What does it care if it waits a few months?"

Haycock grunted.

"And imagine how confused it must be, how upset it must be, how sick it must make it to be what it is now. To be *imperfect.*"

Haycock just shrugged. In fact Haycock's question had been one that Arjun had not considered, even for a moment, all winter long; his surprising facility in answering made him doubt his own words. He said quickly, "I will pay for books, Mr. Haycock, on the Typhon. Or I suppose on Shay, if there are any, or anyone doing Shay's business, whatever it was. Or whatever you think suitable. I have to go. It'll be dark soon."

He took a carriage back to Stammer Gate. The driver went too close to the water, but Arjun held his tongue. Night fell. The carriage passed briskly by a long lonely street to the left of the main thoroughfare, and down the brick terraces and railings and weeds of the street it was possible to see the edge of the River, and an unhealthy light playing across the heavy water, and by that light for an instant Arjun saw the tiny figures of a man and a child down by the water. Arjun said nothing, and felt terribly ashamed.

Three days later Haycock brought Arjun a sackful of books.

There was a nasty and sadistic fiction called *The Murders of Doctor MacLaglan,* in which a repellent man who lived in a narrow dark house whose unwashed windows opened over the river carried out a series of lovingly described murders, by strangling, or drowning, or poison, all at the command of a gurgling voice that rose up from the

cold water every night and called itself *Timon*. First MacLaglan murdered neighborhood street-children, and then his nieces, then a succession of prostitutes, then his own beautiful sister. He did it
joylessly, resolutely. One by one he brought the bodies down to the
water.

Arjun was unable to finish the book. It seemed inevitable that
either the protagonist would prosper without consequences for his
murders, or he would be devoured himself by the monster. Either
outcome would be unbearable to imagine. Arjun was not surprised
when Haycock told him that the book had been banned as blasphemous, and for the most part destroyed, and *that* was why Haycock's
expenses for the book were so great.

Along with *Doctor MacLaglan,* there were two histories of the
River. One alluded vaguely to the rituals of the Bargemen, back in
the hard old days, who would gather at midwinter in the tunnels
and draw lots to determine whose child would be offered to the
water that year, so that the Bargemen might be spared drowning or
sickness or loss of business. Another noted casually, as if it were
something everyone knew, that "of course, the first bridges had bodies in their foundations." Both referred in passing to the Typhon,
but there were a dozen other gods of the River and they dwelled on
those instead.

There was a short, poorly written *Memoir of the Life of a Bargeman.*
It began:

*I was born into a hard life, my mother said I came early in the Cut
under Tyn Wald and the lanterns had burned out and every bargeman knows how in the tunnels the day at the end is only a speck, it
gives no light, to see by. In the dark the horses panicked along the
narrow towpath when she cried out in her labor and my father, who
was slow sometimes she said because of the ague, tangled his foot in
the towropes and fell in, and though my uncles came back with poles
and lanterns to look for him he was never found. We say, another for
TYPHON's coils, when that happens, and that is how a Bargeman
goes, or by the ague. Father was taking coal from Unger to the Wald
for the heating of Baths, by contract to the HOLCROFT Combine,
who never paid a penny for the death of him because they said, the*

GOD willed it. So when I could first walk I had to become a Bargeman my own self.

The *Memoir*, too, had been banned, for injudicious remarks about the Holcroft Combine and its ultimate owner, the Gerent of Stross End.

Those four exhausted Arjun's budget; Haycock packed up the rest of his books with a shrug. As he was leaving, Haycock stopped to offer a range of charms and amulets against evil and drowning, purchased, he said, from secret but impeccable sources. Arjun bought two of them, which he could not afford to do. He spent the rest of the day wearing a bracelet of white feathers and a dull pewter ring with a paste gem and feeling increasingly ridiculous. The books answered none of his questions.

His purchases left him almost without money for food for the rest of the week, and so when Olympia came by three days later and suggested they go to a café, he was delighted to say yes. She had Hoxton take them to a snug and warm and smoky place full of students. Olympia drank heavily and cheerfully, and Arjun drank, too, until his head reeled. When Arjun wondered out loud what had happened to that painter, that "Mochai, was it?" she laughed and said, "We had a *disagreement*. No more Mochai!" and his spirits rose immensely. The students at the next table sang a drinking song that used part of the melody that was the Voice for its chorus. For the next two days Arjun's mood was good, and he was productive and happy, and noticed music again; on the third day it rained and the fear washed filthily back over him.

Winter dragged on. It seemed to Arjun that it lasted for an uncommonly long time, as if slowly gathering its strength; no one else seemed to find it unusual. Two more students drowned, an apparent suicide was found floating in the Calder Canal, and there was an outbreak of Black Lung in the Missionary Shelter at Hailie Circle.

TWENTY-SIX

Jack did not go back to Shutlow at once. It would have seemed like a waste of the gift he had been given. He set out wildly over the city, slicing great arcs across its map. The whole sky was his. He shared it with smoke and startled birds. Sometimes he saw the *Thunderer* on the horizon, but he kept his distance.

He decided to go *out,* as far as he could. He faced west and went forward. For every acre of city he put behind him, there was another ahead on the horizon. And as he moved away from the River and the Mountain, the effort required to keep his balance grew more exhausting. He gave it up around evening, afraid that if he kept going he would find his power failing in midair.

He came to rest on a flat roof in a part of the city where huge standing mirrors flashed at each other across the rooftops, and rested for a time. Then he came back in toward the River, navigating by the Mountain's great starless shadow. It seemed that he didn't need to sleep, as if flight took the place of sleep. He wondered several times if he was in fact dreaming.

At first he felt a strong urge to treat this gift reverently, to make it an act of worship, although he was not sure to whom or what, so he kept a solemn face and tried to think deep thoughts. He couldn't keep it up for long. He went up to Goshen Tor, and drifted among the high windows of the banks, scaring the pigeons off the ledges. He rapped on the windows, then fell laughing away when the clerks turned to look. He found a plush office at the building's peak, and knocked on the window and called, "Excuse me, sir, shine yer shoes,

sir? Sir? Buy the *Era,* sir!" A pale fat man in a brown suit gaped
at him; Jack stared wide-eyed and innocent back, then laughed
and fell back into the air. That sort of thing amused him all afternoon.

Since he was on the Tor, he drifted up to the temple of Tiber,
where he had hidden months ago, and sat for a while, thinking,
Catch me now, you bastards! But no one came for him.

He sat on a north-facing slope of cold tin. As the winter evening
darkened, a red light waxed on the horizon. The Pillar of Fire. The
god of his gaolers. It was always there, a faint glow on vision's edge
by which one could navigate at night, but he had never been there.
He ran to the edge of the roof with quick steps and threw himself
into the air, going north.

It was perhaps midnight, but it made no difference. Red, fluxing
light bathed everything, smoldered in the glass of all the windows,
sparked in the air. The tall bone-bleached buildings around the
Plaza were tortured into pillars and flutes and proud statues; they
strove for grandeur, but could not compete with the thing rising
from the center of the Plaza. But it was hard to look at that, so the
eye was always drawn back to the buildings. Their polished marble
reflected the flames.

The Fire poured endlessly up. It was as thick perhaps as the
arm-span of a half a dozen men, and taller than the tallest buildings.
Rigid but flowing. The Church taught that all those who died right
would be born again as flickers in the Fire, endlessly purified and
rarified. Maybe; who knew? It stung the eyes. It gave off much less
warmth than one would expect.

It was like an exclamation mark, or an admonishing finger. It
demanded attention. It had to *mean* something. But the flame curled
silently in on itself. The courthouses and prison-houses around it
captured its reflection and imposed meaning on it. Their stern facades spoke: it stood for *justice* and *punishment.*

Jack approached it on foot, through the crowd. He did not want
to draw attention to himself. There were priests all around, and
guards with rifles shouldered through the crowds. Irreverence would

not be tolerated. Not that it was likely to be offered, in that sacred place; the crowds drifting around the Fire in the un-night looked dazed with worship.

The crowd parted. A group of priests came through, followed by marshals, leading a man in chains. He was absurdly small and thin and old. His head was shaved and his beard hacked off. The crowd hissed at him. The lead priest clapped his hands and the crowd cleared a path. Jack stepped back, too.

The priests wore the ornate red and gold robes of the Church of Tiber. They led the prisoner up to a scaffold, slightly off the plaza's center, near to the Fire. The scaffold, and the men on it, cast long shadows across the stones.

Jack knew this ritual. His teachers had described it in detail and with relish. The Church would take men who were to be hanged. They did one a day, chosen at random from all the city's many prisons. They would bring them to the Fire to be ended, so that they could contemplate it in their last moments, and then, afterwards, be purified within it.

The marshals held back the crowd with bayonets. Jack got as close as he could. He was too late to hear the first part of the ritual, the denunciation of the man's crimes. Now the man was weeping, lamenting the sins and follies that had led him to the scaffold. He was reading from a script, of course. Jack knew the words. The priest raised the noose over the man's shaved head.

Jack started running before he knew he was going to do it. The marshal in front of him lowered his rifle and raised his hand, shouting. When Jack kept coming, the marshal lifted the gun again, but too late. Jack leaped up and over his head.

Two marshals stepped down to block the scaffold's steps. Jack rose up over the structure's side. Landing lightly, he grabbed the condemned man's arm. He stumbled. The man's weight was too much, scrawny as he was. For a moment they were in motion, and maybe if the man had not fought him they would have been airborne. But his bloodshot eyes went wide with fear, and he scrambled back and fell; Jack wanted to slap him. Someone grabbed Jack's arm from behind. Jack snapped his head back into bone and the hand released.

The condemned man tried to run out into the crowd, but a bullet tore at his hip, and he fell. Two marshals threw themselves on him and pinned his arms. A priest behind Jack was on his knees, clutching his bloody nose and moaning. Two more stood nervously around. Riflemen were cutting through the crowd.

The crowd yelled: "It's his son, come back to save him!" and "It's an accomplice! Stop him!"

Too late to do anything now; he had mistimed everything. Jack hurled himself up, arcing into the air, to gasps from the crowd. One woman screamed, "It's the Key Himself!"

A shot was fired. Jack turned himself toward the Fire, where they could not look and dared not shoot. He swerved around it at the last minute. It stung but did not warm his skin.

When he was far enough away, he turned himself back around and headed south, to Moore Street, with a new sense of purpose. He knew what the Thunderers could do and be.

It was a long journey, even for him, and he stopped often in the night and the day, pacing up and down on high roofs, gesturing and talking to himself, preparing his speech. He wanted to say: they were brought together by the Bird's casual gift of freedom, of the *will* to freedom. They were betraying it if they stopped where they fell, settling into petty crime, waiting to be arrested again, or going with the press-gangs, or . . . Only if they kept moving forward, sharing the gift, becoming greater and wilder, could they be worthy of the miracle. There was a whole city of prisons and workhouses, a city of chains to be broken. Now he had the power to do it. He could take them with him. They would be a dream of freedom. There was a final perpetual escape to be made. Those were the sort of things he wanted to say.

And yes, true, all right, his first attempt had not been a success, and perhaps he shouldn't mention it; but with an army behind him, a growing army . . . That could be their purpose. They could all be saved.

And so on: cobbling together a fervent harangue, out of half-remembered playhouse picaresques and rogue-ballads, and out of the prayers and prophecies beaten into him in the House—unhampered by knowledge of anything else in the world, and with the power, the gift, whispering inside his head and bearing up his feet.

He landed near the river, south of the Heath, and walked the rest of the way to the Black Moon with his hands in his pockets.

It was morning when he reached Moore Street. A couple of old men from the boardinghouses at the north end of the street were starting their dull days. Lagger was setting up his hurdy-gurdy on the corner, smoking a roll-up with his gnarled left hand. His bruises were healing.

Someone had torn the boards off the Moon's front windows, opening the interior to the morning. Its innards looked pale and raw, and very small and shabby. The garden gate was smashed off its hinges. There was no one visible in the exposed interior.

Jack ran around the back and into the empty bar. He ran upstairs, shouting, "Who's there? What happened?"

The upper floors were empty. Someone should have been there, always, whatever the time of day: he and Fiss had put a lot of effort into organizing them in shifts. "Fiss?" he called, banging the walls, his voice breaking. Their stuff was gone; their supplies, their reserves. All their small trophies.

He went up to the roof and looked down. There was no one around. In the corner of the garden was a heap of fresh ashes. He dropped down from the roof and poked through the cold ash. There were some scraps of unburned fabric in there: their blankets.

He walked around the front of the building again, and sat in the street, under the hanging sign. A few people looked at him, but he didn't care who saw him now: he could no longer be caught or held. But the others could. And he had not been there. Let them report him; *let* them try to catch him.

He was hungry, and there was only so long he could ignore it. Around noon he went back into the Black Moon. They'd had food there. Perhaps the watch had left it untouched.

As soon as he stepped back inside, the building felt different. Before it had felt naked and exposed; now it felt furtive. Someone was hiding. Someone had returned while he'd been out the front. He sensed it before his conscious mind registered the footsteps: a flutter of fleeing feet down the stairs, stopping like held breath as he came in. Down in the cellar.

In the kitchen, the trapdoor was open. Dark steps led down into the floor. Jack stepped down slowly.

A figure rushed out of the darkness at him, holding a knife over its head. Jack had all the time in the world to step calmly aside. He waited until the figure was past him, then seized it by the shoulder, and looked Fiss in his startled and dirty face.

It stank and it was hard to breathe in the unventilated cellar. Fiss had made a small fire there, in the corner, out of a broken crate. They sat side by side against the wall.

"I didn't know I was gone so long," Jack said.

"Only a few days."

"Something happened, Fiss."

"You don't have to apologize. You said you were going and you went. You weren't our keeper, and you couldn't have made a difference. It was never going to last forever, anyway."

"I'm not apologizing. Don't look at me like that: I *didn't* know I was gone so long. Something *did* happen, and I *could* have made a difference. We can make it right again."

Fiss shook his head and stared at his feet.

"So what happened here? How did *you* get away?"

"Day before yesterday. First thing in the morning, while it was still dark. Martin and Elsie were on lookout, I think. It was Elsie shook me awake, said there were men with rifles and lanterns coming. I woke Aiden, and we tried to get everyone out into the garden and over the fence, like last time, like that last time the watch came, but they were out there waiting, in the dark, taking us and dragging us away. So I got a couple of lads and tried to go back out the other way, and then I heard them ripping back the boards out the front, and smashing the door at the back. Though it wasn't even locked."

Fiss looked very thin in the fire's light. He had not eaten or really slept since this happened, Jack guessed. Still, he would have to be strong enough for what Jack needed. They would have to act quickly, and there was no time to rest.

"I got out on the roof—I panicked, Jack, there was nothing I could do. Namdi wanted us to fight, but how were we supposed to fight? They had swords and guns. So I got out on the roof and jumped for it over to the pawnshop. Beth was with me, but she couldn't jump in that skirt. Aiden missed the jump. I made it. I made it out of the street. They had men outside, Jack, they were *mad* to catch us, they could have done it anytime they liked, anytime we made them angry enough to take the trouble."

"Did anyone else get away?"

"I don't know. I don't think so."

"Was anyone hurt?"

"Aiden fell. I saw someone hit on the head. I don't know."

"Whose men was it?"

"The Countess. I think. Yes, the Countess."

"So, it's only been a day. No one will have been moved. They'll still be in the Countess's watchhouse, here in Shutlow."

"I think so."

Jack grew excited. He felt much less sympathy for the others than he thought he probably should. He knew they must be scared, or hurt, and that Fiss was distraught and despairing, but he knew he could make it all right again; no, *better*. He said, "I had a speech prepared to convince you. I wasn't sure how it was going to go. I think it might have been hard to make everyone understand. Now I don't need it. You're going to *have* to do it, and like it. We'll start with ourselves. Sorry, Fiss—don't look at me like that. I'm just excited. Come on up, then. Follow me. I have something to show you."

The Countess's Shutlow watchhouse was a dull, three-story box of ivied stone, flat-roofed and not quite square in shape.

It was one of many. Mass How's Parliament regarded Shutlow as part of its dominion, and maintained a watchhouse in Acker Street. Chairman Cimenti wanted it to be known that he was generously concerned to help keep Shutlow's peace, and although of course he did not claim *authority,* by any means, he sponsored a civilian force based in Seven Wheels Market. A half-dozen other Estates kept their men around somewhere or other.

The Countess's watchhouse was on Deacon Street. Two guards stood out the front. In other parts of the city—in Fourth Ward, in Garhide, in Ar-Mouth—it was not uncommon for riots to strike the gaols, whenever some criminal managed to win the mob's affection; but there was no danger of that sort of thing in Shutlow, where the locals had never easily been stirred into action. The gate-guards were really only there for show.

Both men jumped as a tile shattered into red dust on the stones in front of their feet. They looked up, and then ducked, shielding their eyes with their arms, as a second tile came plummeting toward them. It broke over one man's mailed back, dropping him to his knees. A third hit his shoulder and broke sharply, buckling the mail and piercing the flesh. His colleague scrambled crabwise through the door, shouting, "There's some bastard up on the roof throwing things! Hinton's hurt!"

Jack dropped fast, scattering the rest of the tiles as he landed by the gate. He had been far above the roof: far enough, he had guessed, that the dropped tiles would incapacitate but not kill. He felt a little sick to see the mess he had made of the watchman's shoulder. Blood welled between the broken chain links; the arm hung at a bad angle; bone ground against tile as the man stood, screaming and bellowing. It was all much less clean than Jack had imagined. Next time, he would do better.

He made himself unsentimental, and grabbed the rifle in both hands and placed a foot on the man's back, and pulled, so that the rifle's strap snapped. The man screamed again. Jack reached for the bandolier. Holding the weapon, the charges, and the bullet-bag, he leaped into flight across the street.

Down the street, people were poking their heads from their windows. This was not Fourth Ward, where people knew to keep their heads down when they heard screaming; this was Shutlow, shabby and damp but *quiet,* where people believed they were not the sort of people to whom violence happened. *They* screamed, too, when they saw Jack leap, like an actor lifted aloft by wires and pulleys, but climbing much higher, and, impossibly, out there under the naked sky.

Jack landed on the high flat roof of a warehouse on the opposite side of the street. Fiss was there, watching. "Here," Jack said, handing him the rifle and the bandolier.

Jack looked at Fiss's tired, sunken eyes. "Remember: you don't have to hit anyone. Just fire as fast as you can, and make them afraid. Don't get shot yourself." Impulsively, Jack hugged him, then kicked himself off the roof again.

As Jack flew back over, a group of watchmen burst out into the street, spreading out, angling their rifles into the air, scanning the skyline. There were five of them. One picked up the wounded man and helped him indoors. Two more ran out onto the roof, truncheons ready. A woman leaning out of the window of the pub three doors down called out, "He's in the air! He's in the air!" The watchmen paid her no attention.

A shot rang out across the open street, breaking the glass in the watchhouse window. Fiss stood out against the sky on the roof opposite, reloading his rifle. The watchmen pointed and fired in his direction, but he ducked behind the parapet. He rose up again to fire and they scrambled for cover.

Jack came around the building's side where a second-floor window stood ajar. He pulled the window open and slipped through into someone's office. He ran out the door and down the stairs.

There was a hall downstairs, with weapons along the walls: swords and rifles and spears. A kitchen opened off the hall, and inside it, the wounded watchman lay on the table, moaning. There was a lot of blood on the floor. Another man, the one who had dragged him inside, was trying gingerly to remove his armor.

The wounded man leaned up on his good arm as Jack came in, pointing at the intruder and yelling hoarsely in alarm. The other watchman picked up his club and came running for Jack. Jack sidestepped him and kicked the back of his leg. The watchman fell to one knee, then got back up and lunged again. He was huge, but much, much slower than Jack, who jumped away over the man's head and pushed him in the back, sending him sprawling.

The wounded man was leaning off the table, stretching for a

cleaver on the counter. Jack kicked the table; the wounded man's weight unbalanced it and it fell. The man rolled into a corner, holding his arm and yelling. He did not try to get up again.

Jack drew his beautiful stolen knife and held it under the other man's chin till he froze, and spat, "The cells. The cells and the keys to the cells. Now."

The man lifted shaking arms over his head and slowly stood, and walked cautiously backward to the hall, and led Jack down the stairs into the cellar. Jack followed, the knife at the man's throat. He felt all the man's fight leave him.

A fetid tunnel led away from the cellar. There were cells all along it. Jack had the watchman take the keys and go down it, opening the cells. The first one contained an ancient-looking woman, a drunk probably, or a whore (*Gods help her if she is,* Jack thought), asleep on the straw. The next contained several of the Thunderers; Jack saw Turyk, the carpenter's apprentice; Een, the little thief from the docks.

"Jack! Bloody *Fire,* Jack!"

"Just stand together, out in the corridor. Don't move until I tell you to. Be quick."

When all the cells were open, there was a group of maybe a dozen boys standing in the tunnel. They were not all there—and no girls at all, for that matter—but there was no time to count. No Aiden, no Namdi. "Where are the others?" he asked, and a babble of voices told him that they had been taken, the night before, processed to this workhouse or that. "We'll find them later, then," he said. "That's enough for now."

When they were ready, Jack snatched the rifle off his hostage's back and handed it to Turyk. They went up into the hall, where Jack said, "Take a moment. Arm yourselves. Knives, guns, all you can carry. Bullets. No pikes or anything stupid."

Two watchmen peeked around the door to see a thicket of brandished rifles, and dodged back out onto the street. Jack followed, leading his hostage before him, arms up. Outside, he saw the two watchmen in the street. Three more (*where did the fifth man come from?*) had made it across the street, braving Fiss's fire, and were battering down the door of the warehouse.

Jack grabbed Turyk and said, "Go," pushing him in one direction, and Martin in the other. In each boy's ear, he whispered the name of a different market in Fourth Ward. They ran, the group splitting up to follow one or the other. Jack stood in the door, still holding the knife to his hostage's throat. The watchmen looked at the escaping children, and at Jack and his hostage. Jack stepped back into the building, and they made their decision and chased him. In the hall, he dragged the watchman halfway up the stairs and then shoved him to his knees. He leaned to whisper in his ear, "Soon, there will be more of us than you can count."

Then the others came in and pointed their rifles, but Jack was already running up and around the stairs and onto the next floor, where he ran to the window and threw himself out. And after that, it was easy to fly across to the roof where Fiss waited and lift him away before the watchmen could break down the door. It was all easy, so far.

Almost all of them made it to one of the rendezvous places Jack had named. Only one boy was unaccounted for. A recent recruit, by the name of Will. No one knew when he had fallen behind. "There's nothing to be done about it now," Jack said, after they had waited as long as they dared, hanging around the waste-heaps at the corners of the market. "If he's still free, maybe he'll find us. If they took him, we'll find him soon enough."

That left an even dozen. They were tired and frightened. Two had been beaten, badly, by the guards. One had a swollen eye; another was nursing a twisted shoulder and a useless arm. Jack's guilt over the man he had injured burned violently away.

Fiss was no help: silent and withdrawn and weak. He had not eaten or slept in too many nights. The diversion back at the watchhouse had taken the last of his strength. With Fiss in that state, Jack had to organize the boys himself. Fortunately, they were tired and scared, easy to lead. He was so full of plans and excitement that he could barely remember their names.

"It's not safe to go back to Shutlow," Jack said. No one was inclined to argue. So he chose a direction at random, as he had done before and always, he thought, with good luck, and led them west across Fourth Ward. "Don't steal anything, don't touch anything, don't *look* at anything. Keep to the shadows, keep your heads down. We leave no trail."

They were all very hungry. It was torture to stand in the markets, even the sparse, stale markets of Fourth Ward, and touch nothing. "There's food for us when we get where we're going," he said, although it was a lie.

He grabbed a boy called Rauf and shook his arm. "Remember how you were marching up and down, playing at soldiers for the Countess? I told you to stop? You're a soldier *now*, Rauf, and I'm telling you, *march*. Show us what you can take."

They were not such an odd sight in the streets of the Ward. Just another dog-pack of ragged children, scrabbling through the refuse. They slipped through the backstreets, the ditches cut in the sprawling mess, scrambling over the heaps of filth swept up by the sides of the road. They kept their hands in their pockets, if they had them, and stayed together, like obedient schoolchildren shuffling from one schoolroom to another.

Jack went ahead, scouting the way. He remained grounded, not wanting to make himself conspicuous, but his feet tingled with pent-up excitement, and he broke constantly into a run.

There were no special patrols, no armies of watch combing the city for the escapees. Perhaps none of the men in the watchhouse had dared confess their humiliation to their superiors. Or maybe the patrols *were* on their way, but just not organized yet. He urged the lads to move faster.

No more press-gangs in the street, either, he noticed. Did that mean there was going to be peace, or did it mean that the Countess had all the men she needed for war?

He led them by a circuitous route. He didn't know the Ward very well, and they were going further west than he had ever been. He tried to navigate by the Mountain, but it was often obscured by the blighted buildings, and he got off course. He didn't admit that he was sometimes lost. And he didn't talk about his plans for them; it was too early.

Night fell and they were still crossing Fourth Ward. A light

snow began to fall, slowly making the shoulders and backs of their
jackets sodden and heavy. He wouldn't let them sleep. There was
nowhere for a dozen boys to sleep, anyway. Local gangs and tribes
were watching them out of the darkness, out of blank windows and
holes in crumbling walls.

No one attacked them. Anyone who tried would have had a terrible surprise. They had not left the spoils of the watchhouse behind. They carried rifles and swords, wrapped in rags taken from the
waste-heaps at the edge of the market. There were pistols and
knives under their jackets. Their pockets were full of powder and
bullets. They had the makings of an army now.

In the night, they passed through rag-hung courtyards under a
great wall of concrete towerblocks. Snaking tunnels in the concrete
opened onto deeper plazas. Jack scouted ahead, leaving Fiss in
charge—and, on a second look at Fiss's grey face, Turyk, too. And
he hid behind a pile of broken bricks and looked ahead, down a tunnel into the deepest clearing, where a parade was passing, bearing
torches and drums. Whirling women danced at the van. There was
drumming deep in the earth. Maned men at the back came on all
fours. A dreadful red giant stamped joyfully in their midst. Lights
sparked in all the windows. Jack dug his dirty nails into his palms
so that he would not join the dance. In the morning, he was not sure
that it was not a dream.

They stopped at the end of the night, on the debatable border between the Ward and Agdon Deep. "That's far enough," Jack said.

"We're into the Combine's territory now," Turyk agreed. "The
Countess won't extend her forces this far across the Ward. Not for
the likes of us. She'd be too exposed."

Jack looked at Turyk with surprise. "That's right," he said. At
least, it *sounded* right.

They had found an abandoned stretch of canal. Its water had
been diverted elsewhere, and its stones were dry. A ramshackle mess
of empty boathouses stood by the water, their bricks and timbers

not yet altogether stripped and carted away. There was a wide expanse of muddy ground all around them, crept over by growths of scrub and weed. The steel forges of Agdon sounded distantly down the hill. It was empty, lonely space: if they hid in the boathouses, they would see enemies approaching but would not themselves be seen coming and going. They began again.

Food was the first priority. Across the mudflat, and a short walk through unfamiliar streets into Agdon, there was a great metal barn where the overseers of the forges doled out bread and beer to the workers. Jack's boys knew how to do this very well by now, and came away with enough for all, with no alarm raised. They ate and drank and slept on the dirt for almost a day, even Jack.

For a week, Jack let them get stronger. Agdon Deep was not rich—it made no luxuries and consumed none, and the wealth its factories earned went elsewhere—but it made useful goods, and its warehouses were full. It brought in simple food in bulk for its workers. Everything the Thunderers needed was there to be taken.

He still didn't discuss his plans for them. Safest to take one step at a time. They still had to rescue Aiden, and Beth, and the others; that would force them along the path he wanted.

He was thinner now than he had been when he escaped from Barbotin. His limbs seemed lighter, and his face sharper. His eyes were brighter. Sometimes when he caught his reflection in windows, in water, there was a frightening shine in his eyes that brought him up short; he smiled brilliantly and confirmed to himself that he was in fact *beautiful,* and increasingly so, with every day of waiting, every day of holding his vision fluttering inside.

One morning, when he couldn't wait any longer, he came into the room where they sat on the dirt floor, playing with stolen cards, and said, "Stop that, and look at me. It's all true. What you thought I could do. Look." He stepped forward and up, into the rafters above them, and smiled down. They were stunned, then they started to cheer: *Silk! Silk! Jack bloody Silk!* When they were done, he settled to earth again, and said, "That's how I got you out. That's how we're going back for them. I need you all with me. To search around, spy for our missing brothers; to be

my lookouts; to take these"—hefting a rifle—"and be my army, if
need be."

Turyk, nervously, said, "That's mad, Jack. It's great, but it's
mad. We were lucky to get away once. It's good, what you did for
us. But they'll kill us if we try it again."

"You'd leave them behind? You're free, so you'll take it for yourself and leave behind those who took you in?"

Turyk looked around for support, saying, "We just want to be
left alone, find something to eat. What's wrong with that?"

Martin started to speak, but Jack cut him off. "You can go then.
Be alone. Get out of here. This time I mean it. Get *out*."

Jack would accept no apology. This was important. After a few
moments, Fiss stepped forward to say, "Like Jack says, Turyk. Get
out. Martin, bring him some food, and a blanket and a knife, to take
with him. Then that's it."

The rest were his.

Beth was back in Ma Fossett's, the same place she had escaped from
before. They'd added bars to the lower windows since she last got
out, and wire around the outer fence, but they hadn't troubled to
bar the upper windows.

Jack came to the high window of her dormitory at night and
called for her, waking a roomful of girls who started to shriek, "It's
a ghost! A vampire!" They banged on the room's bolted door.

Beth came slowly to the window through the panicking flock,
in her grey nightshirt, rubbing her eyes. "Are you real?"

"Of course."

She looked down, beneath his hanging feet, and said, "You can
fly. Like the little ones always thought you could."

"Yes."

"Well, *that's* a bit of news."

"The noise will bring guards. Take my hand."

She leaned out the window and looked down. They were on the
fifth floor; the bushes below were barely visible.

"We'll come back for everyone else later. I just need you for now.

If you come with me alone, just you, it'll be like you were never here. I don't want to raise any alarms. Yet."

"What are you talking about?"

"Just take my hand."

There was the sound of someone unlocking the door, from the outside, shouting, "Quiet, you stupid girls! Be quiet!" Closing her eyes, Beth took Jack's hand, and stepped out of the window.

They hit Barbotin a few days later. It was easy. The House was utterly unprepared for anything like this. Jack brought a group of them up onto the roof, where they waited with pistols, to ambush the laundry party when they unlocked the iron door and emerged into the light. The workhouse boys dropped their baskets and ducked for cover, but the invaders were not there for them.

Mr. Tar and Mr. Renfrew were with the laundry detail. They were overwhelmed at once. The Masters carried knuckledusters, and vicious barbed clubs, but no guns. They were used to beating down angry, frightened, underfed boys; they had never faced anything like this. Jack would have no killing—but he took their keys, and shot both men in the leg, to make sure they couldn't follow him, and also for the sake of his feelings.

Carswell, who had been his friend when they were both prisoners, was still with the laundry detail. Jack clapped the stunned boy on the shoulder and gave him a pistol, telling him, "You're with us now." Then they all went down into the shadows.

He had heard that the Masters had a locked case of guns on the ground floor, where no boy was ever allowed to tread. But the Masters didn't even try to arm themselves; when they heard what was coming through the House's dark corridors, gaining numbers as it went, methodical and angry, inflicting measured repayment in blood, they ran, not stopping to lock the doors behind them. A great flood of pale youths followed, bursting out through the last, narrow door onto the wasteground around the House.

Outside, more of the Thunderers waited, and tried to channel the flood, but most of the escapees vanished at once into the streets, like rats going to ground, like ghosts. "That's all right," Jack said. "We gave them their chance."

A few—the ones Jack knew were reliable—came with them across the Ward, back to the boathouse, where Jack explained that they could stay, so long as they helped with the next job, and the next.

TWENTY-SEVEN

It was a pleasant day for walking, at last, after months of winter; cool but bright and clear. On the way to Holbach's house, Arjun stopped in a café in Foyle's Ward for lunch. He sat under a linden tree, checking over his notes.

A group of young men at the table behind him talked politics and war. Was the Gerent alive or dead? There had been no further violence for more than two months. Would the *Thunderer* strike again, or had the Countess made her point? It was all well-worn ground, discussed to death all over the city for months. They were very loud, though, perhaps drunk too early in the day. Unwisely loud for such a conversation; for all they knew, Arjun might have been a spy for the Countess.

It was best not to be too close to people like that. You never knew. He paid the bill and headed around to Fallon Circle.

An excellent start," Holbach said. "This will be very helpful. Now, was there anything of any interest in Sethre's *Daybook*?"

"Nothing of interest to you, I don't think," Arjun said. "Largely a matter of disputes over parish politics. Sethre felt strongly about simony. I doubt that you do."

They sat in Holbach's study, drinking coffee and discussing Arjun's work. The pile of books on and around the table was impossible—the city in microcosm, full of precarious towers and shadowed valleys; one day it might grow to swallow the real city. Piles of neglected correspondence sat on the outskirts like ghost towns. Holbach's project had wind in its sails.

The soldiers were gone now, leaving Holbach, to his great relief, to take his own chances. Their place had been taken by an army of scholars. The economist Dr. Kamminer had marked out a permanent ghetto within the book-city for his own texts. Dr. Branken kept a laboratory in Holbach's attic, a tangle of glass and mirror and copper tubing that to Arjun's eye looked like an exploded pipe organ. The playwright Liancourt seemed to live in the kitchen. Two jurists sat in the library, shouting at each other about the nature and purposes of the right of property.

These were formal men, but in Holbach's house, they left their wigs by the side of their chairs and threw aside their coats. They sat around the fire scribbling in their dingy undershirts. Paper flew back and forth between them like birds flocking from tree to tree, spire to spire.

Arjun knew that he was only a small part of Holbach's project. The expertise he had acquired was a narrow, peculiar one; a small immigrant population, centuries gone and forgotten. A single street in Holbach's city of scholarship. Still, once a week or so, Holbach found time to hold these meetings, where they came back again and again to the Black Bull, and to the Tuvar's theories about their vanished god.

"Heirophant Teitu's *Daybook,* on the other hand, was a real find. Haycock did well." Arjun passed a pile of papers across the table. He fumbled in his jacket pockets, produced a sheaf of scribbled notes. "I've begun to translate. Teitu had the misfortune to live in the last days of the Bull."

"Distressing for him, but it serves us very nicely."

Arjun described the book. Teitu had been one of the Tuvar's Hierophants in the community's dying days, when the Bull had appeared less and less often, and finally stopped coming altogether. It had been painful for Arjun to read.

A man Arjun had never seen before came into the study and rummaged in the books. Holbach introduced him. The man was an architect, apparently, and an engineer, and very famous. Arjun failed to catch his name.

He found the buzz in Holbach's house overwhelming after the silence and solitude of his scholar's room in Stammer Gate. People grabbed him as he passed and lectured passionately on their research; everyone expected him to be an expert on everything, fascinated by everything. In the little anteroom to Holbach's study, Branken had talked to him at length about the structure of the human eye (lenses, apparently, not unlike a telescope). In the hall downstairs, Arjun had asked Liancourt about the progress of his latest play, and was subjected to a bitter analysis of the travails of theatrical fund-raising. And not just scholars: three painters sat in the billiards room, drinking Holbach's wine and smoking his cigars. Holbach was too busy to add to his collection, but his hospitality was still open. "When is the big man going to be *done* with all this, eh?" they'd asked Arjun, who'd shrugged and passed by.

The explorers and the scholars met in corners, and whispered urgently to one another. They spoke in hints and codes and raised eyebrows and sly, electric smiles. They gathered upstairs, in the ballroom, where something was being built, something to which Arjun was not privy. He didn't ask.

And young men, students, or struggling artists, Arjun's age, came to the house from distant reaches of the city, bringing charts and facts back with them, staying a few days before they were dispatched again. Explorers. Mapmakers. They came back with surveyor's theodolites slung over their backs, the way a soldier might wear a rifle or a broadsword. Sometimes they wore those, too; they were often called on to visit dangerous places.

The house celebrated when an expedition returned from the slums of Dreshkel, late but unscathed. There was grave concern when an expedition to the Mountain failed to return on time. The house's occupants slowly accepted that it would not return at all. "No one's yet gone that close to the Mountain and come back," Arjun had heard the historian Rothermere saying, leaning over the billiard-table, lining up his shot; his coat was the same rich green as the felt. "I hear the streets fold in on you, up there, and you end up lost in strange places. You can meet mirror-selves, strange new versions of yourself in foreign streets, and you get confused or stolen, and *never* come back. It's reckless. I'm sorry, but it is."

"What are we here for," his opponent had replied, "if not to be reckless?"

"Don't see you sending *yourself* out," Rothermere said, unthinkingly, and the mood froze; but Arjun was on his way out of the room anyway.

Holbach observed that the coffeepot was empty, and rang the bell to summon his housekeeper. He filled the pause, as he often did, with praise for Arjun's efforts. It was his instinct, Arjun thought, to ingratiate. "Again, I'm amazed by your facility, the mastery you display of this really rather alien culture. Remarkable progress. I think we've learned a lot of good stuff."

"If it comes naturally, it's because I sympathize with their search for the Bull. They are not so alien to me."

"Oh? How goes your own search? Are you still searching?"

"I don't know. My . . . experience with the Typhon wounded me. I don't know. I am wary of throwing myself back into my search. Of being *possessed* again. But I can't forget the Voice. I want to find It, to hear It, to know what It is. Does that make sense?"

"By the standards of the things people say about their gods, yes. I promised I would help you, didn't I? Of course I did. And I will, as soon as this"—he waved a hand to indicate the piles of paper and the scholarly occupation of his house—"is done with again for a time. Gods, and this!" He strode to the window and took a pile of broadsheets off the sill; he clutched them to his head in a pantomime of horror. "She demands I do something about this. Reports of some flying child breaking open gaols and workhouses, all over the city. Yes, flying."

"Is that possible?"

"Does it sound *probable?*"

"A great many things in this city strike me as improbable."

"Well, I haven't looked into it yet. I'm sure it's nonsense. Certainly there've been riots, escapes, as there always are, but the more colorful details: *no*. The papers are always full of that sort of nonsense. Well, no, no"—he rolled a paper thoughtfully into a cone as he spoke—"I shouldn't say *nonsense*. It's an expression of the city's deep feelings. This stuff *rises* up. Childlike dreams of freedom, of insurrection. Notice that they cast this ridiculous winged savior as a child?"

He slumped in the green leather of his chair. "And gods know that I sympathize. If you knew how caged one feels as a scholar in this city, Arjun. How many lords and ladies and jumped-up little *councils* breathe down your neck, checking your every word for heresy or dissent, itching to give you a spell in the Rose, or to clip your ears or clap you in the stocks. We have too many gods, too many lords; more laws than people. If you stay here, Arjun, as a young man of some promise, you too may find your head high enough one day to fear for your neck. Sometimes one just wants to, oh, *knock* it all down."

He swung a thick arm across the table for emphasis, and visited catastrophe upon a parish of the book-city. He cleared the rubble sheepishly, with Arjun's help.

Every so often, Arjun reminded Holbach of his promise. Arjun's wounds were healing. He had not forgotten the Voice; he *could* not. The man he was, was made of its echoes. The bitterness and doubt the Typhon had inflicted on him, down in the tunnels, were still there, discords that might never be resolved, but it made no difference. If he gave up the search, he would be nothing; there would be nothing to fill him. Still, for the time being, he was content to help Holbach, occasionally reminding the Professor that he would one day have to help Arjun in return. He didn't delude himself: he was stalling, treading water, afraid to begin again, to fail again. But it was not unpleasant, in the meantime.

Haycock vanished one day. Arjun didn't notice until Olympia mentioned it, as they sat outside a café, enjoying the shaft of cool sunlight that came through the trees. "He came to the mansion a few days ago. I tried to give him Holbach's orders for the month, and he made some *remarkably* improper suggestions. Apparently half the people in his lodgings are dead of the lung-rot, and he's going to go to ground somewhere in the north."

Lung-rot, again. Arjun hadn't known; he hadn't been back to the Cypress in weeks. He went there that afternoon, to find the place almost empty. Defour remained in her place; he understood now that it would insult her to ask why. Heady had gone, too, she said, and the lodger who had taken Arjun's room had died.

"Haycock left this for you," Defour said, removing a heavy old book from the desk drawer in her office. "Excuse *me,* young man! I didn't hold this for you for free, you know."

They haggled. Eventually, grudgingly, she let go.

Arjun spent the afternoon visiting graves all around the outer precincts of the Cere House. Having made the observance for Norris, he felt he had to do it for them all; he had a fine sense of justice.

Shutlow felt dark and close. Winter would not let it go. He remembered how, in the hills, they had feared the wolves in winter; there was that sense of something prowling, hungry and mad, around the edge of sight; a sense of time held back, of violence deferred. People looked tense and wary. He pulled his collar up, shoved his hands in his pockets, and got out.

The book Haycock had left behind was called *Thinkers of Our Age: Thirty-Five Collected Profiles in Invention.* What Age, exactly? It was hard to say. The date of publication was not in any form Arjun recognized, which generally meant—he had learned—that the book was either exceedingly old or from very far away. It was made of a finely cut glossy paper, and was so unblemished it might have been printed yesterday. Back in his flat, Arjun flicked quickly through it, and recognized none of the names of people or places anywhere in its pages. He began to think that Defour had made a mistake, had given him the wrong book, until he came to the splendid full-page picture—it seemed too clear, too precise, too sharply colorful to be an ordinary illustration—of *The Enigmatic Mr. Cuttle, Welcoming Us to His Laboratory.*

The man in the picture, wearing a smart grey suit, smiling wryly, gesturing with a many-ringed hand at a shadowy background of cages and contraptions and clockfaces and greasy lights, was—unquestionably—Shay.

The text accompanying the picture was both nonsensical and

deeply disturbing. It was made even more confusing by the fact that someone—Haycock?—had neatly sliced out a half-dozen pages.

Arjun ran down to the street and took the first carriage he could find back to the Cypress. He caught Defour on her way out the door, dressed in her finest shawl, attempting to carry a folding chair under one arm and an umbrella under the other.

"Where did he go? Where did Haycock go?"

"Young man," she snapped, "am I not already *quite* late enough?"

"Please. Anything. I must find him."

"Hmm. Come with me and I'll see what I remember. You can carry the chair. Yes, *and* the umbrella."

They walked together down Moore Street, down Millward, down Stevenson, and came to a grassy hill overlooking the River. A shabby little patch of slum huddled on the banks below.

It was late in the evening, and there was already a crowd spread out waiting on the grass of the hill.

Defour said, "You made us late!" Then she retrieved and unfolded her chair. "All the good spots are gone." She made Arjun erect the umbrella over her chair: "They say there's going to be ash and bits blowing." Finally she admitted, grudgingly, that she did not in fact have the faintest idea where Haycock was.

Arjun waited anyway, and watched, with the crowd, as the *Thunderer* appeared from behind the tall blocks across the River, and came to hang over the ugly little sprawl on the riverbanks. "Black Lung," Defour explained. "Another outbreak in the Bargeman's Mission down there. About time they did something about it. *Burn* it out. Oh, the new ideas people have these days! It's not *all* bad, is it?"

Down at the foot of the hill, another crowd, a small sad little group, stood in the shadow of the condemned buildings and waved tiny illegible signs.

Apparently the *Thunderer* had arrived earlier than the appointed hour. There was some confusing delay as it lowered itself with weightless ease to the roof of the tallest building, then rose again, up and up, until it was well clear; and then it rained down fire. There was a tremendous crash and roar as one by one the buildings collapsed into the haze of smoke and flame. Red light shimmered out over the water. The crowd on the hill clapped and cheered and stamped their feet, and Arjun cheered, too: *Take that, monster!* He went downhill caught up in the embrace of the crowd, and it seemed there was nothing at all frightening or mysterious in the busy spring night.

TWENTY-EIGHT

AT HOME WITH THE ENIGMATIC MR. CUTTLE

In the old days we called them Gods—and if your grandparents are like mine, then I suppose we all know someone who still does. (I kid, I kid, Granddad!) And yet today we hardly think about them, do we? I know I never did until I met the famous—some might say notorious!—Mr. Cuttle, who is surely one of the most intriguing figures to be profiled here.

I went to see him in his laboratory, on a sunny day in Slinndo Hill. The flowers were in heat and the air was warm and thick with spores. He says he doesn't mind them, and he laughed openly at my mask—if you ask him to explain things like that, he'll just say, "You should see some of the places I've been! Some of the things I've had to breathe! It toughens the lungs." Or something similarly enigmatic. But I get ahead of myself!

Perhaps you wouldn't imagine him working in Slinndo Hill—too everyday, too pretty-pretty, simply too middle-management, my dear! But the man himself is just as you might expect. He's small, but seems, whenever he speaks, to fill the room. His movements are sharp and precise. There is always a smile on his face, as if he's already had this conversation, and it amuses him that you're too slow to think of anything new to say.

He ushered me into his shadowy chambers with a click of his fingers. In all the years I've been profiling for the *Times,* I don't think I've been greeted in that way, and I don't think I would stand for it from any politician, or actor, or any ordinary businessman. (So be warned!)

But of course the usual rules hardly apply to Mr. Cuttle—as he took every opportunity to remind me. Is there a richer man in the city today? If there is, I don't know who it is! Is there anything in Ararat that hasn't been transformed—for better or worse—since that day he turned up, briefcase in hand, a total stranger, in the lobby of the Bishop Hotel and presented himself to Lord Monboddo?

"Was it difficult," I ask him, "doing business with Lord Monboddo? Was it frightening?" His only answer is a barking laugh—one might almost think it contemptuous. And that sets all the birds and rats and monkeys in all of the cages barking, and howling, and laughing, and muttering the little scraps of nonsense that are all the words, Mr. Cuttle says, that they know.

"They're not finished yet," he explains.

And the noise sets the fields of those unique and subtle energies, the energies that have transformed our city, into shimmering and swaying, waxing and waning, flickering and sparking.

Can I describe the sensation—the cavalcade of sensations—that this awakes? I don't know that I can, honestly.

And Mr. Cuttle grins, with the light playing over his glasses and his white hair, and he says, "So let's talk about them, then. You people used to call them *Gods.*"

Mr. Cuttle's laboratory is a hard thing to describe. The clutter, the strangeness—the sense that the whole thing is a display, like a storefront, and the real secrets are hidden. There's a kind of showmanship even in the cages themselves, which are . . .

✵　✵　✵

. . . truly learned anything? It's hard to say. Mr. Cuttle is a baffling and extraordinary subject to interview. In a way his origins and methods seem more mysterious now than they did before; certainly, as I write this, I don't seem to have a single straight answer in the notes before me. As we talked, messengers came from Lord Monboddo; from ministers and magnates of all kinds, and he said yes and no to them as if he owned this city. And perhaps he does! As I walked down Slinndo Hill, it wasn't only the flowers that made my head reel. His plans, his ambitions, beggar belief—if anyone else spoke of the Mountain that way, I'd say they were mad. So have we made the right deal? We'll see. These are interesting times!

Editors' note: The preceding Profile was, of course, conducted prior to the recent Cuttle Scandal, which exploded shortly before this book went to press. After much discussion it was decided that the Profile should remain, if only as a historical curiosity. We do not, of course, condone Mr. Cuttle's abominable actions, and we apologize to anyone for whom this Profile may be a painful reminder of that dreadful incident.

TWENTY-NINE

The *Thunderer* came in low over the River, in the late evening, approaching a huddle of buildings by the banks east of Shutlow. The Bargeman's Mission was there, and a few other buildings, including two warehouses that had belonged to the Gerent, and were now no longer needed. Whatever else was there hardly mattered. Arlandes had his orders. If there were residents in the buildings, they had been given fair warning to depart. It would all burn.

The matter had been decided. The Countess had spoken to her advisors. Some friend of Holbach's had advanced notions regarding the control of disease through fire and quarantine. Other advisors told the Countess it was blasphemy to interrupt the natural order of the city, and that the disease would spread according to the gods' designs. A man from the transportation concerns complained that the sickness was bad, it was bad every winter but this winter it had been worse, and now it was dragging on into spring and eating into profits. Captain Arlandes sat in stony indifferent silence through the whole debate, and spoke only when Holbach's friend asked: *Will you do it, Captain?* Arlandes had grunted in surprise. *Of course.*

There was a new kind of weapon. There had been a general feeling that the proceedings at Stross End had been messy, had been unclean. Over Holbach's objections, the thin and eager Professor Bradbury had offered his plans for a new flaming liquid, suitable for delivery by cast-iron shell, and capable, Bradbury promised, of rivaling the Fire itself for the ruthlessness with which it would burn and burn.

One of the Countess's elderly cousins, Sir Brice—under whom Arlandes had served on his first ship—had observed that there were conventions in close-packed Ararat against the use of arson as a weapon of princes. "But this is not *war*," the Countess had explained. "This is *cleansing*. This is a public service. This is *modernity*." Sir Brice had looked pleadingly at Arlandes, and Arlandes was not sure what Brice wanted him to say, so he said nothing. "Then the matter is decided," the Countess said.

But Arlandes had no particular taste for watching the thing be done. He dined alone in his quarters, and when Lieutenant Duncan knocked on his door to say "We're there, sir," Arlandes didn't look up.

"Then you know what to do, Mr. Duncan."

"Yes, sir. Sir, there appears to be a crowd watching. An audience, sir, on Hailie Hill. They should be at a safe distance."

"Disgusting. Continue."

"There's a group down by the banks. They have signs, sir, and they appear to be residents of the condemned area, and aggrieved, sir. Someone tried to fire on us, sir, with a rifle, but of course we were unharmed. Ah—they may *not* be at a safe distance, sir."

"They were warned, weren't they? Go and do your job, Mr. Duncan."

A short while later Duncan returned.

"Ah—Captain? There's a man on the roof of the Mission."

"More fool him."

"He's waving a white dress, sir."

"...Let me see this, Mr. Duncan."

The process by which one descended from the *Thunderer* was a cumbersome one, involving ropes, shouting, the nervous shifting motion of the kite-boats as they came down among the chimneys and water towers, and a final hard *jump* onto the rooftops. Mr. Lemuel—the man in the brown suit on the roof of the old Mission building, holding the white dress, was most certainly Lemuel—watched the process with obvious amusement.

When Arlandes was finally down, and approaching rapidly

and angrily across the rooftop, Lemuel shouted, "Good evening, Captain!"

"What are you doing with that dress, Lemuel?"

"This old thing? Rummaging. Downstairs. Captain, it's amazing what people leave behind when they're in a hurry. Do you want it?"

Lemuel held the dress up by the shoulders. It was clearly not Lucia's dress; it was faded, and worn, and in a fussy style that had not been in fashion for several generations.

Arlandes snarled and turned back to the waiting kite-boat, signaling his men to let down the ladder for him.

Lemuel called, "Aren't you going to ask why I'm here?"

Arlandes turned again, and approached Lemuel, with his hand on his saber. "Why are you here?"

"Professional curiosity! I had to see this for myself. By the way, if you put that thing down, we can talk more easily."

Arlandes was holding a red camphor-fragranced handkerchief to his mouth.

"It's not here anymore, Captain. You don't have to worry. It's moved on. Trust me, Captain, do you see me looking worried?"

Arlandes slowly lowered the handkerchief.

"Someone's made a right fucking mess," Lemuel said. "Shocking. Irresponsible. Playing with dangerous forces. How's your ship going these days, Captain?"

"What are you talking about, Lemuel?"

"I came here to make some observations, and I made them. I've been taking soundings. Sniffing the air. You won't understand my instruments or my methods. I can tell you a few interesting things, Captain, if you still want to do business."

"I told you I do not want to do business with you, Lemuel."

"But here you are talking to me. Are you happy here, Captain?"

"What?"

"Are you happy here? You don't look happy. Have you ever considered taking that big ship and going, oh, let's say, west? To the walls, and the outside? Or let's say going north, and *in,* and to the Mountain. Maybe there's a better life for you there. Have you never thought about it? You see, Captain, I'm interested in your ship. It's no skin off my nose if you want to come along. In fact I could use a man like you. I keep thinking, you're a difficult man, but there must be a deal to be made here. There just *has* to be."

"I'm returning to my ship, Lemuel. Stay here for the fire or don't; it's all one to me."

"Just think about it, Captain. Now would be a good time to travel. From what I've seen here today, life's going to become very unpleasant in this part of the city—and sooner than you might think."

Later—as the fire crashed down and sparks and smoke poured up over the decks—Arlandes remembered shouting, *No, Lemuel, no, leave me alone!* but he couldn't remember how he'd ascended back up into the ship, nor where or how Lemuel had gone.

THIRTY

Where did they *go?*" Holbach said, booming across his study. "Our mysterious old friends the Tuvar. That's a question *I'd* like to have answered. Rothermere?"

"I've never made much study of them. My line's more, shall we say, *mainstream* history. The Tuvar were never very numerous, and they kept themselves to themselves, once they'd settled in. No one much noted their passing. I expect they just sort of interbred with the rest of us. So if that's all you called me over for, I don't think I'll be much use to you. Your young chap probably knows more than I do by now. Arjun?"

Arjun leaned back and thought; as he often did when thinking hard, he tapped out a simple unconscious rhythm on the table's black wood; the rhythm gathered speed and complexity until he spoke. "I don't know. In the last days, when their god had left them—the second time, when the Black Bull vanished, and they were left alone in Ararat—some of their Hierophants despaired. Others searched for it. They went out all over the city. But there's no book you've shown me that says what happened. Maybe they found it in some district far to the east or west, but they'd taken on a new name by the time they'd walked that far."

"Any other Bull-worshippers around, Holbach?" Rothermere asked.

"Ha! Do you want a list? We'll be here all evening."

"But some stayed where they were, I think; their journals say that they searched the same streets again and again."

"Running in circles?"

"I don't know. The Hierophant Worora kept a journal; there's a diagram in it of a, a *spiral,* going down into the city beneath their streets. And he said he kept walking the same streets every day, but sometimes, he thought they were different, he thought he could see different cities behind the one he knew; he said what the Bull had shown them was that Ararat was fertile soil, and that most of it was buried; and he thought they had further to go, to go *inward,* to follow their god. He thought the Bull was posing them a test. That was all he said; he said he wasn't ready to say any more. That was near the end of his journal. And I think it's the last of their books. Professor, does that mean anything to you?"

"Well, now, maybe. There are certain, ah, *anomalies* on the Big Map. If you'll let me finish up with Rothermere for a minute, we'll take a look and talk further."

Arjun glanced at the little clock balanced on the edge of Holbach's desk, like a gleaming brass dome atop a piled cathedral of books. Worora's story made him uncomfortable; it made him think of Shay and his talk of secret ways, and he had no taste for the conversation. Besides, he recalled: "I can't. I've an appointment. I promised Olympia I'd go with her to some exhibition in the Arcades."

Holbach raised a bushy eyebrow. Rothermere smirked.

"Ah. Yes. I'm sorry, Professor. Tomorrow, perhaps."

You know, I've been wondering when you'd ask." Olympia poured out the last of the wine, and held up the bottle, signaling to the waiter for more. "It's no big secret, really."

"I've had other interests," Arjun said. "And it *seemed* like a secret. With all your whispering, and the code-words, and the locked ballroom upstairs, and all the lengths Holbach and all of you went to never to speak in front of Ilona's soldiers."

"Oh, it's a secret from *them,* of course. But no one's trying to keep it secret from *you.* You can't be a spy. You're too odd. I think the only reason Holbach hasn't already told you all about it is that he's forgotten you don't already know. I think he thinks everyone already knows and cares intimately about all his projects. Genius can be like that."

"Am I really that odd?"

"So this is what you're working toward: the mighty ship of scholarship on which you are a sailor, which Holbach steers these days, since Nicolas was taken from us, and I try to keep off the rocks of gaol. Ha-ha. Sorry. Bit drunk. The *Atlas,* Arjun. Your work will be a part of the Atlas. Hadn't you guessed?"

"Oh."

"Oh? Is that all?"

"I've heard of it. A book of maps. Isn't it banned?"

"Not just maps. *Everything;* where it is, where it stands, and what it means, how it's ordered. And *gods* yes, it's banned."

"Should we be talking about it here?"

Olympia gestured around the café. At the next table, a group of unshaven young men and pale, glamorous women looked up. "These are freethinkers here. We are safe enough." She leaned in and whispered. "Besides, Arjun, I was joking about the spies."

"You don't think you're being spied on?"

"Oh no, I know for a fact that I am. But so what? They won't *learn* anything. The censors know what we're doing and who we are already. Do you think the Countess doesn't know exactly what Holbach does with every moment of his day? No, we hide our names from the mob, lest we have riots at our doorsteps and the censors are forced to act. But the spies and the spymasters know what's what, and know that we know that they know. So long as the common people remain ignorant, and I pay the right bribes, we are safe from the censors. They don't want to make martyrs: there are those who support us, too, who would rally to us if they put us down. The censors will lock up the occasional printer or dealer, to frighten the others into line, and they exiled Nicolas, who was proud and would not hide his name, but our class of people are safe. More or less." She leaned back and shouted, to no one in particular, "Isn't that right?" She looked back to Arjun. "You look non-plussed."

"I thought you were building a weapon. Like the *Thunderer.*"

"Some sort of giant-Bull-inspired weapon?"

"Ah. Yes, perhaps. I'm afraid perhaps I did."
"We think the Atlas is more powerful. Let me explain."

Nicolas Maine began it. He was born into Chairman Cimenti's family: the older one, the current Chairman's father. He was raised to be a lord of Goshen Tor's banks and mercantiles and combines, but he had no head for business. He bored too easily.

The Chairs of the Tor's banks were always great patrons of the city's arts and sciences. That became Nicolas's life. But he was more than just a fund of money and a thrower of parties: he was himself an essayist, a thinker, a wit. He was full of a great passion for the city, and he inspired that passion in others, including Olympia, then the youngest daughter of one of the Cimenti families—a family of middling distance from the Chair, of solid but not magnificent prospects.

"I never knew him, you understand, though I sometimes managed to sneak myself into the salons to hear him speak. He was much older than me, and far above me anyway by birth: he might have been Chairman, had he cared. And then he was exiled before I was old enough and skilled enough to have anything to offer to him. But, if you'd ever seen him speak, Arjun—the most amazing energy and curiosity. No mind like his in all the city."

He was no more than a student himself when he conceived the great work. It would be a great glory to the Cimenti family: he would bring together all the city's scholars and create a single account-book, in which all knowledge would be tallied, all arguments resoved; all science reduced to a handful of axioms, all politics and philosophy, art and religion, filleted down to a volume's worth of epigrams. Everything in the world in its place. He had pictured something that might fit in a gentleman's coat pocket, to be referred to in the event of disputes. In later years he would talk about those naïve early ambitions at parties, just to get a laugh.

The real thing didn't come into existence for twenty years. The city had no single school—nothing like the Choristry—to organize all its scholars. They were scattered in churches, in towers, in the banks, tutoring princes in palaces or starving in garrets. He had to bring them together, soothe clashing egos, fire up their passion for his dream. He had to learn enough about everyone else's field of study to judge who was truly great, who was a hack or a lunatic. "Or at least weed out the worst lunatics," Olympia added. "Scholarship being apparently only loosely compatible with sanity."

And they needed teams of cartographers, explorers to go out into the city's vast reaches, and they needed to arm them.

An encyclopedia, of sorts, and a map, the *one* map. No one, so far as they knew, had ever attempted to map Ararat in its entirety. The map stretched out across many volumes, far past the parts of the city Arjun knew, and out into strange places. Its entries dug back into the city's history, and into its thoughts and dreams and gods. In the course of their studies, they found whole forgotten fields of thought, even new languages, new tribes, in remote parts of the city. "And the city changed under them," Olympia said. "*That's* why it took so long. It changes under us all the time, Arjun. With everything that we do—that's the historians' work to untangle—and with every move the gods make across our map. And it changes more the harder you look. A very uncertain geography. That's what's up in the ballroom—our work-in-progress. The Big Map, always being updated. You should see it sometime."

When the first edition came out (named *Atlas* in honor of the long-dead ruler who had charted the Peaceful Sea), it was in twenty-two volumes. It mapped the city as far as Egolf to the north, Ambruton to the west, and the Puppeteer Council in the east. Further editions followed, interspersed with endless supplements, each bringing new districts or concepts within the Atlas's scope, or capturing some shift in the city's map. Olympia counted them off on her fingers: "It depends on how you count, but we're at edition four now. At least, that's what we're calling it. The first new edition since Nicolas left."

"People bought all of these? They wanted them?"

"Everyone who was anyone, anyone with the least pretension to scholarship or fashion."

"So why was it banned?"

"It happened after the second edition. Their ambitions expanded; they wanted to change the city, not just to record it. They

thought if everyone could see where everything was, how everything connected to everything else, it would mean an end to confusion and to division. To isolation and impotence. To fear and
clutching for comfort at the familiar. And they wanted to tell the
city how to do things better, how to stop being so *stupid* and so
cruel."

"Who would object to that?"

"Is that *irony*? Are you joking? That's new. Well, different things
upset different people. Nicolas had a sharp wit and he made unkind
remarks about a lot of powerful people. Then there was the political
material: essays on all the ways in which other parts of the world organize themselves. Better ways, not so arbitrary and cruel. And then
just the thought of mapping the city angered its powers; they like
us as we are, divided, lost.

"They—*we*—had to be subtle, of course; we couldn't launch a
frontal attack on anyone who counted; we had to make our attacks
by implication, irony, sleight of hand. It made us a lot of powerful
enemies, but so long as we kept it subtle, coded, there was nothing
that the censors could prosecute. But then it was the gods that
really ruined things, as always. The first edition had nothing uncon-
ventional to say about the gods: just names, portfolio, aspect.
Nicolas wasn't mad, not at first. But then we got more daring. And
that's where Holbach got involved."

Elsewhere in the city, two days' ride to the southeast, Holbach held
forth for a group of young men leaning angularly against the fluted
green glass walls of their meeting hall. They were impeccably
dressed, with the most precisely judged element of the feminine
to their clothing: estranged and rebellious kin of First Citizen Gull,
of East Midian. They were potential sources of funding, maybe even
a measure of protection, and rich enough to demand the attention
of the big man himself. They looked at him covetously, like a fashionable new hat. He was tired and rambling, his charm stretched
thin.

"Many people ask how I first met Nicolas Maine. I was not political, you know, in those days—and even now, my dedication is to

truth, and no other cause. I was working in a garret, under a guttering candle. As in a hack painting or a poor play." He laughed; they didn't. "Ah. So, at the time, Nicolas was far above my head. I was poor then, and young. And I was thrilled by what he had to say. I recall his first edition's entry on the regime of the Director Caulkot"—a safe target, now as it was when Nicolas first wrote it; the Directors had last held sway a century ago, and had no friends in this room—"and I believe I can still quote it: 'Society should first of all be happy. To that end, it should be rational. To call oneself *Director* is to invite question as to one's *direction.* Let us ask...'"

Holbach was dissembling. He had never been able to care much for politics, even when he was young. He meant well, distantly; that was the best he could do. It was not Nicolas's political writings that had fired Holbach's blood, back then; it was the promise of science, and truth, and a full and final understanding of the entities and forces that Holbach studied; their subjection under reason. And, yes, the thought that *he* might be the one to write those final words.... But that wasn't what these pretty young wolves wanted to hear. This was: "A *rational* ordering to society. And to government. New leadership. I think we've all dreamed of that." Their ears perked. *Though gods help us if it's you lot,* he did not say.

"Ah, but perhaps you're too young to remember how it was when the first edition came out. But there I was, sneaking out of my attic to read those dangerous volumes in my patron's library. And I published my *Critique.* Merely a technical piece of theology," he rambled to their blank, bored-again faces, "but it had some small success. And I was working under a pile of paper in the back of some temple, when a kindly old man—he looked old to me *then*—sat next to me and asked if I was Gracien Holbach. And he offered gentle criticism of my work, from the cuff, things I had never thought of, and then he told me who he was, and I fell all over myself to shake his hand. He told me that he needed men like me, that he knew the Atlas was weak on theology, and he said, 'Every time I try to show the city how it could be, be *better* than it is, someone says, "The gods made it so, and they have their reasons." But I don't believe they do. I think they are walls in our path, and I need men who can strike at their foundations.' Someone to track their paths across the city's map; to chip away at their mystery, and bring them within our understanding. And that remains central to the great work today, though it has made us many enemies, and left us in dire need of friends, friends among the enlightened and those who love the future, such as I hope you may be. Which brings us, regrettably, to the vulgar matter of money."

Well," Olympia said, "Holbach's told you about his theories. You can imagine how people reacted to the third edition."

"I suppose so. Not easily."

"Well, then take my word for it. He rubbed their faces in their folly. There were riots. Outrage. Like a thousand Mr. Shays; worse, it was like a thousand *rich* and *privileged* Mr. Shays mocking everything the city held dear. Those who loved us were too quiet, too afraid, to act.

"It had been safe enough until then. It all went out under Nicolas's name, you see—everyone else was anonymous—and Nicolas Maine was too close to the Chair to be easily challenged. But the third edition went too far. The churches were breathing fire; the scandal sheets were never silent. The censors broke our presses and strung up our printers, and the mob set fire to dealers' stalls in every market in the city, but it wasn't enough for them. And anyway, as I said, there were a lot of powerful people waiting for the right moment to move against Nicolas. Guess which of the Estates moved first. *Guess.*"

"You'll say his own family. The Chairman."

"*Yes.* An order of exile, to an island in the Peaceful Sea. Under certain humiliating conditions of confinement. Then the other Estates piled on, each one adding their own conditions—forbidding him this or that food or requiring this or that daily atonement from him. His life on that island is very strange, Arjun, and perhaps he may never come back. But they *never* stopped us. And later, when I'd completed my studies—which is a story in itself; the Chairmen don't regard the law as women's work, I'm afraid—I offered my services to those who still loved him, and now I spend a *very* great deal of my time fighting in all the city's courts to have him returned to us."

"I'm sorry it hasn't worked yet."

"Maybe I don't expect it to anymore. And of course, while we wait, Holbach has been keeping us working. And I do what I can to keep us safe from the noose. And sometimes I swear they want me to be a fucking mother to a dozen grey-haired bachelor scholars, gods help me. But together all of us keep it in motion. Hence all the recent efforts: we hope to produce the fourth edition in the next months. Our first since Nicolas was taken from us. It will go out under no name and in secret, but it won't be silenced. There are many people waiting. And more who'll come round, one day."

"So Holbach is your leader now?"

"He's not our leader. Only, say, our central point. He's brilliant, he knows *everyone,* he's very rich: why not him? Lucky for you that he is who he is, or you'd never have found us."

The bottle was empty again. Arjun considered it for a moment, then raised it up to signal for more. He smiled and said, "I suppose it *is* lucky."

THIRTY-ONE

Four things changed for Arjun in the first weeks of spring. He could count them off on his fingers, reflecting, as he did so, on how little control it seemed he had over his own life, outside his one great mission. And even that, perhaps, had been given to him, not chosen.

The first change was that he learned the nature of Holbach's project, and the purpose of the work he had been engaged in since leaving the Nessenes. After Olympia told him, Arjun went home from the café very drunk and very excited, and lay awake on the hard bed in his flat in Stammer Gate, his head reeling. It was a wonderful purpose, insanely ambitious and wild. To take everything the city knew and reflect it back, like light in a signal-mirror, so the city could change itself and be wiser: it was the kind of thing to which a man could give over a life. He was glad to be even the tiniest part of it.

The next morning, hungover and grey-faced, he sat at his desk, rubbing his aching temples, and wondered how on earth he had come to be involved in Olympia's nonsense. He stared out of the window, over the graveyard and the sea of roofs beyond, and thought what an absurd vanity it was. Nothing could capture all the city's knowledge, not in a thousand years, nothing could map that chaos, and certainly no mere book could *change* it. It was idiocy to think that it could; a consuming delusion. The weapon Holbach had created, the dreadful thing that had laid waste to Stross End: *that* could change the city, though only for the worse. But a book? And how was it that his own pure passion, that had borne him from edge to summit of the world, had been soiled and stamped to ash, and the wound in him filled with this city-trash? He had *failed*.

Still, he had some notes to drop off with Holbach that morning, so he dragged himself out of his flat and through the streets. And once he was there, in the thick of it, with lively people around him, the thrill of it caught him up again.

"Rough night of it?" Liancourt asked him as he passed the kitchen. The playwright was sitting at the table with one of the painters—Mochai, Olympia's lover, the young artist whose daring bird-shit-spattered canvases were creating quite a stir in the press . . . Arjun fell gratefully on the coffee, and joined their conversation.

Liancourt was explaining how his play in progress—*The Marriage Blessing*—would dramatize the themes of the new Atlas. "The scholars can *tell* the citizens how they're used and lied to and divided and confused," Liancourt said, "but we can make them *feel* it. And oh, the lords and their censors will hate it! With this and the new edition out at the same time, they won't know what hit 'em! They'll feel like the whole city is rising up and speaking against them, from the very stones! They'll *howl,* boys! But are we scared?"

Mochai thumped the table, laughing, and shouted, "No, sir!"

Arjun smiled, too. "Excuse me," he said. "I have to see something." He left them, and went up to the ballroom.

It was locked, but the housekeeper opened it for him, saying, "Remember, no candles. The Professor'll kill you if you take fire in there. And take off your shoes, of course."

The pine floor was buried under sheets of thick paper, overlaid end to end and side to side all across the huge bright room, densely etched with charcoal lines and circles that ran across one sheet to the next. A variety of hands had annotated it in tiny script. These were the notes they made toward the great work; this *was* the work. Place-names, street-names. The names of prominent persons. Lines of string in many colors were pinned across the map. Arjun followed a red line to the note that explained that it marked out the borders of the Countess's power. He imagined she would hate to see her limits delineated so starkly.

There were other circles of red, here and there, marking other parts of the Countess's domains, overlapping with the yellow of Cimenti and the brown of Mass How, and others. Further from what Arjun thought of as the city's core (though he supposed there was no reason to), the Atlas-makers had reused the red for other Estates. Not enough colors, he supposed, not nearly.

He followed a grey-green line, stepping very carefully on or between the papers. A note on that string read, in Holbach's hand, *Course of the Motions of Atenu, '47–'56, '61–'67.* There were many tiny knots in the string, some with little tags of paper tied to them, with dates on them.

It made him dizzy to look so closely at the tiny details of it, so he stood up straight and looked around the room. Ar-Mouth and the Bay were near the door. The sheets of paper nearby were very thickly detailed, and full of pins and strings and tags. Piles of notepaper containing relevant essays and entries from the Atlas sat on top of each map-sheet.

The map-sheets got less and less detailed as they moved away from the Bay. It was very easy to see where the Atlas-makers were based. Further out, there were patches of detail, surrounded by blank sheets, or sheets marked only with a name and a question mark. In the distance, there were more rivers, Arjun saw, with disorienting shock; one came down in a thick line of charcoal from Ar-Mount and ran west, and another ran east. There were other docks along them.

Concentric circles of string on the far side of the room marked the rising slopes of the Mountain. A few sheets within the outer circles were marked up—Arjun saw that Stross End's map had been redrawn recently, on fresh white paper—but the inner circles were all blank. There was nothing north of the Mountain except the room's wide bay windows.

At the room's other edges, past wide stretches of blank whiteness, thick rough lines sketched out the city's walls. There were question marks next to them.

Some of the pages were fresh, recent changes to what was clearly a work in progress; others were stiff and faded golden-brown, the black lines like cracks in leather. It was, Arjun thought, the color of the city's thick fogs; the color of its stained brick and stone when, from a hill, one watched the sun set behind the towers. He felt briefly dizzy.

A couple of weeks ago, Arjun had spoken to Holbach in the study. There was yet another story in the *Sentinel,* headlined *Survivors of Stross End Rebuild in Wreckage.* Holbach had sunk over it, and said, "Maybe Olympia's right. Maybe Nicolas *would* have told me not to make the *Thunderer.* Maybe he'd have *known* they would make it a weapon. But I thought we could see everything at once, from above. See how it all fits together, and what it all means. I thought I was working for his dream." Arjun hadn't understood, and Holbach had gone back to work without explaining. Arjun understood now. He went back downstairs, locking the door behind him, thinking of how Julah had locked the door behind him as they came down from the Voice's Chamber.

The second change was that he took Olympia to bed, or perhaps she took him; his memory was unclear.

Like all of them, Olympia was very busy, in those last months of the Atlas. There were deals to be made with printers and distributors and dealers, and there were a thousand censors and regulators and licensing authorities to be bribed, or converted, or tangled up with legal trickery; everything had to be ready. The free-love advocate Mr. Brace-Bel—a sinister, arrogant little man; he preferred to be called *debaucher*—angered the censors with a new volume of letters and was charged in blasphemy and sedition in seven separate jurisdictions, and tried in two, and, despite Olympia's best efforts, convicted in one, and returned to the Iron Rose by order of the Duke of Baltic Street. "No great loss," she said, philosophically; "He comes and goes." The battle took her all over the city. But the gathering speed of the work filled her with energy, as it did for them all, and she was never busy enough. She burned off that energy drinking in the bars of opulent hotels, or in lupine dives, depending on where she found herself at the end of the day. She was often in places where women were not welcome, and so she kept Hoxton with her for protection, but she had—she told Arjun, as they sat on deep red leather seats in the bar of the Hotel Nareau, looking out on

Lake Kuyt—exhausted most topics of conversation with her driver. So she took Arjun along, for the company. "Come on," she had said, as she passed him that morning, leaving Holbach's office with an armful of books. "The Tuvar will be just as dead tomorrow. You should see more of the city while it's alive."

He sat back, warmly creaking the hotel's red leather, and asked her, "Why me? I hadn't thought I was good company."

"Fishing for compliments? You're a good listener. You're honest. You're not un-handsome, now that you've put some weight back on after your, shall we say, *sickness,* so I needn't be embarrassed to be seen with you. And you're so, well, *foreign.* So *fresh.* You probably haven't had time yet to see how very irritating and silly we all are. I want to know how we impress you. Do we?"

"Very much." And they did. They were much more alive than the Choristry had been. The Choristry had only had one moment of vibrant life, and that had vanished. He started to tell her that, but he realized that *he* wanted to be the one to impress *her.* So he got drunkenly up and walked over to the corner of the bar, where the band played, and leaned over the (incompetent, sadly) pianist, and said, "I can pay you, sir, if you will please move aside for a moment."

The maître d' started to glide over to Arjun, to usher him back to his seat, but Hoxton stopped him with a look. Arjun took no notice. He sat at the piano and played. Like all his music, there was an echo of the Voice in it, but it was different from anything he had played for years. It did not draw on the Voice in its melancholy and fragile aspect, or its demanding and austere aspect; it was the Voice in joy and elation. He had forgotten. It was wonderful. The room was full of laughter. After a while, he returned control of the instrument to the anxious pianist, fumbling an absurdly excessive tip into the man's hands, and joined Olympia on the polished dance floor.

They woke up together in the hotel's deep bed, her leg lying across his. They made themselves late for Olympia's morning appointment. She was demanding, and laughed a lot. Arjun was very serious; it had been a long time. They did not speak, until Atenu's temple, two streets over, banged the big hammers to signal noon, and Olympia said, "Shit!" and rolled out of bed and clutched at her clothes.

It became a habit. They were spending the days together anyway, traveling the city, as she carried out her business. And when she wasn't traveling, she was a fixture in the cafés and salons of Ebon Fields and Faugère, where they talked radical politics and enthusiastic blasphemy. She passed off Nicolas's wit as her own, but she coined her own, too. She needed every weapon she could bring to bear. She was very determined to shock and to impress.

Sometimes they crossed water; sometimes they drank in cafés on the banks of the pleasure-canals. Arjun was nervous at first but she dared him to go near the water, and nothing dreadful happened to him, so he began to think that perhaps he had imagined the Typhon's hatred of him. Perhaps it had gone back into the water to gnaw at its wounds. Perhaps it had died of its own sickness, and good riddance. In the spring it was hard to believe in the monster; in the elegant and lively places Olympia took him, it was impossible.

Perhaps Olympia liked to bring Arjun with her because he was not witty, and would not outshine her. Or, he thought sometimes, she was an outsider to the Atlas, too, in a way, for all her efforts on its behalf. She served it, but she had added nothing to it. And he thought perhaps she enjoyed drawing him into it, that it made her feel more central to things to have him in her orbit. Those were both just guesses; he was quite sure he didn't altogether understand her. She was much more sophisticated than him; or, at least, sophisticated in a way he wasn't. She was very clever and strange. He found her interesting.

They were not in love—not even in the cool and abstract way the Choirmen loved, and certainly not according to the city's theatrical and sentimental understanding of the condition. On that first morning, as he sat at the back of the room and watched her conduct her delayed meeting with the Brattle Printers' and Pressmens' Collective, shouting them down one moment and cajoling them the next, he had worried that she might be (why not? Passions of all kinds were sparked too quickly, it seemed to him, in this strange city), but he was relieved by her good sense. Her first dedication was to the Atlas. And he knew that she had other lovers, some of whom he thought she still saw. He was not jealous. His own highest love was still the Voice; she'd never understand that or share it with him. Still, it was a pleasant arrangement. He had, he realized, been lonely.

He talked to her in a way that was new to him (*I've found a new Voice,* he thought, *ha-ha*). It wasn't just the drink that loosened his tongue, or the stuff they breathed in from the bubbling glass bellies on the tables in the bars in certain parts of the city to the west; it was the way *she* talked, the way they all talked: quick, argumentative, as if always questioning themselves, joking with themselves. He tried to explain to her, leaning across the smoky buzzing space above their table in the back room of Vittorio's, that he'd seen how they, the Atlas-makers, were all prepared to give their lives over to their work, but how they laughed at it, too, and at themselves. And of course, he said, he knew that he probably gave the impression, with his silence, that he couldn't exercise the same self-scrutiny, but that wasn't true. He must seem like a very simple creature, but he wasn't. He could imagine how his quest looked to them. He could say it himself: it was an obsession, it was an addiction, it was selfish and shut-in. People in the city had so many gods and purposes to choose from; the Choristry had had no choices. They'd never had a place from which to stand outside their lives and look in and laugh. He was what he was. But he didn't want her to think he was stupid. He was well-traveled, remember, he said. He was learning; he'd find a way to make it *mean* something.

She kept nodding while he talked, and smiling. He didn't think he could talk that way with anyone else, he told her. She told him he was sweet to say so; but he hadn't meant it as flattery, but as simple truth. The smoke from the glass on the table made his tongue feel fat and numb, and his head charged but slippery. He'd lost his train of thought. No matter; it was there to be picked up again some other night.

She was fond of telling him, quite kindly, that he was mad. "Of course," he observed, "to me *you* are mad, and foreign." She remained unconvinced.

He spent most nights, when they weren't off in some distant part of the city, at Olympia's flat in Ebon Fields.

The Atlas-makers were libertines to a man, and were not shocked. Olympia had long had a prominent place in their daily gossip; they were happy enough to add Arjun to its cast.

Not everyone was happy. One of her other lovers, the painter Mochai, waited in Holbach's hall, drinking rough wine, and threw himself weeping and cursing on Arjun as he passed, shouting, "She's mine! Who the fuck are you? What've you got?"

He took a clumsy swing at Arjun's head. It was not hard for Arjun to knock the man's arm aside, and hold him until he stopped weeping. He had learned a little about violence in his travels. More than Mochai, at least. "I'm sorry," they both said. Mochai picked himself up and stalked away with wounded pride, and stopped coming to Holbach's house.

"Well, *I'm* not sorry," Olympia said, when Arjun told her what had happened. "All that nonsense with birdshit. *Yuck.*" He mentioned it only in passing; he saw no reason to dwell on it.

And the third thing that changed was that, after all his excitement about the work of the Atlas, his own work ran out, and he was left idle and aimless again.

He had a long meeting with Holbach on a sunny morning, in the downstairs study, where they had retreated to escape a foul smell Dr. Branken's experiments had produced, which pervaded all the top floors of the mansion. They spent the morning finalizing Arjun's contributions to the Atlas. With Arjun's help, Holbach drafted a short entry on the Black Bull, with a brief summary of the theories of the Tuvar theologians. It ran to a page or two. They went up to the map-room, and added a few notations to the stretches of the map in which the Tuvar had lived.

"There's still much more to be read," Arjun said.

Holbach shook his head. "I don't think we need more. The Bull and its folk are long gone from the city; little more than a footnote. Sufficiency will do, here, not perfection, I think."

Holbach was also preparing a new version of an essay from the previous edition. "The death and the dying of gods, the how and the why of it. Or perhaps one should say that they *fade,* or are *extinguished,* or *resolved.* As with all the most interesting problems, it is hard to know even how to name our inquiry." Over a long, late lunch, they worked a few references to the disappearance of the Bull into the essay. It didn't require any changes to be made to its argument. The conclusion still amounted, essentially, to *Who knows?* It was, Holbach observed, defensively, a nascent science, regarding recalcitrant subjects.

Then it was over. Holbach laughed. "You worked too fast and too well! Put yourself out of a job!" Then he saw the expression on Arjun's face, and scrambled to say, "I'll tell you what, though. I think we barely have an entry on the Tuvar's history."

"I have it memorized. It reads, 'Immigrant population circa 1100 to 1200; we presume assimilated or deceased.'"

"Oh, dear. And not a mark on the Big Map, either, I think. Hundreds of thousands of lives, perhaps. And some very worthy scholars, to judge from what you've translated. How sad. Well?"

"An entry on the Tuvar?"

"Why not? Who else? At this point, there's no one who knows the Tuvar better. Talk to the historians, if you need advice. They were *people,* Arjun: do them justice! Have a crack at it."

Arjun went back to his flat on foot, feeling suddenly guilty about taking a carriage on Holbach's money. He started the slow work of writing an account of the Tuvar's history. It didn't come easily to him. He had no experience of writing anything but music. It was hard to know where to start. He could feel that he had many frustrating days ahead. He gave up in the evening, and took a carriage (*the Fire with it!*) to Olympia's flat in Ebon Fields.

And the days ahead were frustrating, until the fourth thing changed for him, and he found a new purpose.

Arjun had no idea how to order his thoughts on the Tuvar, and he was unable, after a fortnight, to produce a single satisfactory paragraph. He did not try very hard. When he could, he traveled around the city with Olympia. When he couldn't, he spent most of his days at the mansion, joining in the rambling arguments of the painters and poets and other hangers-on. He surprised them and himself with his ferocity of argument.

He tried to tell Holbach that the man should stop paying his salary, but Holbach wouldn't hear of it: with all the work for the Atlas and the Countess consuming his time, Holbach couldn't afford to let anyone go. So Arjun hung on. He talked to the explorers who came back from distant parts of the city. None of them, in their travels, had ever heard of anything like the Voice.

He talked to Rothet, a hard man, older and tougher than the rest of the students and aspiring scholars who formed the cartographers' ranks, a man who had come back from the forbidden precincts of Red Barrow with dreadful stories of the Barrow's brutal Thane and a fresh scar on his face from the Barrow's militia. Arjun described the Voice; he sang an echo of its song. Shaking his head, slight tears on his scarred cheeks, Rothet said, "Never. No. No music in the Barrow. I'll keep an ear out, though. It's lovely. I'm not ashamed to say that. What is it?"

On a bright Bell-day afternoon, Arjun was sitting in the kitchen talking to Alwhill, a young man who had come back from charting a district called Ton-Pei, made of warrens built into the side of a cliff, near to the Mountain—"but not dangerously near. I'm not being paid enough to go too close."

"It would be an insubstantial spirit," Arjun said, "that sings, or makes music. If it has found worshippers, they would devote themselves to echoing it. Have you heard of it?"

"Sorry. They weren't very musical. They had a sort of, ah, spiderthing. I don't know if it's the same as what we in these parts call the Spider, or different—they said it lived deep in their tunnels. Holbach says he needs more data to decide what it was. They did everything as a gamble, because they said it pleased the spider. They wanted me to take my chances before they'd give me any interviews, and some of their forfeits were bloody nasty, so you can imagine I didn't talk to anyone much more than I had to. I just mapped their tunnels and got out. Bloody stupid way to live, whatever kind of spider their spider is. This singing thing, is that what you're studying?"

"In a manner of speaking." Arjun shook his head. "I'm sorry, I don't mean to be cryptic. I'm..." He was distracted by the sight, through the window, of Liancourt leading a group of unfamiliar people across Holbach's lawn and into the pine-gabled building behind the rose garden.

"The new play," Alwhill said. "*The Marriage Blessing*. Liancourt wants it to be a musical performance. He thinks he'll rouse more people with music than with words. The state of *his* words, he may have a point. I'm sorry, but I frankly think he's overrated. Don't tell anyone I said that, all right? Anyway, our host had a lot of musical instruments brought into the conservatory, a few years back, when he was working on some study of some music-spirit. Liancourt's going to work there."

"Can we talk later? I want to see this."

Arjun followed them into the conservatory—white-walled, rose-trellised, at the end of a gentle path. Inside, a flock of actors and actresses stood around while Liancourt auditioned a group of composers, who one by one tried out their offerings on the clutter of dusty instruments. "No, no. That's too weak. We want *anger;* our hero has been kicked in the face by the city *yet again*! I'm sorry, but no. Do you have anything else?"

One after another, Liancourt rejected all their suggestions: too slow, too derivative, lacking in zest. He tugged in frustration on a grey fistful of his own hair. He threw himself into his chair, sullenly, like a child, then threw himself up out again and paced like a drill-sergeant.

Finally, one of them sat at the piano, tried playing the echo of the Voice that Arjun had set loose in the city, months before. Liancourt had one of the actresses sing some nonsense syllables to it, to see how it sounded for voice. "It's very pretty," he said. "And I like the thought of adapting a popular piece, something *familiar;* I want people to feel this play is *theirs*. But it's not quite perfect."

"It's an echo of an echo," Arjun said. "Of an echo. It's been corrupted since I gave it out to the city."

"That's yours?" Liancourt said. "Really?"

"I can do better than these men. Give me a few days."

Liancourt agreed. Arjun asked Liancourt to have food and bedding brought to him in the summerhouse, and to leave word for

Olympia that he was well, but not to be disturbed. Liancourt left a copy of the play, and his first draft of the libretto, and left Arjun to his work.

This *did* come naturally to him. He felt himself reaching out and back across time to the Chamber of the Voice, and he let it echo through him and through the music.

He paid very little attention to what Liancourt's play was supposed to be about; what he read of it had a vicious wit that was not altogether to his taste. Leafing through, he saw there was something about an angry young man; something about a much put-upon young woman; various cruel lords and ladies. Anger, then, was appropriate, and also sadness. He put everything that mattered into it: all of his longing for the Voice; all of his sadness when it vanished; all of his bitter anger when it never returned; everything he remembered of joy.

"Music," Holbach said, "is wonderful stuff." (Holbach appeared behind Arjun's shoulder from time to time, a genial paterfamilias, taking an interest in his household.) "I don't know why we don't have more musicians. We have painters, and poets, and playwrights, and Mr. Tilbury dabbles in sculpture, to rather daring effect. But a dearth of musicians. But it's such an esoteric art, don't you think? It draws the mind away from the material things of the city, and from the hurly-burly of political life, and from the company of one's fellows, and from nattering old fools like myself, I suppose, and on to higher things. And yet at the same time it is so remarkably *compelling.* So powerfully moving, and on such a deep and primal and inarticulate level. It rouses the masses in a way that all the words and science in the Atlas can't manage. It touches the passions and the sentiments. Wonderful stuff. Wonderfully effective. May I hear a piece of it? I promise not to steal your thunder; I won't repeat it. I wouldn't know how; I can barely whistle."

Holbach's visits made Arjun uneasy, and oddly guilty, for reasons he could not quite articulate, and for hours afterwards he could not quite hear the music. After the third visit he took to locking the door to the summerhouse. As soon as the bolt slid home, the music flowed back into him, as if he'd unlocked something within himself, and he ran back to his chair with his head spinning.

He emerged a few days later with sheaves of paper, and played Liancourt the main theme. "It needs work," Liancourt said. "I mean, it's not perfect." His voice was slightly hoarse, and his eyes wet and gleaming. "But we can get it into shape. We have a few weeks. Let's get to work, then."

THIRTY-TWO

Bright green shoots cracked out of the flat grey earth by the Thunderers' new hiding place. Spring brought white birds to flock around the lonely bushes. The boathouse buzzed with life and excitement. Jack was very proud of them and full of pure fierce love. Months had passed since the attack on Barbotin. They had never slowed since.

The week after Barbotin, Jack went back to Ma Fossett's and unlocked all its gates and windows. His boys held the matrons helplessly at bay, glowering, while their girls made their choice. Some of them chose to stay; others seized their moment and ran. All Jack could do was offer them that moment, he thought.

As Jack watched the girls flee the workhouse, into the winter night in streets in their nightdresses, Beth said, "For the gods' sake, Jack, they'll need better clothes than that, it's winter." He took some of the lads to hunt out the laundry room, and steal a heap of the thick grey wool dresses. "Grow up," Beth told them as they sniggered over the undergarments.

They brought some of the girls back to the boathouse. Jack had let Beth suggest which ones were sound. She marked out a separate wing for them, which Jack agreed was sensible.

The next week they hit 34 Lime Street. The Masters had heard the stories, and tried to be ready; they had armed themselves and thought they would be brave, but when Jack came down out of the sky, the setting sun behind him, bright silk threads trailing in the wind, and his savage children rose up with rifles on the rooftops all around, they gave up without a fight. No one had to be hurt.

They found Aiden there. He had been given a terrible beating, to mark him as an escaper, and to warn the other boys; his face was still bruised and his left eye would not stop bleeding. He didn't say anything, but his cracked and swollen face beamed and he hugged them fiercely.

"There's nothing special about Shutlow," Jack said. "There's a whole city of prisons out there. Anyway, they're expecting us in Shutlow now. They're ready for us. They can't stop us, but they can slow us down. They can make it expensive."

So they struck out into Agdon Deep, and broke open the iron doors of the forge, and gave the boys who worked the machines their freedom, if they wanted it; and they stole the keys to the leg-irons on the chain gangs that scavenged the burnt-over ruins of Stross End for fragments of brick and timber.

At first they only struck the places where children were held. But on the day the year turned over (by most reckonings), they opened the concrete hulk of Mensonge's prison in Fourth Ward. They gave all the men there their freedom, without asking what their crime was. "It's not our place to pick and choose who goes free," Jack said. "We're not gaolers." They did not, however, bring any of them back to the boathouse; it would have seemed wrong, somehow.

As they worked, Jack got stronger and stronger, faster and faster. At first it was hard for him to bear a single boy aloft; by the end of winter, he could, with an effort of will, bring a whole group of them briefly into the air, like the *Thunderer* leading its fleet. At first they went arms linked, each bearing his brother, the hilarious, ecstatic gift passing from hand to hand. They'd thought that was the greatest wonder the city could offer, but the power was still growing, unfurling. Slowly, and at first without noticing it, they found that the gift was in Jack's wake: that when they followed in his footsteps, it passed into them, and like him they ran and leaped from rooftop to rooftop, crossing from tower to tower with weight-less loose-limbed strides. None of them could be sure when it had started—had it been there when they'd chased the *Thunderer* across

Shutlow? To some degree, surely: how else could they have survived those headlong vertiginous dashes with their necks and backs unbroken? Nor could they be sure when or whether it would end.

The unnatural power the Bird had gifted to Jack couldn't be contained within one person, even if he'd wanted to keep it for himself. He knew of course that it was a basic principle of theological science: that the changes the gods made to the fabric of the city each entrained further changes, expanding outward unpredictably like ripples in a pond. It was an extraordinary demonstration, though. His teachers could never have imagined it.

But for the time being, all he and his followers needed to know was that the power was there. He was electric with it; he sparked it in those around him. But only, Jack noted with satisfaction, so long as they kept to his course, kept faith with his purpose.

They took their first wound in the last week of winter, when they struck the chainhouse of the Crawling Stone, in Third Ward. The priests had hired a group of bravos from Garhide, who knew how to use their weapons and how to set an ambush. They were still no match for the speed and power Jack had stolen from the Bird, but they managed to kill two of the escaping boys and to place a bullet in the bone of Namdi's leg. Two of the bravos were also killed, to Jack's regret. It could not be helped.

Jack brought Namdi through the night to a sawbones in the 'Machy; he judged that to be far enough from home for safety. Jack held the patient's arm as the man dug in the meat of Namdi's leg. Namdi bore his scars and his limp with pride, prematurely elevated into an honored old soldier.

The chainhouse was the first time they had to kill, but there were other incidents, as their targets got better prepared, and as Jack's forces swelled, taking in angry new blood. They tried not to kill, or at least Jack told them to try, but mistakes were inevitable. They were only boys, after all. Jack could lend them speed and flight, but not wisdom or patience or self-control. He found it easy to forgive them, so long as they did his work.

Jack hardly ate anymore, but the others needed to be fed, and there were more of them all the time. So they still stole. They were more organized, now; they never went thieving near to the boathouse, and they would go a full day's walk to find fences. Fiss handled all that sort of thing. Feeding, organizing, caring; Jack lacked the patience.

He and Fiss didn't talk much that winter. Fiss was quiet and drawn tight. "This is your purpose, not mine," Fiss told him one evening, standing out on the cold mudflats. "It can't last; you'll get us all killed soon enough. *My* job is to keep them fed. Just try to let me do that, if you can, will you?"

Jack couldn't bring himself to get rid of Fiss. He owed him too much. And he needed him, he knew. But he kept an eye on him, anyway, after that, and he made his plans with Namdi instead.

Spring brought a flowering of ballads about the Thunderers. Jack would slip out over the city, dressed plainly so that no one would know him, and listen to the songs. When anyone asked him who he was, he would say that he was an apprentice, out to make purchases for his master. There were children running free in the streets singing the songs; they leaped from stone to stone in the broken streets, arms outstretched as if in flight, shouting the words. He watched a crowd sing "The Ballad of Jack Silk" outside the Ironwood Gaol, until the militia rode out and scattered them with whips. He resolved to come back.

All the various militias were searching for him and for the Thunderers. He hid in alleys or on fire escapes and watched them questioning confused bystanders. They were clumsy and heavy-footed, and he did not fear them. He followed the watchmen back to their barracks and listened at their windows; they never had anything to report to their superiors. The Thunderers never struck near their home, and the militia would not find them.

In the first weeks of spring, he noticed new pursuers on his trail. Young men, asking around in the pubs and markets of Fourth Ward and Shutlow. They were not soldiers or watch. They were soft, unscarred, with quiet, precise voices. They had journals, and they took careful notes, not the half-literate scratchings of the watch. They didn't seem interested in where to find him: they asked questions like "Were they all wearing silk, or only one boy? Did he flap his wings, like a bird, or did he move according to his own nature, as the *Thunderer* does? What I mean is, did he appear to be *walking* on air?"

One of them was asking around in Seven Wheels Market, on the corner near Mensonge's gaol. A slight young man, with a wispy beard and glasses. Jack followed him back that evening.

Holbach was dreaming of dark streets that roared out flame and swirling clouds of broken bone, under a black moon and the thunder of guns; and as he walked slowly—he couldn't run—through what he knew was Stross End, the bloody arms of corpses clutched his legs, and ragged jaws yawned open to tell him that he had missed yet another deadline, and that the printers had lost his manuscript in any case.

He awoke sweating and cold. There was a slight figure moving in the darkness of his bedroom. No, his study; he was on the sofa, a book open across his belly. It must be one of his colleagues. He considered pretending still to be asleep, to avoid embarrassment at having fallen asleep in his study again, like a student, at his age.

He sensed the figure turning toward him, although the moonlight was too weak to make out its features. "Don't move," it said. "Look at the ceiling, not at me. If you turn your head toward me, I'll kill you. I can *see* you."

Holbach's gut froze. He snapped his head rigidly to the ceiling, and babbled, "I have money, a lot of money, in a safe across the hall. Do you know who I am? If you kill me, the Countess will hunt you down."

"I don't need your money, and I don't fear your Countess. I know who you are. I've been watching and listening. Do you know who I am?"

Holbach was silent. The invader was trying hard to speak deeply and roughly, but it was overdone: underneath the imposture, it was still a boy's voice; not a child, but by no means a man. It was familiar, somehow. "Jack, ah, Jack Silk?"

"That's right. I followed one of your spies here."

"Ah. Ah, not spies, exactly, Master Silk, so much as they are students. Oh, I do hope you didn't hurt him."

"Not yet. Why are your spies out following me? Asking around about me? Is it for the Countess? She's hunting me?"

"Well, yes, strictly speaking, she wants me to investigate you, and yes, of course she wants to catch you, Jack, may I call you Jack? After all you've done, of course she does. But no, *I'm* not trying to trap you or catch you. I promise you. I only want to know how it works, what you do. If it's true."

"You're the one who made the *Thunderer.*"

"Yes, I am."

"Did you make me?"

"I'm sorry?"

"Why the Bird's gift never left me. Like the *Thunderer.* What they say is true, you know; I can fly. It's not much like walking on air at all, if you must know. Was it your doing?"

"I promise you it wasn't."

The figure was silent. Holbach listened to sixty slow ticks of the clock and tried to will his pulse to slow with them. He asked, "May I see you do it?"

"No. I won't be your weapon."

"Oh gods, boy, that's not what I want. I—"

"I'll keep breaking open your prisons as long as I can. There are more and more who follow me every day. We'll kill you if you try to stop us or slow us. We *will.*"

"Oh, no. I don't mean to stop you, even if I could. I just want to know how you do what you do. No, in fact I've written, well, not me personally, but a man under my direction, on reform of our penal institutions; our practices of incarceration are a horror, Jack, yes, and I've campaigned against them since before you were born, ah, so I do understand what you're doing—"

"Shut up. You don't. I followed the ship across the city. I saw what it did to Stross End."

"Oh. I'm so very, very sorry, Jack."

The clock measured out a further span of silence. Jack sat silhouetted in the window. Gusts of feeling twisted his thin shoulders. He was not in control of himself, Holbach could see.

"So how does it work, then, wise man?"

"I don't know, Jack. I wish I did. If you could tell me how it started. Was it when the Bird returned? Did you call on it? The gods' purposes are obscure, but they can be understood. . . ."

"How long will it last?"

"I have no idea. If I could examine you..."

"No. Don't look."

Holbach snapped his head back to the ceiling. The molding was a dark map of shadows.

"What would you do with it, if you knew how it worked?"

"I'd share it, if I could. Find how it's done and share it. If it works that way. I'd lift us all up, the whole city."

"That's what I'm doing. I'll free everyone, every prison in the city, and I'll bring them with me. The power just gets stronger, the more I do it."

"But what you're doing—something like it, maybe, yes, but what you're doing makes no sense, Jack. I understand that you're angry, but what's going to happen to the people you free? Hundreds of them—are they going to starve? Or what? And they'll kill you all if you keep doing it. You're still just one boy. You're building nothing that'll last. And the balladeers will be just as happy to sing of your death as they are your fight. Perhaps I can *help* you: tomorrow we can talk about—"

The door opened, and light came in, and the dark figure at the window fell away at once. In an ink-stained nightshirt and cap, holding a candle, the botanist Dr. Grishman shuffled into the room to rummage among the books on the table. He didn't notice Jack; his eyes were fixed on the dark cluttered floor.

Holbach did not bother to go to the window to look out after Jack. Instead, he roused his aching bones, and said, "Midnight oil, Grishman? Good for you. Can I help you look?"

THIRTY-THREE

Haycock spent the spring moving from place to place, burrowing furtively north, and west, and north, and east for a week or two, and then north again. He took two cases with him. One was full of books, which he sold off for food and lodgings as he went—and, traveling well away from all his usual haunts and his regular clients, he was reminded again, every fucking day, how cheap, how greedy, how ignorant his fellow citizens were, what thieving vermin they were, how they took every opportunity to gouge and cheat a fellow down on his luck.

The other case contained Haycock's three ratty suits, and a wide assortment of charms and amulets and fetishes and inscriptions and philters and wards against evil. He picked up more as he traveled. He stank alternately of incense and booze.

If he drank enough, maybe he could forget the *shape* he had seen, coiling and seething coldly in the grey mists that pooled in the Cypress's lonely beer garden; he could forget how it had *looked* at him, how it had *hated* him. He could forget how his skin crawled with the knowledge that he had been *marked*.

In his jacket pocket Haycock carried, crumpled now, the pages he'd cut from *Thinkers of Our Age*. Cuttle! There was a man one could deal with. There was a man who knew how things worked—a man who might save Haycock's hide, in return for which there was nothing, *nothing* Haycock would not sell. If only Haycock could *find* Cuttle. For the time being, the important thing was to put as much distance as possible between himself and that little foreign Arjun bastard whose fault this all was.

North again, then, toward the Mountain. Haycock wasn't sure why, but it seemed like just plain common sense that that was the way to find Cuttle, or someone, anyone, who might know what the score was. After a couple of months Haycock's money ran out. He swore and cursed his own kindness, his own damn fool kindness, in leaving the rest of the book behind to warn Arjun—Haycock could have bought lodging for *days* more with that fucking thing! Haycock slept in the parks or under the arches. He was too old for sleeping rough. He came down with a cough, and a dead numbness in his legs. He tried to sweat the fever out, sleeping in an abandoned lockup full of damp and rust and mold, in the shadow of a disused rendering plant. He knew it was a mistake—the god was always at home in abandoned and ugly places—but what fucking choice did he have? His lungs burned and unpleasant visions came and went. When the door banged open and leaves and rain swirled in and behind them he saw that unspeakable formless poisonous *thing,* all he could do was croak in despair: *Fuck you, then, monster.*

THIRTY-FOUR

Arjun woke up on a cool Bounds-day morning, on the edge of Olympia's bed. There was a sticky splash of red wine across the tangled sheets. Olympia was not there. She was an early riser, as Arjun himself had always been, back in the Choristry, and during his time of hard travel. *I'm becoming dissolute in my idleness,* he thought.

Olympia's girl, Pieta, had filled the ewer in the toilet with warm water. Arjun shaved with a crisp blade, then pulled on black trousers and a loose white shirt. On his way out, he passed Pieta, and spoke with her for a while. Olympia always addressed Pieta by name, and encouraged her opinions, and Arjun saw no reason not to follow Olympia's practices in her house.

"I saw *The Blessing* again," she said. "At the Palace. I took my sister. I had to have her see it. She cried and cried when the little girl's father was taken from her."

"Good. We wanted tears. Was the singer adequate?"

"She did you proud, Mr. A. Pretty, too."

"No riots? No torch-bearing savages? No censors?"

"Some loony Lavilokine stood up at the back, and held this big mirror around, shouting 'Look at your blasphemy and repent!' like they do, but a bunch of lads from the soap-works—you know 'em by the smell, you know?—gave him a knock on the head. And there were militia sniffing around the edges, a few of 'em trying to look like normal people, you know, but they weren't doing anything. Miss O. says they're scared to do anything. Says the play is too popular to put it down."

"Maybe. If they ever stop being scared, though, it'll take more than the soap-works lads to save us."

"Ah, I'm not frightened. Oh—not that I mean to say you are, Mr. A."

"No offense taken, Pieta."

No, he could see that she wasn't frightened; but then, she was very young. Arjun wished her a good day, and went out.

The Marriage Blessing was a ridiculous, triumphant, blazing success. It had its first night at the Radiant Crown, on the fringes of Harp Street—a boxy little outfit, whose name was a joke at the expense of its spare grey space, and whose underfed and urgent impresarios were thrilled beyond belief to be launching the new play of the great Joseph Liancourt. Arjun could see their thin shoulders square and their chests inflate as Liancourt told them of his plan, and as they realized that he meant it, it was not some cruel joke. Arjun had not, until then, understood how famous and well-loved Liancourt was.

When the first night opened, the Crown was so packed that it seemed people were hanging from the rafters. Many more were turned aside at the gate. "It has to be this way," Liancourt had explained. "The larger theaters won't take it, even for me. Too dangerous. But it's better this way, anyway. Open small at first. Let it gather momentum. Sneak up on the censors. Make people beg to come and see it. Make it seem like a secret, something they have to *work* for. It worked for *The Sign,* and by gods it'll work for this." But his confidence broke on opening night, and he fretted and tugged at his hair, back in the wings, peeking out at the seething dark hall as if every person in it wore a white robe and carried a flaming brand just for him.

Arjun stood near him. Unlike Liancourt, he had nothing to do and no one to fuss over: he trusted the musicians they'd hired. And he had no reputation at stake: he'd refused to be named anywhere as the play's composer, saying that the music was not his creation, that he'd only echoed it—which he knew Liancourt found aggravatingly pious, but the truth was the truth. Still, he was almost as nervous as

Liancourt, and he was listening more to the crowd than to the music. He wanted very badly to be understood. He liked to think it was more than vanity.

The Blessing followed two stories. One was a sentimental piece, a story of a girl whose father was taken into the Iron Rose for crimes that were not specified, but were strongly implied to be a matter of subversive or blasphemous speech; her mother died quickly of an illness that could not, due to the family's straitened circumstances, be treated, leaving the poor girl to be cast out into the city's streets, among criminal folk. She would find that all her attempts to better her situation and, later, to find a husband, would be thwarted by the machinations of shadowy figures. And the second story was a comic one, with flashes of anger: a solid craftsman, plump, a little bald, and not-so-young, whose own attempts to marry were frustrated again and again by mocking aristocrats and his own shabby status. Arjun lent both characters the Voice's song.

This was the sting: Liancourt had added a chorus to the play, masked figures resembling no particular god, but clearly godlike in nature, who mocked all of his heroes' efforts to escape their situation, who moved the city's powers around like chess-pieces to thwart them. And every time a cruel boss or a smirking lord or a criminal thug denied something to Liancourt's heroes, those avatars of repression would shrug and point to the chorus behind them, and say, "But the gods say no"—and, on a good night, the audience would yell back at the stage in anger.

This was the promise: both protagonists were saved by the discovery of a book of wisdom and wit, with a magical map that plotted the way out of their respective traps. It was not safe for Liancourt explicitly to propagandize for the Atlas, but the play's code was not subtle: it was easily understood that *The Blessing* was heralding the Atlas's return, was clearing its way.

It closed, of course, with dual weddings, and a birth, and the overthrow of the wicked and the unmasking of false gods, and with the jubilant pouring of the cast onto the crowded stage, and then with the most tremendous crescendo of bells. An *extraordinary* number of bells. Arjun had insisted on the bells. They used neighborhood children to bang them. Wedding bells, prayer bells, fire bells, warning bells, tinkling chimes and deep bass notes, all rising and spiraling and rejoicing and raging together like a lightning-storm from which emerged—slowly, imperceptibly, at last—the simple pure melody of the Voice.

(Arjun had studied the acoustics of the theater intently, and experimented carefully. He'd wanted to make it overwhelming, but not—not quite—intolerable.)

The first-night crowd wept and howled and, at the end, stamped their feet. Liancourt hugged cast and crew, then collapsed in a prop chair, exhausted with relief and joy. He beckoned Arjun and Olympia, and in an exaggerated croak of exhaustion, said, "Come here. Don't make me get up; I'm too old, and you're too young. We reached 'em, no? There's something in them that was ready to be moved."

Over the next few weeks, the play moved out of the Crown and into the Key, the street's largest playhouse. Then Liancourt was happy to let it out of his hands, and allowed companies all over the city to stage their own performances, hastily knocking together scenery, making work for even the worst singers and actors. The play made it as far north (at least) as Stross End, in an iron-walled hall at the base of one of the surviving clocktowers, and as far west as the Sacral Wall, as far east as the docks of Red Mire. Some stripped-down versions, with minor characters cut away and ambiguities resolved, made their way into the streets, and were performed by enthusiastic amateurs from the backs of carts, for tossed pennies or food. The street-players cut out the orchestra, but they always kept in the main themes of the music. It worked well even on crude instruments. Sometimes they banged out the bells on pots and kettles; it was a bloody awful noise but the crowds stamped and cheered anyway. There was an energy to it that persisted even in the shabbiest circumstances.

The churches staged protests and vigils, but for every passerby they drove away, they drew another curious one in.

The white robes closed down a few productions with fire, but others sprang up. At the Summit, the robed children rushed the stage and beat the heroine with brands in the glare of the stagelight, then fled into the crowd before the watch could come. Olympia had known the actress, and she and Arjun went to visit the poor woman in the hospital, to promise that the Atlas-makers, by which they meant Holbach, would compensate her for her ruined career.

The *Era*'s editor warned that the play was a dangerous and reckless subversion of the city's fragile order, and should be stamped out forthwith, while the *Sentinel* praised it rapturously, as a fine flowering of the polyphony and creativity that was Ararat at its best. After a couple of weeks, the papers reversed their positions, to keep the fight fresh.

The censors sniffed around—stood disapprovingly at the back of the theaters, sent Liancourt threatening letters on thick official paper—but the play was too popular to be closed down, and too artfully vague. Besides, the censors were too busy with the ballads of Jack Silk, liberator, gaolbreaker, and the sudden parades of citizens dressed in brightly dyed tatters and rags, the wild anarchic street theater. That was far more blantantly subversive than Liancourt's play, and took all their attention.

Arjun went to a few performances, to see how the singers handled their parts, but otherwise he took no part in it. It was not his job to train them or direct them. It was no longer his business. He directed inquisitive journalists from the *Era* and the *Herald* to talk to Liancourt instead.

He took to walking the streets again, renewing his old search. For two days, he went out by himself, rising in the morning, taking a carriage north until midday, then wandering, following whatever music he heard.

On the third day, he slept late, and when he woke, he found that Olympia was already back from her morning's meeting with an official of the First Citizen's Office of Doctrinal Correction, and was sorting her files in the study. "Oh, it ended almost before it began," she said, "with screaming and impotent threats on both sides. Not dignified, sadly. Horrid little man."

She was free for the rest of the day, so he pulled her away from her papers, and they took a carriage together; Arjun told the driver to choose a direction at random. They went north, until they passed a wedding on the banks of the river. The wedding party were dressed in white and gold, and protected by a heavy guard: it was a joining of great houses. The party danced stiffly to an orchestra on the pier. Arjun stopped the carriage, and they sat by the river's edge, listening to the music.

The grim black prison-bulk of the Iron Rose loomed incongruously in the distance behind the stately dancers. Further down the river's banks, the RiverHouse Theater's banners advertised *The Blessing*. Olmypia pointed to the banners. "So, do you want to hear my theory?"

"Certainly."

"It's rather good. I think the play's success comes down to this: the threat of war is over. No further attacks for months. Stross End was the first and the last. The *Thunderer* is almost vanished from the skies. The Countess rolled dice with the city; she could have sparked total war, great rolling waves of blood and fire back and forth across our streets, but it didn't happen. Renegotiation of borders and tribute went on over our heads, secret moves in the great game. And then after months of fear, without any official word, without any surrender or treaty, we all realized that it was over, forgotten, and who knows when that happened? I have *superb* sources of information, Arjun, and I was in the dark, too. But if it hasn't happened now, it won't. And so all that pent-up tension and fear had to go somewhere. What first presented itself? *The Blessing.* And the Thunderers, too, I suppose. The city's new obsessions: both ways for everyone to say, 'It's over, we can, we *will*, move on.' "

"I don't think that can be all of it."

She laughed. "Is that injured pride of authorship? Holbach's hangers-on rubbing off on you at last? Of course your music is important, too."

"I meant that the city's very big; I'm sure many people find many different things in the play. As many people hate it as love it. Anyway, it wasn't *my* music. I just echoed it."

"Oh *gods*. How *pious*. Oh." She looked at him. "That's what we're out for today, isn't it? Looking for your Voice. You're starting that again. I thought you'd lost interest. I thought we'd given you something else to think about."

He looked out over the grey water. "The Atlas has been a pleasant diversion. I don't mean to insult you by putting it that way. But

I've done what I can for you. When I wrote that music for Liancourt, I looked inside myself, and the Voice was still there, waiting. It's time to move on, and there's nowhere else I can go, nothing else I can do, but search for it."

"Oh, well. I knew you were mad. We could have talked about it, you know. I wouldn't have understood, but I would have made sympathetic noises. So, let's get up and get on with it, then."

They wandered along the river until it started to get dark. They found nothing, of course. She teased him, but that was all right. He didn't mind. He saw no reason why his quest should be a solemn matter, and it was pleasant not to be alone.

A few days later, Olympia was woken by a messenger from Cimenti's Bureau of Printing and Publication, who left behind an official letter on plain grey paper, in the ugly print of Cimenti's typing-machines. It read: *Prisonr's Request is GRANTED. Sentence is Liftd. Prepartions for Prsioner's Release Are To Proceed Accordinlgy.* The date-stamp was weeks old. She stared at it blankly, then said, tentatively, "Nicolas?"

She spent the day at Cimenti's courthouse and at the Bureau's offices, trying to find out what had happened. The letter was real. Some wheel in the machine had jerked into sudden motion; no one could say why. She left the premises quickly, not wanting to ask too many questions, afraid it was a mistake that might still be corrected. "It's real," she said, to the hushed and awed assembly in Holbach's dining room that evening. "And strictly speaking, no other Estate but Cimenti's has sentenced him to *exile,* only to certain *conditions of exile,* so by itself this is effective to secure his release, if we act quickly. But I have *no* idea how this happened."

"Who bloody cares how?" said one of the poets.

The Atlas-makers celebrated. Holbach and the professors and wise old men made speeches. The poets and painters and the young explorers raided Holbach's wine cellar, and shouted down the speechifying. They carried Holbach through the hall on their shoulders, then Olympia, though she kept telling them it had nothing to do with her. At the end of the evening, Arjun and Olympia fell into bed in one of the upstairs rooms.

Two days later, Holbach received a letter, this one from Nicolas himself, and addressed to *All My Brothers and Sisters*. It said, *Today they opened the gates of my tower. Tomorrow a ship will take me from my is-land and return me to life. They will not tell me what miracle has secured my freedom. This letter may precede my return. . . .* It was over a week old.

Nicolas himself appeared the next morning. They had made a place for him in Holbach's house. A carriage brought him up from Ar-Mouth, and the house's occupants poured out into the garden to see him. The shock of his return had not worn off. It was like a god manifesting before them. They clapped and cheered as he emerged, a frail, tiny old man in a plain brown coat, shaved head just starting to bristle again, all bony hooked nose and elbows, sharp, darting eyes. Holbach had the honor of supporting the sage's shaking arm out of the carriage.

Arjun was around the house that day, and the next, as Nicolas held court in the study, and the assembled artists and thinkers came to pay him tribute. Exile had not mellowed him; it had burned him pure. In an angry, wounded rasp, he urged them on to greater defi-ance, greater outrage. He tore through Holbach's piles of newspa-pers, quite literally, taking pages that enraged him in both bony hands and ripping them effortlessly to shreds. "This boy has the idea!" he said, waving a page headlined *"Thunderer" Outlaws Strike Again: Can They Be Stopped?* "No compromise or cowardice. Not anymore. I am too old to be wise."

He called them all around him, and said, "I have had so much time to think, gentlemen, and I am tired of it. My gaolers may snap me back at any moment; I am determined to *act*. I have great plans, gentlemen. We must organize." A few of the scholars found Nicolas's new talk too incautious, too frightening: they left the house, making weak excuses about their own neglected projects, and did not come back. Most of them stayed, waiting around the house, for the great sage to call them up into the study to be inter-viewed. Nicolas was inspecting his troops.

Arjun spoke to Nicolas only briefly, on the second day. Holbach, fussing around Nicolas like an anxious courtier, gave Arjun a brief introduction, as his translator and Liancourt's composer. Nicolas turned sharp, angry eyes on him and said, "Yes, I've heard your name. The one who came here to look for his missing god. The one who tried to sneak a lot of religious nonsense into Liancourt's play. The one who keeps demanding that the Professor waste his valuable time on some selfish obsession. Some *addiction.* I shall have to think carefully whether you have a place in the project. Now, Holbach, who's next?"

Arjun was not offended. Nicolas was right. He was not truly part of the Atlas, and never would be or could be. He excused himself politely. He came back on the fourth day, just to see Olympia, but found that she was shut in the study with Nicolas. He waited for her in the lower library, reading the papers. He sat alone; all the life in the house had been drawn up into Nicolas's presence, upstairs. He listened to a light rain scatter across the windows and the gravel paths outside.

The rain grew insistent; thick heavy bursts abused the trees and rattled the windows. The sky was suddenly very dark for a spring morning, or even, then, for a winter night, and the room was very cold. He heard the servants running around, closing the windows to keep out the downpour, and the sound was like doors slamming, like hull-timbers breaking—he felt like a trap had closed on him. He ran to the window. The path out of the garden seemed to stretch far into the dark.

There was a smell, stale and familiar. He knew what was coming down that dark path. He had felt it before.

He ran upstairs, almost bowling the housekeeper over on the landing, and burst into the study. He tried to shout, but his voice was constricted: "Something's coming. You have to leave, all of you. It's the—"

Nicolas cut him off. "We're at work. We've no time for—"

"—the Typhon, the river-thing, *please,* come on, I can feel it, I remember it, it's finally followed me here—"

"Quiet." Nicolas turned to Holbach. "Holbach, is there any reason to imagine that the Typhon would manifest itself here?"

"Well, no. I would know if something were to manifest in my

own house, and there've been no signs. Anyway, we're far from any waterway. Arjun, the gods move in a predictable manner, rule-bound, as I've explained. Perhaps you're—"

"See? Now please settle down or leave us."

Arjun looked around in horror. They couldn't feel it. *Yet.* Holbach was gesturing for him to calm down. Liancourt would not meet his gaze. Olympia was leaning against the wall, looking horrified and embarrassed. He grabbed her arm and dragged her out the door, protesting. She shouted at him and tried to push him away on the landing, but he barely noticed. He pulled her behind him down the stairs, saying, "I'm sorry, I'm sorry, but we have to get *out.*" She nearly fell trying to keep up.

Hoxton appeared at the foot of the stairs, with a sudden blow to Arjun's gut that floored him, sobbing and choking. He stood over Arjun, rubbing his knuckles.

"Sorry about that, sir. For what it's worth, I always thought you were one of her better ones. Miss O.?"

"Hoxton, it's not like that. Leave him. Arjun?"

He pulled himself to his feet, and tried to gasp out, "Please." The pain and the fear were crushing his throat.

"All right, Arjun, I'll come with you. All right." Her voice was light, as if to humor him, but there was an edge of doubt and fear in it. "We'll go for a ride, clear our heads. Hoxton?"

Hoxton wrapped a hairy arm around Arjun's wheezing chest and helped him out through the garden and into the carriage.

"To Arjun's place, Hoxton."

"It's the Typhon. I feel it. It'll kill them all."

"You heard Holbach, Arjun, it can't be. You make it sound like a, I don't know, a starved wolf. It's not like that."

Just a few streets away, the rain stopped and the cold lifted. Olympia's mood was calm again, now that they were out of the house, and she said, "You're reacting to the weather. We've all been under pressure. You should sleep. We'll take you home."

She sat by him for a while in his room, until she was sure he was no danger to himself. He was silent and exhausted. He would not go back to the house with her, so she left him with a troubled kiss, which he did not return.

* * *

I'm so sorry, Nicolas." Holbach shook his head sadly. "He's not a bad young man. He just had a very nasty experience." Nicolas grunted and indicated with a wave of his bony hand that the meeting should continue. Liancourt attempted to pick up where he had left off—with his proposal that the Atlas-makers form an alliance with certain dissident factions in remote Red Barrow, with whom he was in occasional secret contact through the medium of an actress, a defector—but the mood quickly soured. Branken objected that no one from Red Barrow could be trusted under any circumstances; Rothermere told Branken he was a fool; and a bitter squabble broke out.

Holbach sighed. He hoped Olympia would get back soon.

The sky continued to blacken as the storm seethed outside. Nicolas cursed the darkness and ordered candles to be lit; they promptly flickered out. The Atlas-makers sat in the shadows and sneered and sniped at each other's pathetic plans. Holbach slumped in his chair and a sense of hopelessness settled on him. The room grew cold and for a moment the long shadow of a chair's heavy back swayed against the far wall and took on an angular shape that was both monstrous and tortured, and Holbach felt an instant of stupid, demoralizing terror.

Soon Nicolas started to cough, damply, miserably, painfully, and the old man retired to bed. Soon after that, both Branken and Grishman complained of headaches and fever, and the meeting was adjourned. Holbach had a stiff drink to steady his nerves.

THIRTY-FIVE

Olympia came to Arjun's flat the next morning.

"What happened?" he asked. "Are they all right?"

"Nothing happened. Yes, they are. Are you?"

He looked glumly at her. "You don't believe me."

"Arjun, nothing happened. I'll admit, I was unnerved at the time. But *nothing happened*. It's all right: I told Nicolas you'd had a terrible experience with the Typhon, and that the rain must have brought it back to you. He understands. More or less."

"I don't need his understanding. It was *there*. I remember how it felt. I can't go back."

"We've talked about this. Arjun, the Typhon couldn't possibly come to Holbach's house. It's not part of its path, he says. It couldn't happen without signs, portents; and Holbach would know. He knows about these forces, Arjun. They are bound by rules. I thought you understood. You were so much better."

"I forgot. I let myself be distracted. Now I remember. Olympia, I *felt* the Typhon, down in the tunnels. *I* know it, better than Holbach or you. It's sick. It's not like the others, not at all, not anymore, if it ever was. Not after what Shay did to it. Not after what I did to it. I don't know what it might be able to do."

"You're not making sense."

"I'm sorry."

Irritation and sympathy clashed on her face. She wouldn't be understanding for long. They did not have, he had not sought, that sort of relationship. "I have a meeting," she said. "I'll check on you tomorrow. Don't just sit here worrying all day."

He visited the herbalist on the corner, and bought a pouch of leaf-wrapped pellets that would, he was assured, bring sleep and prevent dreams. Many of Stammer Gate's scholars had bad dreams, the herbalist told him. Arjun spent the day darting from one café to another. He went back to his flat that night reluctantly, but it was—to his desperate relief—free of the monster's mark. It had not followed him.

Olympia came again the next evening. "You look terrible," she said. "Bloodshot eyes and bloodless everything else. Are you eating? You should come back to the house. Don't you want to see what Nicolas is going to do next?"

"I can't. I'm sorry."

She couldn't stay long. There was too much to be done. As she was leaving, he said, "Tell Holbach to come and see me. He promised me, months ago, he could help me find the Voice. It's time now. It has to be now. Tell him to come."

"I'll try. I'll be back again soon."

She did not come the next day. Nor did Holbach. Was it so hard for them to believe him? They were too proud of what they thought they knew; they had lost their fear of the city.

To pass the time, he went back to work on the last of his Tuvar texts. The pile was small now. At noon, a boy came bearing a note from Liancourt, expressing Liancourt's hopes for a swift recovery, and telling him not to worry that Nicolas would be angry with him: the great sage knew how highly strung creative temperaments like Arjun's could be, and would understand, soon.

The next day passed in the same way, and the next, and the next. In the evening, he gave up waiting, and went walking, east across Stammer Gate, past the Surgeons' College that marked the border with Rywhill. He tried to listen for the sound of the Voice, but it was hard to keep himself open for it. Every draft, every scent of rot

or mud or the city's sewers, made him think of the Typhon. The city
felt like a toothed trap, its spring winding down. The Typhon was
coming for him. He felt it.

Holbach came to the flat the next morning. Arjun had no place
to entertain guests, so they went for a walk. The sun was high and
hot, and the street smelled rank.

"Thank you for coming, Professor."

"I have only a little time, Arjun. We're very busy now, of
course. We have new plans now. Arjun—Olympia says you won't be
coming back. I don't mean any offense, but you understand, don't
you, that you must not talk of our work or our plans to anyone?"

"Of course."

"Nothing happened, you know."

"I know what I felt. You were lucky to escape unharmed, if you
did. You should leave that place, or you should think of ways to protect yourself from it, if you have that science."

"There's nothing to protect against. And we have other concerns."

"So do I, Professor. You promised me you would help me find
the Voice if I worked for you. And I have. I faced Shay for you; I
have worked for months on your Atlas. The play you're all so proud
of is as much my work as it is Liancourt's."

"I know, I know."

"It's time for you to help me."

"Gods, there's just so much *else* to do. With Nicolas's return,
we've moved the deadline for the new edition back a month, but we
have so much more to do; and the Countess demands that I do
something about the Thunderers, find the source of their power
somehow, and that I do something about the lung-rot epidemic,
which is *entirely* outside of my field, but she doesn't understand that
I have limits, too. Gods. *Soon,* I promise."

"I may not have much more time in this city. It's turning
against me. I feel it. It's only a matter of time. Because *you* sent me
to Shay, the Typhon has *seen* me, and *hates* me, and it's *marked* me."

"It doesn't work like that. And anyway, I couldn't possibly have
known you would meet the Typhon when I sent you. I meant to do
you a favor. I thought Shay could help you."

"Nevertheless. What happened, happened."

"All right. Yes. I'll think. That's all I can do just now. It's a strange problem. I never meant to waste your time, you know. I'll think and I'll let you know if I make any progress. I may know some people who can help. I may send you some books."

"That's all I can ask. On your honor, don't forget, Professor."

They shook hands stiffly at the end of the street.

The heat got worse. Summer, too, was coming. Nagging clouds of midges and mosquitoes hatched out of the earth, out of the cracked brickwork. The air was hazy with them, reminding Arjun of the swamps through which he had passed in the south. The herbalist on the corner spat in disgust out of his door, into the street: "Fucking things. Last summer it was clear, and we had the Bird, Praise Be; this year it's this vermin. No wonder no one can sleep."

Arjun thanked him, and pocketed his pills, then he went down to the docks, where the water was a very deep green, and the fish-stench was thick and greasy, and the dockhands sweated and reddened and swore at each other. Down by the docks' edge, in the spray, there was some relief to be had from the heat.

The familiar strains of *The Blessing*'s opening theme were playing from a makeshift stage by the water, then a weak, vulgar voice started knocking the heroine's song about. A small crowd gathered, and Arjun joined them.

The players were rough, untrained but forceful. The men had the look of dockhands, sailors, toughs. The heroine looked brazen, slatternly. They looked, in fact, like criminals, like convicts, and probably were. It was a bad summer for crime and for random violence in the streets. The beneficiaries of Silk's campaign were all over the place. Some found work in the docks or the factories, some were snatched back into their gaols, and some ended up begging or starving; but too many formed brazen packs in the streets. "Money with menaces," that was the legal term. The newspapers were quite hysterical about it.

And the play itself had been rewritten by some hack's hand. It was similar, but not quite the same. In Liancourt's original, the protagonists had been abused by cruel, arbitrary aristocrats, but those powers had been left artfully unnamed: they could have been any of the city's rulers, or, if the censors asked, none of them. To Arjun's surprise, in this version, the enemy was quite clearly identified as the Countess Ilona. She commanded a flying ship, with a ghoulish, death-obsessed Captain, who flew about the city to place obstacles in the heroes' way.

Where Liancourt had used a chorus of the gods to comment on the action, this version used conversations between the Countess and her Captain. They were crudely sexual, the Countess throwing herself, humiliatingly, at the frigid Captain.

The street-players had slashed the play's length greatly. Wit was replaced by curt sloganeering. The music had been truncated brutally; this bastardized version used only the songs into which Arjun had poured his anger and bitterness, his fear, his abandonment. The players had cut the gentler, wiser music entirely. Arjun was appalled to recognize sour notes—sour notes that *he* had written, but never really heard—that owed more to the Typhon than the Voice.

Then, at the end, he was astonished to see, they made it explicit that the book that saved the heroes was the Atlas. They called it by name. Liancourt had not dared to do so, before. They were inviting retribution. What had made them so reckless?

It was quickly over. A few angry hecklers had gathered, but it finished before there could be violence. The players took away their props with them on the back of a cart, disappearing at once into the shadowed streets of Barbary. The crowd, too, quickly dispersed, and Arjun with them. It was safest not to linger after such a performance.

Olympia came to see him a few days later. "Holbach says you think you need to leave the city soon."

"You knew I didn't plan to stay forever."

"Of course I did. Don't flatter yourself. I'm just sorry to see you go for no reason. For a mad reason."

"I'm not going yet. I'll stay as long as I must, to find what I came for." He noticed that there were lines of worry on her face; she had not been sleeping well either. "There's something else troubling you. Are the plans going badly?"

"Things are very tense in the house. We're all working very hard. And Nicolas is sick, and he's taking it out on us. He's very old, and the strain . . . It's all very sudden for him. Oh, I don't know, he'll be all right. It's just hard, at the moment."

"I don't like the changes to *The Blessing.* It's out of my hands now, of course, but I regret what Nicolas has done to it. It's very crude. Is that all that his plans amount to?"

"Oh, no. That's nothing to do with Nicolas, or any of us, for that matter. It just started to appear, early last week. Liancourt is furious. So is Nicolas: he thinks it'll bring retribution down on us, before we're ready to move. They want me to put a stop to it, but I'm no censor. I don't have the power. There's no one to sue; the play crops up in one place for a day, and vanishes. They don't use actors, they just hire whatever they can dredge up from the pubs. I try to tell Liancourt, if you let something like that play loose in the city, it's not yours anymore. It *changes.* I'm just busy now trying to persuade the censors it's not our work. I'm not sure they believe me."

"Be careful, please, Olympia. Not just of the censors, but of the Typhon. You should leave that house."

"Stop it. *You* should come back. Dangerous times are exciting times. This is what we've all been working for."

"I can't."

They had sex, their first time in Arjun's austere flat. They both seemed to need it very badly, but their moods were not greatly different afterwards. Olympia seemed irritated that it had not lifted Arjun's dread or changed his mind. She left.

That afternoon, he went down to the docks again, but the play was gone, the rude stage dismantled. Arjun bought lunch, meat wrapped in thick leaves, from a stall.

There was an empty half-circle in the crowd, against the looming wooden wall of a shipyard. A man lay moaning against the wall. Blackish-green drool ran from his slack mouth. The crowd gave him a wide berth, pressing handkerchiefs to their faces if they had them, or the tails of their shirts. "Oh gods, it's lung-rot," said a clerk by Arjun's side. "Don't get too near."

The smell was dreadful: cold and wet and deathly. It made Arjun think of the smell of the canal-tunnels. And he recalled that Olympia had said Nicolas was sick, and he suddenly could not believe how stupid he had been, how thoughtless. He had been within its mind, and he knew what sort of thing it was. It had pursued him in Shutlow, and taken Norris and the others, and then to Holbach's house. *And it has put its mark on Nicolas. Maybe on all of them.* He turned and ran toward the Tor and Foyle's Ward.

But he could not do it. He got near to Holbach's street, and fear buckled his knees. He could not face it. He would rather die, and let everyone he had ever cared for die, than face the creature again. But they had to know.

There was a carriage rank nearby, and he found one of the stable-boys, and gave him a message. He had no paper or pen, so he made the boy memorize it: *The Typhon has caused Nicolas's sickness. It may be the source of the lung-rot. It may be the lung-rot itself. It may have marked you all. It may still be there. I beg you to leave the house now.*

The boy repeated it back one last time. Arjun said, "Now, deliver that message to the first person you find, and see that they give it to Olympia—*Olympia*—or Holbach—*Holbach.* Will you remember that? And swear to me, on your mother, that you'll leave as soon as you've done that, and got your money. Don't stay there, for any reason."

The boy nodded and ran off. Arjun hated himself for sending a child into that place. He watched him turn the corner.

He sent a second boy to the Cypress, to warn Defour. Then he went to Olympia's rooms, to wait for her.

"She's not here, sir," Pieta told him. "We're not expecting her back for days."

"Is she at Holbach's house?"

"Dunno. Could be anywhere. You know how she is, sir."

"I'll wait."

She let him sit on the sofa, drumming his fingers nervously on a glass-topped table.

"Do you mind if I ask, sir? Is there trouble between you and the mistress?"

He glared at her. She left him alone. He regretted his coldness, but could not face calling her back. He sat alone all day, and went home in the evening, when it was clear Olympia wasn't coming.

The next day, he sent another messenger to Holbach's house, in case the first had run off with his money. Still no reply.

He went back to Olympia's flat the following afternoon. To reach it, he had to cross the delicate carved bridges over the pleasure-canals of Ebon Fields. The Fields lay between the canals: sharp-edged, gleaming jags of ebony set on a background of verdant grass, jeweled with bright flowers. And on a wide flat mound of ebony, beneath the bridge, a crew of players was performing the bastardized *Blessing*. Arjun told the driver to rein his horses, and leaned over the bridge to watch. The crowd here was well-dressed, the spoiled pleasure-seekers of the Fields. They seemed to find the play a guilty thrill. It was cut short quickly, the pantomime-villain-Countess in mid-sneer, when a boy came running to the foot of the black rock stage to shout, "Watch! Coming quick!"

The players and the crowd ran for it. Arjun got back in the carriage and proceeded to Ebon Fields. She was still not there.

Two days later, he was woken by a banging on his door. It was very late in the morning. The pellets helped him sleep, but made it hard to rise. He waited, warily, until he heard Olympia's voice call, "Arjun?"

He let her in. Holbach was with her. Both looked tired and grey. He asked them, "Well?"

"Nicolas died in the night," Holbach said. Olympia choked back a sob and put a tense fist against the wall.

Arjun shook his head. "I'm sorry." It was sad news, but he had resigned himself to it days ago.

Holbach said, "It was the lung-rot, in the end. Like all the other cases I've studied, in the end, but slower. A week ago, it was a cough and a shortness of temper, then it grew, and grew, and last night... I got your messages. I've sent everyone away. We need to talk, Arjun. Tell me again: what did you see in that tunnel? This time I promise to listen."

Arjun took a deep breath, and began to describe it, leaving nothing out. When he was done, Holbach was shaking his head. "That's very wrong. What you say you felt. Very strange, and very wrong. The sickness, the division you describe, between the divine and the impure elements. I've never heard of anything like it. If Shay affected it somehow, changed it, then, well...I don't know how it might behave. I suppose it might behave the way you describe."

"Shay poisoned it," Olympia spat.

"That seems most likely," Holbach said.

"It followed you to us," Olympia said.

"I'm sorry. I tried to warn you."

They were silent for a time. Arjun asked, "Professor, can you defend against it? Hide from it? Fight it?"

"I have no idea how to even begin to answer that question. I have no idea what sort of condition the Typhon may be in. I've never heard of one of its kind being, ah, *corrupted* like this. I'm not even convinced that you're right; it may be a mere coincidence, and your recollection may be confused. I don't even know all that much about the Typhon, even in what you might call a *healthy* state. I told you once, I think, that I prefer to study the useful powers of the city. What use is the Typhon? Let it sit in its tunnels and be forgotten, was always my view. But now..."

"Don't go back to your house, Professor."

"Gods no. I'll take rooms somewhere."

"Find some way to fight it or ward it off. I release you from your promise to me. You have to work on this, instead."

"Oh, yes. Ah, thank you. Yes, I will, of course."

"If it hunts me down, I'll never find the Voice. If you can fight it, I'll be able to search again."

"Ah. I see."

"I'm sorry about Nicolas. I hope the Atlas survives."

They talked a little longer, awkwardly, painfully. There was nothing much to say. Olympia and Holbach were still too shocked, too sad, to know what they would do next.

"Ah, no," Holbach said. "No funeral plans, yet. Not yet."

They left. Arjun shook Holbach's hand. Olympia moved behind Holbach and out the door, not meeting Arjun's eyes.

Next afternoon, a messenger delivered a note with the address of Holbach's hotel, and instructions that Arjun should contact Holbach if anything happened, or if he remembered anything important, and a promise that Holbach would be in touch as soon as he made any progress.

Arjun sat at his desk, taking stock. He now had two impossible goals. First, to find the Voice; he would not leave without it. Second, to hide from or destroy the Typhon; he could not stay so long as it hunted him. He had no inkling of how to do either. He was mortal, and they were not. He could not touch or reach them. And, too, he was afraid for Olympia and Holbach and all the Atlas-makers. They had been kind to him, and their dream was a good one. He was afraid their time, too, was short.

That night he leafed through one of the last of his books, the Hierophant Vikar's record of his theological debates. It was tiresome and self-serving, perfect to induce sleep.

The last thing he read was Vikar's penultimate chapter, in which Vikar soundly defeated (he claimed) the heresy of a city-native who had denied that the gods were deserving of worship. Vikar explained:

> *That man's confusion had many sources, for every street in this city may lead a man into confusion. But above all, it was his reading of a certain ancient text, a* Riddle-Book *(which he unearthed in a manner it may be safest not to discuss) that addled him. It was a very foolish book, the product of many dozens of this city's scholars, proof, if any were needed, that numbers are no guarantee of wisdom, and that folly compounds with folly. In the form of a riddle-book, though one swollen to monstrous size, they thought to pose and answer all the city's questions and paradoxes.* They dreamed of explaining the joke of the city to the city, *my unwise friend told me,* and so

help it rise above its own absurdity, and set it aside. *There can be no better answer to those Riddlers' foolishness than this: they are gone, their book burned and their names expunged from history. Thus the city refuted them.*

Arjun put the book aside and slept, badly.

He waited for three days before deciding that he needed to see Holbach. He needed to speak to Olympia, too, he didn't want to leave things between them as they were, but Holbach had to be first. Arjun was going mad waiting to hear from him.

So he headed down to the carriage rank. There was a message-post there, always full of announcements and offerings, pronouncements of blessing or anathema. A small crowd gathered around it. He pushed gently through, and started to ask, "What are we looking at?" but it was obvious. Thick black print on a half-dozen posters shouted:

> *All Citizens Are Warned: The Performance Known as*
> **THE MARRIAGE BLESSING** *Has Been Found by the*
> *Authority of the Countess* **ILONA** *to Be Both Seditious and*
> *Libelous. The Following Persons Involved in This Libel,*
> *and in the Proscribed Work* **THE ATLAS,** *Are to Be Questioned.*
> *Possession or Performance of the Proscribed Works Are*
> *Forbidden Within Our Territories. By* **ILONA'S** *Order.*
> *By the* **GODS'** *Will and The* **CITY'S.**

A list of some twenty names followed. Nicolas Maine's topped it, followed by Holbach's and Liancourt's and, near the bottom, Olympia's. Arjun's name was not on the list.

He had not imagined Ilona would act with such unseemly haste. He extricated himself carefully from the crowd, staring at his feet, willing himself invisible. He took the first free carriage, and when the man asked "Where to?" he could not decide for a moment whom he was most frightened for. After a second, he gave the man Olympia's address.

He waited in her street for a while, watching. When he saw Pieta at the window, emptying out the chamber pots, he judged that there were no watchmen waiting there. But Olympia wasn't there, either. And when Arjun told Pieta what had happened, she dropped the vase she was dusting in shock, and held her pale hand to her face: she hadn't known. Olympia had not been back for days, and the Countess's men had not been to the flat. "Go home to your family," Arjun said, and, as an afterthought, he opened his wallet, saying, "She may not be back for a time. I can give you some money to tide you over."

The desk clerk at Holbach's hotel told Arjun that Holbach was gone. Arjun left at once, before the clerk could report him.

Three days later he stood at the back of a tight-pressed crowd out on the Heath, hot animal bodies packing onto the grass, stinking together of sweat and fear and anger. The sun burned the backs of their necks, except in the middle of the crowd, where a swath of shadow lay over them, cast by the low-hanging *Thunderer.* At the edge of the West Meadow, a wooden platform raised distant figures above the audiences' craning heads.

At the front of the stage were two men on their knees. Arjun could not make out their features, but he knew that they were Holbach and Liancourt. Behind them, dozens of armed men.

The Countess stood among her soldiers, her high collar making a halo of diamonds and gold behind her head. To Arjun, she looked like the monstrous lizards he had seen in the southern desert, which opened collars of scaled skin around their heads and spat poison. She stepped forward, and a footman screamed for silence, and she spat out the sentence that the crowd had gathered to see carried out.

The verdict had been rendered in sealed proceedings, in the Countess's chambers, and made public the day before. The Atlas was still under investigation, but there could be no question that *The Blessing* was both libelous and seditious. The sentence was death for Liancourt, whipping and imprisonment for Holbach.

She wouldn't want to lose Holbach's services, Arjun thought.

Some of the crowd cheered her, others booed, quietly at first, then with gathering courage as others joined them. Two burly men next to Arjun started to hum a theme from *The Blessing*, in a deep, defiant drone. When they saw him watching, they went silent and stared at their feet. He wanted to signal to them, *Don't worry, I am no spy.* He wanted to say, *Do something, for the love of the Voice, do something to stop this.*

The Countess screamed her proclamation louder, her voice hoarse. She was taking the insult very personally.

A man next to Arjun, a thick-necked laborer in a grey cap, fingered a knot of bright silk threads in his dirty left hand. Arjun thought, *Silk's here!* but the man was at least forty; he was not the famous prison-breaker.

For a moment, Arjun pictured himself as Silk, rushing up to the stage, casting the executioners down, and carrying the condemned men to freedom, but it was only a childish fantasy. He would not indulge himself in it.

He would attend solemnly. He would suffer along with them.

The Countess screamed, "Be warned!" She turned her back on the crowd, then turned again, with a shaking, pointing claw, and shrieked, "Be warned!" Then she gestured to one of her men, who stepped up behind Liancourt, drew his pistol, and fired it into the back of the playwright's head. The bellowing of the crowd was senseless and terrible.

Holbach's scourging was a more drawn-out affair. Arjun could not keep his word, and turned his eyes away.

The crowd's mood grew ugly as the punishment dragged on. The man next to him was openly raising his fistful of silk over his head, and shouting, "Silk!" and "Shame! Shame!"

There was some commotion at the front of the crowd, and the man in front of Arjun stumbled back against him, and Arjun nearly fell. There was screaming. He craned around the head in front of him, and saw men trying to climb onto the stage, the soldiers stamping on their heads and hands. A shot was fired. Soldiers with rifles converged on the front of the crowd, hunching against a hail of thrown objects. A curtain of soldiers drew around the Countess and the pale, bloody mess that was Holbach.

A signal ran through the crowd and shocked it into ugly life.

Arjun stood his ground, jostled by frightened and angry people surging in all directions. He didn't know whether to push forward, to join in the riot, though it was certainly a doomed gesture, or back, to get clear, before something terrible happened. He felt fixed in place, the whirlwind's still center.

More shots, more screams. A group of men with convicts' shaven heads rushed past, charging forward, brandishing knives and hammers; an elderly woman tried to lead a group of screaming, sobbing schoolchildren out through the crowd to safety. He wondered who could be attacking the stage. He had not thought the Atlas-makers had so many friends in the city, or at least not friends of this sort.

The press of the crowd took him under the *Thunderer's* shadow, and he looked up with holy dread at its great black guns. If the riot was not stopped soon, would it turn those guns on the crowd? He stared up at the warship, feet planted widely to keep his balance in the blindly surging throng. As he stared, there was an explosion across the Heath, though the guns had not fired. Then there was another explosion, closer to him. Each was followed by silence, a cloud of dust, then screaming.

The crowd was thinning now. Men ran through a fog of dust and smoke. The white wood of the bandstand, where Arjun had so often watched the city's musicians, was in flame. Soldiers on horseback rode over the Heath, striking fleeing men on their heads and necks with sticks. Arjun was not sure which way he was facing anymore. He thought he could see the skyline of the river's bank, and ran that way. He stumbled over a hole in the torn earth, and fell, his leg twisted beneath him.

Behind Arjun, one of the Countess's redcoats turned his horse, its legs knitting in a fine circle, and set it into a charge toward him. The soldier's face was resolute, and he held his sword level. Arjun could not quite manage to stand.

A heavyset figure stepped over him and fired two pistols, one in each hand, with a crash and a stink of powder. One shot at least did its work, tearing the rider from his saddle to hang tangled in the reins. The horse reared in terror as Hoxton bent down, firmly gripped Arjun's arm, and dragged him away.

THIRTY-SIX

Hoxton let go of Arjun's arm as soon as he was upright, and strode off, reloading his guns, calling over his shoulder, "Hurry up if you're coming." Arjun limped after him. A group of young men in factory uniforms ran between them, holding iron pipes, charging the front; for a moment, Arjun was afraid that he had lost Hoxton, but he saw him again when the mob passed.

No one stopped them. The Heath was emptying out. The riot-front had moved west, where the soldiers dismounted to pursue the hard core of the rioters into the dark of the Widow's Bower. A few men and soldiers ran here and there in Hoxton's path, but he hid his guns and kept his head down, and they left him alone.

Arjun followed Hoxton to a copse by the edge of the Heath, where Olympia waited behind the trees. She no longer affected her eye-catching and finely tailored masculine dress, Arjun saw: instead, she wore a shapeless, anonymous grey-white smock.

"Got 'im," Hoxton said. "You were right, it *was* him. Took some finding; he'd walked himself into the thick of it."

"Thank you, Hoxton. *Thank* you. Olympia . . ."

She cut Arjun off with a wave of her hand, and said, "We should get away from here." They climbed over a low wall, and into a dark alley that ran between two rows of restaurants, and ran through the smells of spices and the stench of rotting food.

✵　✵　✵

They took a circuitous route back to an attic room in a backstreet in the docks, over a sailors' pub. "I have given the landlord to understand that I am a whore," she said, "and Hoxton my pimp. That makes you custom. Try to look the part. Call me Julia, if you need to call me anything."

The room was bare, except for a bed, and a blanket in the corner that, to judge from the weapons arranged around it, was Hoxton's. Olympia sat on the bed and rubbed her brow.

"You should go further away," Arjun said. "We're still in the Countess's territory. If you go north, you may be safe."

"He's not wrong," Hoxton said.

"Not yet. Holbach's still alive. That bitch kept him alive, and you can bet she's keeping him close to her."

"What can you do for Holbach now?"

"I don't know yet. I saved some of the others. I persuaded the prosecutors that Branken and Rothermere, and a few others, weren't involved in the play. I made sure your name never came up. I persuaded them to hold off on condemning the Atlas itself, and that gave some of the others time to go to ground. But then they charged me, too, to shut me up, and no, I don't know if there's anything more I can do, not from hiding. But I can't leave Holbach. We might still recover one day, if we still have Holbach. *You* should go. There's no reason for you to stay here. I don't think they're looking for you, too, but they might."

"Holbach'll give 'em your name sooner or later, if they question him," Hoxton said.

"No," Arjun said. "I won't leave Holbach either. Or you."

"Because you think he'll help you find your fucking *Voice*?"

"Partly, yes. Only partly. I'm sorry. I do want to help. Him, and you."

She glared at him. "We were trying to change the whole city. All you ever cared about was that, that *nothing*."

"That's not true."

Hoxton checked over his weapons. He held up a heavy black pistol by its barrel, and asked Arjun, "Can you handle this?"

"A little."

"Ever shot a man?"

"I'm afraid I have."

"Really? You? Right then, good." He handed it over. "Keep it hidden. You're not a child or a fool, so I don't have to tell you that if you ever have to use it against the watch, you're already as good as dead."

They were quiet for a while longer in the hot little room. Olympia's face was very pale and grim. Hoxton, by contrast, had acquired an efficient, soldierly sangfroid. There was clearly something military in his background, and he reverted to it wholeheartedly. He went out for food, and brought back beer, and vinegary fish in stale batter and newspaper.

Arjun asked, "Did Holbach learn anything about the Typhon?"

"I don't know," Olympia said. "There was so little time. And it's the least of our problems now, anyway."

"I hope so."

"You had me worrying about ghosts and phantoms and monsters. *This* is what's important: power and politics and princes, and the laws, and the gaols, and the censors, and the watch."

It seemed that any answer would only infuriate Olympia further. Arjun took a swig of beer, and said, "I saw Pieta."

"Oh gods, is she all right?"

"Yes. I gave her some money and sent her home."

"Thank you. I'm sorry. Gods, I didn't even *think* about her. I was with Holbach, busy trying to fight off those charges, and then when they arrested him I was here, hiding. I didn't think."

They ate in silence for a time, then Olympia said, "It was that fucking play. It wasn't even anything to do with us. We were so careful, and we had such plans, and then that thing got out of our control and went bad, and we paid for it."

"It was a strange thing," Arjun said. "It was as if the play's new authors wanted to goad the Countess into destroying the play, and the Atlas. I wondered at first how Nicolas could be so reckless, but if you say he wasn't responsible, who *was*?"

"I don't know. I tried to tell the Countess's men we didn't have anything to do with it, that we even tried to stop it, but they didn't believe us. But I agree. I think someone was trying to force the Countess to act. Trying to destroy us."

"I wasn't expecting the riot. I hadn't thought the Atlas was so well-loved. Did you have a hand in that?"

"No. I was just there to watch. What else could I do but fucking watch? But there were always people who loved us, people who had hopes for what we were doing. And they loved the play, you know? *Your* play, too. For them to see what that woman did to Liancourt . . . Gods, I can't believe she turned the *Thunderer*'s cannons on the crowd. She had soldiers there, it was under control, she didn't need that, that *abomination*."

"She didn't. I was watching the guns when the explosions hit. They never fired. I'm sure."

"Then somebody brought powder-charges into the crowd."

"It did *look* as though the *Thunderer* attacked the crowd."

"Perhaps it was meant to. If you're sure of what you saw. Perhaps even the Countess wouldn't be that reckless. But people will think she did it, and they'll never forgive her. Perhaps someone meant them to, to make them hate her."

They sat in silence for a while longer. "Gods," Olympia said, "what use am I like this? I can do *nothing* from hiding."

Arjun turned the bottle between his fingertips, and thought. There was shouting in the street. He went to the window, and watched a group of men stagger down the street. There were about a dozen of them. They were too drunk to agree on a slogan, so some of them cursed the Countess and her monstrous weapon, and some cried for Jack Silk, some for the Atlas or Liancourt, and some for freedom, or truth. The man at the front waved a fistful of silk threads. They went into the Red Lion.

"Jack Silk could free Holbach," he said.

"Well, yes, if he exists. Sadly, none of *us* have been gifted with miraculous powers, or an army of wild children, or any of the rest of the things they say he has."

"Maybe we can find him. I think I may have seen him once, before he became notorious. Did I ever tell you? It was just before I first met you. The Flame, the white robes, attacked the street I was staying on. There was a fight. There were some boys, who I think drove the Flame off. One of them . . . I only saw his back, but he was wearing a shirt that streamed with bright silk, the way they describe Jack

Silk. There were always gangs of children around Moore Street, hiding in the derelict buildings. I think he might have been one of them. He might be somewhere in Shutlow. We can look for him there."

"We'll never find him. That's a fantasy. We might as well wait for your Voice to rescue Holbach."

"I don't *want* to go to Shutlow. The Typhon was there once. It may still be. But do you have a better idea?"

Every day for the next week, they crept up from the docks into Shutlow, and split up, and hung around in the pubs and halls and churches, asking after Jack Silk.

Hoxton took to the work easily. He made a convincing dockhand or factory-rat, or laborer, or criminal, depending on the company. He bought drinks and made crude jokes. If anyone had known anything, they'd have told him, but they didn't.

Arjun couldn't easily pass for a local or fake nonchalance the way Hoxton could, but he was good at making himself inconspicuous, and listening. He had a well-trained ear; if he focused, he could listen to a half-dozen conversations at once.

Olympia found it frustrating. She needed to shine, to shock; it was hard for her to be forgettable. Conversation dried up around her. She was asking about a dangerous subject. She seemed like a dangerous person, and it was a dangerous time. It was hard for her, and it was made worse by the sense that she was neglecting her duty to the Atlas. There was a report in the *Era* that the Countess had arrested fourteen book-dealers, all over the city, on suspicion of conspiracy to circulate and sell the forthcoming edition of the Atlas. Olympia knew that the Countess was right about eleven of them.

On the second day, on her way through the streets, Olympia passed the building that had been the Great York Printworks; it was boarded up, BY ORDER OF THE COUNTESS. "I should be doing something," she said, back at the docks that night. "They were our people. I was the one who brought half of them into the Atlas. I should be fighting for them."

"You're a fugitive, too," Arjun pointed out. "You know there's nothing you can do. You know that." She glared silently.

On the second night, all three of them went to Moore Street to search the ruins. Hoxton crowbarred a way in for them. There was a tiny group of starveling infants in the Black Moon; Hoxton caught one by the arm as they fled, but he knew nothing of the Thunderers, only the same stories as everyone else.

They heard a lot of grumbling about the Countess, which turned, with drink, into angry denunciations of her tyranny. And they heard empty fantasizing about Jack Silk, who would lead an army of children to take revenge on whomever the speaker saw as his or her particular oppressor—but nothing useful.

It was hard. They must have looked like spies. People were suspicious, and rightly so: all week, Shutlow was rocked by violence. The riot on the Heath was followed by another the next day, during which much of the Widow's Bower was burned. Smaller disturbances broke out constantly. The Countess's soldiers marched in force in the streets, and crowds formed to hurl bricks and ordure at them, before running back into the alleys.

It was not how Arjun remembered Shutlow. Its citizens were angry—angry and full of frustrated hope. When the Countess's soldiers marched down the street, shouting at the windows that the city's good order, and the will of the gods, required that the citizens remain peaceful and quiet, Shutlow had something to throw back at them: the Atlas, the Thunderers, *The Blessing*.

Even so, it would probably have gone nowhere, the citizens would probably all have choked back their anger and sulked silently into their beers, same as always; but now, after months of Silk's prison-breaking, the backstreets and the flophouses and the bars were full of desperate and rootless young men, with nothing to do and no fear of the watch. It was as if they'd been waiting. Arjun wondered if the Bird—it was Holbach's theory that the Bird was responsible for the Silk phenomenon—if the Bird had intended that consequence when it had worked its change on the boy. Maybe, maybe not. But the scum Silk had freed were natural recruits for the rioters. Possibly natural leaders, too; Arjun didn't investigate them too closely. Once, he was sitting in the Grey Goose, listening, when a line of soldiers marched past outside, and all the pub's people got up at once and ran out to pelt the soldiers with glasses and run for their lives. Arjun fled through the back door.

He read the *Era* and learned that the riots were by no means confined to Shutlow. They were much worse in Fourth Ward. Huge crowds gathered on the Heath. The docks roiled with it. The rioters wanted Holbach released; they wanted the play and the Atlas un-banned; they wanted the *Thunderer* scrapped. Mostly, though, they made no demands. They were just angry. The Countess was burned in effigy a hundred times.

Sometimes, Arjun heard secrets, whispered in the back of pubs: meeting-places and times, a man who could provide guns, plans for protests, rumors that other protests had been compromised. Never the secret he was looking for. For all the talk about Silk, there was no hint that anyone knew where he was or how to reach him: he might not have been real at all.

Businesses closed down. Their owners watched the streets nervously from behind boarded windows, clutching their guns. The mills of Fourth Ward shut down and locked their gates, rather than take the risk of allowing in workers in a machine-breaking mood. The idle weavers of the Ward took to making banners.

The Countess did not sit still. Arjun saw more than one riot put down with force. She had special soldiers for that sort of work; he saw them around more and more often. Her regular forces wore red coats and plumes; these men wore mottled grey and flat caps. These men were not for show; they were for killing.

Arjun recalled that Girolamo had written of his experiences as a soldier in Ararat. He had said that it was not like being a soldier anywhere else in the world. Ararat's wars were fought between city-lords, in city streets. No serried ranks clashing in open fields; instead, there were dark-clad men shooting each other from high windows, or hacking at each other in alleys. Girolamo had said that it was worse than any sort of warfare he had ever seen. Seeing the bloody aftermath of a protest that had met the grey men, Arjun could believe it. He wished there was something he could do for the survivors, but there was nothing. He no longer belonged in the city. It was not his affair.

In the narrow streets, stray bullets might smash in your window and kill you. The advice of those who had seen that sort of thing before was to pile up furniture in the window: an upturned table, a mattress, the dusty back of a heavy armoire. It made the streets claustrophobic and unfriendly.

The Countess was not the only Estate to claim authority over the rioting territories, but her rivals did not help her. For the time being, the crowd's anger was directed solely at the Countess, and perhaps her rivals preferred not to become targets themselves. Perhaps they were enjoying her humiliation. Chairman Cimenti issued a statement to the effect that he regretted the loss of life and damage to property, and hoped that the proper authorities would achieve a peaceful and equitable resolution of the situation, with all dispatch. It must have infuriated her.

The churches were split. The priests of Lavilokan issued sermons in coded support of the rioters. Lavilokan was a spirit of masks and mirrors and smoke, prone to manifestation among theaters and theater-folk, and her priests took the suppression of *The Blessing* and the execution of Liancourt as an affront. The order of Uktena celebrated both sides' ferocity for its own sake. Tiber demanded submission to the lawful authorities; Tiber's priests preached it in the streets, suffering the catcalls and projectiles of the mob with patient disdain.

Some groups of rioters took to carrying banners marked with the Pillar of Fire. Arjun overheard an unusually articulate protestor explaining the symbolism to a reporter from the *Sentinel:* "What do the priests know? Tiber stands for *justice* and *punishment*. We want justice. The Countess went too far, she's lawless now. We want justice. That's all we want." Arjun checked later; the *Sentinel* had not dared to publish the story.

He heard some of the rioters singing songs he had written for *The Blessing*. Liancourt's words—asking why decent people should be at the mercy of arbitrary and cruel powers, cloaked in the authority of the city and the gods—but Arjun's music. His own anger and pain fueling Liancourt's complaints, and now those of the crowds. It bothered him.

"You know there's a hundred other reasons why they're rioting,"

Olympia said as they walked quickly away from the scene of a clash between rioters and militia, heads down. "You've been here long enough to understand that. They didn't do it just because you gave them a good protest song."

"I know. But I shouldn't have been a part of it. I shouldn't have made the Voice part of this violence."

"Maybe you *should* have. Maybe it's about time for something like this."

"It's terrible."

"It was terrible before, too. Weren't you paying attention?"

"I've stayed too long. I've done the wrong things."

On the fifth day, Arjun was the first of them to return to the room in the docks. He had passed the Cypress earlier, wondering whether Defour was still there, still alive, but had not dared to go in; he couldn't trust her not to report him. Besides, he felt a gathering darkness about the building's windows that put him in mind of the Typhon, and though he was sure that it was only imagination, he could not concentrate for the rest of the day. He went back to think.

Hoxton came back early, too, his only explanation: "Got into a fight. Lot of wrong things were said. Best not to stay on the scene, you know?" He sat in the room's sagging sofa, and said, "So there's bad news, Mr. A. Three watchmen in the Red Lion, asking around after you. Wanted on charges of sedition, by order of the Countess. Inflaming the populace."

"It was only a matter of time."

"You're taking it calmly, sir. That's good. You might want to grow a beard or something, or dye your hair. The Countess is busy right now, what with all this foolishness in the streets. But it won't last forever; people get tired. They forget why they were angry. They decide they can live with things, after all. I've seen it happen. And then she'll turn her attention to those who she'll hold responsible, and that'll be us. If you don't mind my asking, sir, and you're not in a position to mind these days, if you don't mind my saying: why are you staying? Suppose we find Silk, suppose we do get the Professor out, suppose he can find you your Voice, what then?"

"I don't know. Why do *you* stay, Hoxton? You never seemed to care much for the Atlas. If you don't mind my saying."

"Not your business, sir, I'm afraid. There's a debt owed to the mistress. We'll not discuss its nature. I got some history, not the kind you discuss. Ask her, maybe. But that brings me back to my point. Seems the mistress is following you for the moment. We'll see how long that lasts. Let me say this: you're not thinking more than one step ahead. You're not *planning*. You're waiting to be *saved,* and you think then you won't have to wake up the next morning and take a shit. I've followed people like that in my time, in all kinds of capacities. Leads to undesirable consequences, you understand? Time to look to the real world. You got enemies, now, real ones. Think on it."

Toward the end of the week, things got worse. Preceded by rumor and frightened whispers, the white robes came to Shutlow. They boiled up from the Ward, or they came down by the river. It was hard to say. There were so many of them. At first, no one was sure what side they were on; they clashed with the rioters and the soldiers alike. But they made their position clear; they shouted it in hoarse voices as they marched down the street, so that there could be no confusion. They were there in the name of the Fire; in the name of order, and justice, to stamp out riot and insurrection. That their activities also put them in conflict with the Countess's men did not seem to trouble them.

They had guns now. That was new. They were dreadfully vicious. They tore into protests, wounding and killing, then remained, after they had driven off the protestors, to fight the soldiers. They struck from the rooftops sometimes, and sometimes they swaggered down the street, carrying their flaming brands, enforcing their strict code.

They did not like to see unaccompanied women, and they left scars to remind transgressors of their views. It was no longer safe for Olympia to go anywhere without Hoxton's protection.

By the middle of the second week, the white robes were on every street corner. They tore books off the market stalls, and burned them. They torched the gambling dens and the whorehouses, and made a spectacle of beating the whores in the street.

The soldiers struck back at them, and killed many. The white robes were only children, and too fanatical to be good soldiers, but there were so *many* of them, and the Countess was only one of the city's many rulers. She didn't control very much, really: Shutlow, a share of Ar-Mouth, Barbary and the Ward, most of the Heath, a few other streets, here and there. The Flame poured in from all over the city. There were far more of them than of the Countess's men. They were an angry ocean.

Arjun watched them from the high window of the room in the docks. The white robes, the grey soldiers, the dirty prison clothes of the desperate escapees, the drab of Shutlow's angry citizens, the filthy brown rags of the Ward. It was as if the hand of a stupid and thoughtless god had taken hold of the Atlas-makers' great map, and crushed it all together so that its colors ran together and its lines were all torn and ruined.

When, early in the next week, the bright colors of the Thunderers joined the clash, it came as no surprise.

Jack had come to Mass How to watch the movements of the guards at the Parliament's Oak Street Gaol. The Thunderers had opened it before, more than a month ago, but he wanted to do it again. It was a fine game. He watched from the neighboring rooftops, and from the night sky.

Mass How had closed its borders. It stationed its citizen militia along the escarpment to keep out the rioters.

Jack had barely heard of the riots before leaving the hideout and crossing Fourth Ward to come to watch the Oak Street Gaol. Fiss and Aiden had been talking about the news out of Shutlow, but he'd barely paid attention; he had other obsessions.

Now, though, he looked down from Mass How into Shutlow, stretched out at the foot of the escarpment, and watched the fires dotting the dark streets. He drifted down the hill and watched from behind the chimneys. He saw the rioters clash with the grey-coated soldiers. He saw a man at the front of the mob raising a fistful of bright fabric, and shout, "Silk! Thunder!"

"*Yes,*" he hissed. When the man fell, and a grey coat loomed over him with his club raised, Jack shot down from the roof and cut the club from the soldier's hand, then disappeared onto the other side of the street so fast no one could have been sure what happened.

He watched the arrival of the white robes with hate. He saw them set up their barricades in the streets, demanding gestures of submission from anyone who tried to pass. He saw them bludgeon down the rioters who wore *his* colors. They were willing and eager gaolers. He could not abide them.

When he had seen enough, he crossed back over Fourth Ward, and entered the boathouse through an upper window, into the loft, where Fiss was talking to Aiden. "I saw the riots," Jack said. "It's *magnificent.* Like they're all with us, at last. But the white robes are there, too. Hundreds of 'em. Putting the riots down, in Tiber's name. Ashes, and they call it order."

"Gods," Fiss said. "How bad is it?"

"Bad. But it doesn't have to be. We can do something about it. We beat them before, remember? We're so much stronger now. We can bring them all under our wing."

The boys gathered in the room below, at the foot of the loft's ladder, listening up to Jack and Fiss's conversation. Jack stepped out to the edge overlooking them. "What are we for, if we allow this? Is this our city or theirs?"

Fiss and Aiden looked at each other nervously, but the boys below cheered. Namdi cheered loudest, at the front.

They had to wait a while for some of their number to come back from thieving in the market, and to check over their weapons, then they followed Jack back across the Ward. In Jack's widening wake, they moved almost like he did, unaware of their own speed and grace, over the crumbling roofs, under dark scudding clouds.

THIRTY-SEVEN

They no longer went out alone. It was less efficient to go everywhere as a threesome, and they were more likely to draw attention from those who might be hunting them, but the streets were simply too dangerous and too frightening to be alone.

They were in the Ghentian Hall, on the edge of Barbary, not far from Moore Street. It was a cavernous, many-leveled terra-cotta structure, aping the Mass How style, but uglier, cheaper, cracked and dirty. The interior was smoky and hot and noisy, sticky with spilled beer. Barmaids hustled through the crowd in a state of half-undress, dodging and slapping at pawing hands. Grey-coated soldiers roved in groups of two or three, holding pistols or pikes, glaring suspiciously. Some in the crowd glared back. Others were happy to see them; at least they kept the Flame away.

The three of them did not sit together—that would have made them conspicuous—but they kept an eye on one another. Hoxton was down in the pit, backslapping and joking with an even larger man, a Ghentian, brown-suited and walrus-mustached, both of them roaring and laughing. Olympia was talking to one of the barmaids. Arjun could see them both from where he sat, on one of the raised platforms, by one of the bars, listening.

"...not going to that temple again, not after that. I won't be told it's Atenu's will that I bow down to that bitch, after what she's done. She turned a bloody *warship* on that crowd. I hear there's a preacher in Chalk Street has some bloody balls. Who'll come with me?"

"... lost another to the lung-rot. We'll have to shut up shop if we lose another, not that there's any custom now. That's what drives me mad: they say that those Atlas-makers were working on a cure, could have saved us all, and then the Countess smashes 'em down just because they dared hurt her feelings. I don't know, I just don't know."

"Tomorrow night. Greycloak Court. There's a man; you'll know him when you see him. We'll go from there."

"It's no joke. How do you think I got here tonight? The Flame had a barricade at the end of our street, and you think they'd have let me pass if I said I was going out boozing with you lot? No, they're real: they came running down the street, and I swear to you, *flying* off the roofs, all bright and fast, and they *swept them away*. I was out on the Heath when the Bird passed, and I remember how it felt; it felt that way. I swear."

That sounded promising, perhaps, but Arjun had heard a lot of stories like that in the last couple of days. He was sure now that Silk was here, somewhere, and apparently locked in battle with the white robes. Just knowing that Silk was around was no help, though: Arjun needed to know *where*. Just in case, he picked up his drink and moved toward the speaker, through the crowds, trying to look as if he was just looking for somewhere to sit.

"... how dare she. That Liancourt was right, gods bear him to glory, he was bloody *right*. She can't hold us back now."

"... I mean, look at the bastards. Fucking *look* at them, with their guns and that sneer ..."

"I just want it to *stop*. I have daughters, and they haven't been out for days. I need *money*. It's too hard."

"... recover from this. She pushed things too far, and now she's paying the price. She can't stop it. It makes her look weak. What use is the *Thunderer* against this sort of thing? And if I can see she's weak, then you can bet the Parliament can, or the Chairman, or somebody. I tell you. Just wait."

"Remember when Monan appeared in the sky, a few weeks back? I think he was warning us about this. I think the stars spelled out how to stop it, make it right again, if only we could read them. No, I'm serious, I really do. I do. Well, fuck you then."

"I'm not going to stand here and tell you that you shouldn't be angry. You're *men,* aren't you? Of *course* you're angry. Who isn't? Who wouldn't be? *Yes.* All I'll say is, I can tell you how to make that anger useful. Wait, shut up, *shush*..."

Arjun stopped. He knew that voice. It was Mr. Heady, from the Cypress. The Typhon hadn't got him, then.

"...All right, I was saying. You're not much use by yourselves. But you *want* to be useful. Course you do. These are times for brave men, they say. There's a place, and a man can get you arms. Listen, now..." He leaned in and whispered.

Arjun turned around, and made his way over to Olympia. "There's a man over there—don't look—recruiting for some sort of riot, or sabotage, or strike against the Countess."

"This place is full of that sort of thing."

"But I know this man. I lodged with him. He was...he was no radical. No rioter, no rebel. He was very proud of his deference to power. It's very odd. He can't be doing this out of anger. Someone must be paying him. I would like to know who."

Heady got up, shaking the hands of the other men, who remained at the table. He walked toward the door.

"He's leaving. I'm going to follow."

"We should get Hoxton." But they couldn't see him. He was lost in the throng down in the Hall's drinking pit.

Arjun felt a tug at the back of his mind. There was a path and a connection before him. He thought of the Spider's letter. An image of incurious, manipulating spider-eyes clicked quickly across his mind. "I'm following him. I'll come back and find you later." He pushed out through the crowd, and Olympia, after a moment of nervous scanning for Hoxton, followed.

All their numbers meant nothing. All their hate meant nothing. The Thunderers fell on the white robes with fierce joy. The white robes were earthbound, and the Thunderers were not. The Thunderers came at them from the rooftops; they hurtled down the streets to topple their barricades. They moved with the speed and freedom of the Bird's gift. As he led the charge, Jack could turn his head and see them behind him, moving brightly across the drab of Shutlow's roofs. Their clothes were grey or brown, dirty and ragged, but each was marked with a blue, red, or gold crest of the *Thunderer,* and each of them trailed brilliant silk. It made him sure that he was doing the right thing. His power was widening. If it ever stopped, he would know he was no longer worthy of it.

"Don't be afraid of killing," he'd said as they left the boathouse, "if you can. If you can't bring yourself to do it, think of this: they chose it. They live for this. For the cruelty. They're not just doing their job. This is their *purpose*. There's hundreds, thousands of them. Many, many more than us. We can't share the city. We have to *put them down*."

On the first night, Jack had seen a dozen of the white robes striking into a crowd on the Heath, gathered around a fire of broken wood, the remains of the barricade the Countess's men had erected on Gauzy Street. A trio of young women danced in time to the crowd's clapping. The crowd was drunk, and off-rhythm, and the girls sometimes stumbled, laughing.

From behind the trees, the white robes fired on the crowd, felling several, then forced their way through, stabbing, to the dancers. One tall one grabbed one of the dancers by the hair, and spat on her screaming face.

Jack came at them over the heads of the terrified crowd. He drew his knife, and struck quickly. He killed three; those who ran he only marked. The rest of the Thunderers were approaching through the crowd by the time he was done. They started to clap and cheer, and the crowd joined in. Jack found himself in a firelit circle surrounded by applause. He held the arm of the sobbing dancer and pulled her up, and, impetuously, kissed her, dipping her flamboyantly, like they did on the stage.

The crowd loved it, and roared his name. The girl tolerated it stiffly for only a moment, then pulled away from him, sobbing. He left bloody fingerprints on her arm and face.

Fiss died two days later.

He wasn't the first; the Thunderers had lost a boy called Gantley in Rudder Street, when a fight with the white robes had been interrupted by the Countess's grey-coated soldiers, and a lucky bullet had caught Gantley in his beardless throat. Martin's skull had been cracked by a white robe's brand. Jack had brought him back, sleeping, to the locked-out factory they were using as a base, but he had never woken up. Fiss wasn't the first, or the last, but he was the first to give Jack pause.

He had died pointlessly. The Thunderers had routed one of the white robes' barricades from Akely Street; as the white robes ran down the street, one of them turned and fired wildly behind his back, and the bullet hit Fiss in the chest. Jack leaped on the shooter instantly, crossing the intervening space in a single weightless step, and cut his throat.

Jack ran back across the street, letting the others go, his steps seeming very heavy. It seemed to take him a very long time to reach Fiss. He held him for a moment, saying, "It's all right, Fiss, there are doctors, don't try to speak, don't . . ." Then Fiss jerked, choked up blood, and died.

Jack hunched over Fiss's heavy body for a long time. He was sad for Fiss, but more, he was sad for the Thunderers. Without Fiss, how could he keep them going? He had *needed* Fiss. "Our time is nearly up now," he whispered. Namdi, kneeling next to him, stared, but Jack didn't explain. It was clear to him. Fiss's vision was dead; Jack's had swallowed it. Without Fiss, there would be no more of them. Their ranks could not grow. There was no promise of peace and shelter to hold them together. There was only Jack's war. That could not last forever. Soon they would be worn out, and then they would fall apart.

He supposed that had been bound to happen, anyway. They would not have been young forever. But this was cruel.

Thirty-two of them there: that was what he had to work with. He would do what he could with the time that he had. He brought them back to the factory to mourn and regroup. Mourning should be a joyful thing, he told them; they should stoke their anger. Aiden slipped away, without speaking; Jack did not see him go. Thirty-*one.* Over the next few days, they redoubled their efforts.

* * *

The Thunderers still needed sleep, and food, but Jack didn't. He left them in the factory at night and went out into the dark streets. The lamps had been extinguished all over the Countess's territories, to help enforce curfew. He took note of where his enemies' strengths and weaknesses were.

It was a quiet night. Perhaps people were tired of the violence; perhaps they were at home, plotting more. Small squads of soldiers carried lanterns and pikes through the streets. Citizens scurried here and there, from pub to pub, always in twos or threes: to travel alone was to risk violence from the white robes, and any larger group might be stopped by the Countess's men on suspicion of seditious intent, and taken for questioning. There were rumors about the questioning.

From atop the hammer-tower of Atenu's temple on Bow Street, Jack watched five white robes gathered in an alley around a fire of broken boards, checking over their guns, practicing holding their rifles. He had never seen them smiling before. It made him uncomfortable. He left them alone, that once.

In the alley on the other side of the building, a group of men stood around a tall, hard-looking man with a lantern, who was saying, "... are you serious? There's no point if you aren't serious. But if you are—that's right, yes, but keep it down—if you are, I know a man who can get you guns. That's right. Come back here tomorrow if you mean it. We'll talk."

The tall man left the others behind in the alley. Jack watched him go. He was not especially interested. He was aware of all the plotting going on around him that week, but he had paid little attention. He had recognized men he had freed from a dozen gaols among the rioters, and he was pleased to see what they were doing with his gift, but it was their fight, not his. Still, it was a quiet night, and he was a little curious, and he followed behind the man as he walked quickly through the streets. He felt a certain tug, a certain urgency; he felt that there were many calculating blank eyes appraising him.

They followed Heady at a distance. At Olympia's suggestion, they put their arms around each other so that they looked like a couple out for a walk. She was warm; Arjun suddenly missed their former intimacy very badly.

Heady was not alone. Outside the pub's door, a second man met him, a big man, heavy shoulders under a long dark coat. Heady nodded to him, and said, "All right then? No rest for the wicked, eh?" The second man followed Heady silently, at a couple of paces behind.

While his bodyguard waited, Heady stopped in another pub to give a similar speech, and a similar promise: "*Guns.* That's what you need. Good lads. You have friends, you know." He was very slick, very ingratiating. Arjun felt a certain respect.

Heady and his bodyguard left, and walked east, and down through the docks, and onto a street of warehouses in the shadow of the Jaw. Heady's bodyguard carried a lantern; Arjun and Olympia followed in darkness. Heady approached an iron gate in a chain-link fence, unlocked it, and walked through a rubble-strewn yard and into one of the warehouses. After a moment, Arjun followed them up to the fence, crouching, and tested the gate.

"It's locked. Can we climb this, do you think?" he asked.

"Are you mad? Someone will hear us, and then we'll be trapped on the other side."

"Ah. I suppose you're right."

"We should go."

"Wait. There's someone at the window. I can hear them. If you're quiet."

Olympia crouched behind Arjun as he leaned against the fence and listened, filtering out the city's noise, honing in on Heady's voice, by the window, saying, "...you can expect maybe a dozen men tomorrow morning. Another dozen may, may not."

"Wait your turn, Mr., ah, Healey, is it? There's other business to be done."

"Oh, no, of course, I understand, sir, it's Heady, by the way, I'm sure it's good work that you're doing, sir, but it's just that it's late, sir, and it's dangerous work, sir, round here, these days, and I'd like to be paid, if you don't mind."

"When they turn up, Heady. Not until. There's no money for promises. You can hang on here a day longer. Go home now."

Heady's voice tailed off, mumbling. The other man, the one
Heady had been speaking to, started to talk to someone else,
who had apparently been suborning a disaffected member of the
Countess's own militia: "He's nearly ready. He wants to help us, he
just doesn't know it yet. Give me a little more time."

"They're preparing for something," Arjun said.

Olympia leaned over him, and stared across the dark yard at the
lamp-lit window. She gasped and dropped down, with her back
against the fence. "That man at the window, the blond man, is that
the one who's talking, who's in charge?" Arjun nodded. "Then we
shouldn't be here. We shouldn't see this. Get down."

"Who is it?

"Marius Vittellan. One of Chairman Cimenti's personal secretaries. A distant relation. I've argued cases against him."

"He's a lawyer?"

"Yes. No. An agent. He *arranges* things for the Chairman. If he's
here . . . These riots, the Chairman's using them. Feeding them.
Gods, maybe he started the bloody thing. Maybe he's the one who
had that bastard version of *The Blessing* set loose. He could have had
his agents do it, and make it look spontaneous. To make people hate
her, then to force her hand, right? Against *us*. And then he sent his
agents out, and he hired people, like this *Heady,* and they angered
everyone up, he brought guns in for them, too, convinced them how
much they loved us, gave them courage, so all this would burst back
in her face. And there's nothing her *Thunderer* can do about it; no
fortress to attack. No leader to kill. The whole bloody city's an army
against her now. Maybe he's behind Silk, that's why the streets are
full of escapees . . . Gods, maybe that's why they let Nicolas go.
Cimenti could have secured his release with nothing but a wink. So
he'd be there, to push us too far, only that monster killed him . . . or
so that he'd be there, to die with the rest of us when she turned
against us, to get rid of him once and for all."

"Maybe Cimenti's just taking advantage of the riots to humili-
ate her. You don't know he *started* all this."

"Don't be fucking naïve. This is *him,* this is all *him*. He made
this. Remember there was an explosion in the crowd, on the Heath,
on that first day, and you were sure the *Thunderer* never fired? He

made us into a weapon, against her, so she would have to destroy us, and destroy herself doing it. Oh *gods*."

"You don't know that."

"I'll *tell* you what I fucking know. And there's nothing we can do about it. We shouldn't know this. I don't want to know. I don't want to know we were *tools*. We have to get away."

She stood into a half-crouch, and stepped away from the fence. As she stood, the gate opened, and Heady and his bodyguard stepped through. Olympia froze as the bodyguard said, "Night, Mr. Heady. Go careful on your way home."

Heady took a few steps in Olympia's direction, then stopped and shouted, "There's someone there!"

The bodyguard yelled, "Who...?" and lunged for Olympia, who turned and ran. He caught her arm quickly.

Arjun stepped away from the fence, drew his gun and aimed at the bodyguard, who dropped his lantern and pulled Olympia in front of himself as a shield. Heady ran for it, without a word.

Jack had entered the warehouse through an upper window, and settled among the dusty and cobwebbed rafters. The room below was stacked with boxes, among which men moved purposefully, by the light of shuttered lamps. The tall man he had followed had come in by a back door, talked to a blond man by the window, been given a pouch of coins or possibly bullets; it was hard to see and impossible to hear. Jack tried to get closer. He heard a lot of talk about weapons, explosives, movements of the guard, coordination of activities, who was sound and who was not. It was exciting; for a moment he considered revealing himself to them, offering them his leadership.

One of the men—a greasy little person with his greying hair combed over his head, hardly Jack's idea of a revolutionary, but still—was leaving, followed by a big man in a coat. Jack decided to follow. He hopped from rafter to rafter to a grey window, scattering pigeons. He waited for the pigeon-noises to settle, then creaked the window open, very carefully, and stepped out into the night.

There was some kind of altercation in the street. The big man was holding a woman in a grey dress. He had a gun to her head. Jack did not like to see her held and struggling. A young man was standing a few paces away, holding a gun of his own, trying to get a clear shot. Jack made his decision quickly. He shot down from the roof and scored his knife across the bodyguard's arm, and snatched the gun from his stunned fingers.

More men ran outside to see what the noise was. Jack grabbed the woman's arm, and pulled her away, calling to the young man, "I can take you to safety. Don't just stand there!"

As the boy ran down the dark street away from Arjun, light from a window-lamp fell on him for a moment and his bright clothes glittered; Olympia, pulled behind him, was almost rushing off her feet, and her grey skirt billowed. Arjun followed, thinking he would never catch them—they were dwindling so fast—but he found himself somehow keeping pace. Lightly, *effortlessly.* It was something in the strange boy's wake; it was like the way music had come to him so easily while he was within the echoes of the Voice. The shouts of their pursuers echoed distantly, then vanished. They were far away into the city's maze when the boy stopped and let go of Olympia's arm, and Arjun staggered to a halt, and leaned against a wall, feeling something leaving him.

They were in the courtyard of a temple of Orillia, spirit of the lights; an apron of glass-stained firelight welled out into the night from the temple's windows, green and gold. In that light, the boy was a patchwork of bright colors. He looked them up and down, shrugged, and said, "You'll be all right here." He turned as if to go, then said, "Why did those men in the warehouse attack you? Were you with them, or against them?"

Olympia said, "I don't know. I think we have an enemy in common, at least. Jack—are you Jack?—were you watching them? Are *you* with them or against them?"

Jack shook his head. "Same enemy as them, maybe, same as you. I don't know." He stared at her. "You don't need to look frightened of me. You can go home."

Olympia began to protest, but the boy was already turning to go. Arjun tore himself away from the wall, reached out for the boy's sleeve, and said, "Jack, wait. Please. Don't go just yet. We need your help. We've been looking for you for a long time. Just hear us out."

Met with a sharp glare, he dropped the boy's sleeve and stepped back, holding up his hands.

"Just give us a few minutes," Olympia said. "We're on your side. We *know* things. Help us and we can help you."

Jack stared at them for a long moment. Then he shook his head, and launched himself up and instantly out of the halo of light cast by the temple's lamps and into the night. Arjun could not stop himself from reaching pointlessly up as if to catch him. He and Olympia looked at each other in shock and despair.

Then they heard the bolts on the inside of the church door scraping back. The doors opened and Jack stepped out. "They never lock the upper windows." He smirked. "They're still never ready for me. Come on, then: we'll talk inside. Make it good."

Olympia disliked this arrogant boy. He frightened her. His power frightened her. It was not entirely under his control. It *rode* him. She did not know what he might do. Apart from the face, that strange face, he did not remind her very much of Arjun. But she swallowed her dislike easily. She was used to negotiating with dangerous and disagreeable people.

"They say you rescue people from the gaols. You and your Thunderers. We've read about you, we've heard all the songs and the plays. We represent an organization that tries to do something similar. We want to bring freedom to people; to break them out of prisons of ignorance and confusion. We represent the Atlas. Have you heard of it?"

"It's blasphemous," Jack said. "That's all they ever told me." He sat cross-legged on the altar. He had sat there with exaggerated casualness, as if he chose that seat because it was comfortable, not because it was shocking and dramatic. Olympia had not been fooled, but had not commented.

The room was full of candles, lamps, colored glass, and mirrors.

During the service, the room would burst with light, like the city at night, seen from a hill. For now it was dark.

Olympia said, "Some people call it blasphemous. But the same people call you a criminal, and—"

"I don't care if it's blasphemous. Why should I?"

"Ah, right. Well, we've been looking for you. We want to *help* you. There are a great many of us, famous scholars, journalists, printers, playwrights. Arjun here is the composer of the music for *The Blessing*. Do you know it? We can tell people what you're doing, and why. But we need your help first. Our leader is a man called Professor Holbach, and he—"

"I know who he is."

"Right, then you must know that he would support you if he could. But he's been taken prisoner. We don't know where. By order of the Countess Ilona. I know you've freed a lot of her prisoners. We need you to free one more. That's all, Jack."

Jack looked at her skeptically. Arjun said, "The Professor is the creator of the *Thunderer*. You know that, don't you? The thing from which you take your name. Why did you do that?"

"No reason you'd understand. I don't owe him anything, or the Countess, or you. I *took* the *Thunderer*'s name. He didn't make it for me. I don't have to do anything for him or for you."

"But perhaps he could make something for you," Olympia said. "Or he can help you with this power you have."

"I don't think you know how your own power works," Arjun said. "Or what to do with it. Do you? I can tell. Holbach can help. If you free him."

"Gods, there's no reason not to," Olympia said. "It's what you've done for hundreds of prisoners, all over the city. We know you don't owe Holbach anything, or us. You don't have to refuse to help just because someone's asking."

Jack jumped down off the altar. "All right. That's enough. We'll do it. Why not? We need to get away from here, though. We need to find a place to talk about this. Where are you staying?"

✵ ✵ ✵

They walked back to the room at the docks. Hoxton was pacing nervously outside; when he saw them return, with Jack following, he said, "Bloody hell, is that him? Is that you? Gods, you really *are* young. An honor, Mr. Silk. Will he help, Miss O.?"

They went inside, and tried to tell Jack everything they might know about where Holbach might be held. They could not be sure; there were many gaols the Countess might have used for him. "Perhaps I can find out," Olympia said. "There are still people I know who might have an idea. They might not want to help me, but they probably won't turn me in. I can try, anyway."

Jack left in the morning, when everyone but him was ready to drop. "There are people waiting for me," he said. "I have to be there when they wake. I'll come back here soon. Wait for me."

Jack went back to the factory where the Thunderers waited on foot. The streets were silent in the cold dawn. Arjun and Olympia had told him what they had seen and heard in the warehouse; that the rioting, and the causes of the rioting, might all be some ploy of Cimenti's, some subtle strike against the Countess. He didn't know whether he believed it or not. He felt out of his depth. It was dirty, and he needed to believe that everything was pure of purpose. He decided he would not mention it to the others, and put it from his mind.

It got hot and stinking around noon, and the boys were drenched with sweat as they chased the white robes away from Amber Street. In the afternoon, Jack followed the *Thunderer,* from rooftop to rooftop, keeping a careful distance, watching the great ship cast its shadow on the crowds below. There was a distant crack and a tiny puff of muzzle-smoke from up on the edge of the deck, and a chimney pot not twenty feet away from Jack exploded. A good shot! Eventually Jack got bored and let the ship go on its way. He sat on a flat roof among empty wire pigeon-coops and watched the sun go down.

And in the evening, he decided that it was time to help them, if he was going to. He told Namdi to lead the boys back to the factory, and he began to visit the prisons of Shutlow and Fourth Ward, watching from the sky, darting through the shadows, looking for Holbach or some sign of his trail.

Arlandes heard the crack of the rifle through the locked door to his quarters. He heard the men cheering. He did not get up. He was busy writing a letter to the Countess urging—with all due respect and humility—that she consider permitting him to make full and unrestrained use of the *Thunderer* against the rioters and criminal conspiracies and seditious vermin in the streets below.

For weeks the *Thunderer* had been idle, useless, drifting like a sullen cloud. The Countess's attention was focused on her own noisily crumbling territories, and she had no time to threaten and bully and poke and jab at her rivals' districts. And there was nothing for the *Thunderer* to do at home in Shutlow or Barbary or Fourth Ward: what good was a weapon like that against rioters, and stone-throwers, and slogan-chanters?

At least, that was what the Countess said. With a brittle and cold smile, she'd ordered Arlandes to keep the *Thunderer*'s guns in check; she cautioned *patience* and dreamed her people would learn to love her again.

And now she would not talk to Arlandes at all. Three days ago Arlandes had received orders, by messenger, and not even under her signature, but under that of her cousin Sir Brice, commanding him to return the *Thunderer* to drydock at the palace on Laud Heath, and to abandon his pointless patrols of the sky. Arlandes had complained and Brice had explained that it sapped the *Thunderer* of its menace, its authority, for it to be seen to be ineffective against the rioters. Arlandes had continued regular patrols anyway, and Brice had said nothing further.

Above Arlandes there was a general breakdown in order and will. Below him, too, discipline decayed. There had been desertions and defections even among the sounder men: Bradley, at least, and possibly Yager, had left their red coats folded on their bunk beds and gone over to the rioters. Or gone to hide in some shabby hole with their wives, which was, to Arlandes' mind, an equal dereliction of duty.

And the plague had killed Lieutenant Duncan two weeks ago; he'd choked and puked and curled up and died, and they'd thrown his body over the *Thunderer*'s edge, somewhere over the River, for fear of infection. Dautry had gone the same way. Their bodies, rotten before they were even dead, had dropped and spattered like birdshit from the warship's arse. Bad times all round.

And so the remaining men, with nothing better to do, had made it into a sport to take potshots with their rifles over the edge of the deck whenever they saw, far below on the rooftops, one of those unholy children in the robes or ribbons or what-have-you. They were yet to claim a scalp, the distances being what they were.

Arlandes let the men be. His attention was absorbed by his letter—in which he urged the Countess to consider, with all respect *et cetera,* that perhaps things would *not* get better, that her people would *not* learn to love her again, that everything might be irretrievably ruined and broken and poisoned, and that therefore the best option might be to unleash whatever fire they still had at their command and damn the consequences. Of course he wouldn't send it, any more than he had sent any of his previous drafts. But it sickened him to see the great weapon reduced to impotence; so much had been sacrificed for it.

Olympia went with Hoxton to visit a man she knew in the Countess's countinghouse, who had been a good source of rumor in the past. The next day, she visited a woman who filed documents for the Countess's court, and who could sometimes be bribed to disclose their contents. There was nothing Arjun could do to help, so he sat alone in the room in the docks, cross-legged on the bare floor, meditating on the Voice and its song.

Jack came back three days later, through the window, in the morning. Olympia was asleep in the bed; the others in blankets on the floor. Jack rapped on the rusty bedframe to wake them.

Olympia jerked awake, and choked down her shock at Jack's intrusion. *We need him,* she reminded herself. She said, "Jack. Jack, I know where they're keeping him. It's confidential, but I know someone—she let me see the order of transfer to the—"

"The Iron Rose," Jack said. "I know. I don't have to know any-one. I can break into their file-rooms myself, as I please."

"Then will you do it?" Arjun asked.

"It's far to the north," Jack said. "And my Thunderers have busi-ness here, with the white robes. We'd have to give up the fight, or split our forces. They could do it without me, of course they could," he said quickly, "but still."

"It's the greatest prison in the city," Arjun said. "In the parts of the city we know, at least. And you've never struck at it, have you? If you have, I've never heard of it. Will you let it stand?"

"I said I'll do it, and I'll do it. I do what I say I will. Don't you? You can come north with me, if you like."

"Yes," Olympia said. "We'll be there."

"Then I'll come back in the evening. We'll go at night."

When he came back that night, they were waiting, tensely. They collected their few possessions—the handful of things Olympia and Hoxton had been able to snatch from their homes, a few necessities Arjun had purchased from the markets in the docks, some food and other provisions—left the room behind, and set out. Jack walked with them, a jacket over his bright shirt.

They went west and north, across Fourth Ward. A squad of sol-diers stopped them, once, and told them to turn away from Piven Street; there was violence there, and it was safest for a family like them to stay clear of it. They were just an ordinary family, weren't they? They weren't looking for trouble? With apologies for wasting the soldiers' time, Arjun led the group away, and they took another route west. There was a fire on the skyline, a few streets over, and broken bricks under their feet.

Jack pointed the way—walking at the back of the procession, light-footed, nervous, eager; sheepdog-like, Olympia thought, warming to him for a moment before she reminded herself to be wary—until, after a few hours' walk, they were on the east end of Fourth Ward, at an empty street of factories, closed and locked away behind chain-link fences. "This is it," Jack said. "Wait here. I'll be back for you."

He disappeared down the dark street, and over a fence.

"Can he be trusted, do you think?" Hoxton asked.

"I don't think it's a trap, if that's what you mean," Olympia said. "If he wanted to rob us, he could have killed us at any time."

Hoxton snorted, skeptically.

"He'll help us," Arjun said. "He has to. He can't not."

They waited perhaps another twenty minutes. Then Jack returned. There were a dozen youths behind him. Thin, dressed in dirty grey, with bright crests. A couple were really children; most, like Jack, were nearly young men. There was one square-jawed girl. They stared suspiciously, defiantly. "This is all the help I'll need," Jack said. "Now, follow us if you want to."

Together, the two groups headed back across the docks, and crossed the Jaw. On the other side, it was like a different world. The streets were quiet, and unmarked. They had almost forgotten what streets free of violence looked like. The windows were not barricaded. There were washing-lines hung across the streets again, unmolested. The lamps were lit.

They walked north, up Cato Road, Jack and the adults in the lead, the Thunderers following behind, in the shadows. As they crested the hill, the black shape of the Iron Rose became visible in the distance, rising in front of the grey clouds.

The Iron Rose was one of the city's most recognizable structures. At least, in the part of the city Arjun knew, he reminded himself: there were certainly reaches of the city where it was unheard of. Five great ancient towers of black stone had leaned slowly into each other as the rocks beneath the city shifted until they fell against each other, and were, to everyone's surprise, able to check each other's collapse. They formed a circle, a crown, a rose. Later generations had bound the slumping giants in place with a web of iron struts and girders. They had built bridges and walkways between the towers, high above the streets. They had tunneled the towers together into a maze of strange angles.

It was a fortress for a while, then a temple, then finally a prison. It was vast, far larger than any single one of the city's powers, even the cruelest, could make use of. No one had that many enemies. Instead, they shared it. It belonged to all the city, by complex treaty. Its labyrinthine interior was divided into a thousand precincts, in each of which the guards enforced the punitive regimes of different churches or lords.

They said it was possible to escape into the tunnels or across the bridges, from one zone into another, so that a person arrested on the authority of, say, the Thane of Red Barrow might escape from his cruel justice into, say, the more lenient, whimsical regime of Lavilokan's halls. One of the printers who hung around Holbach's house had claimed to have done just that.

As with everything else in Ararat, the Rose was shaped by its gods. Two presences fought through its dark corridors. The Key passed through, opening the gates, breaking shackles; if you could find it, and follow it, you might escape. The Chain was a power of confinement and duress, to be avoided at all costs: it locked doors, turned passages that might have led into the light into closed circles, buried the prisoners deeper in confinement. They crossed each others' paths endlessly, folding and unfolding the shifting tunnels behind them.

There was a rumor that the Atlas-makers had a map of the Rose, that they had somehow smuggled an explorer in to chart its tunnels, but that they had never published it; to do so would undoubtedly have brought down retribution on them. Arjun didn't know whether that was true. He supposed it didn't matter now.

"Not that way," Jack said, when they reached the great golden archway that led north onto Goshen Tor. "Too well-guarded." They turned west, down the hill, to the River, where the Rose was no longer visible. It was a relief; the presence on the horizon had been troubling. Arjun dreaded entering it.

They followed the river's banks north, scrambling through wild stretches of scrap and scrub, quickly past loading-docks and jetties quiet for the night, cautiously past riverside pleasure-districts and palaces. Jack shuttled back and forth between the two groups, planning with the Thunderers, walking with Arjun's group in silence, except when he needed to discuss directions with Hoxton, who knew the river well.

Arjun walked next to Jack as they crossed an expanse of stone, sparsely dotted with statues of robed women walking down to the river, arms raised before them, as if bringing some sacrifice down to the water, or beckoning something up from it. The boy—he was nearly a man, really, but there was something incurably not-adult about the boy's presence, with his ridiculous clothes, his feverish intensity, his grace—the *boy* both fascinated Arjun and repelled him. The boy was in the grip of an obsession, he could see. A very peculiar and personal mission. Arjun wondered if he looked as strange to others as the boy did to him.

He had to ask. "Jack. Listen a moment. I know you grew up here, in this city. You have many gods here. You love them and hate them at the same time, in ways I don't fully understand. We had only one god, and it was *everything* to us. I want to know if you can understand this. Why I've done what I've done."

Jack listened silently as Arjun told his story, beginning down on the plains, where he first heard the Voice's echoes in the song Mother Abayla sang to him as an infant. He whispered: this was between the two of them. "Do you understand why I had to come here? Would you have done it?"

They walked past one of the statues, so that it passed between them. On the other side, Jack shook his head and looked coldly at Arjun. "It's a waste. It's selfish. You're not doing anything. No one knows or cares. You're alone." It stung, but Arjun had been expecting it, he supposed. It changed nothing.

After a few minutes, Jack said, whispering, "When *I* was young, there was this monster on the Heath. A *hyena*. And I followed it...." Arjun listened as Jack described his confinement in and escape from Barbotin, his slow discovery of the Bird's gifts to him, the disciplining and naming of the Thunderers, the purpose to which he had put them.

At the end, Arjun could only say, "I'm sorry. I don't understand. You can't provide for the people you free. They'll only end up locked up again. You can't change the city this way. It won't last forever, and they'll just start again as soon as you stop. You can't change that. It makes no sense. I'm sorry."

Jack shrugged. "I didn't think you'd understand. It doesn't change anything."

"No. I suppose it doesn't."

There was a distant red glow on the horizon. Even after all his months in the city, Arjun for a moment thought that it was dawn. But the glow was in the far north: it was Tiber. It was the Fire. Dawn was not coming. They were in the darkest hours of a night that seemed like the deepest and longest of his life.

The river was a very long dark tunnel into black emptiness. Although it was a summer night, there was a chill around Arjun's feet. They were passing through vacant industrial space. Rusty cranes towered overhead; it was as if Arjun were sunk on the riverbed, and the cranes were thick waving weeds. It was as if . . .

He knew the signs. In his head, his wounds throbbed in response to the approaching presence. It was coming down the river. Why had he been stupid enough to go near the river? Had he simply not wanted to look like a coward in front of the boy?

He stopped walking suddenly, turned to Olympia, and said, "It's coming. Again. We have to get away from the water."

He waved to Jack and the Thunderers behind him. Jack ran up to him (so *quickly*), and Arjun said, "There's something coming. A monster. The river-god. The plague. It's found us. Please don't argue. We have to get away from the water, go uphill."

"Believe him," Olympia said. "He can feel it."

There was a bad, stale smell rolling up. Jack sniffed, and his face wrinkled with distaste. Waving the rest of the boys up, he said, "We have to get away from the water. Something bad's coming. This one here, he'll explain later. Come on, quick."

The boys all took knives or pistols out of their clothes and dropped into a ready crouch as they took the road east, away from the docks and cranes. Arjun's group went ahead. They had to climb over a fence. One of the boys had a stiff leg, and his fellows had to lift him over.

A cobbled road ran east up Hood Hill. The buildings around

were blank and dark. They saw lights going out as they went by, windows being shuttered, and Arjun wondered whether that was the presence's doing, or whether the people inside could feel it coming, and were hiding their own lights for fear of it. The road seemed very steep, and the cobbles wet. They moved slowly, as if always sliding back down toward the hungry water.

They all sensed it at once, when it was nearly on them, and turned.

The street behind them was dark and there were no stars. There was an icy cold and a terrible sense of pressure. There was no wind but the trees all down the street quaked and thrashed and snapped.

Foul water trickled between the cobbles underfoot.

Jack said, "I *see* it."

Some of the boys started to cry. Olympia staggered back and slipped on the wet cobbles. Arjun stood in front of her. He could not think what to do. He had a sudden mad urge to sing. Music might sting the monster. At least, he would die with the Voice in his ears. But his throat constricted silently.

"It's huge," Jack said. "It's so *ugly*." His gaze was fixed on some invisible point high above the darkened street. His wide eyes darted, as if whatever he was seeing was twisting and writhing. "Gods, look at it; it's in so much *pain*."

Hoxton grabbed Jack's arm and said, "What do you see?" Jack pointed. Then Hoxton grunted and stepped forward. He grabbed a fallen child by his collar and half-pushed, half-threw the sobbing boy back, away, into Arjun's arms. Then he drew both his guns and fired into the blackness.

There was a long silence, swallowing the echo of the guns. The darkness neither lifted nor deepened. Further down the street, there was the sound of a window breaking, and another, and another.

Hoxton fumbled for more bullets, found nothing, swore, turned to the others and shouted, "*Run,* you idiots!"

Jack quivered with feverish fascination and stood almost on tiptoe to stare down the street. "Gods," he moaned, "it *sees* us."

Now nothing could be seen in the dark; the street behind them was a stinking void.

Hoxton threw both empty guns into the darkness, pistoning his right arm forward, then his left, roaring incoherently. Then he drew his heavy knife from his back, and turned and shouted again, *"Run!"*

Arjun and Olympia slipped and staggered away, stumbling in the dark, on the slick mossy stones, dragging and being dragged by the children and each other. Arjun could not stop himself looking back, again and again, but there was nothing to see except darkness.

And now Hoxton turned and ran, too, but he took only three steps away from the black cloud before the slime under his feet cost him his footing. The cloud rose around him. To Arjun, it seemed that Hoxton was falling far away, into empty darkness, though he was still there, kneeling on the cobbles, reaching for help, terribly alone.

The darkness rose into the sky. The street was spattered with muck and reeking water. Weed and wet leaves spun and drifted in the still, windless air. Underfoot there was decaying wreckage; timbers, old worn bricks, slimy with moss. It seemed the street was crumbling; as Arjun stumbled slowly backwards, a pub-sign snapped from rusted chains and fell at his feet. The rotten wood snapped in two. There was screaming; Olympia, the boys, the people in the buildings all around, perhaps Arjun himself.

Hoxton fell away at the center of the darkness. A deeper darkness seemed to cover him, as if the black mud beneath the cobblestones was rising, flooding, seizing him. Darkness covered his roaring mouth and he choked. Darkness covered his eyes.

Hoxton drowned. It was only moments, but seemed to take a very long time. *(Long enough for everyone to forget you,* Arjun thought, *that's how long the thing takes to kill.)*

Someone pushed past Arjun. Then there was a speck of white in the air, trailing brightness, in front of the inky cloud, hanging high over Arjun's head. "Chase me, monster," Jack yelled. *"Chase me."* He threw his beautiful stolen knife into the darkness, and turned in the air, like a tropical fish twisting in the water, and streaked over the darkness, and west, across the river and into the stars. The night followed, flowing after him.

The street was empty again. The stars were out and there was a cool summer breeze. A few people looked out of their broken windows. Filth and debris were strewn everywhere. Hoxton's slime-swaddled body lay on the cobbles. Olympia ran to him, and touched his chest, and sobbed.

The Thunderers stood around in shock, looking at the sky. Without their leader, there was nothing much to them. They were ill-fed and scared boys. *I have to speak quickly,* Arjun thought, *before they panic.* He tried not to let them see how nervous they made him.

"We need to keep going," he said. "Jack would want you to keep going."

The boy with the bad leg snapped, "We need to wait for him. He'll be back. If we go, how will he find us?"

"Do you have no faith in him? He'll find us. He'll escape that thing and find us. But if we wait here, that thing may lose interest in him, and come back, and kill us. Do you want to leave him alone? Do you want him to come back here, and find he's *alone?* I know what he'd want you to do. *Think.*"

They looked at him, murmuring.

"What's your name?" Arjun asked the boy who had spoken.

"Namdi."

"Namdi. Think of what he's risking, leading that thing away from us. You need to take a risk now, and go on without him. He'll find us. But we can't stay."

They were unhappy about it, but they didn't want to stay either, really. The monster's mark was on that place.

There was a glint in the grime of the street: Jack's fallen knife. Arjun picked it up. Then he tenderly helped Olympia to her feet, and they walked silently together, the boys following them, up the hill, east, and then north again, to the Iron Rose.

THIRTY-EIGHT

Not far east of the Iron Rose was a small park. There was a café in the middle of it, by the pond. It was a depressing place; the prison's complex shadow fell across the water for the best hours of the day. Arjun and Olympia sat out at the wrought-iron tables in the café's garden all morning, sipping coffee.

"I'm very sorry about Hoxton—" Arjun started to say.

She cut him off. "It's not your fault. No, wait, we don't *know* that it's your fault. Maybe the monster was chasing you, but maybe it's chasing us all. It killed Nicolas, after all. Maybe it has a taste for us. Maybe we *offend* it."

"Olympia, even if it is me it's chasing, I didn't ask for it. I'm trying to help. I can leave you, if you like, if you think I'm a danger to you."

"I know. I'm sorry."

She lit a cigarette, and inhaled and exhaled deeply. She looked very tired in the morning light, under the grey shadow.

She asked, "Is that what it was like before?"

He shrugged. "No. Yes. It's getting worse, I think. Every day. It's in pain; you heard what Jack said. It's only going to get angrier and angrier. I saw it before and it *watched* me. This time it reached out and . . . It's learning to kill."

"Fucking *Shay*." She rubbed her temples. "This gives me a headache."

"Waiting here is hard," Arjun said. "We're well outside of the Countess's sphere of operations, but still . . ."

"Never mind her. The Chairman will want us dead, too. If he

really did use us to provoke her, like that . . . well, we're a loose end. His agents will be looking. I'm more afraid of *them*."

They both looked around nervously. It was painful to be exposed in the open air, but they needed to wait somewhere where Jack might see them from the sky. The boys were doing the same nearby, on the rooftops around the park, wearing their crests. Silk had sharp eyes, they had told Arjun.

"I hadn't thought of that. Olympia, what will you do if we do free Holbach? Can you still operate in this city?"

"Maybe. Maybe if we move further away. Out west or east. We'd have to start all over again. I don't know. We'll see."

They ordered more coffee. The proprietor looked at them suspiciously as she took their order. "Our brother is in there," Olympia lied. "We just came to be close to him. I think maybe he can feel us, even if he can't see us. Don't you, Simon?"

"I hope so," Arjun agreed.

They did not see Jack until he sat down next to them and swigged down Olympia's coffee. He wiped his mouth with his sleeve and smiled. "Led it away. Lost it somewhere miles out in the west, around dawn. It wasn't so fast." A thought troubled his brow, and he said, "I'm sorry about your bodyguard." He leaned forward. "So what was that thing? It was like a god, but no god behaves like that. No god gets *lost,* for one thing, but that's what I did with it."

Arjun tried to explain.

Jack shook his head. "Fuck. Did you *see* it?"

"Not really," Arjun said.

"*I* saw it. I have good eyes. Do you want to hear what it looked like?"

"Not really," Olympia said.

"Suit yourself." Somehow, without his hands seeming to move, he had stolen and lit one of Olympia's cigarettes. "So now it'll come after me, too?"

"Perhaps, Jack. We don't know. We don't understand how it thinks. *If* it thinks. Perhaps Holbach can find a way of stopping it. He knows a lot about these things."

"You should have told me."

"I didn't think we'd be together long enough for you to be in danger. It's very slow, Jack. It's not as though it jumps out at us from every corner, every day."

"It's slow, and I'm fast. But you still should have told me."

"We're sorry," Olympia said. "But we need you. Holbach can stop it. I believe he can. It's getting stronger and you'd have been in danger even if you'd never met us. Everyone is. You just wouldn't have known it, yet. But it's true that you're in more danger while you're with us. We don't want to put your people at risk. Finish it quickly and we'll be done with each other. We should get started at once."

Jack gave Olympia a condescending look. "I *have* started. With the Thunderers. They're getting what we need right now. Did you think I was going to take you, too? I can't use you. You're too old and too slow. Do you have a place to wait while we work?"

Arjun patted his pockets. He pulled out a loose mass of paper from his jacket pocket. He shuffled through the heap. There were pages of musical notation. There were pages scribbled with strange languages, strange untranslated words and complex declensions and conjugations of Tuvar and Kael and Ghentian. There were old scraps of paper on which he'd nervously scribbled his income and expenses. Olympia raised an eyebrow; he shrugged. Jack's eyes studied the proceedings coolly; Arjun wondered if the boy could read. "Can you read, Jack?" The boy nodded. "Good."

There were pages, neatly folded, on which he'd drawn maps. During his wanderings—back a long time ago, now—he'd tried to map the city. To map each day's fruitless search. He wondered how much the city had changed since he'd wasted that ink. He opened the folded pages and one by one put them aside. Olympia picked them up as he put them down, and she flicked through them lightly. There was a page half-full of a map of Faugère. Arjun tore it in two, and on the blank half he wrote:

THE HOTEL MACLEOD, 141 BOTANY STREET, ROOM 11
SOUTH OF THE IRON ROSE
NORTH OF THE TEMPLE MIRRORS
WEST OF MUNDY WAY
(DOWNHILL FROM THE THREE TALL WINDMILLS,
UPHILL FROM THE MISSION)

Olympia reached out and gripped the paper. "If he's captured with that, they'll come for us."

"He won't be captured. Will you, Jack? You won't be captured and you won't forget us." Arjun gently eased the paper from Olympia's grip. He handed the paper to Jack, who folded it and placed it in his own jacket pocket with great silent solemnity.

Jack nodded once. Then he turned, rising from his chair, vaulted the railings, and disappeared into the bushes. A moment later they heard the rushing of footsteps over the roof-tiles.

High girders of pitted and rusting iron held together the Rose's towers and vanes, its shuttered bridges and disused walkways. The thick iron sagged and bowed with age. Cables cut across the sky like rigging, binding the whole creaking mass together.

Sometimes the Rose's guards would shove a prisoner out there and lock the door behind them, leave them for the birds. Here and there rust-swollen cages hung from the cables, were bolted to the spires and girders; bones turned yellow in them.

Namdi and Een sat on a girder that stuck out at the crazy angle of a broken rib from the southeast tower. They'd been quite alone up there all morning—since Jack left them there—but now Jack was back and they were all waiting, and still waiting, all through the hot afternoon, for night to come.

Someone had painted most of the girders' length black, many years ago; only a few flaking black leaves remained. Jack idly plucked at them, chipped them off from the iron, sent them drifting slowly down onto the rooftops below. His nails were long and dirty, and he got rust under them. It was windless and his long black hair hung greasily.

Namdi sat on Jack's left, smoking, his back leaning against a knot of cables, his bad leg stretched out along the girder. Little Een sat cross-legged on his right, his rifle (ridiculously oversized) in his lap.

Beneath them—far beneath them—was a flat expanse of roof, heaped with gravel. Below that the roof fell away in a tiled slope, and below that—at the edge of Namdi's and Een's rifles' range—the tower walls were studded with the dull mirrors of windows.

A door opened below with a distant scrape and clang of bolts and chains. Three guards with guns and billy clubs led a troupe of pale and bony men out onto the rooftop. The prisoners carried what Jack thought at first might have been weapons of their own, but were apparently brooms. For an hour they swept the gravel across the roof's surface. None of them bothered to look up. The afternoon wore on sweltering hot and windless.

Namdi shielded his eyes from the glare of the setting sun and studied the men below. "Don't suppose he's one of them, is he?"

"He's fatter. A lot fatter."

"Could have lost weight."

"True. Not that much, though, not that fast."

"True. Poor bastards."

"Yeah."

"Would have saved time. Could've just plucked him off and no one would have had to go in, down there. Would have been easier."

"What are we, shopkeepers? Looking for the easy deal? This is going to be *sport*."

"For you, maybe." Namdi stiffly shifted his leg. "For me it's a long wait."

"Shut your whining. You've got a gun, soldier-boy. You get to shoot it. What else would you rather be doing?"

Namdi shrugged. "Don't know. True enough." He looked Jack briefly in the eye; Jack was angry again, for no reason. He'd been worse than ever since Fiss died. "Redcoats wouldn't have me now, anyway. This'll be sport, like you said. Look at that great black iron bastard." As the prisoners filed back in through the door, their guards kicking and shouting, Namdi flicked his cigarette down onto the roof. "I mean, if we don't come back from this, it's not a bad way to go."

Jack scowled, then smiled.

A few minutes later Jack stood, balancing on the iron beam. He covered his eyes and stared at the northeast tower. "I'm going to check on Beth's lot. Namdi, Een, will you be ready?"

"We'll be ready. Right, Een?"

"Good lads." Jack stepped off the iron; he fell ten feet to a cable and ran up its quivering length and at its tight arcing apex he launched himself into the sky. Namdi watched the speck of him recede and vanish among the cables and rusting iron.

The sun passed behind one of the towers.

Namdi looked down at the drop. "Well, that's us fucked if he doesn't come back."

"He'll come back."

"Unless he doesn't."

Een screwed up his face into an expression of great resolution and loyalty, and said nothing.

Namdi rolled two cigarettes, and gave one to Een. Een tossed one of the bombs to Namdi, and Namdi tossed it back, and so on, for a while. Later, Namdi sat rolling the bomb back and forth in his lap, until he worried that the sweat of his palms would soak the paper and dampen the flash-powder.

He kept thinking about that . . . thing. The thing that had come at them out of the river. The thing that Jack had fought. Sickness and plague and drowning, raging through the city. Namdi's own mother had died of a cancer that rotted and hollowed her and made her stink and go mad. It scared him dreadfully. He looked at Een's face, round and tiny and dirty. Een was little; probably he'd forgotten it already, or at least grown used to it. Grown used to a city that contained that madness.

Maybe this fat scholar Holbach could stop it. He'd bossed the Bird around to make that ship; maybe he could order that monster back to the river. But in the meantime the thing was out there somewhere, and angry, and no city that contained it made any kind of sense. Something very bad was going to happen. Maybe not to him, and he hoped not to Een, who wasn't a bad lad, and he prayed not to Jack, because he loved him fiercely, but somewhere, to someone.

Sunset would be the signal to get ready. The first flash and distant thunderclap from the northwest tower would be the signal to *begin.* Namdi checked his rifle over again, and again.

✳   ✳   ✳

Arjun waved for the proprietor. He ordered bread and cheese and water.

"And wine," Olympia said. "I bloody well intend to get drunk."

"We should stay alert."

"We're *superfluous,* Arjun. You heard that awful boy. Nothing to do but wait." The proprietor placed a jug on the table, and two rough clay mugs. Olympia waved him away. "To Holbach! He'd want us to have a drink ready for him." She filled her mug and knocked it back, and made a sour face. "To Hoxton, too. It's probably best he's dead. If he were still alive, the humiliation of this would kill him."

"You'd rather take up a knife and a gun and storm the Rose yourself?"

"I'd rather be *acting* than waiting."

"This is a bad business. I'd rather be waiting."

"Easy for you to say. Why don't you sing us a song to pass the time?"

He put a finger to his lips. "Quiet. We should listen and wait."

"You infuriating man."

Arjun leafed through the spill of papers. A map of the northern edge of Fourth Ward; he ran his finger along the black borderline of the canal. He picked up a long yellow strip torn from the *Era:* he'd jotted down in the margin a dozen different possible translations for *Black Bull. Black* could equally have been *fertile* or *rich* or *ancient* in Tuvar. *Bull* could have been *king* or *father* or *night;* in fact it might equally have been *horse* or *ox.* Scribbled notes toward an inconsequential puzzle. He'd enjoyed those months.

"Ha! See? You," Olympia said, "cannot let things go. You *cannot* put things down. An obsessive. Professor Almuth had theories about people like you; he says it begins in childhood, with toilet training. We printed his theory in the Atlas, and a censor from Mass How went quite mad over it. It's very sad to see it in action."

He smiled, balled up the paper in his hand, and dropped it on his plate.

Olympia nodded. "Keep going. You are a man badly in need of throwing things away."

He tore up a page of music and scattered it.

"Progress!" she said.

"But not what you're looking for. Not what you're looking for me to give up. These are just empty gestures. Don't confuse symbols with the world."

"As Holbach liked to say."

"Exactly." He took a drink. "To Holbach. And Hoxton, of course."

"To Holbach."

They both drank.

"And what about you?" Arjun asked. "What will you do if we can't get him back?"

"Something different, I suppose. Something new."

They finished the bottle. Olympia didn't like the way the proprietor was looking at them; he had an informant's calculating eyes. They switched cafés. Two hours later they switched again. When they were drunk enough to be past caution of eavesdroppers, Olympia started telling stories about Holbach, then about Nicolas, and the Atlas, and the enemies they'd made, the wonderful trouble they'd caused. Stories about herself. As the sun was setting and they sat by the railings, she confessed that *Olympia* was not her real name. She'd taken it from a painting. She'd made herself over and if she had to she'd do it again, she told him. If she could, she'd make the whole city over.

Before Arjun could press her to give up her real name, there was a flash on the edge of his vision—it was over in the north, up on the Rose's towers—and a distant thunderclap, and another, and another, going off like fireworks, like gunshots.

Arjun jumped up from his chair to watch. Another and another, flaring red, from the east tower and the west. After a while the explosions stopped, but there were still gunshots: distant, muffled, quiet enough that probably only he could hear them.

Olympia grabbed his arm. He turned and looked south. Across the hills, the river, the squares, days to the south—unless he missed his guess, back down by the docks, by Shutlow, by Foyle's Ward, by the Heath—the sky was a lurid bonfire red.

They sobered up quickly.

☀ ☀ ☀

Arlandes snapped awake suddenly and with a sense of dread. A sense of having fallen and struck the ground with great violence. Something terrible echoed in his ears.

He'd fallen asleep in the black leather armchair in his office. When he wasn't on the *Thunderer,* he generally just slept in his office; what else did he have to do but sleep?

Someone was shouting in the corridors outside. He replayed the sound that had woken him and concluded that it had been an explosion. Confirmation: from behind the thick curtains on his window there was a glowering red light in the darkness.

As he woke and stood and stretched his aching neck and walked over to the window, he daydreamed that someone had taken the *Thunderer* and turned it on the crowds, and he thought, *Good. Shut their mouths once and for all.*

Footsteps running in the corridor, and more shouting. Leoden's voice, and Gibson's. Soon there would be someone banging on his door; he could feel it.

He pulled back the curtain. Fire over the rooftops, over northeast. There'd hardly been a night without fire for weeks, but this was a big one. Black smoke clouded out the sunset. Unless he missed his guess, it was the magazine of the North Shutlow barracks. Behind that squat brick building's iron doors were shelves and shelves of powder, rifle and artillery. That would account for the explosion echoing in his ears.

Arlandes was in Barbary barracks. Not the barracks at the Countess's estate; not anymore. In light of the filthy slurs in those plays and pamphlets—the Atlas-makers' nasty sneaking insinuations regarding Arlandes' relationship with the Countess—the Countess had thought it politic to keep him distant.

The *Thunderer* was far from Barbary barracks, and Arlandes had not set foot on its boards in—two days? Three? The days blurred into one now. The great ship drifted on its tether at its elevated dry dock, overlooking the Countess's palace on Laud Heath—orbiting, as the Countess liked to put it, the sun of her glory.

Barbary barracks was on that district's western edge, by the livestock sheds. There were twenty-three men in it. None of them were his best.

A bad business if the rioters had gotten into the magazine. They were getting ambitious. It was time to restore order. It was time to put an end to softness. If they wanted fire, it was time to give them fire. He would talk to the Countess in the morning. He would organize a punitive force. Arlandes let the curtain go and reached for his sword, which rested against the desk.

Another explosion sounded outside, so close and so loud that it shattered the window-glass behind him and blew open the curtains. He staggered and fell against the desk. The walls rocked and the door crashed open and the bookshelf by the window rocked and swayed and fell with a crash. The room was full of sudden blazing heat and light and the stink of gunpowder, then the air was full of brick-dust.

The Barbary magazine.

Not twenty yards outside my own fucking door.

Arlandes, lying on his back on the floor, touched the back of his head; it was bleeding where he'd struck it on the desk. He felt suddenly very terribly tired.

The Thunderers all had pocketwatches, or the wrist-worn watches that were fashionable in Soutine and Albermarle and other northern districts, or some other stolen timepiece; but none of the devices told quite the same time and none of the boys or girls had any idea how to fix that. Atlay had been a clockmaker's apprentice, but Atlay had succumbed to the plague two weeks ago; they'd wrapped his poor body in a blanket, doused him in oil, and burned him clean away. Fiss had been clever with locks and trinkets and he'd always known how to fix stolen things up nice for the fences, but Fiss was dead, too. So Jack had abandoned the idea of using watches to coordinate, and instead the signal they'd chosen was sunset, behind the Rose's western tower. It was better that way, anyway. It *felt* better—*purer*.

Sunset stained the tower rose-petal red. Roosting next to Jack on the high iron beam were Beth, Caul, Wood, Kuyo, and Dait.

They had guns over their shoulders but knives in their hands; these were the ones who'd volunteered for the *close* work. Who'd chosen to see it through to the end, all the way to the end, while Namdi and Een and Taine and the others perched up out of harm's way, in the rigging, dropping their flash-powder parcels and firing their stolen rifles and playing a diversion, a distraction, a *chorus.*

When the sun fell all the way behind the tower and it was black again, Jack stood. There was a flash and a bang from away over on the southeast tower: Namdi. There was another flash over near the southwest tower: Simeon. There were gunshots. More flashes and bangs from the north and the east, and all over.

When he heard distant shouting, doors banging open, guards running and panicking, he stepped off the perch and dropped. Beth and Caul and Wood and Kuyo and Dait dropped with him, their silks fluttering in the night air.

Below them was a gaping black chimney-vent, wide as a river. They dropped soundlessly into its mouth.

Captain?"

"Captain?"

Arlandes groaned and swore. The stink of blood in his nostrils almost covered the stink of fire and smoke from outside.

"Captain? Are you in there?"

Arlandes reached for his chair, which had fallen, and pulled himself up so that he was sitting against the desk. The voice was Sub-Lieutenant Gibson's. Gibson himself came round the edge of the desk a moment later. The man was pale and unshaven and sweating filthily, but he was in uniform, red-coated, sword in hand.

There was a dull thud and crash from outside, and another. One to the west, one to the east.

"Captain? They've struck the magazines. They've blown up our magazines."

"I can see that, man."

"They've blown up one of the Countess's countinghouses. They've blown up one of her gun-towers. I don't know what else, sir. Sir, we're on fire downstairs. Let me help you up."

Gibson reached out a hand and Arlandes snarled at him to get back; to leave him alone. Arlandes stood, leaning on the edge of the desk, swaying slightly. He could not think what to do. He wanted to sink into his armchair again and wait for it to be over, for whatever was happening, to happen.

"Sir, it's all happening at once, sir. We have to get out of here, sir." Gibson stepped closer and stretched out his hand again, reaching for Arlandes' arm.

There was something terribly wrong in the Sub-Lieutenant's eyes: sickly fear and anticipation giving way to coldness, to resolve, and then a sudden wild surrender to decision and *action*.

Gibson's left hand reached for Arlandes' arm, and his right hand brought the saber back and drove it savagely forward at Arlandes' gut. But Arlandes was already falling back and away, twisting out of Gibson's reach, and the point pierced his shirt and grazed his side but did not, he thought, he hoped, do more than scratch him. And in the next moment, while Gibson staggered forward, Arlandes lunged forward and grabbed Gibson's head by his ears and slammed it down hard, with a ripping and cracking sound, onto the desk's surface.

Gibson fell back, bleeding from his nose and forehead, and tried to swing the saber again. He was stumbling and slow and quite comical. Gibson was no gentleman and had never been properly taught how to wield a saber. Gibson was more a carpenter than a warrior and held his saber like a hammer. Arlandes grabbed the nearest implement from the desk, which turned out to be a silver letter-opener, and speared Gibson under his armpit, and again in his throat, and twisted Gibson's suddenly weak wrist until the saber fell from it. He stabbed Gibson one more time, in the gut, before thinking to question him.

He lowered Gibson's quivering body into the armchair. He held the man's jaw so that he could look into his terrified eyes. "Who *bought* you, Gibson? Who bought you?"

Blood poured from Gibson's mouth and from his throat and covered Arlandes' shirtsleeves. Gibson croaked and whined; he seemed unable to speak.

Arlandes tore open the brass buttons of the man's jacket and emptied his pockets. A chapbook copy of *The Marriage Blessing,* with a lurid frontispiece showing the Countess draping her bony body around Arlandes' stiff brutish shoulders, in a cruel parody of seduction. A pamphlet demanding the release of Professor Holbach in the name of the Atlas and the city and the future and progressivism and all the other usual nonsense. A scrap of paper with an address in Ebon Fields, and the name *Olympia Autun,* which was, if Arlandes remembered rightly, the name of that sneering bitch who'd dragged Holbach's fat carcass around all those years. Arlandes snorted and scattered the papers and gripped Gibson's jaw again.

"Ridiculous. Absurd. Do you take me for a fool? You are not one of Holbach's people. Shutlow magazine and Barbary magazine and the countinghouses and who knows what else, all in one night. Holbach's people don't have the will to do that. They only talk and talk. They write *plays,* for the gods' sake. They don't get their hands dirty. Someone *real* bought you. Who? Was it the Stross Mercantile? Was it the Thane of Red Barrow? Was it Mensonge? Was it Cimenti and his bloody bankers? Was it bankers' money that bought you, Gibson? Was it the Combine? Or was it somebody's church? Did you do this for some god, Gibson? Were you a *pawn,* or a *sacrifice?*"

Gibson's eyes had gone dull and the bleeding had stopped. Arlandes let go and let the dead man's head loll. Then he picked up his own saber and ran out into the hallway, shouting, "To me! To me! Redcoats, on your feet!"

The corridors of the Iron Rose were lined with iron cells and cages. Most were empty, or contained men who were blind or mad or perhaps dead, but every few yards they would pass pale hands reaching out to them, pleading or moaning.

Some of the prisoners even knew who Jack was; they saw the bright silk and called out his name. It pained him to pass them by, but he had no keys for their bars. Indeed the cages seemed to be opened not by locks, but by machinery hidden within the thick walls, by levers and gears hidden in the heart of the Rose somewhere. Or perhaps they couldn't be opened at all. Jack and Beth and Kuyo gripped the bony hands as they went past, and they asked, *Where is the warden? Where's the heart of this place?*

Some of the prisoners walked around the corridors freely—if you could call it freedom, lost in the Rose's half-lit maze. They wore badges or collars or chains; many were branded. They drifted alone and apparently mad, or swaggered around in gangs. Jack tried to · avoid them, if he could. He suspected they might have bought their comparative freedom with promises of loyalty to the guards. He didn't know; the place made no sense to him.

Even in the Rose there were white robes, dressed in robes cut from greyish blankets but still identifiable by their shaved heads and burn-marks; little feral packs of them, snarling and bullying the weaker prisoners, strutting around like little wardens themselves. Jack felt a kind of pity for them, and he left them alone.

There was a lightless pit, behind bars, where the sick were thrown, in their dozens. There was a terrible stench from the pit's mouth: a variety of human and animal stinks, and over it all the cold, alien, mossy stink of the river-god's black-lunged plague. After he saw that, Jack stopped touching the prisoners' hands.

The ceilings everywhere were oppressively low and dark. It reminded him of Barbotin. He'd learned how Barbotin worked, over the years, learned its puzzle so well he'd broken it open, but every prison was different. The city contained cruelty in infinite variety.

For a while they had it easy, as the Rose's guards panicked, running up and down through the corridors; word had gone out that they were under attack, from all quarters at once, from above, from within, from nowhere. Near the foot of a wide staircase that led down through the upper levels, Jack skulked in the shadows, Beth leaning over his shoulder, and they watched two groups of armored men run up to each other at a junction of gas-lit corridors and shout, "We're under attack at the north tower!" and "To the east tower!" and practically fall over each other's pikes and bayonets trying to work out where to go.

But before the Thunderers had gone too much further down, they had to get their hands dirty. On the sixth level down—maybe seventh; the place was mazy and the floors and walls seemed to shift—there was a wide inner courtyard lit by bonfires. Jack watched from high arches of blood-red brick that hung over the yard as a group of guards, their senses seemingly addled by panic, drew their rifles and opened fire on a huddled pleading mass of prisoners, who they'd apparently mistaken for their attackers. Jack and the others dropped from the arches. They threw their knives as they crossed the yard's dark interior space. They landed as the knives struck and they pulled them from the guards' flesh and they struck again. When there were only a handful of guards left alive, they asked, *Where's your warden? Where's your boss? Who runs this place? Where's the heart of it?*

Arjun and Olympia went northeast up Mundy Way, and north round Glabber Crescent, until they found a hill from which they could see the Rose more clearly.

The hill was covered in broken and graffiti-etched marble pillars, and equestrian statues of dead rulers with broken arms and heads and swords. There were stone benches, but they were already full; the hill was crowded with gawkers, passing around jugs and bottles, watching the flames and the explosions and the echoes of distant gunshots. Whispering: *That's right, burn the fucker down* and *What if they all get loose? What if those scum get loose? What happens to us then?* and *What's happening to this city?*

There were intermittent flashes and bangs from the southern towers. The northernmost tower seemed to be quite seriously ablaze.

Arjun and Olympia watched it with fascination, and horror, and exhilaration, and guilt, and shame.

"This is horrible," Olympia said. "This is a horrible thing to be involved with."

"This is a terrible city. A terrible cruel city. Even those who try to do good for it are tarnished."

"What do you think's happening back south?"

"More of the same, I expect. Fire and riot and madness."

"Gods, maybe they'll finally kill that bitch Ilona. Maybe she'll finally kill Cimenti. Maybe they'll kill each other."

"That won't stop it. Someone else will take their place. Or some*thing* else. The river-thing will take what's left. It will get worse and worse. Discord only grows and grows. This ugliness will not stop it. Only silence and peace can stop it. Olympia, did I ever tell you about the Thunderer? I don't know what else to call you except Olympia. It fits you well, real or unreal. I wonder if I ever told you about the Thunderer. Not the ship, but what it makes me think of. Olympia, there was one of the Fathers of the Choristry, a Father Hari—many cycles of our song before I was born—who had a theory regarding the Voice. That it had an opposite, that its existence implied an opposite somewhere. Or perhaps merely an *absence*. Dynamically, so to speak, its existence implied its absence, and that absence would be everything the Voice was not: it would be loud, and violent, and senseless, and chaotic. It would be the most terrible discord in the world, sounding eternally but without purpose, and everyone who heard it would go mad. It would crash and smash and shake loose the sanity of all those who heard it. Hari named it Thunder. It was only a theory, of course. Hari did not really believe in its existence in a literal sense. I think perhaps Hari and Holbach would have liked each other. Though Hari did not attempt to bring his fear into being. I wonder if I ever told you this."

Olympia had stopped listening, and Arjun's voice had long since trailed off into a murmur anyway. Olympia was staring north, and biting the nail of her thumb.

"Arjun. I can't watch this anymore. Those poor children. Those horrible vicious children. What if it all burns down? Those poor people back in Shutlow, and Foyle, and Barbary, and gods know where else. Sometimes I think we've done everything wrong, Arjun."

Captain, what . . ."

"Sub-Lieutenant Gibson is dead. He was a traitor and this is his blood on my hands. If there are any other traitors present, I suggest you come forward now and we'll resolve the matter."

He was weeping, but it was only from the smoke that filled the drill-yard. Smoke invaded his lungs and he bent double, coughing, but he wasn't the only one; all the men were crouching and wheez-ing and holding rags and cloths to their faces.

The barracks were ablaze. Auterton and Lane and Kay were dead; they'd been trapped in the kitchen, which had been next to the magazine, and had gone up first and fiercest.

Lieutenant Leoden had been leading a group of the men in fight-ing the blaze, with buckets and the drill-yard's well. It was a doomed effort but a good one; however, there was more important work to be done.

"The fire'll spread, Captain. If the wind changes, the fire'll spread to the rest of the street. We have to stop the fire, sir, or—" Leoden was a good man. Nevertheless, Arlandes had cuffed his face, collared him, thrown him to the floor in front of all the rest of the men. He'd told them: "*Forget* the fire. The enemy has betrayed his hand. This is no accident. Tonight we save our Countess. Tonight we save the *Thunderer*. Tonight we take revenge. In the morning we rebuild. Do you understand?"

They'd asked, "What enemy, sir?" And he hadn't been able to answer, but of course it hardly mattered.

There were twenty of them. They formed two columns, and Arlandes took the lead, and rifles in hand they marched through the streets.

On Sheppey Street a boy threw a half a brick at them, and Arlandes shot him as he fled back into the alley's trash-heaps.

On Exhibition Street someone threw a piss-bottle from an upper window, which tumbled spilling its foul contents down through the washing-lines and, seeming now incongruous and absurd, a line of tattered red flags. It broke quite precisely before Arlandes' black boots. If nothing else, the riots had taught the Countess's people good aim. There was no time to chase the offender down, so Arlandes signaled *Ignore it.*

They turned down Silden Street, and into the mirror-cracks of unnamed alleys that ran between Barbary's warehouses. In the shadow of the warehouses, they couldn't see the fires burning all around them. In the deep ravines of brick and slate and sagging timber, they could barely hear the distant thunder of the Countess's third and last magazine going up.

Huddled under the loading-arches of the Great West Ferry &
Freight warehouse, they found a group of the plague-sick. Great
West had closed its Barbary operations three weeks ago, and the
warehouse was empty. The plague-sick—their eyes black and their
bodies thin—were gathered around a bonfire of chairs. They stank
of weeds and rot. They stared blankly, resentfully, at Arlandes' shining black coat, his bright saber, at his men in their rooster-red coats.
Leoden swore and spat. Arlandes shook with horror and for an instant it seemed the dying men's black eyes were *hunting* him; the
lung-rot seemed a malign and purposive thing. He wondered if all
the forgotten and abandoned places of the city were filling with that
rotten filth. *Fire and flood,* he thought, nonsensically, *the River has
burst its banks.*

He gave the order and his redcoats—from a safe distance, handkerchiefs or gun-cloths to their faces—opened fire, and reloaded
their muzzles, and fired again, and put the ghastly creatures out of
their misery.

The warden of the Iron Rose was a fat man, very fat, and he'd worn
a ridiculous hat shaped like a locked box; the hat had rolled off into
a corner and the man himself lay dead on his desk like a fat fish
flopped on a market stall. His suite was more like a priest's chambers than a warden's offices. His hat was a priest's kind of hat, and
he'd worn black robes hung and wrapped with chains, like a priest
of the Chain, which was presumably what he really was.

He'd begged for his life. When Jack had come bursting into his
chambers, he'd begged and whined. He'd run (puffing and wad-
dling) across the floor, from the side of the room that was dark and
lacquered jet-black and into the side of the room that was painted
white, and full of wide-open windows. There he'd thrown open his
closet and shown Jack his *white* robes, hung with golden chains, *broken,* and with golden keys. He'd babbled about the *Chain,* and the
Runagate, and the sacred cycle of the Iron Rose and of confinement
and release and confinement again and release . . . .

Beth's parents had died in the Rose. They'd been arrested, when
she was very small, by the police of the Parliament of Mass How, for

subversive activities. Or at least so she remembered it; Jack suspected it was something less heroic. Probably they were debtors or something stupid—it was none of his business. But they'd been taken, and locked away, and the cycle for them had ended right there, so Jack let *her* shoot the warden. "I am only a servant," he'd whined. "Only a servant of the Rose. Only—"

Afterwards, while Jack and Wood and Dait went through the warden's ledgers, she was sick behind the warden's closet. It was hardly the first time she'd shot someone, but she was sick anyway. Dait laughed and Jack cuffed his ear.

The ledgers said that those who had offended against the Countess were held seven stories down. The Countess's entries in the ledgers were only a tiny, tiny part of the whole. To Jack's surprise, she was not close to the heaviest user of the Rose's services. Even so, she had an extensive maze of cells to her name; Holbach was at the heart of it.

Seven stories down. The stairs were crowded with rushing guards and panicking prisoners, so they dropped the first three stories down an air-shaft.

Arlandes' redcoats left the alleys and crossed Gull Street, which was a wide river of panic. All the bars were closed. The market-carts were stopped in the streets, and fruit and fresh butcher's meat had spilled all over the paving stones, and splattered and slid under trampling, panicking feet.

The crowds parted for the redcoats.

Some of them came running up to Arlandes, pleading and whining: *What's happening? There's fire everywhere! What's happening? Who's doing this?* A grey-haired woman in a ragged grey dress, four fat children in tow, clutched at Arlandes' sleeve and begged: "They burned my street. Why won't you help us?"

He shoved her aside. *Now* they begged for his help! After weeks of slurs, and slander, and riot and sedition, *now* they wanted his protection again. Now that some foreign enemy was there on the streets, skulking in among the crowds. Now that the game of riot had become the reality of war. He despised them.

Was it Mensonge? Was it Cimenti? Cimenti was a tricky bastard and it was his style to use proxies and subterfuge; Mensonge was a degenerate and Arlandes would not put it past him to use slander and dirty plays and the passions of the mob. There was no way of knowing, and Arlandes could not think straight; the streets were too busy and too noisy.

There were more redcoats among the crowds—little scattered bands of them, confused and leaderless. They rallied round Arlandes; they made their panicked reports. Bad news was general all over Shutlow and Barbary and Fourth and Foyle's. More than one of Arlandes' fellow captains had vanished mysteriously, most likely assassinated. There'd been explosions and fires all over, at barracks and magazines and watchhouses and countinghouses and court-houses. It was too coordinated to be mere riot, but the perpetrators were invisible, uncatchable; they wore no uniforms, they vanished among the angry and frightened crowds.

On Gissing Street the fences were plastered all along their length with fresh wet posters: FREE HOLBACH and UNBIND THE ATLAS and NO GODS, NO MASTERS, AWAY WITH THE OLD MAPS. Arlandes, striding through the wet leaves heaped in the street, thought *Holbach!* Was it possible that fat old fool had planned this? The men torching Shutlow were no scholars, whoever they were, none of Holbach's degenerate clique of playwrights and intellectuals, but Holbach was rich; he could have hired them. Holbach may have been unworldly, but he had worldly people around him. That woman, the one who'd escaped the arrests; she'd had a cunning look about her.

The redcoats did not know whom to shoot. On Quay Back Row, Arlandes passed a group of young men moving with a purposiveness he found suspicious, and he ordered them shot on general principles. A quick search of their pockets found nothing more than ordinarily incriminating. Leoden looked sick; Arlandes told him, "Keep moving. The Countess'll pay their families compensation in the morning, if she's still alive."

On Grossmarket Street they passed the body of a woman, black-haired, facedown, and broken in the dirt. The crowds rushed past ignoring her, eyes on the fires on the skyline, just as they'd rushed past Lucia's body, eyes turned to the sky and the *Thunderer*. Arlandes held back tears; he pretended it was only the smoke.

On Barium Street they passed a flock of those white-robed hooligans putting the torch to a public house. Arlandes couldn't recall which mob was which, or what they called themselves: the white-robed shaved-head creatures and the chattering shrieking children in silk blended in his mind into one swirling slurry of gutter filth. One more sign that the city was falling into ruin. For a moment he speculated, absurdly, that those evil children were his hidden enemy; that this new mutant generation of bastards and freaks was rising to take the city from him and from the Countess. Leoden fired a single shot and the white robes scattered like pigeons. (Their white robes fluttered away like her dress, as she fell.)

Arlandes' numbers swelled. He had some twenty-five men with him when he went through Seven Wheels Market. A bomb had toppled Coney Wheel: the great stone wheel lay split in two, carts and stalls crushed beneath it. Arlandes rallied two redcoats who'd been trying to fight the fires. Near Saddler Wheel he picked up a prowling half-dozen of the grey-coated Irregulars. The Irregulars were, in his view, little better than thugs and murderers, their mere existence a symptom of decay in the body politic, but it was no night to stand too nicely on scruple. Thirty-two men. Too few, far too few. Their numbers were too few, their resources strained and scattered, after long weeks of policing and patrolling and *pleading,* almost, for order. He kept thinking, *How has it come to this? What god did we offend?* He started thinking, *How did the Countess fail us so badly?*

He had forty men with him by the time they passed under the arch on Ruby Street—the gates of which it appeared some entrepreneur had unhinged and carried away for their iron—and forty-two when he stepped onto Laud Heath.

Up the hill, over the lawns, behind the tree line, the Countess's estates were burning.

Arlandes broke into a run, and his redcoats followed.

Long, thin shadows came flying over the lawns down the Heath toward them, and then past them; men and women fleeing, tumbling down the hill, back-lit by the bonfire of the palace: *servants,* disloyal, rats fleeing from the burning building. The servants' arms were full of stolen silverware and furnishings. A girl in a maid's dress came careening down the hill, candlesticks stacked in her arms like firewood; she blundered into the redcoats and spilled her burden. A man in a butler's black suit fell on his face, almost cartwheeling downslope, and put his foot right through the painting he'd stolen, which was of the Countess's grey-bearded grandfather, and snapped its golden frame beneath his weight; Arlandes cuffed him aside and kept running.

Perhaps there was no true enemy; perhaps it was only the plague. Perhaps the plague had driven the city mad, and the city was turning on itself. *Fire and flood.*

They ran through the Widow's Bower, trampling the neatly graveled paths. The lanterns had fallen from the trees and they stamped them under their boots.

At the crest of the hill, the hill just southeast of the palace, they stumbled into a group of men who were running through the trees on a course aslant of them. Both sides were briefly startled, but only briefly. They drew swords and pistols and lit into each other. The interlopers, whoever they were, dressed in neat black suits; they fought efficiently, quietly, brutally. They carried nasty barbed brass rapiers; they lunged again and again at Arlandes' head like ravenous mosquitoes. They were outnumbered—they left behind no more than a dozen bodies—and they went down quickly. There was no time to search the bodies to see whom they'd served.

Arlandes cut through the trees, and burst through the bushes, and left the Bower, and looked down on the Countess's estate.

Neither Arjun nor Olympia could sleep. They walked through the streets, around and around in aimless circles. They went arm-in-arm; it was cold, and they were frightened.

They turned down a street with no name that they could see any sign of, because there were lampposts among the trees and lights on in the brownstones, and there was the sound of conversation and laughter from one of the windows.

"I can't stay," Arjun said. "I've decided. If they bring Holbach back to you, and you and he go on to bring back the Atlas, I can't stay with you. Or if they *don't* bring Holbach back, and you go on anyway."

"Nicolas is dead. Liancourt is dead. If they don't bring Holbach back, the Atlas is over."

"You'll find a way. You won't be alone. Holbach's friends and your friends are still around. They weren't all arrested, were they? Hidden, maybe, for now, but still around. Aren't they? You'll begin it all again. Things go away and come back again; that's how this city works. You won't be able to walk away from it, Olympia."

"But you can?"

"It isn't why I came here." He shrugged his thin shoulders. "I do not want to be misunderstood; your work is a better and braver thing than anything I may ever do. Even though sometimes terrible things must be done, must happen." He gestured vaguely in the direction of the Rose, and then south toward Shutlow. "All this will pass. But I cannot stay. I have no business in this world. Perhaps I am not brave enough."

They turned off onto a narrower street, less well-lit, without trees. He held her closer; they leaned against each other.

She shook her head. "What will you do? How will you go on searching? What if that *monster* finds you? What if Holbach can't stop it? What if it just keeps feeding until it's swallowed the whole city? Will you give up then?"

"I have some ideas. I have been thinking. I have been thinking that I have been going about things all wrong. I have fought against the city when I should have bent with it, and bent with it when I should have fought. I have certain ideas as to how I should proceed. I think no one further needs to be hurt. Or hardly anyone. After tonight, I think, if we all make it through tonight, there need be no further cruelty, or violence. Or hardly any. Perfection eludes our grasp, of course, but we can do better. I'll begin again. If I tell you what I plan you will think I am mad."

On the corner of the street, there was a theater, closed and shuttered for the night. Out the front of the unlit ticket-office was a wooden statue of a little boy, stiffly and blindly holding out a wooden tray. Olympia ran her hand over its painted head as they turned left onto a street of seedy haberdashers and gin-houses and warehouses.

She told him, "I already think you're mad. Remember? But it's a gentle enough madness. Maybe there'll be a place for that kind of madness when we remake the city. Why does the world have to make sense when we remake it? We'll make it beautiful, and large enough for everyone. You're right, you know; we'll begin again, and better. No Countess or Chairman or any other bastard'll crush us. If not the Atlas anymore, something else, something better. This is Ararat, after all; what's the Countess or the Chairman in the great scheme of things? What's some stinking forgotten river-god? There's a thousand rivers out there somewhere and a thousand gods of it. What's the Atlas, for that matter? There's a thousand movements and revolutions, all the time. There are things dying and being born again everywhere, in a thousand different ways. What matters is the *future*. We'll go *north,* maybe. There's people in the High Parliament of Dewey Hill who're friendly to new ideas."

She stopped and peered ahead. As the street curved crookedly round south by southwest, and downslope, a circle of flickering gaslight came into view, and dark figures moving in it.

"Maybe we'll go east. I've been in correspondence with a man in Millom-Bry. A banker, an inventor, he wrote for the Atlas on *Quicksilver* and *Nitre* and I don't know what else. He's rich; he'll take us in, maybe."

As they got closer, they saw that the gaslights stood in a circle around a row of tables, on which were heaped food and blankets. On one side of the tables a small group of women in robes bustled and fussed; on the other a queue, a procession, a slow dismal tide of men, shuffling, in rags. Some women, also, and children.

"Maybe we'll stay right here. We'll hide in burned-out buildings like those awful children; we'll live like wild animals, and *fuck* anyone who tries to stop us."

As they entered the circle of lamplight, everything became clear; sheer black silhouettes took on faces, lined and tired. The building on the street corner proclaimed itself a Nessene Mission. The ragged people, bent double, coughing and sighing, bore the signs of lung-rot, in their black eyes, their glistening fish-belly skin. Their *stink*.

Behind the tables worked the Nessenes, the healers, in their blue robes, the little golden trident-pins glittering in the gaslight. They wore breathing-masks of blue cloth and charms to keep out the sickness. The little women looked like delicate industrious beetles. They barely looked up as Olympia and Arjun approached. There were only four of them, and there were so very many of the plague-sick.

"Enough talk," Olympia said. "We've talked enough and I'm sick of it. If we can't sleep, let's make ourselves useful. Sisters," she called out, "can we help you?"

From the hilltop, Arlandes looked down northwest onto the palace. He looked down north onto the *Thunderer,* and its great complex wooden dry dock. The palace was in flames; the *Thunderer* was not. Men scurried back and forth in the firelight, antlike, vicious, purposive. They climbed the dry dock and swarmed the *Thunderer's* rigging.

Leoden stood at his side, sword in his hand. "Captain?" Arlandes shushed him.

The fire in the palace was in the west wing, and in the conservatory, and parts of the arboretum. There was fighting at the east wing. Muzzle-flashes at the windows, barricades on the lawns. He watched the invaders launch a charge, a brief sally, coming round by the carp-pond and up the ornamental steps. The charge failed. The south wing, however, had clearly fallen to the invaders, and its occupants had been lined up on the lawns, and were being—searched? Suborned? Charged and tried and executed, perhaps? But by whom?

It occurred to Arlandes that he'd recognized the barbed brass rapiers of the men he'd killed in the Widow's Bower. He'd fought a duel once against one of Chairman Cimenti's half brothers, or nephews, or managers, or something; that was the weapon the man had chosen. Were those Cimenti's men down there? But there were so many of them: could Cimenti field so many men?

Leoden stepped closer. "Captain? The *Countess*, Captain, the Countess needs us." Arlandes held up his hand for silence.

There were men crawling over the deck of the *Thunderer;* at least thirty men. More on the dry dock. More belowdecks, no doubt. They didn't know how to launch it, clearly. They were not perfect, whoever they were. They did not know everything. They were blundering in the same darkness as Arlandes.

Who were they? It could have been Cimenti. But it could have been any of a dozen others. Red Barrow could deploy that many men; Red Barrow's Thane liked *fire*. He had no territorial ambitions this far south, surely, but would regard death and chaos as its own reward.

It could have been Mass How; there'd been subversive elements in Mass How's Parliament that had had truck with the Atlas.

It could have been the city itself; it could have been the city turning against the Countess and her people.

Arlandes' eyes darted back and forth across the battlefield. There, down by the doors to the south wing: a woman being dragged down the stairs, and onto the croquet lawn. Her clothes appeared gold and her face white, but perhaps it was only the firelight. She was so tiny and distant. Leoden stepped forward and Arlandes held his shoulder, pulled him back. There were black-suited men holding her arms and one of her legs. It might have been the Countess or it might have been a serving-girl; it might have been anyone. A crowd of men in black surged around her, grabbing her, dragging her down, obscuring her from view.

Arlandes sagged. He held tightly to Leoden's shoulder to support himself; his legs felt suddenly weak. *If she is gone, I am next*. He whispered it out loud—"If she is gone, I am next"—and Leoden looked at him in shock.

And if he saved her—if he charged down there and hacked about him left and right and dragged her from the melee, if somehow they escaped—then what? Then she would begin again, of course. Her face white and stiff and implacable, she would begin again. And there would be revenge, and more sacrifices, and more death, and he could not stand it; he could not stand the thought of it. What was the point? There was nothing worthwhile left to save. Her terrible white face, red-lipped, ordering him *Begin again. Build again*. Cold as a statue, heartless as a god. And beneath that white face could be anyone; it hardly mattered. It was the cruel mask that mattered, and the orders it would give. He felt his courage and the last of his dignity tremble and break at the thought of it.

He pulled himself up straight again and drew his sword, and pointed with it north, past the palace, at the *Thunderer,* and the dry dock, and the men swarming over it.

"The *Thunderer,* gentlemen. We must take the ship. The *Thunderer* is everything. Our last and best weapon. If we assault the palace, we give up the *Thunderer;* we give up our only escape. She would *want* us to save the *Thunderer* first. Those were her orders, gentlemen." He hated the sound of his own voice, pleading and whining like a shop-keeper, a condemned man, a coward, a deserter. The men shuffled uneasily.

"If we take the *Thunderer,* we can avenge her," he lied. "Do you understand?"

His redcoats put up no real resistance. It was shameful.

Jack had Holbach's floor and cell number, from the warden's files, and it should have been easy to find him, but it wasn't; it wasn't at all; in fact they all felt as though they'd been in the Rose for ten nights, or a hundred, or a thousand. They went down and down and the Rose unfolded beneath them. Petals of rust and iron; barred walls and bloody spikes and the dragging of chains over stone.

There were very few guards to challenge them—they'd all gone up, it seemed, into the upper floors, drawn up by Jack's diversion. The Thunderers wiped off their knives on the bedding of an empty cell and stuck them back in their belts. There was no one left to fight. But the Rose itself turned deadly beneath them. Grinding its gears like jaws, it slid open pitfalls and spike-traps. It spun and tilted its corridors like a slow-motion knife-juggler. Chains would pull and drag across the floor and—suddenly—the ceiling might fall, or a wall might draw itself across Jack's path, or blades might whisk across the floor. They danced and leaped and fleeted over the

blades and the spikes and chains; without the Bird's gift, they'd
each have been skewered a dozen times. Sometimes the floor would
shake and groan and *shift* beneath their feet, and they'd soon find
themselves back again descending a staircase they'd already descended once, twice, three times. Once, an iron curtain descended
across the corridor they were running down and cut Beth off from
the pack, and it seemed that it was hours later that they found her
again and she threw herself into Jack's arms sobbing with relief.
When the same thing happened to Coit, they searched and searched
but they never found him.

Some of it was just clever engineering—walls shifting and sliding on hidden and oiled gears like scene-changes at the theater.
Inside one suddenly opening pit there was an immense slowly spinning device of chains and pinions and crankshafts and steam-
pistons; Jack jammed it with a guard's pike and it screamed to a
juddering halt. There were trip wires and pressure plates and similar bits of machinery. But some of it, most of it, maybe, was nothing
to do with human ingenuity; it was the god, the Chain, rushing
through its lair, reshaping it. Bars grew out of nothing, across the
hallways, right in front of them, in brazen defiance of sense; bars
that, when Jack touched them, were fixed stiffly in place by centuries of rust and dust and cobwebs and dried blood.

The corridor that led between cells 110 and 130 of Mensonge's
fief turned, and turned, and circled back on itself without exits, or
windows, or escape. They walked round it a dozen times, hearts
sinking. They ran helter-skelter round and round it and there was
still no escape from it, and the wind of their passing as they went
faster and faster and faster blew out the torches and they were
in darkness and at the mercy of the god's will. Caul and Wood
screamed and sobbed as they ran. Caul went silent quite suddenly as
he hurtled into something sharp in the dark. The rest of them kept
running anyway, as if they could outrun the god's mindless grip.
Which was madness; the realization settled coldly on Jack that it
was madness. All he had was the tiniest stolen scrap of the Bird-
God's power, the tiniest rag torn from its hem as it passed, a single
bright coin stolen from its purse. In the face of the city's true ancient Powers, he was *nothing;* he shouldn't have come into the

Chain's place of power. He kept running anyway. And quite suddenly there was a doorway, and the beautiful, brilliant glare of
torchlight, and they stumbled out into the new passage that opened
before them. They weren't sure whether they'd been released or
driven further into confinement; which of the Rose's two gods had
blown past them—the Chain or the Key? There was no way of
knowing, and it hardly mattered.

A little later, Wood sat down and refused to move, or be moved.
Beth cried and slapped his face, but he would not explain himself,
and in the end he had to be left behind.

They went deeper and saw stranger things with every turn. The
prisoners in the cells on every wall babbled and begged in strange
new languages, tongues Jack had never heard. Most of them were in
rags; some of them were in stranger clothes, things cut in a style
Jack had never seen. There were shiny fabrics he'd never seen before,
more like metal than cloth. The people themselves were often
strange. He'd seen dark-skinned folk before, of course. Namdi and
poor Coit, for two; that funny little man Arjun, for three. Ararat
was a big city and it was full of all sorts of people. But there were
stranger shades; copper and nightshade and sky. There was a row of
cells in which the prisoners had eyes like cats, yellow and hungry;
he'd never seen that before. There were prisoners who went on all
fours, and not, apparently, from madness, but from habit; their arms
were long like spiders' legs and their legs by comparison quite
stubby. There were tunnels and tunnels and deeper tunnels, windowless, musty-smelling, where red roots as thick around as Jack's
waist twisted through the walls, and coiled and knotted underfoot
like guts, as if Jack was crawling into the innards of some gigantic
impossible tree. It was at that point that Jack had to concede that
they'd gotten lost. That they'd taken a wrong turn, and more than
one wrong turn. Beth was for turning back, but "We have to keep
going," he told her; and he ran on and carried them all with him,
through corridors of black marble. There were corridors that
creaked and swayed like an old ship, and smelled of saltwater and
rot. Always there was the sound of heavy chains, dragging, sometimes right over their heads, crashingly loud, sometimes distant,
stealthy, and ominous; always there was the sound of doors swing-

ing open and slamming closed. Torchlight gave way to gaslight gave way to white-walled corridors where tubes of cold dead light buzzed and hummed. A woman in white, in a peaked white hat, stepped out of a white cell as they ran past, and she gasped in shock and dropped her white tray of pill-bottles and needles, and she called after them: "Children, children, you shouldn't be here; there are sick people here, you mustn't frighten them..." They passed her, left her behind, rushing on through chambers of glass, through shuffling chambers of thin white card-paper. Jack thought of the weight above them, the Rose's terrible dark density; he thought of the world and the order of things buckling under the pressure. He thought of coal crushed into diamonds, of old dense stars collapsing into swirling hungry blackness. The thought of those black stars flitted across his mind as he ran, and he didn't know why, or what it meant; it was no thought that belonged in *his* city. The Rose was misnamed; it was a star, not a flower. No; it was a wound, not a star—it was a great infected wound cut into the city's flank. Purple and red and wormy; as they went down, they sliced further and further into torn city-flesh, broken and mis-set city-bones, all shards and odd angles, the city-tissues swollen and distended. They dug up buried strangenesses like writhing maggots.

Two more levels down from the nurse in white, there was a man in a steel-lined cell whose face and bare arms were stitched and woven with silver wires. He sat cross-legged next to the bars, and reached through pleadingly, curiously. His golden eyes glittered and irises clicked open and closed. The flesh around the wires looked infected. The wires themselves carried a faint glow. He spoke in a language none of them understood, and in fact they were not sure the noises he made were language at all; they seemed almost involuntary. The glow of the wires blinked on and off in stained-glass shades, the sparks of color pulsing up and down the man's arms and face. He looked at them expectantly, patiently, as if the lights were a message, a code, as if he hoped they would understand him. Jack shrugged; the man's golden eyes blinked shut, blankly. They could not find a way to open his cell. When he fell silent, despairing, the wires still hummed and hissed.

There was *nothing* like him in Ararat—Jack would have sworn to it. But there the man was. Jack resented him; he couldn't help it. They left him behind (humming and clicking and hissing and blinking) and went down, and down, but Jack could not put the poor bastard out of his mind. Could the same city that held Jack, and Barbotin, and the Palace Cabaret and Shutlow and the hideout in the Black Moon pub and all that, also hold that creature? It seemed impossible. If they ever escaped the Rose, would it be to the same city they'd woken up in that morning?

Jack's breath came ragged and raggeder. He stumbled over cables and chains. The scale of the Rose and everything contained within it overwhelmed him. He thought about the dwindling numbers of the Thunderers; he thought how tired and ragged and pathetic they were, and how vast the city was. He thought of himself beating his tiny wings against a vast thunderstorm, pointlessly, forever; his futile motions changing nothing, *nothing*. He staggered and slowed. He was on the point of sitting down, like Wood, and just *stopping*, when Beth cried out and grabbed his arm.

She pointed down the corridor. An archway at the end of it was hung with a beautiful familiarity, the comfort of something he'd always, always hated: the Countess's arrogant red flags. He grinned, hugged Beth tightly, inhaling the wonderful bitterness of her sweat. "We're not done yet, then."

THIRTY-NINE

In the early evening of the next day, they were woken by a knock on the door of their hotel room. Olympia jumped from the bed, pulled the dirty sheet around herself, and ran stiffly to the door. Arjun woke slowly and watched from the bed as she opened it to reveal the hotel's fat manager, fist raised in mid-knock.

"Boy here says he has a message for you. Little bastard woke me up. Don't do it again."

It was the smallest of Jack's Thunderers. Arjun thought his name was Een. He said, "Someone wants to see you. Follow me." They followed. He stayed well ahead of them, waiting for them at the end of each street they turned onto. He led them onto a street of imposing office buildings, and in through a door under a partially dismantled sign that marked the building as an abandoned outpost of the Gerent's commercial empire.

The foyer inside had probably once been grand, but the steel and marble had been stripped by thieves. Now it was dusty and grey. The Thunderers stood around in the room's shadows. A heavy-set figure slumped on one of the room's stone benches, his head lowered. He was writing something in a notebook in his lap.

"Professor," Olympia called, and ran toward him.

Jack stepped in front of her. He looked pained, sympathetic—older, somehow. His awkward face announced that he was trying to be kind. "We got him out. We found him. It wasn't easy but we found him. But they'd beaten him badly. We didn't want to bring him to your hotel. He, well, he'd attract attention. He must have made the Countess very angry. I'm sorry. You'll need this for him." Jack handed her an empty notebook. "The bitch let him write, so he could work his science for her, but she took his tongue. I'm sorry."

Olympia went and sat next to Holbach. When he got closer, Arjun could see that Holbach's whole face was purpled, bruised and swollen. The wound was quite new. Olympia put her arm round his shoulder, and held his hand. No one spoke.

They waited a little longer. Holbach was writing something in the notebook for Jack. When he was finished, Jack took the notebook, and said to Arjun, "I got what I wanted. And it was good, to take someone out of that place. We'll come back, one day, and smash it all down. I'm sorry they did what they did to him. I'll wish you good luck, I suppose."

"Thank you, Jack. Was it very terrible? Did your own people come out unscathed?"

Jack didn't answer.

"What about the Rose's guards?"

"What do you think?"

"I see. I'm sorry, Jack."

Jack shrugged. Arjun shook his hand, then Jack led his boys away, into the street.

Holbach's legs were weak. Not broken, but badly bruised by his shackles. Together, they helped him outside.

Olympia had a place near the warrens, on the edge of the 'Machy's huge walls, not far north of the Rose. It was a square stone building, in a neighborhood of empty shops. It had once been a pumphouse. "Hoxton picked it out," she said. "He used to have connections in the 'Machy. Not quite legal ones. I kept it in case of something like this. In case I ever needed to hide."

She didn't dare to visit any of the banks where she had accounts, but she had hidden a few caches of money about the city. "I always

knew we might need to begin again one day," she said. They re-
claimed the money under cover of darkness.

Before she had gone into hiding, before she had had Hoxton rescue Arjun from the riot on the Heath, she had been able to help a
few of the Atlas-makers into hiding. Now she went out across the
city and brought them back. Several of the explorers had survived;
so had Branken the optical scientist, Marchant the jurist, Mellarmé
the surgeon, a few others. They found rooms nearby.

Holbach was sick. At first Arjun feared it was the god's touch,
but it was just the result of Holbach's wounds and exhaustion.
Arjun cared for him as best he could, with what he remembered of
the Choir's medicine, until Olympia brought Dr. Mellarmé out of
his hiding place to take over.

Some of the Atlas-makers had refused to come with Olympia.
Others had been missing when she had looked for them; murdered,
or gone deeper into hiding. Those who remained needed very badly
for someone to lead them. They hovered nervously around Holbach.

Arjun spoke to Holbach twice. He asked, "Professor, did you
learn anything of the Typhon? Any way to fight it?"

Holbach held his pencil weakly and scratched, *No. Need my books
to learn anything. Can do nothing here.*

"Did you learn anything of the Voice? Anything that might
help me find it?"

No. I am sorry.

Arjun held the sick man's arm and squeezed it, saying, "That's
all right, Professor. That's all right."

They were far north of the Countess's territories, safely out of the
storm of unrest. The news of what had happened reached them
slowly. They avidly collected rumors and newspapers, keen to see
their worst fears confirmed.

There'd been a quiet week. The *Thunderer* had sat idle in dry
dock. The greycoats had retreated into the shadows. The streets had
been empty. The newspapers had begun to ask whether the violence
had burned itself out.

But then there'd been some further protest, reports of explosions in Seven Wheels Market, a rash of plague deaths, some intolerable outrage by the white robes. Whatever the cause was, something sparked it all off again.

It was worse the second time. Even allowing for the newspapers' exaggeration and hysteria, it was clearly worse. Everyone, on all sides, had guns and explosives and the will to use them. It was not tolerable; it could not last.

Piecing together a half-dozen papers, it was possible to pinpoint the night when it all burst and broke. In one night, it seemed, the rioters had struck each of the Countess's barracks, shipyards, watchtowers, gun-towers, and countinghouses. Her forces maintained three magazines around Shutlow and Barbary, squat buildings behind whose barred iron doors were shelves and shelves of powder, rifle and artillery; in one terrible hour they were all exploded, spraying fountains of fire and brick-dust across the streets, blasting out every window for blocks. Casualty reports were unclear: some people said that the magazines' neighbors had been warned and had slipped safely away with their children and valuables just before the fatal hour. Olympia shook her head and said, "People always say things like that." Certain scholars had tried to calculate the theological significance of the triangle of fire marked out by the explosions, but their results were inconclusive.

And a hundred shocked reports said that the Countess's palace had been sacked, burned, blown up. The blaze was said to be visible all across the Heath for the better part of a day.

Hundreds of people claimed to have been eyewitnesses to the worst fighting. A mob of escaped criminals—*Did we not warn that the anarch Silk would bring unrest and destruction on the city? While our rivals indulged in childish hero-worship of the anarch, did we not warn?* asked the *Sentinel*—had attacked the palace, and the *Thunderer*'s dry dock, without warning, while the bulk of its guards were engaged elsewhere.

In the end, the Countess's forces were spread too thin to protect any of her strongholds.

It was bloody, and confusing. The only thing everyone agreed on was that the *Thunderer* had survived, and so had Captain Arlandes.

They said Arlandes managed to get the ship into the air, though its crew was halved and its cannons unarmed, and had escaped over the Heath, and into the tall buildings to the west.

Over the coming weeks, the *Thunderer* was seen (so they said) all over the city, drifting in and out of the towers. It had gone wild, in the forest of the city's skyline. Its crew descended on ropes in the night (they said) to steal food and supplies from the city's tall buildings.

The Chairman issued a statement to the effect that the fighting in the Countess's territories could no longer be tolerated; that it was a threat to the whole city's good order. With his peers' consent, he sent in his peacekeeping forces.

The rebels were wiped out almost at once, *like an army whose supply-line has been cut,* the *Era* said, skirting perhaps dangerously close to the truth. Knowing what they knew, Arjun and Olympia could not doubt that the Chairman had armed the rioters, stoked their grievances, used them, then cut them off when they were no longer useful. They wondered how many others knew.

It wasn't clear what had happened to the Countess. The Chariman held her territories now (for the city's benefit, of course). The woman herself had fallen into the same abyss of memory as the Gerent. Olympia searched desperately for some news of the Countess's fate, for some vicarious taste of revenge, but she found nothing. Her eyes teared up with frustration.

The Chairman issued a statement promising to restore peace to the affected areas, and to avoid the hubris that had led the Countess to the creation of the *Thunderer* and the repression of the Atlas (though he conspicuously did not lift the ban).

"*That's* the true face of evil in this city," Olympia said. "The true modern monster works entirely through the disingenuous statement to the press. Now he'll turn to the loose ends. To us."

But then that was the last anyone heard of the Chairman. Rumor had it—the papers would not dare print any such thing— that he had been murdered. Some people said that Jack Silk had stolen into his high bedroom window at night and slit his throat, to punish him for trying to end the violence and anarchy in which Silk throve. Others said that Arlandes had had one last shot left in the

Thunderer's cannons, and had fired on the Chairman's tower. Most people preferred not to discuss the subject at all.

When Holbach was strong enough, they brought the newspapers to him. He and Olympia spent long hours passing paper back and forth, trying to determine what had happened to them, trying to plan their next move; Arjun absented himself discreetly from those conversations.

In fact those conversations—which Arjun imagined, as he walked through the streets outside in silence, as intense and brilliant, a flurry of plans and stratagems and wild notions—went nowhere, over and over again.

Olympia said, "She's dead, the one who did this to you. You outlasted her. Are you going to let her silence you now?"

And Holbach's pencil hovered over the paper, and sometimes he'd write out a few words, and then scratch them savagely out—during which operation he made little cattlelike moaning noises, apparently without knowing it. Sometimes he was unable to write at all. Olympia would hold his hand to stop it shaking.

Sometimes he forgot—hard as it was to believe, sometimes he *forgot.* Sometimes he opened his mouth to expose the ruined architecture within—they'd shattered his teeth during the operation—and released a thick moronic wordless bellow. He'd clamp his mouth shut, too late; the shame on his face would be unbearable and Olympia would have to avert her eyes.

At other times his eyes were simply blank and hopeless, and terribly, terribly lonely.

Sometimes Holbach would grab her arm weakly, pull her to the desk, and write, *Then tell me what to do.* He'd press it into her hand. She never knew how to answer.

Arjun and Olympia slept together one last time, both knowing it was the last time, that there was no reason for them to stay together any longer. They were not out of danger, but for one night they both needed to pretend that they were. But when they woke, suddenly, in the dark, both lying silently, stiff and aching, in a bed that now smelled of stale nightmare sweat, neither of them could speak, or move, or breathe, as if they were still drowning in the nightmare that they could not, quite, remember. Something was different in the darkness of the room. Something was different in the darkness of the city. A light they had taken for granted was gone.

FORTY

The Cypress, of course, had gone out of business, and what with all the unpleasantness and unruliness and general wickedness of recent weeks, Defour was not especially sorry. It had always been a burden; it had become *unbearable*.

Heady had been her last lodger. And what a troubling lodger he'd become, who'd once been so nice, with his sinister new friends who came and went at all hours! Until one night he'd come home in a panic, packed his bags, taken a last bath—he always was a fastidious man, at least you could say that for him—and he had somehow contrived to *drown* himself in it, leaving Defour—all on her own!—to move that cold fish-pale body out into an alley to become a Matter for the Authorities. And then there was no one but Defour herself in that big drafty old place. Oh, *because*...

(Madame Defour presently sat on a stone bench at the edge of Tiber's Plaza, shielding her eyes from the red constant glare of the Pillar of Fire at the heart of that wide empty circle. It was nearly midnight, but it was never dark in Tiber's incandescent presence. Defour's bags were packed at her feet and she was very far from home indeed. Her neighbor on the bench was a fat young girl with stringy hair and an expression of sullen troubled self-pity, and Defour was explaining to her that she was far too young to know what trouble really was.)

...*because* the rumor had started that the Cypress was cursed. Gods knew Defour had often privately thought of the boarding-house as a curse, ever since the Spider condemned her to the care of it. But in recent weeks it seemed that the plague had claimed so many of the lodgers—indeed almost all of them—and people were starting to notice. No one wanted to live there. No one wanted to live in Shutlow at all, if they had any choice.

And there *was* something strange in the Cypress. Defour hesitated to use the word *haunted,* but nothing better sprang to mind. For instance, the cellar had flooded, which it had never done before in thirty years, and *remained* flooded no matter how many buckets of stinking black muddy water were removed, until eventually Defour had ceded the cellar to the floodwaters and padlocked the trapdoor, and then there was always a faint creaking and groaning from beneath. Even in the sickly heat of that violent summer, the Cypress was cold and drafty. There were *smells.* All those people died, of course. Sometimes it seemed that there were more rooms than there should be, and all of those rooms were empty and bare and the curtains and carpet were mold-riddled and rotten, and then there were long, darkened hallways that went nowhere and the rooms were unnumbered, and . . .

"That's just how it was when my mum and dad died," the fat young girl said, "and—"

"*Excuse* me!"

. . . and anyway the strange thing was these unusual *phe-nom-en-a* kept getting worse, slowly at first, then faster and faster, as if whatever it was was getting stronger, more confident, was learning new tricks. And once it found something unpleasant to do, for instance causing all of the windows to break to let in freezing winds, or sprouting black weeds out between the floorboards, it would never let up, it would persist with dull unimaginative malevolence, so that after a few weeks, the Cypress was a thoroughly unearthly place, and most of Defour's lodgers would have moved out if they weren't all ailing so badly. Norris had died, and after that it was weeks before Clement passed on; by the end the lodgers were dropping dead as if it had suddenly become fashionable. Misery and anger and bitterness hung in the air like a cold black fog, and matches would not light.

Defour herself would have left weeks ago if not for her holy oath to the Spider-God, which had put her in charge of the Cypress all those years ago. She stayed and made offerings of flies to her god. She knitted a web in her bedroom so that it might feel at home there, and come to protect her. It did not. The Spider's aloof enigmatic indifference, which had always been so fascinating and awe-inspiring, now seemed like a very flimsy and trivial thing by comparison to the haunting presence that she felt *watching* her and *hating* her. And then one day, shortly after the Heady business, she was doing her face in the morning and her dressing-table mirror cracked and in the lonely fragments of her reflection she saw drowned faces pleading and screaming and rotting, and she said, "So much for the bloody Spider, then," and fled, leaving the Cypress unlocked for any child fool enough to squat there.

Defour had no family to stay with. Instead she went north to the distant Plaza where Tiber burned. She spent the last of the fortune she'd saved from her days on the stage on carriages and rickshaws, and practically *flew* along. She traveled by day and by night for nearly a week. She told a succession of drivers to follow the red light of the Fire over the skyline, and be quick about it; her reasoning being that the haunting was a water-thing, was a cold and dark and rot-thing, so perhaps it feared the Fire, perhaps there she would be safe. Now she sat on a bench at the edge of the Fire's Plaza, watching the long shadows of men and women drift back and forth in the god's stark glare. She'd tried to find a room nearby but they all seemed to be taken.

"Well, yeah," the fat young girl said. "That's why we're *all* here." And she waved a grubby hand at the Plaza, and at all the men and women on the stone benches, or huddled together sleeping on the paving stones, or, far off at the heart of the Plaza, kneeling in penitence so close to the Fire that they might very well go blind.

Shut up about the Spider now," the fat young girl hissed. "And get yer head down." She lowered her own greasy head and folded her hands in an attitude of worship. Defour, quite shaken, did likewise.

Six young shaven-headed boys and girls in white robes strutted past. Three of them carried lit torches, a gross superfluity in Tiber's blazing presence. They inspected Defour and the fat girl and appar-

ently found them acceptable, but they kicked awake a man sleeping
nearby with his head on his suitcase, and demanded to know why he
was showing no fucking reverence for the fucking god in its fucking
holy place, and they dragged him away to be beaten.

When the white robes were gone, the fat girl spat. "That's how
it is here, ma'am. Those little shits think they own the place. Don't
make them angry."

"Yes, young lady, *thank you,* I *have* seen these creatures before.
But this is disgraceful! Shouldn't there be priests here, militiamen,
watchmen, *something* to get rid of them?"

"The priests drive the white robes away when it's time for the
morning ritual or the midnight ritual. Otherwise they let them be.
There's too many of them, and it's *our* problem, not the Church's."

"Disgraceful!"

The fat young girl's name turned out to be Delia. She told
Defour all about her own sad story, her own grisly vision of the
Thing, and Defour, only half-listening, watched the white robes
hunt in packs through the crowd.

Defour found that she was muttering to herself: *Oh dear, oh dear.*
The Fire shed harsh light but no warmth, and it offered little com-
fort, and everything was terribly wrong in the city. *Oh dear, oh dear.*
She very much wanted to have someone to complain to.

Delia was now in animated conversation with another girl,
equally unwashed and desperate-looking, whose parents and brother
had apparently drawn their barge into a dark tunnel and *never
emerged.* The other girl was thinking about joining the white robes;
how else was she supposed to feed herself now? Delia, on the other
hand, was resigned to prostitution; she'd heard rumors that some of
Tiber's priests were generous.

It was all terribly wrong, Defour thought. The city was cracking
like her dressing-mirror. It should have been someone's job to prevent it, but apparently there was no one who could be bothered. All
the princes and priests and mayors and councilmen and soldiers
were as distant as the Spider, as cold and useless as the Fire.

Defour, reaching a difficult decision, leaned over and clipped

Delia round the ear. "Girls," Defour said, "stop that talk *at once.* Don't you look at me like that, young madam. I've never *heard* such talk. Don't you have any values? Your poor parents. Now, you both listen to me..."

But neither girl was listening. A sullen scowl had appeared on Delia's face and then vanished, replaced by an expression of confusion and creeping horror. The barge-girl shrieked and pointed across the Plaza. Defour turned her head and at first she couldn't see it. Then she saw how the shadows gathered at the edge of the Plaza; and yet it was *never* dark in Tiber's presence, had never been dark for a thousand years; for a thousand years the Fire had burned away the darkness and glared off the marble and glass of the buildings for a mile all around. But now darkness prowled at the Fire's edge, and deepened, and swelled, and pooled coldly on the stones.

It flowed from all directions, and welled up from the ground. It crept in hungry tendrils toward the Place from which the Fire silently roared. The tendrils burned away into a foul fog, but more came, and more. The night was dreadfully cold now.

Defour watched the crowds of stragglers empty out of the heart of the Plaza; first glancing away from the darkness and trying to pretend that it wasn't there; then, as it crept around them, walking stiffly and nervously away; and now they were running desperately past Defour, and Delia, and the barge-girl.

The Fire *guttered*.

It swayed and flickered as if in an unimaginable wind that might blow away a thousand years in an instant. Long shadows all across the Plaza twisted and lurched.

Bile rose into Defour's throat and her bladder let go.

The barge-girl was already off and running. Delia was staring pale-faced and idiotic at the darkness. "*Stupid* girl," Defour shrieked, and tweaked Delia by the ear to make her *run,* and then they were both fleeing as fast as they could over the slick wet stones, over which shadow and firelight thrashed back and forth in a conflict that Defour could not understand, that she did not want to understand, that it made her sick even to imagine. And it seemed to take a great and unmeasurable depth of time, but before Defour had taken more than a few unsteady steps, the shadow won and there was no more light; the light was *swallowed*.

Defour kept running and she did not look back, not until she reached the mouth of the alley that led between the temple and the courthouse, and she momentarily remembered her abandoned suitcases. She glanced back and the Plaza was just a great empty unlit space in which bitter night winds blew, and there was a darkness at its heart.

A few of the white robes had fled; one had nearly trampled Defour at the alley's mouth. But the greater part of them remained in the Plaza. Defour could see them by their torches, tiny spheres of weak light in that vast shadow. Slowly the white robes approached the darkness that had swallowed their god. There was something reverent about them, something awed. Did they drop to their knees? Defour couldn't be sure. One by one they extinguished their torches, and that was the last Defour could see of them.

"*Fuck*sake," Delia bellowed, standing at the alley's far end, where the streetlights still blazed, "come on, come on, you stupid old woman." And Defour, having nowhere else to go, followed.

FORTY-ONE

Then Arjun sat up, shoving away rank and sweat-drenched sheets, and got to his feet. Olympia was already at the window, leaning out, looking north.

The quality of the room's darkness was subtly changed. Olympia put a name to the nagging absence: "The Fire is gone."

They pulled on clothes and stepped out into the hall. In the next room, Branken and two of the explorers were waking from the same nightmare. Silently, all five went outside, into the night, to join a growing crowd in the street, all murmuring in shock and misery. If they had *all* dreamed it, it must be true. It could not be true. It would not be allowed.

They were south of the Urbomachy, and its towering walls blocked the view to the north. Together they climbed the spiraling stairs of wood and stone that led up the side of the nearest wall. The crowd grew as they passed the stone houses that crusted the sides of the wall, and sleepers came out to join them. There were many resting-places on the side of the wall, but they did not rest. They had to see. Eventually they reached the top of the wall and stood among the battlements. They were high above the city; they could see as far north as it was possible to see. The roofs below bristled with desperate watchers like themselves. For the first time in the city's memory, the horizon was dark, all the way to the Mountain.

✽ ✽ ✽

When it was the Countess," Olympia said, "we could stay and fight, or at least hope to fight one day. Even when it was the Chairman, though that smiling bastard scared me, I won't say he didn't. But this is too much. This is like the *city* turning against us. It doesn't want us. Do you understand? The gods are the city. The city is *us*. Even for people like us, blasphemers, libertines, whatever else they called us. *Do* you understand?"

Olympia could not have been more upset, more confused, if the sun had failed to rise one morning. She paced and fretted.

"Perhaps," Arjun said. "When the Voice departed, it almost destroyed us. I cannot imagine how it would have been if the Voice had stayed, but turned on us, began to hunt us."

"It's not just *hunting* us. It's raised an army against us. It's drowning and devouring the city's other gods, turning them against us, too. Maybe soon it'll be all that there is. I said we'd begin again, and I meant it, but . . . I said everything always begins again, and I meant that, too, but things are different now. Do you understand? This isn't how the city works—everything's ended and begun again for a thousand years, maybe forever, I don't know—but now I think that's all changed. I think it's over. I think everything's broken. I can't stay here; I can't stay if there's no *hope*. No *future*."

In the first days after that night of unanimous dreaming, the papers and the scholars had frantically debated what Tiber was trying to communicate by withdrawing its flame, while its priests sat ashen-faced and blank-eyed in the streets, mourning; Arjun's heart bled for them. The popular theory was that Tiber was expressing its disdain for the recent disorders.

The first rumors of the change in the white robes appeared a few days later. Their eyes were now black and their skin corpse-white. They no longer lit their brands. They were said to have terrible strength, and a stare that could steal breath from your throat, rot the skin from your face. No wound could kill them. They were everywhere, in packs. Hunting for something. Killing those who got in their way.

Preposterous, the *Era* assured everyone; people had always been tempted, it observed, to ascribe supernatural powers to those really rather ordinary and pathetic young hooligans, and the new stories were probably just a confused extension of the stories regarding Jack Silk and the Thunderers. *Et cetera, et cetera:* but the rumors didn't stop. Too many people remembered the nightmare, and couldn't pretend they didn't.

Five days after that night, Arjun saw a trio of the white robes sniffing down the street, slouching, necks craning loosely, their eyes black, blank. They smelled dead. The poisoned god was in them. They had welcomed it in. There were ugly fanged eyeless eels in the canals, Arjun knew; he'd seen them anatomized in the pages of the Atlas; he'd shuddered at the diagrams. That was the sinuous, suggestive, hungry quality of their motion. He shuddered again, and hid in a doorway.

"We can't fight this," Olympia said. "They'll tear us to pieces. And who knows what it might do next? I'm not saying I'm ready to give up on this city. I don't want to abandon it to that monster. But my first duty is to the Atlas. Holbach can't lead us anymore. The others are dreamers, not leaders. I have to take care of Holbach, and what's left of us. We have to leave Ararat. We have to find a safe place. Maybe we'll be able to return. Or maybe we can build again, somewhere else."

"I understand."

"I'll ask one last time. Come with us. You'll die here."

"You know I can't."

"And if it just isn't here? If you're wrong?"

"Then I'm wrong. But this is my last and best chance. If it isn't here, it isn't anywhere. I can't go. I don't have the courage."

She hugged him for a moment. Holbach shook his hand, and Branken clapped him bluffly on the arm. Then they lifted their packs over their shoulders (the explorers showing the more sedentary scholars how it was done), and they left the pumphouse. They would find a ship at the docks—any ship.

He walked with them a little way, though he would not go with them all the way to the docks: "You'll be safer without me," he had said. "I shouldn't go near the water with you."

"I'm scared," Olympia said as they walked. She said it quietly. "I've never left the city. Everything I know is here."

"It won't be so bad. There isn't . . . so *much* as this, anywhere else. But there are places that need scholars and thinkers, and builders. Think: you could map the whole world."

"There's barely a dozen of us left."

"You could start. Or you could continue your old work; you could write it, and smuggle it back into the city."

"No one here cares about anything that comes from outside the city walls. *You* should know that by now." She smiled.

It was an hour's walk to the nearest carriage rank. They would have preferred to walk—it would have been less conspicuous—but Holbach was still too weak for the long trek south. They waited awhile until there were enough carriages for all of them. Arjun shook everyone's hand one last time, before they got into their seats. Olympia did not ask him again.

He watched the carriages go; watched them recede and merge into the general din and haze of the city's traffic, until, as they reached a busy crossroads, he could no longer tell which of the distant carriages going to and fro carried *her,* or poor Holbach, or the Atlas-makers, and which were insignificant, which were only noise.

"I have certain ideas," he said, to no one in particular. "And if I am very lucky, perhaps the city may be saved. But I will have to be very lucky."

FORTY-TWO

The **Urbomachy** was another of the city's monstrous northern landmarks. Hundreds of years ago, the territories of four lords had cornered there. They had fought, with guns of a forgotten design, that launched fire in high curving arcs over the no-man's land of the 'Machy, and with bomb-dropping balloons. Each of them had put up high walls against the guns, and manned them with riflemen against the balloons. The walls had grown monstrous as they fought to overtop each other. They were made of a remarkably durable yellow-white stone, the source of which was also forgotten.

As the tides of war broke back and forth over the streets, the victors built new walls to encompass newly won territories, and the losers were forced to build new walls as they fell back. Some wall-sections crumbled under the guns. New sections were built to corner and buttress the old, fracturing the streets into uncomfortable angles. The warring dynasties were exhausted or intermarried. Then they, too, were forgotten. The walls remained. The warrens grew like weeds at the foot of the walls. Stone steps and wooden ladders led up the walls, past broad out-thrusting platforms. People lived on the platforms. The oldest ones, built to house the wall-builders' armies, were the more expensive districts in the 'Machy; unlike the later additions, they never collapsed, and they often had running water, pumped up by ancient machines. The newer shelves were stacked with the poor and the desperate; they hung over the warrens like vultures in a becalmed ship's rigging.

You could cross from wall to wall, platform to platform, on rope-bridges, or, if you were brave enough, by climbing hand-to-hand along the ropes. The boys who did this would sometimes drop things on passersby below, for a laugh.

It was another of many cities within the city. A good place to hide: many of Ararat's criminal enterprises were headquartered there. The warrens were a thick, dark soil. It was a good place to begin things.

Arjun rented a room on Shelf Seven, Wall Nine. It was one of the wall-builders' shelves. There were only two more above him, and so his room got a little light. Olympia had left him money. He could afford it. He felt safer on the high walls. The white robes sometimes came through the warrens below, terrorizing the inhabitants—who were not easily terrorized—but they never climbed the stairs. They were appendages of the Typhon now, and the Typhon preferred the depths.

He was quite high up, and it did not take long to climb the stairs from his room to Wall Nine's battlements. There, he could look out over the city. Some days he went walking, nervous of the monsters hunting him, trying to listen for the sound of the Voice, but often he just looked out over the city, until the roofs turned red with the setting sun, then blue, then finally black.

Once, from the battlements, he thought he saw the *Thunderer* disappear behind a distant tower, like a wild stag half-glimpsed behind trees. "Look, there," he said to his neighbor, a pleasant young woman with too many children and not enough teeth, who clapped with excitement to see that the thing was still there, still real. He knew she had been hoping to see it. It would be something to tell her children. He was glad she was happy. She had listened generously to the story of his own search, and promised to help him if she ever could.

Some days he felt that he was beginning again; that, after many mistakes and wrong turns, he had found himself back at the start of things, unencumbered, full of promise. Some days he felt that he was at the end of things; *past* the end, that all the orchestra's lively and noisy themes were finished, for better or worse, and he was a mere coda, a single note repeating quietly, in measured isolation, soon to be stilled.

When he spoke to his neighbors, he gave his name as Simon Nelson; a good ordinary local name. The Typhon, he thought, would not be hunting him by means of his name, the Countess was gone, and he was not sure that the Chairman was still alive to pursue him; still, best to be careful. His neighbors assumed his name was false anyway, and that he was hiding from *something;* it was that sort of place.

Some days he went walking, listening for the music. He sometimes saw the monsters the white robes had become loping through the streets. They were grey now. They were like dead dogs forgotten in the gutters, yanked up into unlife by their necks, set loose to drag others into the filth with them. They feared nothing. They had already welcomed the worst in, willingly. It made him sad, as well as fearful.

It took courage for anyone to make music. The white robes had always hated music, and now their childish, callow hatred was joined with the Typhon's bottomless enmity. Anyone who dared to sing or play out in the streets had to be ready to run.

Still, the city couldn't be silenced. Theaters locked up, and the music halls went dark, and all of Harp Street was abandoned, but the music remained. The churches would not give up their hymns. The streets were full of musicians who made their living entertaining the crowds; for them silence meant starvation, and they had no choice but to risk it.

Arjun listened to their music, and when the monsters came from the shadows and the muck, he ran. He didn't stand out; everyone ran. The white robes used their clubs viciously if they caught you. There were rumors that they swallowed souls, which Arjun didn't entirely believe. There were also rumors that they spread disease with their cold breath, which he did. Certainly, the illness was still spreading. The hospitals were always full, even though the victims didn't last long. The Cere House was overburdened with bodies.

A few of the city's lords tried to strike against the white robes, but found that bullets were useless, and that the brutal children, filled with the power that their god had gifted to them, could tear apart a soldier's mail like paper. After a few humiliating losses, most simply denied that the white robes existed, that they were anything more than another of the city's irrational summer panics.

The river itself had turned deadly; there'd been sinking after sinking of barges and boats. The cranes of the loading docks sagged, their timbers rotted through and bolts rusted, and toppled into the water. Mill wheels fell idle, clogged and choked with weeds and muck. Piers and jetties crumbled. The river lapped up over the stones, and reached its fingers into the streets and flooded the cellars with foul water. The city's industry foundered and sank. The city's lords and captains of industry threw money at the problem, sending out boat after boat, crewed by desperate and more desperate men, until finally no danger-money in the city's coffers could pay for a coal-barge to set out on the black water. Some entrepreneurs, it was rumored, attempted to revive the old sacrifices to the river, but the river was not grateful. Businesses closed, boarded up, and so the city was riddled with dark and empty and shuttered places for the monster's dank spirit to fill. The city's streets were clogged with displaced and hungry men—plague-fodder.

Arjun needed, he thought, only to find the one door, the one street, the one line of sweet music, behind which the Voice waited, but the Typhon was bent on closing all doors, drowning all streets, silencing all music. He had been inside its mind, had felt how it tormented the Typhon to be limited to one place, bound to a single body. Now it had broken the bars of its fallen state. Riding the willing bodies of the white robes, it could be a thousand places at once. *Hunting.* And now there were places where no one went, other than the monsters. Dark spaces, holes swallowed out of the city's map. Wounds. Abscesses. A darkness spreading across the city. Time was winding down.

One of the ways he had gone wrong before, he thought, was that he had pinned all his hopes on one source of assistance. He had spent months waiting for Holbach's help, becoming hopelessly entangled in Holbach's own mission. He wouldn't do that again.

Instead, he corresponded with a dozen different scholars. He used a variety of false names, and three different boxes in post offices run by the administrations of three different lords of the city, all of them well outside the warrens.

He offered the scholars his quest as an intriguing problem in applied theology. He hinted that the Choristry could reward them. If that didn't work, he tried to snag their interest by dropping hints about his knowledge of the great theological puzzle of the day: the white robes' infusion of dark power, the plague, and the rumors regarding the Typhon's connection to both. At first he tried to hold back what he knew, to bargain for their attention to his own problem, but the guilt was quickly too much for him; if they could find a way to stop the horror, he wouldn't be the one to slow them down. He gave away what he knew freely, and hoped they would do the same—but he refused all requests to meet in person.

The first replies he received urged him to read books he had already read, or to wander the streets, keeping an ear open, hoping for the best. He wrote again and pressed them for more. He knew they were busy men.

He didn't rely entirely on the city's scholars. He liked them; he had found the Atlas-makers entertaining, he had enjoyed their reckless pursuit of their obsession, and he was well disposed to them and all their colleagues. Even so, he wasn't sure that they really understood how the city worked. The only person he had met who seemed to really understand the city had been Shay. So it made sense to ask for help also from perverts, criminals, and heretics. All he had to do to find them was to take the stairs down into the warrens.

He listened in the corners of disreputable dives until he could identify the fixers, the arrangers of things, the conduits for information. He approached them cautiously, gave them enough time to decide that he was no spy, no censor, no threat. He let them know what he was looking for. Not the Voice; no point in asking that sort of person to find the Voice. He was looking for something else, someone they were well equipped to find, if he was there to be found. He told them he would pay for any rumor.

After long weeks—summer still dragging itself hotly across the city—he came home to his room on the shelf to find a note under his door. *Got a bite. Barker. See me.*

He went down into the warrens. He armed himself first. He had told his contacts that he was merely representing some other, hidden power, that he had no money of his own and was not worth robbing. Still, it was best to go armed. The people he was dealing with expected it; it showed he was serious; not to have taken a gun would have been almost an insult.

Barker could be found at the back of the Alexander Club, near the dancers' stage. He looked a little like a sick dog, of a breed for which there was little demand. He was always sitting behind a table whenever Arjun saw him; if he ever had to get out of his chair, Arjun thought, he might have to walk on all fours.

Barker called Arjun over as he walked into the bar. "*Nelson.* You'd better pay well for this. I don't like it. Have I told you that? I don't. There are limits."

Arjun sat down opposite Barker. "I'm sorry if this is hard for you. But it's very important to my employer."

"Don't take the piss."

Arjun shrugged. He had not been insincere. "What do you have for me?"

"I know you don't think much of me. Looking at me like a criminal. Because of my associations. My business. All right. But I'm a religious man, too, and I don't like this. It's this sort of thing that left the city in the mess it's in today."

"You're probably right. But we need what we need. You've found a man who'll sell what I'm looking for, then?"

"Pay me first. As agreed." When he saw a look of suspicion cross Arjun's face, Barker spat on the floor. "Don't give me that. Don't insult my integrity any more than you already are."

"I don't mean to insult you," Arjun said. "It's just a matter of caution." He looked at Barker's hairy muzzle of a face. There was honest shame on it. Barker wouldn't be troubled by cheating Arjun; shame meant that he meant to help him. "Here," Arjun said, unwrapping a roll of notes. Barker snatched at them.

"I'll be straight with you, Nelson, because I don't like you, and I don't want you as a friend, and I don't want your business in the future. If you'd waited a little, you could have learned this for free.

See, I know you've got other eyes and ears out for this. They'll all hear it in a day or two. You would have heard the rumors soon. You just got *taken*. But you *can't* wait, can you? I can see it in your face. So—this man. Seems he set up business a week ago. He's been putting out feelers. Letting people know. A friend of mine has a friend who works out of the docks, and he heard about it, and he passed it on. The man's down south, so word's taken a few days to get here. That, and most people don't want to get involved."

"He claims to be able to sell gods? As I described? Potent ghost lights, under glass?"

"Rapes 'em, steals 'em, cages 'em, sells 'em to scum like your boss. I don't know the details. There's only hints. It's disgusting."

"What's his name?"

"A Mr. Lemuel."

"Where is he?"

"He works in the Cere House. He's in the Sixteenth Precinct. Room 1104. I'd go quickly if I was you. Rumor travels fast, and it won't be long before enough people hear of this, and the bastard ends up on the end of a rope. I'm thinking I could do it myself, to him and you both, if it wouldn't be bad for my business. Now *fuck* off, and never come back."

It was a day's journey back south to the Cere House, by coach.

The House occupied Cere House Hill, at the southwest corner of the Heath. Arjun had passed it many times, months ago, when he was new to the city. And he had visited it many times, for Norris, then for all the other dead of the Cypress.

Deaths that were on his head, of course. If he had not broken Shay's horrid little cases, the Typhon would not have fallen into the monstrous, fallen state in which it had murdered those men. He shuddered at the thought that he was on his way to visit another man in Shay's line of work. He was excited—he had been relying on a mere hunch that, in a city the size of Ararat, if one man had discovered the science at Shay's command, perhaps there might be others who had done the same, and it was exciting to be proved right—but he was scared, too. He resolved not to make the same mistakes with Lemuel as he had with Shay. He would get what he needed, and try to do no harm.

When he had first heard about the Cere House, he had misunderstood its nature. He had thought that it served the entire city as mortuary, necropolis, place of funeral rites. He had wondered how that was possible; vast as the House was, its cloth-shrouded precincts covering the hill, its spires rising high above and, by all accounts, its vaults burrowing deep below, it could not possibly take in all Ararat's dead.

It didn't, of course. It served only a tiny part of the city. The 'Machy probably marked the northern borders of its jurisdiction, and even the 'Machy's dead rarely ended up within its walls. Probably there were similar institutions elsewhere.

Moreover, it took only certain kinds of dead. The churches disposed of their own faithful. The Cere House disposed of the churchless and lonely poor, with a functional minimum of ritual, and it also took those too great and powerful for any one church to claim, who received the highest honors known to the city, enacted with obsessive and painstaking ceremony.

Still, it was an awesome, solemn sight, as Arjun stepped off the coach at the base of the hill, where the green lawn of the Heath gave way to the grey-white shale of the House's outer precincts. The sun filtered cool and dusty through the waxcloth.

Mourners followed graveled paths away to the outer precincts, to visit their dead. Arjun had business in the inner circles. He lied to the man at the gate, telling him he was a historian, there to make a study of the engravings on the tomb of (selecting a name at random from his vague memories of the Atlas-makers' talk) the Champlain family.

He quickly got lost in the House. It reminded him very much of the Choristry, with its hushed, single-minded dedication to a sacred purpose; then he would turn the corridor into a room lined with skulls, or cross a walkway over a courtyard in which the House's mourners practiced their wailing, a wild sound entirely unlike the measured song of the Choir.

Finally, he asked someone for directions to Mr. Lemuel.

"Who's Lemuel?"

"I think he's probably new here. He's in Room 1104?"

"Oh. Then..." They didn't look twice at him; lost visitors were common in the House.

Room 1104, Lemuel's office, was behind an oak door in one of the lower corridors. Smells of formaldehyde, death, old stone. Arjun knocked on the door. A voice called, "It's open."

Arjun stepped into an empty office. A door at the back was ajar. He went through, into a wide, dark room, full of tables on which what were presumably bodies lay under white cloth. The room was cluttered with ritual paraphernalia of a dozen cults, piled promiscuously together. A man at the back of the room was painting a design onto a corpse's chest, with looping swirls of the brush. He stuck the brush jauntily between the corpse's arm and torso, for safekeeping, and turned to greet Arjun.

"This is Lemuel. Good afternoon. What I can do for you?"

It was Shay. The wild white hair had been razored to a gritty stubble, and the dirty pin-striped suit had been replaced by the grey smock of the Cere House's servants, but it was unquestionably Shay. He even had the same little round glasses.

"If you're here to mourn your dead, you should go wait elsewhere. You don't want to see 'em before I pretty them up. The dead deserve their rituals. Is that it? Speak up!"

Arjun stared frantically at the man's face, hunting for some sign of a scar on the sallow scalp. But no, that was absurd; the wound he'd given Shay was nothing that could be healed; Shay was dead, beyond doubt. But how could it possibly be anyone else?

"Well, I take it from your look of mental disarray that you're not here on Cere House business. You've heard word of some other business, right? Something special?"

Arjun found his voice again. "Yes."

"I'd rather you people would come after hours. I have a job here, you know. It's not as though I expect to keep it for long, but it would be nice to enjoy it for a bit."

"You remind me very much of someone I once knew."

"Well, it's a big city, isn't it?" Lemuel backed toward a table in the corner of the room, under a thick grey tarp, and began untying the tarp's knots.

"Do you know a Mr. Shay?"

Lemuel started. "I've gone by that name at times, and in places. I don't think I've dealt with you before, though."

"You have. Under the name of Shay."

Lemuel pulled back the stiff tarp carefully, winding it under his arm. His wares were underneath, pressing their greasy, ghostly lights against the glass of their cages. Lemuel leaned in close to them, on his haunches, and, in a stagy whisper, said, "Well then, little ones. I don't like the look on this fellow's face. He looks like he doesn't like me. Now, a lot of my customers don't like me, because they're ashamed of what they're here for. But there's no shame on this man. And he knows things he shouldn't. So, little ones, does he mean me harm?"

Lemuel put his ear against the glass as the lights buzzed and clicked. Arjun reached under his jacket for his gun.

"Yes. He means me harm. Or . . . no, he has *done* me harm. But I don't think I know him yet. Isn't that odd?"

Lemuel stood and stared at Arjun, curiously, appraisingly. His left hand was scratching idly at his scalp, just below the hairline, Arjun noticed: was that where the bullet had struck?

"You don't remember me?"

Lemuel sat and lit a cigarette. "I meet a lot of people," he said. "Tell me more."

"Is this a joke? A game?"

"Humor me."

"You were in the Observatory Orphée. On Laud Heath. With your . . . things. You were in a room full of false stars, some old machine, that only you understood. You don't remember this?"

"I don't think I've ever been there."

"I came to you with questions. There was a mob outside, howling for your head . . ."

"Ha! That's life. Mine, anyway. It's a hard road to walk."

"I wanted to know how you did it. How you caught these . . . *things.* I was looking for a god, a ghost. A Voice from my childhood. I thought you might know how to find it. You told me you had a lot of little tricks."

"So did this man who looked like me, did he help you?"

"There wasn't time. The mob was coming. I don't know whether you would have helped or not. I had nothing left to pay you with. There was an . . . altercation. You tried to turn those things in the cases, those reflections you steal, you tried to turn them on me." Arjun drew his gun, and put it on the table before him, resting his hand on it. "I know your tricks. Don't try it again, Shay. It won't work. Move away from them."

Lemuel rolled his eyes, smiling, and scooted his chair a few feet away from the table.

"You turned them on me, and you tried to kill me. I *shot* you. In the head. You died, Shay."

"I really don't think I did."

"I set them free. Your creatures. One of them . . . I followed one of them, as it escaped, and it returned to its source. The Typhon. Do you know what's happening in the city outside, Shay? Do you know what you did?"

"I haven't been here long, but I've read a paper or two."

"It's devouring the city, bit by bit. And it's hunting *me.* It's a plague. There's nothing else like it. Nothing that can stop it from growing, and growing. Did you know that could happen if you set one of these things free?"

"Well, there are always risks, aren't there? In anything anyone really wants? Besides, the way you tell it, *I* wasn't the one who broke the cases. That was bloody stupid of you."

"Stop fucking *smiling,* Shay. How many of these things do you sell? How do you know what people might do with them?"

"The people who buy these things cherish them, hoard them. Hold them close, rocking in the dark. They don't free them."

"You have no idea what they do. You know you'll be well away, though, don't you? Into other places. You're a monster, Shay. The most *reckless* . . . This is *your fault.*"

"You seem to be falling into confusion, young man. That wasn't me. This is a big city, bigger than most people realize; there's probably a great many men who look a great deal like *you* out there. At most, the man you met was a way I might have been, had I walked different streets. We've never met, Mr. . . . ?"

"It was you. It had to have been you. Somehow you survived;

you called on those abominations in your cages to save you, or—or—you said you could walk in secret places, open secret ways; you found some way to walk away from your own death and come back unscarred."

Lemuel scratched his head. "That doesn't sound likely."

"I think that's what you are. And I don't care if you are a different man, anyway. You're in the same filthy business."

"Are you just here to talk rubbish and insult me?"

"No. I need your help. The other one wouldn't help me. But you *will*. I have two questions, and you will answer both. I need to know how to destroy the god that's hunting me. I need to know how to find the god I'm hunting. I need to make the city give up its secrets to me. Tell me, or"—he lifted the gun from the table—"I'll kill you again, Shay. If you came back once, you'll come back again. Or, if somehow there are two of you, there must be three, four, a hundred. Either way, I'll keep killing until I find one who will help me."

Lemuel leaned back and exhaled smoke from the side of his mouth, and smiled toothily, and said, "*Well* then."

The ghost lights pulsed, scattering an oily weave of light across the room, which grew vaster and darker, refracting into strange new angles. Arjun pulled the trigger. Though he had been sure his gun was pointing at Lemuel's chair, the bullet thudded into a corpse-cloth on the other side of the room. It was hard to see where Lemuel was. There seemed to be a thousand possible paths across the room between him and Lemuel's chair. Ghost-light trails wove the floor and the walls and made the space all new and puzzling. Lemuel stood, and a dozen Lemuels around the room stood, too. Some of them approached Arjun; some walked away into the darkness, following trails of pale light. Firm hands reached around from behind Arjun's back and took the gun from him.

Arjun staggered, hands to his head, as some of the Lemuels sat back down in their chairs, and several of them took a moment to calmly reload and prime the weapons.

Each Lemuel uttered a *click* at the back of his throat, and the trails wound their way back home. Arjun fell to the floor. His head was clear again. The room was still. Singularly, Lemuel sat opposite him, holding the pistol on him with a casual hand.

"That's to prove a point. I don't know what happened with this Shay fellow you met. Sounds like a disappointment. But it won't happen with me. That was one of *my* tricks."

He gestured at the cases with his free hand. "These are the weavers of the city. Or, as you put it, reflections of them, which is the next best thing. Fragments of their power. I can unweave and reweave the city's paths with them. I can tie you in knots you can't imagine. What I just did was *nothing*."

Arjun glared at him from the floor, a humiliating reddening sting behind his eyes.

"I should probably kill you. But I won't. Do you know why?"

Arjun didn't answer, not trusting his voice not to shake.

Lemuel went on, cheerily. "Let us suppose I'm *not* the same as the man you killed; he was merely my shadow, let's say. You killed the bugger. As I see it, I owe you for that. I don't need competition. Least of all from someone who may or may not be more or less me. Cunning old bastard that I am."

He raised a finger. "Now let's say it was me you shot. Well, I've been around a long time and I've got a great many tricks. Perhaps you shot me and I came back, or something in me came back, some *essence,* and I don't remember. That's worth something: a chance to start fresh."

"You didn't take it. You're still the same."

"Well, granted. But then, now I know better what sort of man I really am, deep down, and there's value in self-knowledge. So either way, I owe you. If you'd asked respectfully, I would have helped you, you know."

"I don't believe you, Shay. And I don't find you funny."

"Oh dear. Well, what I'll do instead of helping you is, I'll discharge my debt by letting you live. So get up, go on. Sit down, like a civilized man."

There was another chair across the room. Arjun sat in it.

"Now then. Maybe I'll help you anyway, but after that unpleasantness, you'll have to pay. What can you offer me?"

Arjun thought for some time. Was this the same game, or had the rules changed? "I know the secrets of the *Thunderer*."

"Is that that big ugly floating ship? That's of no interest to me.

I'm a man who does his business quietly. I've no interest in an-
nouncing my presence to all the city."

Then the game was changed, and Arjun had few cards. "Money,
then. Or I can promise you service."

"You can do better than that. I can see it; there's something you
don't want to have to promise. Let's hear it."

"I know the makers of the Atlas. The foremost scholars of the
city. I can share their secrets with you."

"They don't have any secrets I want. This is a backward part of
the city, my friend, in a backward time. Look how little you know.
Look how much you've forgotten. None of you here have an inkling
how vast the city is. Whatever this 'Atlas' is, it'll be swallowed and
forgotten soon. I know more than any sad excuse for a scholar you
may have befriended. Do better."

Arjun clenched his fists. There was one thing left. It was a
terrible thing to offer, but he had no choice. Not for the Voice—he
thought that to make this offer would be to make such a terrible
discord in his soul that the Voice might be lost to him anyway—but
for the Typhon. There was nothing he wouldn't sacrifice to end it.
So he said, "I have a final offer. Have you heard of Jack Silk? The an-
archist, the runagate, the prison-breaker? The boy who was touched
by the Bird, nearly a year ago, now, and who still holds on to the
Bird's power? It's still growing in him. He can pass it on to those
around him. I've seen it happen. It's marvelous. He trusts me, I
think. I can bring him to you. Don't you want to know how his
power works?"

Part of Arjun hoped Lemuel would refuse—but he didn't. He
smiled hugely, and put aside the gun, saying, "I don't think I need
this, do I?" and lit another cigarette. "That's very interesting. I've
heard rumors about that boy." He walked over to the caged presences, and whispered to them. They glowed in response. "The Bird's
mark is on you, they say, though weakly. I'm inclined to believe
you've met this boy. I want your promise, young man, that you'll
bring him to me. If you cross me, I'll harry you across this city and
all others, till you wish you were dead. My curse'll be on you. I'll turn
every path you might ever walk against you. Do you doubt me?"

"I promise you, Lemuel, Shay, whatever your name is."

"You know I'll need to keep him? To make him mine? You know I may not be able to treat him kindly?"

"I promise you. Now tell me: how can I destroy the Typhon?"

"You can't. But you can hide. *Run.* Maybe you'll find your Voice, too, on the way. I'll teach you the trick of it."

FORTY-THREE

Arjun did not know how long his apprenticeship to Lemuel lasted. Following in Lemuel's footsteps, it was sometimes day, sometimes night, but according to no natural order. Lemuel wove his own pattern of dark and light across the city. Lemuel's cold rasp was always with him, sneering and snapping when he put a foot wrong. Time could be measured only by the progress of his lessons.

They slept when they were tired. Lemuel could take a turn down certain streets, like so, under certain arches, up a fire escape that led onto a wide white roof where the city was in a lazy tropical summer, where the citizens went shirtless and brown-skinned, and it was possible to sleep blissfully under the open sky, and Arjun woke refreshed. When he wanted night, Lemuel could find that, too; it was always night somewhere.

They ate when they were hungry. Through a maze of alleys, through a stinking tunnel, over a cable-winged bridge of strange design, was a place where Lemuel was known, and restaurateurs ran out from under their awnings to press plates of food on him, for the honor of serving him. Lemuel looked a little shy, as if he had gone too far to impress Arjun, made himself look insecure.

After that, for a while, they ate in parts of the city where meaty fruit grew on the trees by the side of clean streets, to be plucked off by the passing pearl-haired children.

When Lemuel thought Arjun was getting complacent, they started to eat in soup kitchens, among desperate demobbed sailors in mission basements, or laid-off factory workers in grubby church halls, then he made them wait in shambling lines of ruined men, stretching over cratered ground under blasted skeletons of buildings, for scraps of bread handed out by black-armored soldiers with heavy steel guns.

Lemuel moved by subtle navigation, tacking across the city in response to certain signs, unweaving and reweaving its map by act of will.

"It's not *will*," he said, apropos of nothing, as they walked across the bay, in a part of the city where the bay was solidly choked with stationary boats, and you could walk across on planks. "Though I may have told you it was. It's a way to think about it; it gives you confidence. But it's crap, of course. What's one man's will against the city? An infinity of time, an infinity of infinities, has gone into the weaving of it. You know the nature of the entities that weave it as well as any man. Weaving it backwards and forwards, all throughout time and space. Imagine exerting your will against those. You might as well try to fight electricity, or wrestle multiplication.

"No, all we can do is follow in their steps. Look carefully for their signs. For the tangles in the weave. It's a loose weaving they make, great clumsy proud monsters that they are; it has a great many knots and holes in it. As many as there are streets, or doors, or people. Slip through silently. Cunning, not will. It's a trick; no magic to it."

"But, in your office, you forced some change on the room's angles. Or at least on my perceptions. How did you do that?"

Lemuel looked amused. "Well, there's tricks, and then there's *tricks*. I'll show you what you can pay for. For now, that's this. So shut your mouth, follow, and watch, and listen."

They passed through a great many places. Or, as Lemuel put it, they saw the city from a great many angles. Many of them were very different from the city Arjun was familiar with, which he was coming to think of as the city of the Atlas-makers. No point in trying to put them in any order. Some were in the Atlas's future, others in its past. Which was which might depend on the angle at which one walked down the street. "It's all in how you look at it," Lemuel said. "It'll all come round again, somewhere, if you wait long enough, or go far enough in."

On a sunny day, they climbed the wire-mesh steps that spiraled
around a gleaming steel needle on a hill. Curious black butterflies,
the size of a man's fist, nuzzled against them. Lemuel pointed out
over the steel city. "I grew up in a place not much different from
yours. It's always still a shock to see this much gleam and glitter.
Some times shine harder than others. Those are poisonous, by the
way; cover your skin. Sometimes it's hard to believe that these
places are real, even for me, and I'm used to it. But they are. All no
less real than any other. It could all be different, if we had turned
left and not right. You know that. But they don't. Their lives are
real to them. Their *needs* are real. And lucrative, of course."

The city was the only constant; the city, and its vast northern
Mountain. There was an infinite variety of people, and of gods. In
some places, they thought they had only one god, insubstantial and
abstract; in others, the gods strode about far more brazenly even
than they had in the Atlas-makers' city.

"Why does it work this way?" Arjun asked. "Is it that the presence of so many gods opens up these hidden paths, or is it because
the city is built of so many secret places that it gives rise to so many
gods? Or . . ."

"Who gives a shit? Keep your eyes on the path. This way."

There was a place where the men of the city, all pale and tiny and
nervous, traveled in palanquins born by great apes, trained and bred
for the work, caparisoned in their masters' colors. Packs of the apes
broke free and shucked off parts of the uncomfortable armor, and
fought and rutted in the alleys. It was a big problem, Lemuel said;
they weren't sure what to do about it, other than breed more apes
for protection from the apes they had. He thought it was rather
funny.

They stayed in a hotel room the windows of which were heavily
barred against inquisitive primates. Lemuel took the bed by the
door, and snored remarkably loudly for such a little man. Arjun lay
awake in the bed by the window, listening to the jungle sounds of
the street. He felt dizzy, vertiginous; the days (weeks? months?) of
his apprenticeship fell on him in a rush. He was horribly conscious

of the fragility of the city's stuff; he felt that he could fall through at any moment into deeper and more secret places. Nothing was solid or real.

After a time, he realized that Lemuel was sitting up in the gloom, watching him twist and turn, listening to his ragged breathing. There was a half-visible sneer on the man's face.

Arjun found his fear quickly burned away by anger. He sat up and stared at Lemuel. "Who are you really? I'm tired of this game. I think you know I beat you, once, and you're scared to admit it."

"Maybe I know more than I've told you, maybe I don't. That's not the information you've bargained for. Got anything else? Anyone else to betray? Any more friends? A lady-friend, perhaps? A brother? Oh—you don't have any *children,* do you?"

Arjun turned away. "Get some sleep, Shay. I want to finish our business tomorrow."

Lemuel lay back down, saying, "Don't take your guilty conscience out on me, boy. You made your choice."

Arjun lay there. The man was wrong about Arjun's conscience. He misunderstood the nature of Arjun's choice. Arjun had seen Jack fight. He knew what Jack could do. It wasn't Jack whom Arjun had betrayed with his promise. He'd murdered Shay, again, and this time not in combat, but by treachery. And he'd made the boy a weapon; that, too, was sickening.

Sometime later, he said, quietly, "Shay?" There was no answer, but he felt the man was awake and listening. "Shay. There's another possibility. Perhaps you are the same man as the man I shot, but that man is in your future. You say time becomes . . . complex in this city, on these paths."

The man grunted, "Could be."

"Then maybe I *will* kill you. Doesn't that trouble you?"

"We all die one day. If that's how I go, that's how I go."

"So be it, then. I don't forgive you, Shay. But you're not mine to judge. If I am going to kill you, I'm sorry."

The man grunted and rolled over. A stolen and disingenuous apology; it did little to relieve Arjun's guilt.

✳　✳　✳

They made a stop back in the city, in the old familiar city Arjun had come into by sea; stopping at the Cere House, at Lemuel's office.

"Time's not important, as such," Lemuel said, methodically working through the keys on his heavy brass key-chain, like a man investigating the workings of a complex and broken engine. "I try to come back here once a week, every Bridge-day, but it's always Bridge-day somewhere, you know? We could go wandering until we were old and grey, and we could still come back here on Bridge-day." He shuffled up key after key, steel and copper and ivory and iron, teeth like tiny towers rising and falling on the chain's brass loop. "But it's best to have a routine. It's important not to get lost or lose yourself for want of signposts. Aha!" He found the key to his mailbox and flourished it.

There was a single letter in the mailbox. He read it quickly, muttering the words under his breath. Then he tore it up and scattered the pieces.

"We have some business to do, young master Arjun. Come along, then."

Lemuel strode down the corridor, counting off the doors with jerking motions of his bony fingers: one, two, three, four, *ah*! Lemuel lunged for a plain wooden door and darted through. Arjun ran after him and caught the door just before it banged closed. Arjun followed through an unlit stone corridor, through a street at night under washing-lines fluttering in the moon like ragged monstrous moths, through a door in a tower on a bridge over a river of black oily water—and on, and on, always just barely keeping pace with Lemuel's impatient strut—until he ran down a narrow brick hallway toward a slowly closing door, behind which Lemuel's grating, mocking voice was already raised. He caught the door and stumbled through just as Lemuel said, ". . . wasn't sure you'd bother to keep my card, Captain."

Lemuel was pacing back and forth in a bare room, a rough-edged cube of red brick. High arched windows opened out onto a slate sky and wisps of grey cloud.

A man in singed and ragged black sat in the corner, on the room's only chair. His hair was black and filthy, and his head was in his hands. A sword rested against his leg. He answered, "I didn't think I was going to either, Mr. Lemuel. I thought I'd never call on you. I had my duty. But things are different now."

"Duty? Is that right? Is that what you call it? What's so different now, then?"

"The Countess is defeated. I'm ruined. I'm little more than a pirate now. *Nothing* more than a pirate. The *Thunderer* is the most wonderful weapon ever devised in this city, and I've become a pirate with it. I feed my men by raiding. We run, we hide, we lose ourselves among the towers like pirates hiding in rocky shoals. Sometimes I think we could abandon the ship, scurry off like rats, hide in the streets. Turn bandit, turn mercenary, I don't know. But I can *see* what's happening below. From the ship, I can see what's happening to the city below. The stain spreading, the river flooding. The plague's rotten shadow swelling. The fire gone out; I hardly noticed it when it was there, but now it's *gone*. Those savages, those terrible children, swarming over the rooftops, killing and killing. We'd fire on them but we have no shells left. Sometimes we take shots at them with our rifles, when we're hanging low, but they don't care, and they look up at us with those black eyes, and it's as if they're saying *Soon we'll come for you, even you, even up in the sky.* The plague'll reach us soon. I'm sorry, Mr. Lemuel, I haven't slept recently. I don't think I've slept since Lucia died. I can see it: the River-god making itself manifest, growing and never going away. That's not how the city's supposed to work. There's supposed to be a cycle to these things, isn't there? I never made any great study of theological science, but isn't that how it should work? The city's broken and diseased. This place"—he gestured out of the tower window—"is as low to the ground as I dare get now. It's hopeless. My duty is over. I want to escape. I want to be with Lucia again. You said there was some part of the city where she was alive. I want to go there. I want to go to a part of the city where that monster won't reach, just for my lifetime, and hers, and be done with it. You asked for the *Thunderer;* it's yours, Lemuel. Take it to the Mountain, if you like. *Crash* there if you like. Whatever you want."

The man's voice was deep, and cold, and cut from the finest crystal of aristocracy; as he spoke, jagged cracks appeared in the crystal and on *it's yours* it broke, and he almost sobbed; he sounded like a beggar. He moaned deep in his throat. He looked up for the first time, and noticed Arjun.

"Don't I know you? I saw you at the Countess's palace. Weren't you one of Holbach's creatures? You *were.* You were one of Holbach's. Tell me, was it Holbach who planned this? Was it Holbach who planned the Countess's downfall? This monster, this poisoned god loosed on the city—was it his revenge?"

Arjun opened his mouth, and Lemuel motioned for silence.

"There's some dispute over the blame for this development, Captain. Let's let sleeping dogs lie, is what I say. Let's say no more. Let's just say, Captain, that you disappoint me. Is that all you have to offer?"

"*You* came to me, Lemuel, remember. You wanted to trade. For the *Thunderer,* you promised me Lucia. You told me she was out there somewhere. Why not now, damn you?"

"That was a long time ago. Longer for me than for you, I would have said, though you've aged terribly, Captain, now that I come to look at you. I have other interests now. And if I wanted the secret of your ship, well, this young man"—he jerked a thumb at Arjun—"can tell me as well as you. And Captain, let's be frank here. The ship won't be yours for long anyway. Look at you; your days are numbered, as they say. You're nearly done. You're only a loose end. You'll be plucked soon, and I reckon I know how. I reckon I know who your successor will be, and I reckon I'll soon own that young chap, too, and so *no one needs you anymore,* Captain."

Arlandes reached for his sword and stood. Arjun stepped back into the corner of the room, behind Lemuel, who remained in place, hands folded behind his back.

Arlandes held his sword back poised to swing, his feet placed to lunge. He stood like that for a while. He was apparently looking into Lemuel's eyes. Arjun, backed up against the wall, could not see what the Captain saw in those eyes.

After a while Arlandes let his sword clatter to the floor. He sat back down in his chair with his head in his hands.

Lemuel clapped his hands together. "That was a waste of time. It's a good thing I have so bloody much of it. Goodbye, Captain. We

won't see each other again, I don't think. Come along, you little yellow bugger." He stepped out into the hallway.

Arjun crossed the room quickly, silently, and stood over the
Captain's chair. "Captain?" He ventured a hand on the man's tense
and knotted shoulder. "Captain? I can offer you a deal. I cannot offer the same terms as Lemuel. I do not know how to find this Lucia
of yours. I am very lost myself. But I can try. I have a plan, Captain,
to save the city from the flood. I think I can use your ship, and your
sword. Help me and I can try. I can make no promises but I can offer you hope."

Arlandes' shoulder shook. He seemed to shrink into himself.
The Captain was not in fact a big man, though he'd seemed that
way at first sight. He made no sound.

Arjun waited as long as he dared before following Lemuel's fading path, which was not long at all. He left the Captain sitting
silently on his chair in the empty tower.

Lemuel had other business to conduct. He set up in the top of a
ruined gun-tower overlooking a lake full of jostling houseboats.
The squat, bowlegged, grey-faced men who came to see him under
cover of night were, he said, some of the Lake's most prominent
Captains. "You make them nervous," he told Arjun. "You have a
disapproving puritanical look about you. Go make yourself useful
somewhere else." The stairs to the gun-tower crunched underfoot
with moldering bone fragments, remains of some ancient assault.
Arjun made a desultory effort to clear them. The Captains scuttled
down the stairs past him, holding their precious shameful purchases
under their cloaks. Finally Lemuel came down, saying, "Come on,
then, come on," rattling his crowded key-chain, and he locked the
tower behind him, and set out walking down toward the Lake, and
out onto one of the many noisy brightly lit piers. Arjun followed.
Soon the pier was a long, busy Main Street in a wholly different part
of the city.

For two days Lemuel sat in an office above a large railway station
and answered his mail. "Can I trust you with a knife?" Lemuel

asked. "Good, then. Take this and open those envelopes. *Try* not to hurt yourself."

Everything in the office was painted grey or a drab olive-green, and the carpet was covered in cigarette burns. On the mantelpiece there were four large and complex clocks, three of which contained live birds; in the glass window of the fourth was a tiny avian skeleton. The clocks ticked and struck at odd times, and Lemuel's pen scratched, and the trains groaned noisily back and forth underneath.

Arjun slept on the sofa while Lemuel worked through the night. When he woke, a second bird was dead. The remainder seemed to be watching him intently and unhappily.

"Do you have a laboratory, Mr. Lemuel?"

"Slept well, did you? No, I do not. Do you?"

"I read about a Mr. Cuttle once, who looked like you. He had a laboratory, where he had strange lights, and animals and birds that could nearly speak, but not quite."

"Doesn't ring a bell. Cuttle's a good name, though. Efficient. Businesslike."

"I don't know when you're lying to me. I should stop asking you questions, I suppose. Your birds are starving."

"They'll be fine."

"Someone should feed them."

"So go buy birdseed. Maybe I'll still be here when you get back and maybe I won't."

The little birds watched Arjun reproachfully through the dirty glass of their cages, and probably there would in fact have been plenty of time to buy food and return, because Lemuel worked on his mail for *hours* before standing suddenly and saying, "Come on, then, come on."

Some time later, Arjun and Lemuel sat in a park at a long table made of a fallen oak split down the middle, surrounded by hairy red men, under a sky in which the sun was held by a mailed fist. The clutching fingers made shafts of shadow, leagues wide. In the distance, a great black bull, tall as a mountain, stamped its feet into the stuff of the city. Long seconds after each mighty hoof hit the earth, thunder sounded at the table, and the men cheered and clapped, and the towers and windows around the park quivered and re-formed into new shapes.

"I like these people," Lemuel said. "When it's that blatant, you really have to know the score. And they do, and not only have they accepted it, and not gone mad, they've learned to love it. Terrible place for business, can't sell 'em anything, but you have to admire their enthusiasm. Ha! Yes!" He joined the clapping at a particularly violent transformation.

Arjun was listening to the people at the table talk. Their excited chatter, at first, was itchily familiar. Slowly it had resolved itself into words that he knew. Now he was fascinated; so *that* was the melody of their vowels, *that* was the rhythm of their clacking consonants. He'd imagined that Tuvar would sound with sad minor notes; he didn't know why. It wasn't sad at all.

"So, have you been watching me? Are you a good pupil, young man? Have you figured the trick of it yet?"

They had bargained for a while before leaving the Cere House. Lemuel had tried to insist that Arjun bring him Jack before he would teach him anything.

"It can't work that way," Arjun had said. "We can't deal on that basis. I can't trust you to honor your promise. Would you, if you were me? How could I hold you to anything? But you can trust me, because you know I fear you, and you know I can't escape you. That's the only way it can work between us."

Lemuel had tried to argue his way around it, but Arjun had been immovable, and in the end Lemuel had shrugged, and said, "There isn't always a way out, even for me. Very well, then. Come with me, and I'll show you."

They walked for a long time down Lemuel's paths before he announced that Arjun was ready to learn the trick. Lemuel stood up from the long oak table, tossed some coins down, and walked under an arch of trees, across graveled paths, over a bridge across the pond that had not been there before, through a gate in the fence that had not been around the park when they entered, and through the streets, into a concrete tower block, stepping over drug-haggard vagrants, into a rusty box that shook and rattled as it dropped with them in it, then along an antiseptic corridor, through a door that opened into the bone-lined vaults of the Cere House, and back into Lemuel's office.

"Patience, and silence. Openness to even the tiniest sign. The cunning and daring to seize it. There's a certain habit of mind. Not just anyone can do it. If you just start walking randomly, you just stay where you are. You go in circles. To find the secret paths, the hidden doors, to slip into the gods' footsteps—well, there's a trick to that.

"I can't help you to find your Voice. Maybe it's out there, here in the city, maybe it isn't. There's no special way of hunting these things. Never was. At least, not that I've ever learned, in all my travels. If you're patient, and you travel the city widely, sometimes you see them, and then you can snatch away what you need. I could show you *that* trick, but that's not what you want, is it?

"What I can give you is time, and space. I can open up the city to you. You can hide from the Typhon there. And if you wander it long enough, maybe you'll find your Voice."

They left the office again, Arjun following Lemuel, then, at Lemuel's urging, trying to take the lead. It was slow work, at first. There was so much to learn, and to notice. It was like the science by which Holbach predicted the motions and manifestations of the gods, but where Holbach took months of research and calculation to produce an answer, Lemuel darted from street to street, taking signs in at a glance, saying, "That way! Quick, now," and committing himself to a path.

"You have to find a sign that means something to you. If you want to knot and weave the gods' trails into the path *you* want, you have to build it out of the signs that speak to *you*. Make the city yours. *Take* what you need."

For Lemuel, the sign was death, and the accoutrements of death. "I don't think I'm a morbid man," he would say. "I think I'm an *honest* man. Vanity, vanity, all is vanity, you know? Maybe you don't. Well, one likes what one likes. For that *Shay,* who you met in the room of lights in the Observatory, perhaps for him it was stars. Or those secret forgotten machines. Who knows?"

He would walk the streets, head cocked into the air, eyes darting, until he saw a graveyard, or a funeral home; or a bench with a plaque commemorating a beloved husband and father, or a marble pillar honoring the dead of one war or another; or the corpse of a rat or dog in the street; or bones in a gibbet or the meat of a man hung from a lamppost; or a moon-white leafless tree, dead by the side of the road. He would dash into whatever street or tunnel or door the sign marked, with Arjun rushing to keep up. Then he would repeat the process, and again; and soon enough, by a subtle compounding of strangeness, he would find himself in a new city.

For Arjun, of course, it was music. He learned to make all the city's music a sign, a key, a path, a map; he learned to improvise, to descant his own song in and around the city's music. Grudgingly, Lemuel said, "This should have taken you years to learn. I have to admit, you have a knack for this." Of course he did. He had practiced all his life.

Go on, then," Lemuel said, when they were back in his office again. "Go on out. See where it takes you. Spread your wings! But make a note of the way you go: walk it back again, and come back to this place, and this time. I'll be here. Don't betray my trust." Then Lemuel took the brush he had left in the corpse's armpit, dipped it again in the blue paint, which had not yet dried, and resumed his work.

Arjun walked out into the corridors of the Cere House. Turning left down the nearest passage brought him into a courtyard where student mourners practiced a dirge on their dark-wood cellos. A flight of stairs led up to a wall on which plumed trumpeters blasted out a martial honor for a dead princeling, as his mailed body slid from the wall into the firepit below. A ladder down led into a narrow room where an old woman sang a wavering nursery rhyme to her grandson's grave.

Turning and turning, he worked his way out of the Cere House. He was still learning the art. *Art*—he would not call it a *trick,* he cheated nobody by it; Shay and Lemuel had spoken of it as if it was fraud or theft, but the city was ready and willing to unfold its impossible profusion to those who were patient and attentive. It took Arjun a long time to find his path out of the House, and its countless cognates on other angles of the city. Between one passage and another, he walked for a while through a House that took its victims alive, and against their will. He ran through its corridors.

In an overgrown graveyard precinct, he let the hazy song of the grasshoppers direct him through a trail in the thick grass, and then he was out on the Heath, or something much like it, though he felt lumpish and grey among the beautiful, swan-necked young men and women who lounged on the meadows. He walked for a while until he found a band playing by a white bridge.

Most of the places he saw were unremarkable. He passed through a dozen places like Shutlow, where ordinary dull lives were spent. But there was a place where the people all had cats curled around their shoulders, whispering to them, and he walked quickly—instinct told him not to run—to get away from their curious stares; and there was another place where a great bird-god (was it the same one?) held its shining wings over the city's whole sky, their slow beating marking out day and night, and all the people drifted between their city's high arches. But perhaps their own lives were unremarkable to them, too.

He thought about the Atlas. Even if the city's gods and rulers had not turned against them, their project would have been impossible. The city was infinite, and unmappable.

But then again, if the city was infinite, so were the people in it, all of whom the Atlas-makers might turn to their project in time. An infinity of time, and of hands, and of space; which would prevail? The idea of the Atlas could propagate endlessly across the city.

Just as, he was delighted to see, the echoes of the Voice he had released into the city were doing. He heard that song everywhere. It had slipped through the city's cracks and taken new forms. It had gone on ahead of him, to mark his path.

As he walked over a rope-bridge between towers, it crossed his mind that perhaps one of those echoes of the Voice he had released into the city had found its way down some street that led into the past of the Atlas-maker's city, had grown there, swelling into the true god, and had left the city to go south. Unlikely, but possible; he supposed there was no way of knowing.

The echo of the Voice led him to the end of his first journey. He followed behind a group of protestors chanting it, then turned into an alley where a flower girl sang it, then up a broad street where it boomed out from the walls of a grand theater. Then he followed its trail through a number of little streets, until it took on a scratchy and distant sound, as if sung by a tin throat. A tin throat that was only just learning to sing, because it stuck grindingly again and again on the same note, and had to start over. Through a door, and he was in the room where the song was playing.

The sound was coming from a device sitting in the room's window, high above the city; the sound had spilled out into the air. The device was a kind of spinning music box. He poked at it cautiously, and moved some kind of lever, and the music screeched to a halt.

Everything was very silent. The room was spare and empty. He looked out of the window, into silent and empty streets. He had never known the city so quiet.

He stepped out of the room, and walked down a great many winding stairs to get outside. The street was empty. The high windows all around him were empty. The music he had stilled had been the only sound. He walked for some time without seeing or hearing anyone, even a dog or a bird.

There were no signs of sudden abandonment: no half-finished meals, no empty vehicles in the streets. In fact, there were only a handful of signs of human habitation at all, other than the blank grey buildings, and those that there were, were utterly arbitrary. The street had one lamppost, unlit. There was a single black shoe in the road. Looking in through a window, he saw a room containing nothing except a single chair, facing the wall. The next room contained a blank book, half-open on a lectern. The word DELICATESSEN was painted on a third window, in square grey script, but the interior was as empty as all the rest. There weren't even doors in the grey walls.

It was the loneliest place he had ever been. There was no life or

purpose in it. It made him think of the Typhon. Was this lifeless-
ness, this absence, this abscess, what the Typhon would make of the
city? Had he walked into the future of the Atlas-makers' city, after
the Typhon had grown to swallow the life in it? Possibly. There was
no way of knowing. It chilled him, however it had come about. It
was unbearable.

There was one more thing he had to do. He had to turn back,
and finish things. He went back to the room where the machine sat,
and fiddled with it, growing increasingly nervous, until he found
how to move the lever and its needle back onto the spinning disc,
and the music resumed. Passing under its sign, he stepped back
through the door, starting back onto the path.

FORTY-FOUR

Back in the Atlas-makers' city, Arjun left the Cere House and took a coach across the city.

"I won't cross Fourth Ward for you," the coachman said. "It was always a bad place, but now...they say the white robes and the Thunderers fight all over it. With unnatural powers. They say some of 'em can fly, and some can steal your breath with a look. I keep a gun and a club under the seat, but that's only good for drunks, the odd robber. I won't go into *that*."

Arjun entered the Ward on foot. The driver's fears were overblown: the Ward was no battlefield. It was still full of its usual dirty, toothless folk, frightening if they were young, frightened and pitiable if they were old. It was sad; there were so many other ways they might be, in other places. But he knew by now that if he walked firmly, with a hand on his weapon, he was safe enough.

Outside a broken-down cobwebbed smithy, a shark-school of the white robes slouched across the street ahead of him—turning their shaven heads in his direction it seemed, for an awful moment—but he ducked into an archway until they were gone.

In the late afternoon, he reached the street of factories where Jack had brought him, where they had met the Thunderers, and prepared to travel north to the Iron Rose. How long ago had it been? Not that long, apparently, because the factories were all still vacant, the street locked away behind a wire fence. He climbed the fence and walked between the empty buildings. Jack had made him wait at the end of the street; he didn't know which factory exactly was theirs. If they were still there at all. Everything was quiet; a light, warm wind blew dry litter about.

If he tried to blunder about searching, he might come across one of Jack's wild lieutenants, who would probably cut his throat before looking at his face. The safest thing to do was wait. If Jack came there still, he'd see him soon enough. So he sat cross-legged in the dusty street, and cleared his mind.

Jack came down out of a red sunset. He cocked his head, jokingly, as if listening. "So, is that Voice of yours singing here," he said, "or is there some other reason why you're sitting in the middle of my street?"

"I have not found the Voice. How does your battle go?"

"Well." Jack stood for a moment, then sat down. He sprawled loose-limbed and boyish, but his face was lined and troubled. "Yeah, not so well. We don't do anything now but fight the white robes. We haven't touched a prison in ages. It's hard. They've killed . . . they've taken a few of us. And we don't have their numbers. And we'll never have more. They have some terrible new strength. We all had a dream, that it was that monster that follows you that rides them now. Is that true?"

"I believe it is. But there's a way of defeating the monster. I need your help, though. I've found a man who may be the key to defeating it. I need you to come see him with me."

They walked back across the Ward together. Night was the most dangerous time—the white robes, or the thing that had swallowed them, was at home in the darkness—but Jack knew the safe ways to go. Jack pointed out the burnt-out places, the plague-ridden places, the empty black wounds the Typhon and its creatures had made on the Ward's map. "This has to work," he said. "We can't fight it. It'll swallow everything in darkness. It's the worst gaoler in the city."

The gate to the Cere House was locked, but unguarded. Jack lifted them both over the wall and into the inner precincts.

The corridors of the House were not empty: many of the House's ceremonies were conducted at night. But the people who passed them were engrossed in their own rituals, and they passed unchallenged. Jack wore a thick grey jacket to cover his notorious shirt.

The door to Lemuel's office was ajar. Arjun knocked on it and called out, "Mr. Lemuel? I'm back," through the crack.

From the depths of the morgue room behind the office, Lemuel called, "Come in, then! Let's see you!"

Lemuel was standing in the middle of the room. He wore long, bloody gloves, and held a bloody knife; he had apparently been elbow-deep in the guts of the body on the table next to him. Behind his gold-rimmed glasses, his eyes lit up to see Jack.

"Arjun. And a friend." He pulled off his gloves. "Don't mind all this, boy. The followers of Uktena, you see, my boy," he said, adopting an avuncular tone, "won't go into the next life, they don't think, unless they have fresh raw meat in their stomachs. To show their strength. Sometimes they don't have a chance to take a bite before they go, and—well. It's a dirty job, but it has to be done. For the time being, it's *my* job. Are you scared? No, you're not scared, are you? Brave boy like you."

Arjun said, "Jack, this is Mr. Lemuel. Mr. Lemuel, I told Jack about your offer to help him with his gift."

"Did you now? Yes, Jack, that's right. I can teach you a great deal. We can teach each other, can't we, my boy? Come here and let me see what you can do."

Jack glanced at Arjun, who said, "It's all right. I promise."

Jack shrugged. "This had better be worth it, Mr. Lemuel. I have work to do." He crossed the floor, hands insolently in pockets, over to Lemuel, who had moved to his table of cages, and was pulling aside the tarpaulin.

"Don't be scared of these, boy. Has your friend told you about these? They're just lights. Well, not *just* lights. I can help you. Come here."

Jack stopped in the middle of the floor. "I think I'll stay here, Lemuel. You tell me, what is it you can do for me?"

Sadly, Lemuel shook his head as he removed and polished his spectacles. "He should be less suspicious, shouldn't he, little ones?

You stay there, then, suspicious boy. All places are one to me, anyway. *Stay.* You're *mine* now."

The cages pulsed with light. Arjun saw Jack stagger slightly, his eyes darting around the room, suddenly lost, confused. Arjun, too, was lost; he could see the two figures of Lemuel and Jack, but the room was a dark maze, and those two figures spun through strange angles in relation to each other.

Lemuel walked closer to Jack, who took faltering, frightened steps forward, back, and side to side, and reached a clawlike hand to snatch the boy's hair and pull his head back. Both of them were snarling like dogs.

Arjun reached into his jacket and put his hand on his gun, just in case. But it wasn't necessary. As Lemuel pulled at Jack, Jack drew his beautiful knife and lunged to his left and to his right, faster than the eye could see; lunging forward and back and over his shoulder, darting down every path and angle Lemuel opened, seeming to Arjun's slow eyes to be everywhere at once, his speed opening an escape from every trap Lemuel tried to make, blurring into a bursting storm of knives, until blood struck a bright trail out of the empty air behind him. Then that space was occupied by Lemuel, who staggered back, gasping, clutching his reddening shirt to his belly.

The room was just a grubby mortician's parlor again, a big square box. Lemuel choked and fell.

"It was like you said," Jack said. "He tried to get into my head. There were hundreds of him. So"—he kneeled to wipe his blade off on Lemuel's grey smock—"I just had to strike them all. Told you I could do it."

"I didn't doubt it." Arjun knelt by Lemuel's moaning head. "He's too fast, Shay. You shouldn't have tried to chain him."

Together, they walked out of the Cere House, Arjun leading them under the sign of the city's music. The music that had pointed his way was no longer there, but he remembered the route, and he found to his relief that that was all he needed. Jack followed, keeping close to Arjun's heels as they left the city he knew.

The cats in that strange place stopped their whispering, and lifted their flat heads from their bearers' shoulders and hissed at Jack, who spat back. They watched him as he followed Arjun into a street marked by their howling cat-music. The flying folk beckoned to Jack to join them, but he shook his head.

When they were done with what they had to do, they walked back, and into the dark mortician's parlor.

Arjun said, "Then we have just one more thing to do." He looked around the room, and at the eerie glow of the god-cages. "Two more things, I suppose."

Lemuel had two big black suitcases in the corner of the room, like the ones Shay had had. One was empty. The other was half-full of what Arjun guessed was photographic paraphernalia, though it was a little different from Shay's stuff.

They packed the glowing glass cages into the suitcases. It took a long time. They had to hold the cages at arm's length, and even then their fingers tingled and a rush of stolen glory ran up the veins of their arms, filling their heads with thick light, so that they had to go and sit in a corner for a few minutes, heads between their legs, breathing slowly.

When the suitcases were full, heavy and clanking, they each took one and walked out of the Cere House, this time without any special trickery or art. They crossed the dark Heath, and went down to the river, where they walked out onto the jetty. It was, Jack had heard, the place from which the *Thunderer* had been launched. They threw the suitcases in. The suitcases bobbed for a moment in the black water, then sank as their air leaked out.

"They'll rise again," Jack said. "Or be dredged, sooner or later."

"Yes. And perhaps Shay'll come back again, or someone like him, out there somewhere in the city. But this will keep those things down for a good long time, and in this place. That'll have to be enough."

"So what now?"

Arjun leaned against the poles of the jetty to catch his breath, and listened to the river rushing past the mossy timbers below. "Not much further. I think I know the way."

* * *

They left the River and went down through the streets, across the edge of Shutlow, which was silent now, exhausted, and into the looming warehouses of Barbary Ward, and along a street of empty mills. They wriggled under a wire fence and made themselves muddy. They crossed a vacant lot strewn with weeds and dogshit and gnawed bone, under the light of a filthy moon. They came to a great black warehouse straddling a canal. A lightless tunnel cut beneath. The canal smelled stagnant but its waters flowed urgently, powerfully.

Arjun climbed down onto the damp mossy towpath and slowly approached the tunnel's mouth. Jack leaned against the wall and watched.

"This is where you began," Arjun said. "Do you remember?"

Nothing stirred in the dark.

"This is where I made you. I'm sorry for that. This is where Shay and I made you."

Water rushed urgently into the tunnel. The stones hissed and something echoed distantly in the depths.

"I was the first thing you ever saw in the world. No wonder you *hate* me."

The echoes in the tunnel slowly died out. The rushing waters slowed, grew torpid, sluggish, stale.

"You hideous thing."

Arjun turned back to Jack. "Stand close to me. It won't be long now."

The water was still. A cold and foul mist rose from it. Both of them knew the signs of the monster's coming. To stop himself from running or screaming, Arjun clutched the tow-post by the tunnel's mouth so hard that his hand throbbed and stung.

Fog rose off the canal, cutting them off from all the city's lights, so that there was nothing around them but the water.

Beneath Arjun's hand, the wood of the tow-post became slimy and cracked.

Out of the darkness came a small white figure, and another, and another, walking slowly up the towpath. Their shaved heads were cocked at odd angles. As if, Arjun thought, they were listening to a secret signal; as if, Jack thought, their necks were hanging from an invisible noose. Darkness followed them. Each of them was the white crest of a wave of darkness, and darkness poured from their slack mouths and blank eyes, and pooled in their footsteps.

One by one, the white robes halted their approach, and stood slouching around the jetty.

One last sallow creature kept coming. Then it stood before them, alone, and opened its gaping mouth even wider, and freezing silence echoed out of its depths. It was no larger than the others, but it seemed to Arjun that perhaps he was seeing it from very far away, as if he was sinking away into the void while it loomed hugely above him, willing him down.

"I see it," Jack said. "Behind that boy. *Riding* him. Gods, it's so fucking ugly. It's so fucking *sick*."

"Yes." Arjun grabbed Jack's shoulder. "That's it. Love of the Voice, that's it. That's the Typhon itself, inside that one. *Now*."

Jack linked his arm with Arjun's, and ran forward, right at the monster. Arjun stumbled to keep up, but was quickly off his feet, falling; then it didn't matter, because they were both off their feet, hurtling just over the surface of the muddy towpath.

Jack threw his knife at the monster, with impossible silvery speed. It struck the monster in its stolen head, shearing away a part of its jaw. The thing did not flinch.

Then Jack, carrying Arjun, passed over its head, climbing into the sky, away from it, west and over the squat flat warehouses of Barbary, over the chimney pots and slumping roofs of Shutlow, and all of the sleeping city fell away beneath them as they came out over the Heath and across it. And howling, the monster came after them.

The Typhon, too, could be fast, like a flood. It climbed the walls of the warehouses like a spider—like mold, like rot, like a crack running suddenly through a window. It hurtled from rooftop to rooftop. Where it landed, the tiles cracked and ceilings fell in. It took huge, loping leaps over the Heath, cracking and blighting the earth under its feet. Its stride shattered its puppet's ankles to dust, but it didn't slow. Its wake was dark.

Bearing Arjun with him, Jack went west over the meadows, and then over the Widow's Bower. When the Typhon reached the trees, it threw itself up into them and ran across the treetops, reaching up for Jack with its long arms, made longer by tendrils of darkness. A rain of broken branches and blighted leaves fell to earth beneath it.

The Cere House stood at the west end of the Heath, behind the Bower. Jack angled down, and they landed in an open courtyard in the House's inner precincts. Arjun turned, to see the creature howling across the rooftops behind them; there were no stars visible behind it. It threw itself to the ground at the other end of the courtyard, and came running.

That was the most dangerous moment; in the House's tunnels, they would have to go on foot. They would be in its grasp if it caught up to them. But there was no choice. Jack ran through the stone doors into the tunnels, pulling Arjun with him. If any of the House's nightwatchmen had been there, they would have seen only a bright streak crossing their vision, followed a second later by a rush of darkness that would have been the last thing they would ever see.

Into the tunnels, and left, and then right, under cool stone, the flood at their heels.

Right again, then left, Arjun directed them, according to the signs he had remembered.

Down a flight of deep stairs, and through the vaults. Up a narrow shaft, ignoring the long ladder, Jack streaking up the passage under his own power, the monster throwing itself from side to side of the walls, shattering its fingers on the bricks.

They crossed the crumbling graveyard, where Arjun had passed before and the sound of crickets had opened the way onwards. They were under the open sky again, but it was no longer the same city. Through the trail in the grass, then out over the beautiful strange place that was so much like their own Laud Heath.

✳ ✳ ✳

That was where the Typhon scrabbled its body up on top of a white bandstand that crumbled and stained underneath its feet, then hurled itself into the night sky at Jack, and caught his heel with its ruined hand, and pulled him to the earth.

They had not been high in the air, and the fall did not kill them. But Jack landed hard, winded, and the thing was instantly on top of him. Jack wrenched his neck away so that he wouldn't have to look it in the eyes, and tried to crawl out from under it, but it sat on top of him, and put the bloody, bony mess of its hand over his mouth, and pulled his head back, and stared at him, so that he felt himself being devoured.

Jack moaned distantly and went silent; shuddered and went still. The thing twisted slowly and patiently at Jack's limbs until they seemed ready to snap. Arjun staggered to his feet and ran to them, screaming incoherently, and fired his gun. The bullet tore across the thing's back, spraying blood, but without effect.

Desperately, he began to sing. His voice cracked with fear and he emitted a high wavering note. There was very little of the Voice in it, but still it seemed more than the monster could bear—it let go of Jack and *snarled,* a noise like a ship running aground. It leaped up off Jack and loped for Arjun.

Arjun broke into a run, but he knew he couldn't outrun it. He despaired the second he felt hands grabbing his arm, but then he was lifted into the air, and he looked around to see that Jack held him up out of the flood.

After that, they stayed higher in the air, the thing following raveningly beneath them. They made sure not to lose it as they crossed through all the secret ways Arjun pointed out for them, until they came through a plain door into a grey room that was empty except for the scratchy music-machine.

The thing was not far behind. Jack ran to the room's high window, and leaped, pulling Arjun after him. They landed lightly on the grey road far below. The monster, a second later, landed heavily. There was not much left of its puppet anymore.

It pursued them down the empty road. They turned left, then left again, and stopped. The thing roared after them, then stopped, too.

In the middle of a flat circle of concrete, ringed by pointless grey roads, sat Lemuel. He was bound to a plain chair. Blood was just starting to seep through a bandage around his stomach. His face was pale and sick, but raging, and he spat when he saw Arjun.

"You cheating, dishonorable little bastard! How dare you? This won't hold me. You'll pay . . ." He fell silent when he saw the monster enter the courtyard behind his captors.

It pulled up short, and sniffed, and moaned. All its attention was captured by the man in the chair.

When Arjun had planned this, and when he and Jack had bound Lemuel's wound, tied his hands, and carried him across the worlds and lashed him there as bait, he had thought he would have to make a speech; he had imagined himself saying, *Look, great Typhon:* this *man, not me, is the one who stole you and tormented you. This is the one who poisoned you, who made you*—this *is the one you hate. Take him and be revenged.*

But there was no need. The thing *knew.* It forgot about Arjun at once, and advanced on Lemuel.

Lemuel roared with incoherent rage and fear as the broken body approached, surrounded by a cloud of darkness and cold; no, rather, Arjun thought, the cloud approached, pulling the little body along. He thought how stupid the monster was; how crude and narrow its appetites were. It had done so much harm, and it was such a pathetic thing.

As the cloud touched Lemuel's screaming face, his neck twisting away as far as his bonds would allow, Arjun was shocked out of his thoughts. It would not be satisfied with its meal; it would never be satisfied. They had to go, at once, while the monster was busy. Too busy, Arjun hoped, to follow them back.

They flew back down the street while the Typhon was distracted, working its revenge on Lemuel. They did not look, and tried not to listen. It worked slowly; they had plenty of time to get away from it.

In the room where they had entered the empty place, Arjun broke the music-machine. He didn't think it would make a difference—he didn't think the creature would be able to follow the route back without his lead—but he wanted to be sure.

In silence they went back across all the many cities.

Back in Lemuel's office, Jack said, "I'd sooner have killed it. It's been the cause of a lot of evil. It should die."

"It can't die. It's a god, still, as well as a monster. But it can do no more harm where we left it. It's alone there. I think I feel sorry for it. It suffers."

"It should suffer."

"Perhaps."

There was nothing much else to say. Arjun looked at Jack's face, which was pained and drawn, and asked, "Did it hurt you?" Jack shook his head, and forced a smile. They walked out onto the Heath together, and parted with a stiff handshake. They both smiled. Then Jack took off into the air.

FORTY-FIVE

Namdi limped to the factory's door when he saw Jack approach. "Where did you go? Where've you been?" Then he saw the look of exhaustion on Jack's face. "Are you all right?"

Jack looked around. They were alone: the others—those who had survived this far—must have been asleep. Good; he was not ready to talk to them all, yet. He put his arm around Namdi's shoulder, and led him away into the street.

"Namdi, it's over. I mean, well, first, the white robes are over. The power that was in them, their god-monster—it's gone. They're just children again. They'll be forgotten soon. But, Namdi, we're over, too."

"It's not over till no prison stands, you said."

"That was . . . I could say that, because the Bird gave me its power. I had power to spare for you all. But it's done now. The monster *touched* me. Before we trapped it. It made me *look* into it. It *hurts*. Namdi, I can feel the power in me leaking away. It won't last much longer. We have time for one more escape. We have to look to ourselves now. I can take you all with me. Wake them: we have to work fast."

There were fifteen of them in the factory. Another dozen back at the boathouse. That was the remaining strength of the Thunderers. Jack grieved deeply for Fiss, and all the other dead, and Aiden and all the others who had walked away. Now that his war was done, he had time to grieve.

They went up onto the roofs one last time, under Jack's wings, and they ran north in great light steps. Around dawn, they tacked east. Jack went ahead and above them, looking for their prey. They saw it in the evening, after combing gods only knew how many miles of the city's sky: the *Thunderer,* among the ruined towers of Stross End. "*Take* it," Jack said.

They rose in his wake to crest over the warship's side. The effort tore at his heart, but he laughed to see them rise.

The *Thunderer's* crew were ragged, thin. Soldiers reduced to bandits. Had they thought that they would one day restore the Countess's power? Or were they just hiding, running, trying to survive for themselves? It was too late for them, in any case.

Jack led the charge over the *Thunderer's* deck, pulling a saber from the waist of the first soldier to run at him, and cutting him down. He missed his knife, lost back at the canal.

Arlandes came at him. There was no mistaking him; among the redcoats there was only one in ragged black. A true swordsman; his stance was perfect. But he was no match for the Bird's speed, and Jack killed him quickly. Jack let the man lunge with his saber twice, past his left ear and past his right, while he studied his red exhausted eyes. The man swung down and across, jerked his blade back and snapped it forward; Jack was never there. The saber went wild and loose, as if the man had realized that control and skill would never save him, as if he was trusting wildly to luck. Jack suddenly felt sick at himself; he felt that he was playing a cruel and demeaning game with the man. He stepped forward—the saber's blade falling toward him slow and steady as sunset—and drove his own blade up into Arlandes' ribs. It was what the man deserved, for what he had done to Stross End, for the way he had made that beautiful ship into a weapon of tyranny, but it was also, Jack thought, a kindness, if the stories were true. He looked in the Captain's bloodied eyes for signs of relief, but saw only fear, and then nothing. Jack saluted him anyway. It was a gesture he had stolen from the music-hall stage, but there was no mockery in it. The Captain had been a kind of legend, though he'd gone sour long ago, and Jack respected that. He turned to see how the others were doing.

It didn't last long. Most of the warship's few remaining crew-men ran when they saw Arlandes fall. They threw the ropes over the side and slid down, with reckless speed, to escape onto the rooftops. Jack let them go. Only a few stayed to fight.

When they were done, Jack reached into his jacket and took out the notes Holbach had written for him. Among the crabbed lines of handwriting were a great many dauntingly complex diagrams of the ship's helm. Namdi read them over Jack's shoulder, and they tried to work out how to control it.

"It's like the bastard child of an altar and about a dozen spinning-wheels," Namdi said. "Fuck are we supposed to do with this?"

"We'll work it out. We have time."

There was a complex art to steering the *Thunderer*. It would be a long time before they could make it turn sharply, swoop and dive, the way Arlandes had been able to. Holbach's notes were not very clear, which Jack supposed was forgivable, under the circumstances. Still, they figured out enough to rise above all the towers, and point it west, and go forward, and *out*.

Jack leaned over the side and watched the city change below him. As they traveled, he felt the last of the power leak out of him. He was sorry to feel it go, but not heartbroken. There had been enough left in him for the last escape.

Perhaps, too, the monster's touch had set the rot into his lungs, but he did not think so. He was tired, terribly tired, but not dying, he thought; and if he was, even that was all right, so long as there was still a little time.

They could have gone north, but he feared the Mountain. They could have gone south, and been out over the Bay quickly, and across the sea, but he *knew* it was possible to leave the city that way. He wanted to see how far it went to the west and the east. He needed to know that it had limits. He wanted to see the city walls, and break out past them.

The *Thunderer* could go higher than he had ever been able to.

From so far above, the city *flowed*. He was amazed that he had never seen it before. "Look, there!" he said, and the Thunderers crowded around him to watch a god that was a shimmering golden wind work its way across the city, shaping the curve of the streets in its path, until it turned toward the Mountain, and climbed the slopes, and vanished.

Evening turned into night, the city below becoming darkness flecked with fire; then there was a soft dawn. They were in parts of the city Jack had never known. He recalled how his own power had faltered and failed as he traveled further from the Bay, and prayed that the *Thunderer* would not fall from the sky. Praise Be, it didn't. The sun eventually drew down in the west. They sailed on into the red sky.

They saw the western wall from leagues away. It was unthinkably tall, taller than any tower. Almost a mountain in itself. A great glossy line of black scored across the world. There were terrible many-legged gargoyles on top of it, which, as they got closer, resolved themselves into complex mighty guns. If they chose to fire on the ship, it would be defenseless.

All the Thunderers craned over the prow to see what they would see. None of them suggested turning back.

They crossed the wall without incident. It was very thick, and it took a long time to go past. In the shadow of the guns, Jack saw crude thatch huts up on the wall's wide summit, and ragged, stooping primitives, who threw themselves prostrate at the sight of the great ship. He waved to them.

Then they were past everything, and a limitless plain of waving wheat, golden-red in the sunset, stretched out before them. There were little farmhouses down there. It was beautiful. Free space, to begin again. Jack looked back at the city; it looked like broken shackles, cast on the floor behind him. He turned again forward, and smiled.

FORTY-SIX

There was a stationer's shop near the Cere House. Arjun bought
paper, a pen, two envelopes. He wrote,

*Olympia, Professor, my friends. The Typhon is gone. It wasn't big
enough to swallow the city after all; the city swallowed it, instead.
I do not believe it will return in our time, though I may well be
wrong. If you choose to come back, I will not be here. I wish you well.*

Before she left, Olympia had given him the address of a place
she planned to stay, to begin with: the home of a friend of a friend of
a correspondent of Dr. Branken's, on the other side of the Peaceful
Sea, in Ghent. Arjun went down to the docks and gave the letter to
the captain of a departing ship, with the last of his money, and the
promise that Olympia would pay more on receipt. Probably she
would never get it, but you never knew.

He realized that he'd forgotten to ask Jack whether he had in
fact killed the Chairman. *Oh well.*

He gave the captain another letter, for the Choristry, that promised, *I am still searching. Remain hopeful! The city is much larger than we
had thought. There is still time and hope.* He thought it very unlikely
that it would reach its destination.

He listened for a moment, then followed the sound of a sailor's
swaying shanty, and then the sound of church-bells, and then a

drunkard, lying in the gutter, howling a lonely song into his vomit. With every street, he turned inward, and further inward, the city's hidden inner reaches unfolding around him.

He thought of the Typhon, alone in that empty place. Despite what he had said in his letter to the Atlas-makers, he was fairly sure it would never be able to find its way back. It was a crude and stupid monster. Everything depended, then, on the nature of the empty place in which he had left it. Was it a place in the future of the Atlas-makers' city? If so, then every day that passed would lead the city further down into the mouth of a waiting doom. If that place was in Ararat's past, every day would be a step forward and out of the darkness. Perhaps there was no difference; perhaps, as Lemuel had said, everything in the city's past would come round again and again, and so there was darkness on all sides of every brief bright effort its citizens made. If the Atlas-makers did decide to return, he wished them well with whatever time they had.

There was a concert-hall on the corner, from which a droning music escaped. There was a sign on the arch over the door that said ENTER HERE AND KEEP LEFT FOR TICKETING. Under that sign, if you looked properly, was a long silver street under a row of arches. He walked down it.

He turned under an arch where a thing perched that was like pictures he had seen of *angels,* and also like pictures he had seen of *banshees.* It was keening and crooning something that was a distant echo of the Voice's sacred song.

He thought of what he'd done to Shay, Lemuel, Cuttle, whatever the man's name was. He wasn't afraid of Lemuel's curse—he thought it was just bluster—but he regretted his own treachery. True, he had had no choice, and Lemuel had been a terrible, reckless, selfish man, but it was treachery, even so. He feared it might be a discord in him, which would keep him from the Voice. The Voice would not show itself to him while he had that ugliness in him. But he had time to work his music pure again.

The whole city, and all its past and future, was open to him now. What he needed existed *somewhere,* he was sure, and he would find it.

He'd go deeper and deeper behind the fabric of things. He'd make himself a ghost in pursuit of a ghost. Alone again at last, as he had been when he came into the city, and ready to begin, he turned left, and then left again, down a steep golden hill, spiraling always inward.

About the Author

FELIX GILMAN lives with his wife in New York City.
Thunderer is his first novel.